THE STORYBOOK KILLER

KERI BEEVIS

B

Boldwood

First published in 2014 as *D For Dead* and *Dead Write*. This edition published in Great Britain in 2026 by Boldwood Books Ltd.

Copyright © Keri Beevis, 2014

Cover Design by Head Design Ltd

Cover Images: iStock and Shutterstock

The moral right of Keri Beevis to be identified as the author of this work has been asserted in accordance with the Copyright, Designs and Patents Act 1988.

Every effort has been made to obtain the necessary permissions with reference to copyright material, both illustrative and quoted. We apologise for any omissions in this respect and will be pleased to make the appropriate acknowledgements in any future edition.

A CIP catalogue record for this book is available from the British Library.

Paperback ISBN 978-1-80658-872-5

Large Print ISBN 978-1-80658-874-9

Hardback ISBN 978-1-80658-871-8

Trade Paperback ISBN 978-1-80658-873-2

Ebook ISBN 978-1-80658-875-6

Kindle ISBN 978-1-80658-876-3

Audio CD ISBN 978-1-80658-866-4

MP3 CD ISBN 978-1-80658-867-1

Digital audio download ISBN 978-1-80658-868-8

This book is printed on certified sustainable paper. Boldwood Books is dedicated to putting sustainability at the heart of our business. For more information please visit https://www.boldwoodbooks.com/ about-us/sustainability/

Boldwood Books Ltd, 23 Bowerdean Street, London, SW6 3TN

www.boldwoodbooks.com

This book is dedicated to six special ladies: Jo, Ness, Paula, Shell, Chris and Jackie.
Thank you for sharing this journey with me.

PROLOGUE

She screamed, the sound thundering in her ears as she ran up the stairs, heart pounding, threatening to jump into her mouth.

He was behind her, the clip of his boots hitting the stone steps, and she knew he was close.

Don't let him catch me. Don't let him catch me.

Into the kitchen, the room lit by a dull bare bulb, round the heavy oak table. The toe of her sneaker caught the leg of a chair and she stumbled briefly, the clatter of wood hitting the floor sounded as it fell behind her. It would delay him by maybe a second if she was lucky.

Into the hall, towards the safety of the front door.

Please let it open.

She heard his raspy breathing. Knew if he caught her he would take her back down to the basement. She couldn't go down there again, ever.

Her hand grabbed the door handle, yanked it hard, and relief flickered through her as it opened.

Behind her the man grunted and lunged, his fingers skimming her hair, and then she was down the porch step and into the front yard.

'Come back here, you little bitch!'

He sounded mad as hell.

Although he was still behind her, she was younger, smaller, faster.

Up ahead, the blackness of the woods waited to immerse her. If she could make it to their safety, there was a chance she could lose him.

The wind had picked up, rattling the chains of the rusted old swing. Twigs snapped beneath her feet. She was aware of both sounds, though neither drowned out the thundering fear in her head. Her breath was ragged, but still she ran, the adrenaline carrying her.

She thought of the twins. They had left her behind and were probably long gone. She was all alone.

She had to run faster. She had to get away. Her life depended on it.

Into the woods, the thick branches overhead blocking out any light from the moon. Her eyes not yet accustomed, she could barely see three feet ahead, but still she ran, no idea where she was heading, knowing she had to get away.

Behind her he stumbled, cursing as he hit the ground. She ran faster.

The basement. So much blood.

He wouldn't give up trying to catch her. She had seen and he knew she would tell. He would do whatever was necessary to make sure she remained silent.

All around her the trees swayed and whispered. Her foot caught a loose branch and she tripped. Unable to catch herself, she rolled head first down a steep bank, landing uncomfortably in a pile of bushes. Heart in her mouth, she tried to pick herself up. Prickling leaves dug into her back and her ankle throbbed from where it had caught the branch. She knew she had to go, and quickly, but movement was difficult. From overhead came the sound of footsteps crunching twigs.

He's going to find me.

She lay as still as she could, desperately trying to control her panting breath. It was pitch black in the woods. Maybe he hadn't heard her fall. If she was lucky, he wouldn't see her.

The seconds ticked by, each one dragging. There was more rustling from above, then the sound of footsteps again, this time growing distant.

He had gone.

She let out a low shaky breath, still not daring to move. He was not going to give up looking for her and the slightest sound could alert him to where she was. She thought back to the basement, to what had happened, to what she had seen, allowing it to fully sink in for the first time. What would have happened had she not run?

Gagging, she rolled onto her side and threw up into the bush. Backhanding spit from her mouth, she glanced warily around.

Had he heard?

There was no sound other than the whispering trees and her ragged breathing.

Gingerly, she rolled over and started to crawl out of the bushes, knowing she had to get out of there before he came back. Climbing to her feet, she put pressure on her ankle, knowing before the blast of shooting pain that she had sprained it or worse. Grimacing, she felt her way through the branches trying to find a path.

Behind her came a crunch.

Him!

Choking down on a sob, she thrashed her way

madly through the trees, ignoring the white-hot pain each time her busted ankle hit the ground. In the distance she heard the low roar of an engine. A car? Was she near a road? Forcing herself forward, she could make out the low beam of headlights ahead. Behind her, rough hands grabbed at her wrist, yanking her back. She yelped, kicking out and managing to wrench herself free. Dragging her bad ankle behind her she stumbled forward through the trees to the road she could now see ahead. Missing her footing on the embankment, she tripped again, this time falling into the road and straight into the path of the oncoming car. The last thing she was aware of was the thud as her body hit the front grille.

From the darkness of the trees the man watched as the car skidded to a halt in front of the limp body lying in the road.

The problem had taken care of itself.

A grim smile playing on his lips, he turned and started to make his way back through the trees.

He needed to get back to the house, back to his work, and he didn't want to keep his other guest waiting.

1

Tired from her bar shift, Amy Gallaty cursed herself for the hundredth time for agreeing to babysit her friend's dog. She could hear Huckleberry's pitiful whining the second the elevator opened on her floor and was almost sent flying as she opened her apartment door.

It was gone two, her shift had been long, and she wanted nothing more than to crawl into bed. She doubted Huckleberry would make it through till morning without needing to empty his bladder though and so reluctantly she fetched the leash. Ten minutes round the block and she'd be done.

Spotting the leash, Huckleberry let out a joyful bark.

'Hush!'

The disobedient collie gave her a lopsided grin and started panting with excitement as she hooked it onto his collar. Amy made a mental note to have words with Ryan about taking his pooch on a training course when he returned from Europe.

Although the night was warm, she was dismayed to feel a few spits of rain as they exited the apartment building.

Typical.

Huckleberry's ten-minute walk around the block was about to get cut to a quick stroll to the end of the street. Willing him to hurry up and pee, Amy hurried along behind him, oblivious to the pair of eyes watching her from the car parked across from her apartment.

* * *

Victor Boaz finished his shift at eleven and instead of sensibly heading straight home to bed, he had been persuaded by a couple of the other officers to join them for a beer.

It was a foolish move. Pastor Ralph had finally agreed to let him help set up before Sunday service and he was supposed to be at the church early the next morning.

He had been trying to get in on this gig for ages and didn't want to screw it up. This was his big chance to impress Brooke Michaels. So far, she had been friendly but had kept her distance. When she saw how seriously he was taking this church stuff and helping her dad, maybe she would finally agree to go out with him. As for Pastor Ralph, Vic was sure he would approve of him dating his daughter. Vic was a police officer who had embraced his religious side. What was there not to like?

It was almost two when he finally left the bar. Although he had only had one beer, he'd got caught up shooting the breeze, flirting with the new barmaid and playing pool with the guys. He gave a couple of them a lift home and was swinging his car around for the journey back to his townhouse, groaning at the time and knowing he was never going to be able to drag himself out of bed in three hours, when he had an idea.

Pastor Ralph had given him the keys to the church. What difference would it make if he set up tonight instead of in the morning? He could head on over, get everything ready and probably be home in under an hour. Then tomorrow he would get extra time in bed.

Telling himself he was a genius; Vic flipped on the turn signal and took the left-hand fork away from the city.

The New Hope Baptist Church was a ten-minute ride out towards the coast. It was a little out of Vic's neighbourhood, but was the place he had found solitude in his hour of need. The pastor had welcomed him with open arms, been a friendly ear to all his troubles, and offered many words of advice. It also helped that Mrs Michaels was a great cook and always laid out a mouth-watering selection of baked goods for the congregation.

His belly rumbling at the thought of her home-made apple pie and banana bread, he veered into the narrow lane leading to the church. Pulling up outside, he reached into the glovebox for his flashlight, cursing the church for not having any street lighting, and also himself for forgetting to put new batteries in the flashlight. The beam was faint and kept flickering but would hopefully be enough to light his way.

He glanced at the illuminated digital clock on the dashboard before killing the engine and exiting the car.

Fifteen minutes in and out, Vic, buddy. Let's make this quick.

Knowing his bed was waiting, he locked the car door and made his way over to the church gate.

* * *

Usually, Huckleberry liked to pee on everything, but tonight, as if sensing once he had done the deed it would be game over, he was purposely taking his time, stopping to sniff every post and every bush.

Amy sighed and glanced around her. Were it not for the spits of rain it would be a gorgeous night, so quiet and still, a blissful contrast to her busy evening in the bar. Across the road, the trees of the park were illuminated by the faint glow from the street lamps nestled between their branches. In the morning, she would take Huckleberry for a longer walk but keep him on his leash, as last time he'd caused chaos by chasing the ducks. For tonight, he would have to make do with the sidewalk, where she felt safer.

He sniffed for another two minutes before eventually cocking his leg at the bottom of a step leading into one of the neighbouring apartment buildings. As soon as he had finished Amy swung around, eager to get home.

Huckleberry whined and tugged on the leash.

'Come on, you little shit,' Amy hissed.

Ryan owed her big time for this favour.

Huckleberry continued to pull, unhappy at the briefness of the walk. He stared at Amy, brown eyes daring her to make him go back. When she gave the leash another yank, he shook his black and white head from side to side.

'Huckleberry!'

The dog was having none of it and planted his butt firmly on the pavement. As Amy reached for his collar, he started shaking his head more frantically and next thing she knew, he had managed to slip free. He bolted in the direction of the park, leaving her gawping after him, the leash and collar still in her hand.

'Huckleberry!'

This time she was louder than intended and from one of the apartments above came angry shouting.

'Shut the hell up! It's the middle of the night.'

Amy didn't respond; she was already across the street, following the direction she had seen Huckleberry run. The dog was a pain, but she couldn't lose him. Ryan would kill her.

She followed his lead down the path to the river, almost certain this was where she would find him as it was the route they had taken that morning. She only hoped Huckleberry didn't decide to launch himself into the water again.

She was an idiot being out here all alone, but what choice did she have? She could hardly leave the dog and go home. Reassuring herself she was still only minutes from her apartment block and the chances of anyone else being out here in the middle of the night were less than zero, she stopped abruptly as she spotted a shadowy figure, maybe thirty yards ahead, silhouetted against the silvery light bouncing off the water.

Amy caught her breath.

What the hell?

Unsure what to do, she remained where she was, heart thumping and mouth dry, listening to the steadying patter of rain hitting the leaves of the trees overhead.

Had he seen her? What was he doing out here?

Barking distracted her.

Two barks?

A larger pale dog emerged from the bushes, Huckleberry hot on its tail.

The man yelled, 'Hey!' and reached out to stop the pale dog. Letting out a joyous woof, Huckleberry bounded into them both, catching the man off guard and sending him sprawling on his ass. Cursing under her breath, Amy charged down to the scene, embarrassment overcoming her apprehension.

'Huckleberry, come here!'

The man was getting to his feet as she approached, and he looked really pissed. 'Is that your dog?' he demanded.

'Yes... No... Um, well, kind of.'

He stared at her pointedly. He was youngish, maybe mid-thirties, dark hair, and from the way the moonlight was playing with the hollows and angles on his face, attractive... in an angry kind of way.

'Look, I'm sorry, okay. I took him out to pee, and he got off the leash.'

'Well, maybe if you can't control him, you shouldn't own a dog.'

He stared at Huckleberry who had sat his butt down a few feet away and was watching them, tongue hanging out, looking mightily pleased with himself.

'He's not actually mine,' Amy protested, taking a sneaky step towards Huckleberry, hoping to get the collar back on him before he bolted again. The rain was getting heavier, and she didn't have a jacket.

The man wasn't listening. He had turned his back to her and bent down to stroke the ears of the pale Labrador, as he clipped on the leash.

Amy's temper rose a notch. She had apologised and didn't appreciate being lectured at and then ignored. 'He's not my dog,' she repeated.

The man turned back to face her, eyebrows raised. 'So?'

'So, I don't appreciate being accused of not controlling him.'

'Hey, he's with you, he's your responsibility.' He glanced at Huckleberry, who grinned back. 'You need to go on a training course, buddy.'

Huckleberry thumped his tail.

'Look, I apologised. It was an accident. I didn't expect anyone to be out here in the middle of the night.'

'So now you're saying it's my fault for being out here?'

'I never said—'

'How come you're out here in the middle of the night?'

'He needed to pee.'

'Not exactly the safest place to bring him.'

'I didn't come here on purpose. He got off his leash.' Amy sighed, exasperated. It was late, she was tired and – good-looking guy or not – she did not need some stranger giving her grief in the middle of a dark park.

'You might want to rethink your route and walk times if your dog is gonna keep running away. Never know who might be hanging around in these bushes late at night.'

'Like you,' Amy muttered under her breath.

'Sorry?'

'Nothing. Look, I'm tired. I've just finished work, and I want my bed. If you're done lecturing me, I'll take my dog and get out of your hair.'

'So he *is* your dog now?'

'Come on, Huckleberry,' she said to the dog, ignoring the man.

The collie made no attempt to move so Amy went to him. As she reached to slip the collar over his head, Huckleberry quickly moved out of her way.

'Huckleberry!'

She made another couple of unsuccessful attempts to catch hold of him before glancing up to see the man watching her. The rain had slicked his dark hair down to his forehead and was soaking the shoulders of his T-shirt, but he didn't appear to notice. He looked amused.

'What's so funny?' Amy demanded.

Instead of answering her he gave a sharp whistle. Huckleberry's ears pricked and to Amy's surprise – and annoyance – he came charging over to where the man stood, sitting obediently before him.

'You've gotta be kidding me.'

The man held out his hand for the collar. 'Hey, you want me to help or not?'

Grudgingly, Amy passed it to him.

Good as gold, Huckleberry allowed the collar to be slipped over his head. He even had the nerve to glance up adoringly at the man who in turn bent down and scratched his ears. Meanwhile, the placid Labrador sat by, patiently watching.

Amy was fuming.

'If you're done, Doctor Doolittle, I think I can take it from here.' She snatched the leash and gave Huckleberry a sharp yank. He didn't budge and she yanked again.

'Huckleberry!'

Reluctantly the dog got to his feet with a whine. Heat crept into Amy's cheeks, as, with as much dignity as she could muster, she turned and headed back up the path to the road, her feet slipping on the now-muddy ground, a sulking Huckleberry trailing along behind her. She was aware the man was still watching her, no doubt amused he'd made her look an idiot, but she was oblivious to the second pair of eyes watching from within the bushes.

* * *

Vic had the key to the rear door of the church and, too lazy to follow the path round to the back of the building, he decided to cut across the graveyard. He might be doing all this church stuff, but dead was dead and anyone spouting baloney about it being disrespectful to walk over graves was full of shit. Of course these were views he had never shared with Pastor Ralph. No need to go upsetting him.

If he fell out with the pastor, he could kiss goodbye to any chance of getting into Ralph's daughter's pants.

With the faint beam of the flickering flashlight guiding him, Vic made his way across the graveyard. He took care not to step directly on old Mrs Jacoby's plot, knowing her daughters tended it weekly with fresh flowers. He was almost halfway, busy wondering what treats Mrs Michaels would be baking for after the morning service and whether Brooke would be wearing the blue flowery dress with the low neckline, when the flashlight cut out completely.

'Damn, fuck.'

Standing in the middle of the graveyard in the dark, Vic waited for his eyes to adjust. Feeling a damn fool, he cursed himself about the batteries again and slowly started to pick his way forward, careful to avoid the headstones.

Not such a great idea now, hey buddy?

Up ahead he could make out the shadow of the church. There were maybe six or seven more gravestones in his path. Feeling his legs bump the next one, he cautiously stepped around it. As his foot came down, he realised too late there was no ground beneath it.

Crying out as he lost his balance, he toppled forward into the hole in the ground, landing with a thud.

Something squelched beneath him. It wasn't earth. He had landed on something in the grave.

Not something – *someone*.

And he could smell blood.

Lifting his hand, he could feel icky stuff all over it.

He was on top of a body: cold, unmoving and dead.

As the realisation hit him, Victor Boaz started screaming like a baby.

2

Jake Sullivan was getting out of the shower when the phone rang. Grabbing a towel, he made his way through to the bedroom and snatched up the handset as the message kicked in, trying his best to ignore Roxy's pitiful look.

'Sullivan.'

Moments later he was redialling his partner.

Rebecca Angell answered after six rings, sounding groggy. He glanced at the alarm and grinned. 5.45 a.m. Rebecca had been sinking shots of bourbon when he'd left her a few hours ago.

'You sober?'

'Of course,' she muttered unconvincingly.

He heard the creak of the mattress.

'Jeez, Jake, it's not even six yet. This had better be good.'

'We've got a dead body in the graveyard over at the New Hope Church.'

'We've got a dead body in the graveyard?' Rebecca repeated, her tone dry. 'Is this some kind of joke?'

Jake smiled, appreciating the irony. 'I wish.'

Reaching in his closet he pulled out a pair of dark suit pants and a grey shirt. He might not have the hangover, but at least Rebecca had managed a couple of hours sleep. He had arrived home, crawled into bed and found himself wide awake an hour later, unable to settle in the heat of the night. He was tired, but at least sober.

He crossed to the window, drew up the blind. It was already light outside, hurting his tired eyes. He glanced over the lush green of the parkland where the silvery trail of the river snaked a path between the trees.

It was the view that had sold him on the apartment, when things had turned bad with Lara and he had needed to find somewhere fast, and had they not pulled this case he would have been changing into his running gear and heading over to the park before there was too much heat in the sun.

When he was stressed with a case, needed to mull

things over or clear his head, that was his thing; he liked to run. Unfortunately, there was no time now, so it would have to wait.

'Probably best if I drive, eh?'

Rebecca made a grunting sound down the phone which he took to be an agreement.

'Pick you up in fifteen.'

'Jake?'

'Yeah?'

'Can you bring coffee? I'm out.'

* * *

Rebecca was dressed and functioning by the time Jake arrived twenty minutes later, but still not feeling quite human. She had taken the quickest of showers, tied her dark hair back in a low ponytail, and was finishing off a cold slice of pizza she'd found in the refrigerator, when she answered the door.

Spying the two cardboard Starbucks mugs Jake held, she snatched one and took a long luxurious sip.

'Oh, man, this is the best cup of coffee in the world. Thank you, Jake Sullivan. You are my hero.' She grinned and winked at him.

Jake followed her inside, removing his sunglasses

and screwing up his nose at the pizza crust still in her hand.

'You're eating cold pizza for breakfast, seriously?'

'Hey, you said fifteen minutes. I had to improvise.'

'Is that onions I can smell?'

'Maybe,' Rebecca confessed sheepishly, cramming the last bite into her mouth.

'For breakfast? That's gross. You'd better not stink out my car.'

'It's not cold out. You can open the window.'

The man was way too pedantic about his dumb car.

She pushed past him into the kitchen, running through a mental checklist to make sure she hadn't forgotten anything.

Damn, the cats!

She grabbed a can and started opening it.

'Two minutes and I'll be ready.'

Her cats, Sabrina and Shelby, came running at the sound, winding around Jake's legs as she prepared their breakfast. He pulled up a chair while he waited, and Sabrina promptly jumped onto his lap and settled herself down. She loved Jake. Most animals did. Make that animals and women. Sullivan had a way about him.

'So, what time did you leave the bar?' he asked, rubbing the cat's ears, making her purr loudly.

'Around one... I think.'

If she was honest, Rebecca wasn't exactly sure what time she'd arrived home. After the fight with Alan, she'd knocked back a lot of bourbon.

One of the detectives in the department was retiring and they had been out for a few leaving drinks. Everything had been going well until Alan had shown up.

They didn't have plans, and he knew she was going for drinks with some of the guys. That he had chosen to show up uninvited pissed her off. It was as if he didn't trust her. She knew he was jealous of Jake. Not that he had any reason to be; Jake Sullivan was like the brother she'd never had. There was no denying he was a good-looking guy, and yes, it was true he wasn't short of female attention, but it had never been that way between them. Unfortunately, Alan didn't buy it and had been insecure since the moment the two of them had been partnered together.

It didn't help that he wanted to move things faster than Rebecca. They had been dating for six months, introduced by mutual friends; her mother loved him, and he was a good man – safe, reliable and loving. He had been dropping hints they move in together for the past month and was desperate to take her to Florida on vacation with his mother.

Still Rebecca held back.

She had been growing irritated with him over the past couple of weeks. Last night was the final straw and when he had shown up uninvited, believing he could persuade her to leave her friends at the bar and go to dinner with him, she had snapped.

Alan didn't do fighting, which annoyed Rebecca even more, as he had stood in the bar and taken her anger, making her look like the bad guy she knew she was being. Eventually she had told him to go.

He had, calmly, because everything Alan did was calm and methodical, and she had drowned her anger, frustration and guilt in a bottle of bourbon.

Jake had left before her. He had offered her a ride home, but at the time Rebecca was hell-bent on staying. He had left one of the other homicide detectives, his friend and racquet ball partner, Brad Kramer, in charge of getting her home.

It was the getting home bit that was still mostly a blur.

Alan hadn't called since the fight. No doubt he was waiting for her to make the first move.

He could be waiting a while.

'So what do we know about the vic?' she asked,

plucking Sabrina from Jake's lap and setting both cats in front of their food bowls. She was done thinking about last night and Alan, and wanted to focus the few operating brain cells she had on the case at hand.

'Young male, multiple stab wounds. Body was dumped in an open grave. So, have you made things up with Alan?'

'No. Do we know who found the body?'

'Not yet. Caretaker, I guess.'

Rebecca grabbed her sunglasses and keys. 'Best we go find out.'

* * *

Vic was sitting in the back of a squad car, wrapped in a blanket and feeling sorry for himself, when Angell and Sullivan showed up. Mrs Michaels had been fussing around him since she'd arrived with the pastor half an hour before, helping him to get cleaned up, and he was munching his way through the tub of chocolate chip cookies she had made in an attempt to shake off the shock of what had happened.

Angell clocked him as soon as they pulled up at the church in Sullivan's silver Audi and he could see her lips curve as she made her way over to the car.

'Vic? What the hell are you doing here?'

The two of them had been in Mahoney's last night, but only because they were out for drinks at the same leaving party. They didn't frequent each other's company much these days; Angell was too busy hanging out with her detective friends.

While Vic didn't begrudge his former partner's promotion, he knew it was only because of the high-profile Alphabet Murders and the fact she'd happened to be in the right place at the right time that her career had fast tracked so quickly. Had he been the one to unmask the killer, Rebecca Angell would still be in uniform patrolling the streets.

'I was the one who found the body,' he told her through a mouthful of cookie.

'*You* found the body?'

Vic didn't appreciate the slightly amused, almost disbelieving tone in her voice.

'Is there something wrong with that?' he demanded, immediately on the defensive. Six years had passed but Rebecca Angell still had the ability to rub him up the wrong way.

Mrs Michaels, who had been standing close by, choose that moment to pipe up.

'Officer Boaz fell into the grave on top of the body. Poor man, it must have been such a terrible shock.'

'You *fell* in the grave?' This was from Angell's partner, Jake Sullivan, who had joined them and was looking all smug and *GQ* behind his shades. 'Seriously?'

Beside him, Angell tried to disguise her snigger with a cough.

Vic hated Sullivan, Dixie asshole. He'd transferred up from Atlanta a few years back with his cocky, laid-back attitude and stupid cowboy accent and seemed to think he could slot right in.

Vic was a firm believer that outsiders had to earn their place; it had galled him to see Sullivan settling in with that easy way of his and making himself at home on Vic's turf.

After the hellish last few hours all he needed was to have these two idiots laughing at him and questioning every word he was telling them.

The shock of landing in the grave had been bad enough, but when he realised there was a body in there with him, he had panicked, and what with scrambling around in the dark and trying to get out of the muddy and slippery hole, it had taken an eternity to get back to the car. It wasn't until he was back there and reaching for his keys that he realised they were missing. Cold dread had crept up his spine as it dawned on him they must have fallen from his pocket when he landed in the grave. He had looked longingly at his cell phone sitting on the dashboard inside the locked car. His clothes were uncomfortably damp and heavy with dirt and God knew what else, and he couldn't go home until he'd reported the body.

Making a spur of the moment decision, he had used his elbow to break the driver's window and retrieve his phone. Only to find out he didn't have a signal. Cursing loudly, he had wandered up and down the road holding his cell at all different angles, praying for a couple of bars. Just one would have done.

But nothing.

Grim realisation set in. He had two choices: walk back to town or go retrieve his keys.

Had he known the second option would result in a half-an-hour mud wrestle with a corpse and still not produce any keys, he would have started the walk back to town straightaway.

But he hadn't.

It had been nearing five, with the sun already rising, when a mud-caked Victor Boaz had finally managed to wave down a car on the road leading back into the city and raise the alarm.

When he finally got back to his apartment he promised himself a well-deserved beer and the longest, hottest shower ever.

'It was dark,' he pointed out to Sullivan. 'I couldn't see where I was going.'

'So I see.'

'What were you doing in a church graveyard in the middle of the night in the first place?' Angell asked, still sounding incredulous.

Mrs Michaels answered before Vic had a chance. He was noticing she had an annoying habit of doing that.

'Officer Boaz was in charge of setting up for this morning's service and he decided to get here early.'

She left out that he had been planning to go home after setting up, probably because Vic hadn't told her that bit. He had led her and the pastor to believe he had wanted to get to the church early to make sure he did a good job.

By now Angell was barely hiding her amusement at the situation. 'I didn't have you pegged as a church-goer, Vic.'

He was saved further embarrassment by the pathologist, who was standing over by the open grave and now called to Angell and Sullivan.

Sullivan waved back to him before turning to Vic. 'You stay here and munch on those cookies, okay? We'll be back with some questions in a bit.'

Watching the detectives cross the graveyard, Vic

mumbled a few choice swear words through his mouthful.

***

Jake's first thought on seeing the body in the grave was that whoever had inflicted the injuries had been in a hell of a rage. It didn't help that Boaz had messed up the crime scene by landing on the body, smearing blood and mud everywhere, but nonetheless, the stab wounds were apparent and there were a lot of them.

The kid in the grave could have been wearing a Halloween costume. Dark hair, eyes open in terror in a ghoulish face drained of colour, except for the crust of dry blood running from his left nostril down to his top lip.

The pathologist, Greg Withers, had arrived on the scene about fifteen minutes before Jake and Rebecca. A burly man, still in good shape, he was fast approaching retirement and was familiar with both detectives from numerous cases they had worked on. He filled them in on what he knew so far.

The guy was young, probably late teens, and had taken the first stab wound to the chest probably before falling into the grave. Judging from the amount of blood, the wound hadn't been fatal, and the killer had climbed down to finish the job. The death wound had most likely been the one to the throat.

The ground underfoot was still wet, the rain having only stopped an hour or so ago, and the air was fresh with the damp fragrance of flora.

Rebecca walked round the grave. 'Poor kid. Not a nice way to go.'

Jake thought of his own nephews back home. Cody and Travis were about the same age. He imagined his sister's reaction if this had happened to either of them. This kid had a family somewhere and once they ID'd him, they would have the miserable task of breaking the news to his folks. It was a part of the job none of them enjoyed.

Raising his shades, he rubbed at his tired eyes. 'How long before we can get him out of here?' he asked.

Withers raked a hand through his greying, red hair. 'Another hour, I guess. We can see you guys back at the morgue when you're done here.'

Spotting one of his assistants arriving with his camera equipment, he excused himself and hurried over to greet her.

Jake glanced at Boaz, still sitting in the back of the squad car, cramming his face with cookies. 'Guess we'd better get Officer Douchebag to tell us what he knows.'

'There's been a burial here recently,' Rebecca said from behind him.

Jake turned to look at the grave she was studying. The freshly packed earth had been neatly smoothed, not long since. It didn't look like the scene of a recent funeral. 'No flowers,' he noted, brain already on the same track.

'And what about the gravestone?' she said quietly.

Old, greying, weather-beaten with age. They both stepped closer, reading the inscription.

Maria Carpenter
Beloved daughter
Taken too soon
RIP
1969 – 1985

A sliver of dread balled in the pit of Jake's stomach. This grave had been dug over very recently. How long would a person be able to stay alive buried?

He looked grimly at Rebecca. 'We need shovels.'

3

The book signing had been tediously slow for the first hour, with only one purchase and an elderly couple who had stopped for a chat, and Amy was beginning to think she had made a huge mistake.

One of the clerks had thrown her a couple of sympathetic glances between serving customers in the otherwise busy store, while she had sat at her book table, playing with her pen, trying her best not to look bored or embarrassed, and stealing glances at her wristwatch.

Perhaps she had been arrogant to think the small loyal audience who had been following her Zack Maguire series of murder mysteries would embrace her change of direction. Crime fiction fans wanted crime fiction. If Amy was no longer delivering it, there were plenty of other authors who were.

The series had run its course. She had six books under her belt and, while saying goodbye to her beloved characters had been anguish, she had been itching to turn her hand to something new.

Maybe a departure from genre hadn't been such a smart move. Sure, her new book was still a mystery, but it was supernatural instead of a straightforward smart and sassy police thriller. And of course it didn't feature her recurring hero, Zack Maguire. Something a couple of her disappointed fans had already complained about.

Her publishers thought she was on to a good thing and had given the new novel their blessing. The Zack Maguire series of books had been moderately successful, but they were never going to make Amy into a household name, hence her decision to try something different.

Juniper's largest independent bookstore, Too Many Books, had been more than delighted to host the signing. Amy wondered if they were maybe now regretting their decision.

Fortunately, the first-hour lull did not continue,

and she was relieved to see faces, some new, some familiar, by late morning. By the time the signing was drawing to a close, she had sold over sixty copies of her new novel and the nagging doubts that she had made a terrible mistake had long vanished. She had thanked the store owner and was packing up her table when she heard a familiar voice behind her.

'I can't believe you went through with it.'

Oh crap.

Amy's heart sank as she turned to face Nadine Williams. She forced a smile onto her face.

'Hi Nadine, I was wondering if you would show.'

The woman hadn't changed much since Amy had last seen her, which had to have been about a year ago, at the signing for the final Zack Maguire book. Her harshly bleached hair was still backcombed high off her forehead and her pointed face carefully, but heavily, made-up.

Right now, she was staring at Amy, her eyes sharp and her scarlet lips drawn in a thin line.

'It was hard for me to come here today, Amy. Knowing what you *did*.'

The last word was full of accusation.

Amy had known Nadine would be pissed when her series of books came to an end. She was always first in the queue to buy a copy of each novel, gushing about how much she loved Zack Maguire and how the release of each book was the highlight of her year.

At first Amy had been flattered. Knowing her books were being enjoyed and that she had a fan unable to wait for the next instalment gave her a real kick and made the years of struggling worth it. But over the past couple of years Nadine's behaviour had become more obsessive. She was always at book signings, insisting on having her picture taken with Amy, and the way she spoke about the novels and her attachment to the characters didn't seem normal. She had written letters too. Gushing letters about how the books had changed her life.

At the last launch, she had been so excited; Amy had dreaded her finding out the series was ending. She had let Nadine leave with her book, having cravenly dodged her questions about what would happen next, then waited expectantly for a letter to arrive at her publishers berating her for not telling the truth.

Except no letter had arrived.

There hadn't been a single word from Nadine who had appeared to drop off the face of the earth. Until today.

Feeling uncomfortable and hoping Nadine wasn't going to make a scene in the crowded store, Amy fin-

ished loading the unsold books into her one remaining box and picked it up, holding it defensively
against her chest.

'I couldn't keep writing the same story forever,' she
tried to reason, aware her explanation sounded a bit
lame.

'Why not?' Nadine countered.

'The books had run their course. I wanted to try
something new.'

'*New?*' The word was said with contempt.

'Look, I'm sorry you're disappointed, I really am.'
Actually, Amy wasn't sorry at all. She had lost the passion for the Zack Maguire series and hadn't been able
to get the last book finished fast enough. She was only
sorry she had been caught here by Nadine today and
was having to explain her actions. 'Six books were
enough. The story had run its course.'

'You killed him off!' Nadine's eyes flashed angrily.
'Why would you do that? Have you any idea how
upset it made me?'

*Not upset enough that you're gonna go all Kathy Bates
on me, I hope.*

Amy kept the sarcastic retort to herself. Nadine
looked pissed and probably wouldn't react well to the
joke.

'Why did you do it, Amy? Why?'

Her voice was loud enough now to draw attention from the other customers.

Amy hugged her box tighter to her chest with one arm, freeing the other to run her hand back through her hair, a gesture from childhood she tended to repeat when on edge or nervous.

While she was more than capable of holding her own in an argument, public confrontations weren't her style.

'Is everything okay here?'

To her embarrassment, she turned to see the store manager standing beside her, fixing Nadine with a pointed look. Nadine didn't even bother to look at him, continuing instead to scowl at Amy.

'You have no respect for your fans, Amy Gallaty.' As she spat out Amy's name, she poked the box sharply with a long red talon. 'You say you're sorry, but it's a little late for that, isn't it, missy?'

Amy could feel her hackles starting to rise. Who the hell did Nadine think she was? And what right did she have to question her writing choices? This wasn't *Misery* and the woman was starting to piss her off.

'I'm entitled to write what I want, Nadine. I don't have to answer to you.'

Nadine's mouth dropped open in surprise at Amy's apparent sass.

'So that's what you think of your fans, is it? Expect them to support you and buy your books and recommend you to other people, but you don't give a shit about their opinions.'

Her tone was bitter and angry now.

'Madam, I am going to have to ask you to leave.' The store manager had his arm around Nadine, trying to guide her away from Amy.

The woman wasn't going quietly though and wrestled her way out of his grasp.

'Get your horrible little hands off me, you cretin.'

'Madam, please.' The store manager, a neat and meticulous man of about fifty, looked horrified.

He tried to grab her arm again and she shoved him hard, causing him to stumble backwards into a rack of books that all went flying.

'Nadine? What the hell are you doing?'

The voice came from the other side of the store and Amy recognised the man hurrying towards them, a Too Many Books carrier bag in his hand and a look of horror on his face.

Nadine's boyfriend.

Amy had met him a couple of times over the years, and it never failed to surprise her that this quietly attractive, mild-mannered and seemingly intelligent man had chosen to spend his life with a woman like Nadine.

Well, they say opposites attract.

Helping the store manager to his feet, he fixed Nadine with a scathing look. 'What the hell are you doing?' he repeated, his tone calm but with an angry edge.

Nadine stabbed a finger in Amy's direction. 'It's all her fault.'

'Sir, I'd like your lady friend to leave, please, or I will have to call the police.' This was the store manager again, looking frostily at Nadine, although he addressed her boyfriend.

'I am so sorry.' The boyfriend, Todd, Tony... Amy couldn't remember his name, had his wallet out and was thumbing through notes. 'I will pay for any damage.'

'Not necessary,' the store manager said stiffly. 'I just want her out.'

'I can't believe you're trying to give him money,' Nadine hissed. 'I haven't done anything wrong, Troy.'

Troy. That was it.

'You promised, Nadine. You promised you weren't going to come over here.'

'I couldn't help it. I'm so upset. She has a lot to answer for.'

Troy had his arm around Nadine now and was trying to guide her out of the store, despite her protestations.

'I'm sorry,' he mouthed to Amy and the store manager.

'*She* will be sorry,' Nadine snarled, eventually relenting. With a final scowl in Amy's direction, she allowed Troy to lead her from the store.

Amy was quick to leave after the encounter. As well as being embarrassed by the incident, she got the impression the store manager couldn't wait to see the back of her. He had politely asked her if she was okay, but his overall demeanour had changed, and she couldn't help thinking he held her partly responsible.

Her VW Beetle was parked in the lot across the road. She would dump the books in the passenger seat then wander down to the grocery store on the corner of the block, pick up some dinner for later. She wasn't working tonight so she would cook a proper meal. Maybe have some wine with it. She had a couple of bottles in the apartment and, after the encounter with Nadine, felt she deserved a glass or two. Perhaps she would call up her girlfriends, Heidi and Fran, see if they wanted to come over. As she approached her car, the ugly naked word crudely written in red letters across the front windshield stood out.

BITCH.

Amy stopped, rooted to the spot, and glanced around the parking lot, box clutched tightly in one hand, car keys in the other. Bile rose in her throat.

Nadine?

She expected the woman to ambush her again, but as she crossed to the car on shaky legs, no one appeared. Still, she felt sick.

Quickly dropping the books onto the passenger seat, she got a cloth from the glovebox and dabbed at the letters.

It was lipstick or similar.

Had to be Nadine.

Does she hate me that much?

Amy tried her best to wipe the offending word from the windshield. The sticky make-up smeared, but eventually started to lift. The feeling of sickness remained. It was stupid that a silly word could get to her so much.

Climbing behind the wheel and squirting water from the washer over the rest of the sticky goo, she decided to forego the grocery store. She had lost her appetite and if it came back later she would get takeout or make do with whatever was in the refrigerator.

Wine would definitely figure in her plans.

As she pulled out of the parking spot, it occurred to her that Nadine must know the car she drove.

Amy wasn't sure how, unless the woman had been following her.

And if she knew the car she drove, then what else did she know about her?

4

The bodies lay side by side on tables in the morgue: both grey in pallor with dark rings around the eyes and wearing the waxy smooth complexion of death.

The body on the right had been cleaned up, but still carried ugly gash marks from the repeated stabbing, while the body on the left was untouched, but had suffered a possibly more horrific death.

They hadn't been in time to save her and Rebecca dreaded to think what the girl's last moments had been like, buried alive beneath six feet of earth and left to suffocate. Her hands were bloody and her nails torn where she had tried to claw her way out of the coffin. There had been no escape and, according to

Greg Withers, she could have remained alive in that little box, the skeletal remains of Maria Carpenter underneath her, for anything up to two hours.

They were still waiting for an ID on the pair, but both Rebecca and Jake believed they were likely to be a couple, not strangers, as the picture in the locket worn around the girl's neck closely resembled the face of the man lying next to her.

The man who had buried her alive.

Abrasions on his hands suggested he had been the one to have dug up the grave.

What kind of sadistic son of a bitch were they dealing with? Someone who had forced a man to bury his girlfriend alive and then brutally stabbed him to death.

Was it someone known to the couple? Maybe a jealous ex or an enemy they had wronged; or had they been victims of circumstance?

Boaz had been able to give little information. That he had gone to the church straight after leaving the bar to set up for service didn't ring true to Rebecca. Boaz was a lazy cop who liked an easy life. He wasn't the type to lose sleep if hymn books weren't laid out properly.

Then again, you didn't expect to find out he was a regular churchgoer, did you, Rebecca?

She still would never have believed it had the pastor's wife not confirmed it.

Regardless of Boaz's laziness and his family history, he was not a killer. Rebecca and Vic had been partnered for two years and she liked to think she knew him pretty well. When the revelations about Rodney Boone came out, he had taken it hard. Maybe that was why he had turned to the church.

The vibration of her cell shook her from her thoughts. She pulled the phone from her pocket and scowled when she saw Alan's name appear on the screen.

Jerk!

Diverting the call to voicemail, she slipped the phone back, not missing the look Jake shot her.

'What?'

'Nothing,' he replied, grinning.

He had discarded his jacket; the shirt underneath was crumpled, sleeves rolled up, and he was in need of a good shower. They both were, having literally been shovelling soil from the grave.

Jake needed to concentrate on his own love life instead of taking such a keen interest in hers. Since he'd broken up with Lara, he tended to keep his romantic liaisons short and sweet. Rebecca knew the break-up had been messy for him. He and Lara had been childhood sweethearts and had moved to Oregon together, but things hadn't been right between them for a long while. Jake was a cop and worked long hours. Lara found it hard, alone in a strange city, and had strayed. She'd begged forgiveness, but Jake was big on trust and wanted out; he'd ended up walking away with just the clothes on his back and his dog.

He'd fought Lara over Roxy. She could keep all the material stuff, but she wasn't getting his dog. It had been nearly two years and it was time he thought about settling down again. Maybe Rebecca needed to hook him up with someone, take his mind off baiting her about Alan.

'So is there anything else you can tell us at this stage?' she asked Greg Withers, changing the subject and deciding to ignore Jake. Alan could wait also. Her head was pounding, the hangover kicking in, and as soon as they were done here, she needed more coffee and painkillers.

'Not much at the moment,' the pathologist told her. 'I'm waiting on the result of the prints, and I'll let you know as soon as they come through. There is one thing I want you both to look at, though.'

He lifted the girl's left hand. Scribbled in black ink across her palm, the words 'Chapter 26'. Jake frowned.

'She could have written that herself.'

'Possible,' Withers agreed. 'But it's thick ink. Most people who write on their hand use a biro. Besides, why use both hands?'

With that he lifted the right hand to reveal another reference; 'page 323'.

'Okay.' Rebecca nodded, her tired mind working overtime. 'So it's a clue from the killer.'

She thought back to the Alphabet Murders; the killer's calling card had been the victim's initial carved into the back of their neck. Ink pen was less perverse, but didn't match the rest of this killer's MO, whose victims had been dispatched in a particularly cruel way.

'What is he trying to tell us?' she mused.

Withers placed the girl's hands back by her sides.

'Find the book he's referring to,' he said grimly, 'and I'm guessing you will have a much clearer idea of what it is you're dealing with.'

* * *

Finding the book the killer was referring to should have been an impossible task. Fortunately, it had been made easy for them.

The car belonging to the dead boy was found later

that afternoon in a secluded spot on the outskirts of the city, known for courting couples. A squad car had found the abandoned vehicle and called it in. Twenty minutes later, Jake and Rebecca were on the scene.

With the car came ID. Ben Hogan and Kasey Miller were both nineteen and students at the local college. The bodies at the morgue had yet to be formerly identified, but it was looking likely that this was the missing couple. Ben's wallet and Kasey's purse had been left in the car, and the keys were still in the ignition, suggesting the killer had abducted them from this spot and driven them to the New Hope Baptist Church.

Why he had picked that spot had been confusing, until the book had been found.

Jake was on his haunches, using a miniature flashlight to sweep the interior of the car when he found the paperback under the front passenger seat. Slipping on the regulation white gloves, he carefully retrieved the book.

Grave Encounters by Amy Gallaty. A cheap looking novel with a tombstone on the cover.

Nice.

'What have you got?' Rebecca asked, coming up behind him.

'Maybe nothing.' But he didn't think so. He had

worked enough years in homicide to recognise the clues were being set up too neatly. Like a game. 'It was 323, right?'

'Yeah, 323, chapter twenty-six,' Rebecca confirmed.

Carefully he opened the book to the correct page, careful not to disturb any evidence the killer may have left, and began to read.

The words described in gruesome detail the scene they had found at the church. The female victim buried alive; her boyfriend stabbed to death in an open grave beside her.

Jake's lips twisted.

Sick son of a bitch.

Reading over his shoulder, Rebecca let out a low whistle. 'Oh boy. He actually did it word for word.'

Jake closed the book, flipped it over and read the author biography. It was brief, but told them she resided in Oregon.

So she was a local author. Coincidence?

Bagging the book, he passed it to one of the officers combing the crime scene and turned to Rebecca.

'What do you reckon?' he asked, keen to see if her thoughts were on the same track as his own.

She rubbed at her temples and closed her eyes for a brief moment, gathering her thoughts. Jake suspected she was regretting her marathon drinking session.

'Someone with a grudge against the author, perhaps, or a fan of the book? I doubt she is our killer.'

Probably not, but they were going to need to talk to her anyway because, killer or not, Amy Gallaty was somehow involved.

5

If there was one thing Amy loved, it was her friends.

The moment she had called her best pal, Heidi, and told her about the graffiti on her windshield, her friends had rallied round; and they were all now gathered in her apartment, Heidi pouring her wine, Gage making her laugh and Fran cooking her dinner.

Heidi was her oldest friend from college, while Fran and Gage she knew through work. As an only child who had lost her parents to an automobile accident when she was in her early twenties, Amy regarded them as her family.

Fran had brought tortillas and chicken and, using other ingredients in Amy's refrigerator, was making up enchiladas in the kitchen, while Huckleberry sat patiently watching her, eyes pleading and tongue drooling. The smells were drifting through to the living room, reminding Amy she hadn't eaten since breakfast and was pretty hungry.

'Next time you do a signing, I think one of us should go with you,' Gage suggested, glancing up at Heidi, who was pacing the balcony, cigarette in hand. 'In case psycho bitch decides to show again.'

Heidi glanced up at Amy, a look of guilt on her face. 'I'm sorry, honey, I should have been there.'

Amy set down her wine glass. 'Heidi. We've been through this already. It's not your fault. I never asked anyone to go with me.'

Because you didn't think there would be a problem.

Truth be known, she was rattled. She could've handled Nadine showing up and kicking off, but the graffiti had been a step too far. It made it personal.

Maybe she should be flattered her characters meant so much to her fans.

Screw that. Nadine is a nutjob, pure and simple.

'I still should have been there.' Heidi was beating herself up. She'd had the day off and had gone shopping, not knowing her friend was going to need her.

Gage slipped his arm round Amy. 'What's happened has happened. Next time, one of us will be there.' He glanced over at Fran, flipping chicken in the frying pan. 'How much longer until dinner? We're starving over here.'

Fran glanced up and grinned, enjoying herself in Amy's little open-plan kitchen, towel over her shoulder, generous glass of Chablis in her free hand.

'Another fifteen minutes.' She glanced at Huckleberry. 'Behave yourself, buddy, and maybe you'll get lucky.'

Huckleberry grinned, seeming to understand what Fran had said, then woofed loudly as the buzzer sounded.

Amy glanced round as the collie bolted for the door, wondering who it could be when her friends were with her. Getting up from the couch, she followed Huckleberry to the door, expecting to open it to a cold-caller and readying herself to tell them in the politest possible terms to get lost.

What she wasn't expecting to find was the guy from the park standing on the other side, a pretty dark-haired woman beside him.

Huckleberry recognised him instantly and was on his hind legs, woofing his excitement.

The guy glanced at the dog, stroking his head, then back at Amy, his expression one of surprise, as he too recognised her.

'You're Amy Gallaty?'

'Yes... why?'

'You know each other?' This was from the woman standing beside him, who was looking equally surprised and curious.

Girlfriend? Wife?

'Not exactly,' he muttered. Amy got the feeling he wasn't too impressed to see her.

'We ran into each other in the park last night,' she elaborated to the woman. 'My dog got off his leash, knocked him on his ass.'

'Really?' This had the dark-haired woman smiling.

'Because you couldn't control him,' the man added, pointedly.

Was this why they were here – because of Huckleberry? Was the guy after compensation for new pants and a sore butt cheek?

'So, what do you want?' she asked, cutting to the chase. 'You've come here to give me some more tips on dog walking?' He had looked surprised to see her, so maybe it wasn't about Huckleberry. And both he and the woman were dressed in suits: official.

Amy's eyes wandered down, and her insides went cold as she recognised the bulge of the holster underneath his suit jacket. Noting the area to which her attention had gone and wrongly assuming she had been checking him out, he narrowed his eyes, looking unimpressed. Amy's mind was in too much of a spin to correct him. The last time she'd had a visit from the police it had been to say her parents were dead.

'I'm Detective Rebecca Angell,' the woman told her. 'This is Detective Jake Sullivan. We'd like to ask you a few questions if we may. Can we come inside?'

Amy felt sick. 'Has there been an accident?'

Most of the people she cared about were here with her in her apartment. But Ryan was overseas. Had something happened to him?

'Can we come in?' Sullivan was looking at her, eyebrows raised questioningly.

'Yeah, sure.'

She led them into the living room where three pairs of eyes glanced up, all settling on Detective Jake Sullivan with keen interest.

'Cops,' she told her friends, her heart thumping far too fast. Heidi rushed over to stand beside her.

'Is this about the graffiti on her car?'

'Graffiti?' Angell asked.

'Some jerk wrote on her windshield.' This was from Gage, who was still sitting on the couch. Although he addressed Angell, his eyes were all over Sullivan. 'We're pretty sure we know who it is.'

Angell looked at Amy.

'Do you have somewhere we can talk with you for a few minutes, alone?' she asked quietly.

'What's this about?' Heidi demanded.

'It's okay.' Amy touched her friend's arm. 'They have a few questions.' Then to Angell and Sullivan, 'We can go out on the balcony.'

She led the way, uncomfortably aware of the presence of both detectives behind her. The night was warm and a little humid; her fifth-floor balcony was closed in on three sides and overlooked the park where she had run into Detective Sullivan less than twenty-four hours ago.

Pulling the patio doors shut, leaving a distraught Huckleberry inside the apartment with her friends, she turned to face the detectives, arms crossed defensively.

'So, what can I help you with?' she asked, insides knotting, wishing she had brought her glass of wine outside with her. A few sips would have calmed her nerves.

'We need to ask you a few questions about one of your books,' Sullivan told her. He had a slight southern lilt she hadn't noticed before. Not a native Oregonian.

'My *books*?'

Amy hadn't been expecting that. Some of the tension in her shoulders eased, but only a little. Sullivan was observing her through dark eyes. Not necessarily with suspicion, but she could tell he was monitoring her reaction. She would never have figured him for a cop. Well, certainly not based on the ones she had encountered over the years.

'What can you tell us about *Grave Encounters*?'

He caught Amy off guard. She wasn't expecting these kinds of questions at all and had no idea where it could be leading.

'It's the first novel I wrote,' she told him and Angell, not at all sure what kind of information they were after. 'It was published about eight years ago – the first in my Zack Maguire series. Why?'

Sullivan and Angell exchanged a glance.

'Two bodies were found this morning and the way they were killed mirrors a scene in your book,' Angell told her.

What?

'My book?' Amy looked from one detective to the other. Was this some kind of prank?

From the expressions on their faces she knew they weren't fooling around.

'How do you know?' she asked, aware it sounded a

dumb question, but not sure what else to say. She looked to Angell for a response. The way Sullivan was intently watching her as if she'd done something wrong was a little off-putting. His partner was nicer.

'Chapter twenty-six, the murders in the graveyard: girl buried alive, boy stabbed to death.'

'That happened?'

Angell nodded.

'It did, last night.'

'Oh boy.' Amy shoved her hands back through her hair and turned away from the detectives to look out over the park. The sun was setting, creating a dusky pink and orange backdrop, the trees motionless in the still heat. It was a pretty evening. Too pretty to be receiving news like this. 'Why are you connecting it to *Grave Encounters*? It could be a coincidence.'

'The killer left clues leading to your book,' Sullivan told her grimly. 'He didn't make it difficult; he wanted us to know where he got his inspiration.' He waited for Amy to look in his direction, then added, 'He, or of course it could be she.'

Asshole.

'You think I did it?'

Sullivan held her gaze before answering. 'Nope,' he conceded eventually. 'But we would be interested in knowing where you were last night between about eight and eleven.'

'It's a standard question,' Angell added kindly. 'So we can eliminate you from our enquiries.'

Amy was rattled. Why would someone take a scene from her book and use it as a brief to commit murder. It made no sense.

There are plenty of sick people out there.

You can never tell how someone gets their kicks.

Right now, she was experiencing a whole range of emotions.

Guilt, disbelief, a little bit of fear and frustration, and anger, the last mostly directed at Detective Jake Sullivan.

'I was working,' she told Angell. 'Finished my bar shift about one-thirty.' Scowling at Sullivan, she added sarcastically, 'Then, of course, I was busy getting dog training tips from you.'

He didn't react to the jibe. 'Work? I thought you were a writer?'

'I am, but I need more than my books to pay the bills. I waitress at the Velvet Lounge part-time; it's a cocktail bar downtown.'

'I know where it is.'

'Your friend mentioned someone wrote on your

windshield,' Angell said, changing the subject. 'Was that today?'

'Yeah, I was doing a signing for my new novel at Too Many Books this morning. My car was parked across the street, and someone had written on the windshield. I think it was lipstick.'

'What did it say?'

Amy looked at the floor, uncomfortable.

'It said "bitch",' she said quietly. It was one thing telling her friends about it, but these detectives didn't know her and she didn't like the connotations the word implied.

'Any idea who might have done it?'

'There is a woman, Nadine. She's a fan of my books and she got a little mad today because I've ended the series and tried something new. I didn't see her do it and it might not have been her, but I can't think of anyone else.'

'Do you know her last name?'

'Williams. Nadine Williams.'

Angell smiled. 'We'll check her out.'

Sullivan was leaning back against the wall, arms and ankles casually crossed, still regarding Amy intently, most likely trying to figure her out and what part she might play in all of this.

She didn't appreciate the scrutiny. It had been a

long day which had steadily gotten worse as it went along.

'Do you have any more questions?' She made a point of glancing through the patio doors at her friends. 'We were about to eat.' Truth was her appetite had gone. All she wanted to do was to go back to her friends and drink a few more glasses of wine.

'We'll be in touch if we need anything. In the meantime, you call us if you think of any information that might be useful.' Sullivan pulled a card from his jacket pocket and their hands brushed briefly as he handed it to her.

Amy quickly pulled away. 'I'll show you out.'

Closing the door after them, she drew in a deep sigh and turned to face her friends. 'I need more wine in my glass.'

* * *

'You were a little hard on her,' Rebecca noted casually as they left Amy's apartment.

'I guess a little.' Jake was tired; the lack of sleep from the previous night catching up with him and making him grouchy. Still, his mind was working over-time. 'Don't you find it convenient she has a new book out to promote?' he questioned, opening the car door and dropping down into the driver's seat. He turned the ignition and lowered the volume on the stereo as the Foo Fighters blasted out.

'Yeah, I guess the timing is coincidental, but murder to promote a book?'

'They say there is no bad publicity.'

Rebecca looked at him. 'You honestly believe she is somehow involved in the murders?'

Jake thought of the pretty girl they'd been talking to. She didn't come across as your stereotypical nutjob, but that could be a mask. She had appeared genuinely stunned when they'd told her why they were there. And when he'd run into her walking her dog, she hadn't been acting in any way suspicious. There had been nothing in her demeanour to suggest that a couple of hours earlier she had killed two people.

She said she had been working and he had a feeling that, when they checked out her alibi, it would be the truth. Still, something didn't sit right.

'Well, no, not directly involved, although I guess she could've paid someone else to do it.'

Rebecca wasn't having it.

'I don't buy it. She was genuinely shocked when we told her what had happened. She'd have to be a hell of an actress to pull off a performance like that. You're on the wrong track with this one, Jake.'

'Maybe, but she's involved somehow. It wasn't a coincidence the killer left her book for us to find.'

It was getting late and he needed to sleep on it. His apartment was only a block from where Amy Gallaty lived, but first he had to drop Rebecca off; then, when he got home, walk Roxy.

A good night's sleep and he could view the case with fresh eyes and hopefully see the lead they were missing.

* * *

Her friends stayed with her till gone midnight, talking mostly of murder and hot detective, Jake Sullivan. Amy humoured them on both counts and didn't bother to point out that she thought Sullivan was a jerk.

Gage took Huckleberry for his night-time pee while the girls cleared up the kitchen, then there were hugs and kisses before Amy and the collie were alone. Huckleberry was supposed to sleep in the living room, but within two nights of staying with Amy had muscled his way into the bedroom. He whined if she tried to kick him out, so it was easier to let him sleep on the floor beside her bed. She had finished the best part of a bottle of wine and her drunken thoughts of graveside murders and Nadine causing a scene in Too Many Books rolled into one as she drifted to sleep. Those thoughts disappeared as she entered dreamland and an old nightmare surfaced, one she hadn't suffered from in a long time.

Stone stairs leading downwards.

She knew she shouldn't go down them, that something terrible waited at the bottom, but she couldn't stop herself from descending.

The steps went on forever. Lower, closer, the fear suffocating her as she approached the door.

The nightmare always ended in the same place, as she was stepping into the room.

Amy would wake herself up at this point, screaming and soaked in sweat.

It was just a stupid nightmare, she knew that – one she'd had for years. She'd thought she had finally grown out of it, but tonight it returned and when she woke screaming, she scared the bejesus out of Huckleberry.

As the dog woofed and growled, Amy padded to the kitchen for a glass of water, drawing deep breaths to calm her shaky nerves. The dream never failed to unsettle her, and she knew it would be a while before she would drift back to sleep.

As she lay in the darkness in the tangled sheets,

listening to the sound of the crickets buzzing through the open bedroom window, Amy had a premonition. It could be the nightmare had unsettled her, but she had an ominous feeling something bad was about to happen.

6

Rebecca held out on Alan until Wednesday, partly because she was pissed at him, partly because she felt guilty, and partly because she had been up to her neck with work.

They were struggling to catch a break on the church murders; the trail of clues had run cold.

Amy Gallaty's alibi had checked out. She had been working from seven until one-thirty and had about twenty witnesses who could verify her location during the murders. They had delved into her backstory too, and there was nothing suspicious that painted her as the kind of girl to be involved in a murder.

She was squeaky clean, and in her thirty-five years had never had any run-ins with the police, had no points on her licence, and everyone spoke highly of her. She had no family, except a distant aunt she never saw, her own parents having been killed in an automobile accident when she was twenty-two and, from all appearances, she lived quietly in the city, writing her books and waitressing at the Velvet Lounge, a job she had held down for six years.

Her publisher, a small local firm, had worked with her from the publication of her first book, *Grave Encounters*, and portrayed her as a talented writer who'd not yet managed to catch a break. Her employers at the Velvet Lounge also sang her praises, calling her punctual, professional and friendly; a girl with a positive outlook who loved her friends and her life in the city.

She didn't come across as someone with enemies and definitely not as a psychotic killer or someone cold-blooded enough to plan pre-meditated murder.

The fan from the bookstore had also been checked out: Nadine Williams had an alibi for the night of the murder and denied vandalising Amy's car. Rebecca and Jake had paid a visit to the home she shared with her boyfriend, Troy Cunningham, and had seen the signed pictures she had taken of herself with Amy at the launches of each book, while the novels themselves sat proudly on a bookshelf, flanked by A to Z bookends.

Nadine Williams was a little obsessed with the Zack Maguire series, but there was nothing to suggest she was anything more than an over-zealous and disappointed fan.

Rebecca felt most sorry for Troy, who undoubtedly had to live up to Nadine's expectations of Zack Maguire on a day-to-day basis.

The dead kids weren't throwing up any clues. Ben and Kasey had both been students at Juniper College, an establishment with its own grisly history. The campus had moved to a different location four years ago, but Rebecca doubted it would ever shake off its gruesome reputation.

Kasey had been a local girl, born and raised in Juniper, while Ben came from Virginia and was the nephew of Senator Blaine Hogan – an additional headache neither detective needed, as Hogan was already cranking up the pressure to make an arrest.

Ben and Kasey were both clean and nothing in their lives suggested enemies who might want them dead. Kasey had a jealous ex they were checking, but word suggested he was all talk and no action.

It could be a political connection to Blaine Hogan, but Rebecca and Jake didn't think so. The killing was the work of a psychopath, not an assassin.

It was early evening Wednesday when Rebecca returned to her townhouse after a day of questioning more of Ben and Kasey's friends, to find Alan waiting for her, his face partially hidden behind a bouquet of yellow roses.

Her heart sank as she pulled the car to a halt by the curb. It had been a long day and she yearned for a hot shower and a cold beer. She couldn't avoid him forever though and, in truth, knew he didn't deserve the treatment she was giving him.

'You haven't been returning my calls,' he said, by way of greeting, getting to his feet and thrusting the flowers at her.

Her mother would be appalled at the way Rebecca had treated him. Sarah Angell thought highly of Alan and considered him to be by far the most suitable of her youngest daughter's boyfriends. Definite marriage material, that's what she had called him. Rebecca was the only one of her daughters who hadn't yet settled down: her older sister, Jess, was now engaged and her middle sister, Wendy, already married with kids. As her mother liked to point out, Rebecca wasn't getting any younger; if she couldn't persuade her to move back to Swallow Falls, she would at least rest safe knowing she had a stable and solid man like Alan taking care of her.

'I'm sorry, Alan, it's this case. We're crazy busy.'

To make her feel even more guilty he took a sympathetic tone. 'I understand; I've seen the news.'

Ben Hogan's high-profile connections had made it impossible to keep the gory details of the murders out of the press, but so far, they had managed to suppress the link to the book.

'As long as you're not mad at me, that's all that matters.'

Rebecca *had* been mad at him for a while, and it was ridiculous. Alan was a good man. He was kind, considerate and articulate, and he worshipped the ground she walked on. She didn't deserve him.

'I'm not mad at you, I promise. Just really busy.'

'You're not busy now. Let me take you to dinner, Becky. We can catch up and you can tell me about the case.'

Rebecca deliberated for a moment. She just wanted beer and TV, but she guessed she owed him after the way she had shot him down on Saturday night in front of her friends.

'Okay,' she agreed. 'Give me half an hour to freshen up.'

While she showered and changed, Alan made

reservations at the Winchester, an upmarket hotel and restaurant in the city centre. Rebecca would have been happy with a burger bar, but Alan preferred à la carte.

Thinking she had better make an effort, she selected one of the three dresses she owned, a slinky red number that flattered her curves but had a knee-grazing hemline to keep it demure. Freeing her ponytail, she ran a brush quickly through her hair, dabbed her favourite scent, and was good to go.

Her choice of outfit got Alan's seal of approval and he gave her a low wolf whistle as she walked into the living room. Entering the restaurant fifteen minutes later he had his hand placed in the small of her back as he proudly guided her to their table, as if wanting to show her off to every other man in the room. This was what Rebecca hated, being made to feel as if she was some kind of prize. Still, she sucked it up and smiled.

Let Alan have his moment. She'd gotten out of stooping to a full apology and owed him one. For once she would play the dutiful girlfriend instead of being difficult.

The waiter brought menus and took their drinks order. Alan, who was teetotal, had his usual soda water with a twist of lemon, while Rebecca opted for a bottle of Heineken.

They were opposites in every sense of the word: Alan, who was seven years Rebecca's senior, was calm, rational, wore suits for every occasion and liked the finer things in life. Her mother said he was a good influence and balanced her out, while Jake called him safe and stuffy.

Rebecca wouldn't go as far as to call him stuffy, but she agreed he was a safe bet. Nothing wrong with that, as she had enough danger and excitement in her day job. Years of dating unreliable and unpredictable men made 'safe' appealing. And she guessed her mother was right: she was thirty-three now and wasn't getting any younger.

The waiter brought their drinks and Alan took a sip of his soda water, clearly vexed when Rebecca chose to ignore the glass that had been left with her beer and instead drank straight from the bottle. She caught his look.

'What?'

He shook his head, glancing around the busy restaurant as if a little embarrassed.

'This isn't a blue-collar bar, Becky.' He nudged the glass towards her.

Instead of taking it, Rebecca picked up the bottle and took a defiant swig. She'd put on a dress for him, but no way was she going to let anyone tell her how she should drink her beer.

'So how is work?' she asked, diverting the conversation before they fell out again.

Alan relaxed back into his chair. Retrieving a cloth from his suit pocket he took off his glasses and began to clean them while he recounted his day.

Rebecca was only half listening, her mind still preoccupied with the case. There was something they were missing. Jake was still convinced Amy Gallaty was the key to everything, but how did the pieces fit?

'Angell?'

The familiar voice broke through her thoughts and her back stiffened.

No way!

But she knew before she turned, immediately recognising the distinct New York accent even after all this time.

Joel Hickok.

'Jeez, Angell, I thought it was you.'

He hadn't changed. Maybe there were a couple more lines on his face, but the unruly hair remained and he still wore that cocky grin. And had no manners as, without asking, he pulled up a chair and sat down with them.

Rebecca was speechless, having expected to never

lay eyes on him again, and now he was here sitting at the table... with her and Alan. Her boyfriend, Alan.

Alan. God, she'd forgotten all about him.

'What are you doing here, Hickok?' she hissed.

'I'm staying here.'

'Staying here?'

'Staying at the hotel. It's work.' Without asking, he took a piece of bread from the basket in the centre of the table.

'It's work?' Rebecca repeated.

His cocky grin widened. 'What are you, a parrot?' Tearing off a piece of crust he shoved it in his mouth.

Opposite her, Alan cleared his throat, looking uncomfortable. 'Becky, are you going to introduce your friend?'

'*Becky*?' Hickok nearly spat the bread out. 'Since when did you start going by Becky?'

Rebecca scowled, her flaming cheeks matching her dress. She hadn't seen Joel Hickok in six years, yet he thought it was perfectly acceptable to waltz back into her life and start insulting her. Reining in her temper and not wanting him to see how flustered she was, she made the introductions.

'Alan, this is Joel Hickok. He's an FBI agent I worked with a few years back.' She didn't add that she'd also had a six-week fling with him at the end of their investigation. Alan did not need to know that. 'Hickok, this is Alan, my *boyfriend*.' She emphasised the last word for Hickok's benefit.

The two men shook hands, appraising each other.

'FBI agent? Really.' Alan was impressed, but then it didn't take much. He watched a lot of CSI and had been blown away when he'd first met Rebecca and some of her detective friends.

The waiter returned to take their order. He glanced at Hickok, then Rebecca and Alan.

'Will this gentleman be joining you for dinner?' he asked.

Rebecca started to say no, but Hickok was already talking over the top of her.

'Yeah, sure, and I'll have what she's having,' he told the waiter, pointing to Rebecca's bottle of Heineken.

Rebecca was fuming. How dare he come in here and hijack their dinner. She glanced at Alan and shrugged her shoulders by way of apology, but he seemed unperturbed, gratified to be in the presence of an FBI agent.

'FBI. Wow, that must be an interesting career,' he was gushing.

Hickok leaned back in his chair, lapping up the attention. 'So, Adam.'

'Alan.'

'Sorry, Alan. You've never fancied a career in law enforcement?'

Alan almost blushed. 'Oh no, I don't think I'd be cut out for a job like that.'

'You don't say. So what line of business are you in?'

'Oh, I'm in plastics.'

'What, you're a surgeon?' Hickok shot Rebecca a look, sticking another piece of crust in his mouth. 'Moving up in the world, eh, Angell? Little bit different to six years ago, pizza and your couch.' He winked and Rebecca flushed scarlet.

'No, no...' Alan jumped in, so eager to correct he was oblivious to Hickok's insinuation. 'I run a plastics firm. We do picnicking mostly. You know; plastic glasses, plastic plates and plastic cutlery. We're planning a plastic decanter for this year's range.'

Hickok threw another look at Rebecca, a sly smirk pulling at the corners of his mouth.

Ignoring him, she took a long swig of beer.

'So what's the job, Hickok? Why are you in Juniper? Is Max with you?'

'No, no, Max isn't with me. He retired, bought a condo down in Miami. I have a new partner.' The way he emphasised the word 'new' suggested he wasn't particularly impressed.

The waiter returned with his beer and Hickok

picked up the bottle, mirroring her as he took a swig; it didn't escape Rebecca's attention that Alan never berated him for not using a glass.

'You've got a couple of dead kids we've been asked to take a look at.'

Rebecca felt her heart sink.

'Are you talking about the church murders? But that's my investigation.'

Hickok stared at her for a long moment, his expression unreadable. She couldn't figure out if he already knew that.

'It's Senator Hogan's nephew. He's been pulling strings at the top; wants the FBI personally involved.'

'And so they sent you?'

He grinned at her. 'And so they sent me.'

7

Shannon Castle lived her life by routine and Wednesday night was grocery shopping night.

Some people might call her boring, but Shannon liked things in boxes, everything in order. It made life so much less stressful. Monday evening was the gym; Tuesday she would stay home and catch up on her favourite TV shows, Wednesday night was for groceries.

As always, she had her list and spent a pleasant half an hour perusing the aisles of the local grocery store, filling her cart with essentials and a few treats. At the checkout she made small talk with Marcie the cashier while the groceries went through, then loaded her bags, paid for her shop and exited the store, already planning her dinner.

Because Wednesday night was grocery night, it meant she would be home late, so it was also takeout night, and tonight Shannon was favouring Mexican. As she pushed her cart over to her car in the corner of the parking lot, she was trying to decide if she fancied a beef or a chicken burrito, and if it would be greedy to have a side order of nachos. Popping open the trunk of her car, she started to load the grocery bags.

A sound came from behind her.

Shannon started to turn, the nachos dilemma still on her mind, and caught a glimpse of black as something heavy smashed into her face.

The grocery bag in her arms dropped to the floor, cans spilling over the parking lot as she collapsed.

* * *

When she awoke, the first thing she was aware of was the smell of soil: in her face, up her nostrils. Her head was groggy, then the pounding kicked in, bringing with it nausea. Shannon groaned and tried to roll over.

Her arms wouldn't work. Panic kicked in as she tried to move her body. Her arms were behind her, pulled tight, and as consciousness crept back she understood why. Her wrists were tied.

Memories from the grocery store flooded back, of loading the bags from the cart into her trunk, the sound behind her and the glimpse of black. Someone had attacked her. Someone had brought her here.

Hysteria overtook panic and she started screaming.

This did not figure in her Wednesday night plans, did not fit in any of her boxes, and she had no idea how to cope with it.

Where the hell am I?

The earth beneath her told her she was outside, but she couldn't see and the darkness enveloping her suggested she was in some kind of outbuilding or barn.

Who had taken her? What did they want?

Fear bubbled in her throat. She was a good girl. She never broke the rules and always played it safe. This kind of thing wasn't supposed to happen to her.

Her car was at the grocery store. Someone must have found it and realised she was in trouble. They would be looking for her. They would find her, right?

Overhead came a creak: the sound of a door opening. With it came light. Not a lot, but enough to let her know it wasn't completely dark outside and to see she was right about being in a barn. Shadows fell on hay bales stacked high and a wall lined with various rakes and shears.

Shannon shuddered, her eyes moving towards the doorway.

A figure stood silently watching her: dark clothing, features indistinguishable. For a moment she thought her heart had stopped, she was that frightened.

'What do...?' Her voice was a squeak and her mouth so dry she couldn't finish the question. She heard a click; a harsh beam of light blinded her. She couldn't see the figure, but was aware he – she assumed it was a 'he' – was moving towards her.

Shannon whimpered and tried to roll away.

The flashlight beam was in her face and she felt her attacker push her onto her back before straddling her, forcing her legs down and her bound arms to crunch uncomfortably beneath her.

Oh my God. Oh my God. He's going to rape me.

She started screaming and the man smacked her hard in the face with the flashlight. The pain was sharp and white hot as her teeth smashed together; as she tasted blood, her screaming became moaning sobs.

He put the flashlight down and she was aware of him pulling something from a pocket. A knife?

No, dear God no, please don't let him cut me.

Pathetically she wriggled beneath him, going nowhere.

The click of a lid, the shake of an aerosol can. Her heart thumped.

What is he doing?

He began to spray the can at her chest; the smell of fumes filled her nostrils, her sobbing becoming choking. When he was done, he sat back for a moment, as if admiring his handy work, before roughly pushing her over onto her belly, forcing her face into the dirt as he sat on her thighs.

Shannon heard the spray of the aerosol again, this time on her back, and her brain scrambled to understand what was happening.

Eventually the spraying stopped. Again, there was a pause, then another click. This time there was no mistaking the sound of the blade opening.

She started screaming again, now hysterically, waiting for the slice of the knife. How was he going to do it? Was he going to stab her in the back or pull her head back and slice open her throat?

Unexpectedly he went for her wrists, cutting through the binds holding them together. Her arms fell limply by her sides as the weight on her back shifted. She heard footsteps. Were they fading? Was he leaving? For a long moment she lay on the barn floor, barely daring to breathe, let alone move.

Was he gone?

Eventually she pushed herself up onto her elbows. Her arms were hurting from how they had been forced behind her back. She glanced around. The door of the barn was still open and the man nowhere in sight.

Was it a trick, a test to see if she ran?

Tentatively she climbed to her feet, wrapping her arms around her body to check she was still in one piece. Aside from the pain in her banging head and bloody mouth, she was okay. Struggling to stop her heels sinking into the soil, she cautiously made her way towards the door on shaking legs.

From the dusky light outside, Shannon guessed it was about nine, nine-thirty. There was maybe another ten minutes of light before darkness took hold; time for her to establish where she was and get the hell out of here.

Her heart sank as she exited the barn and realised exactly where she was: the middle of nowhere. The only other buildings she could see were two further barns, both large in size. They appeared to be used for storage as she could see no grazing animals nearby. All three were surrounded by open fields, a dirt trail running from the barns past the fields and into woodland in the distance.

Why had he brought her here and then left?

Remembering the aerosol, Shannon glanced down at her blouse. Crude red paint had ruined it. Two red circles, one inside the other.

What was it supposed to mean?

Knowing she was going to struggle in her heels, she removed them. The dirt trail was probably stony, but she would walk better barefoot. Besides, the stiletto heels of her shoes were sharp and the only potential weapon she had should her attacker return.

She was midway along the trail and nearing the end of the first field when the gunshot came. Startled, she dropped her shoes, as the unexpected crack came from nowhere. As she scooped to pick them up, a second bullet whizzed past her head.

Her attacker.

Forgetting about the shoes, Shannon broke into a sprint heading for the woodland that still seemed so far away.

Have to get away. Have to make it to the safety of the woods.

A third and fourth bullet, both close, but not hitting.

Was he missing deliberately?

As she ran, panting heavily, sudden realisation of the significance of the paint dawned.

It was a target. He had been marking her up.

He was never planning to let her go. She was supposed to run; it was part of the game. And the object of the game was for him to kill her.

8

Amy was a couple of blocks from the bar when she realised she was being followed.

After saying goodnight to Gage and Tom and stepping outside the Velvet Lounge, she had an uncomfortable feeling she was being watched, but put it down to paranoia. The vandalism of her car, followed by the visit from the cops, had rattled her, and the return of her nightmare hadn't helped. She hadn't slept properly in three nights, and exhaustion was starting to play tricks on her mind.

The bar was only twelve blocks from her apartment and, apart from when the weather was bad, she tended to walk. The streets were well lit and even at one-thirty in the morning there were usually a few cars about.

Given recent developments, Gage had offered to escort her home, but he had to lock up and Amy, who really needed her bed, didn't fancy staying later than necessary. Besides, it wasn't fair to make him walk all the way to her place only to then have to backtrack to his own home. Half an hour and she would be back in her apartment and ready to attempt sleep.

The evening was warm and humid, the air heavy with warnings of a storm. She had her umbrella but didn't think the rain clouds would break before she reached the safety of home. The Velvet Lounge was on the edge of the city centre, and the surrounding area was still lively with people milling around, which was probably why she hadn't heard the footsteps immediately.

As the streets became less busy, the pedestrians mostly left behind and even the traffic on the road unusually quiet, every sound around her magnified. Normally she took no notice, preoccupied only with getting home, but tonight she was aware of every noise: the clack of her feet hitting the pavement, the distant slam of a door, the screech of a cat, someone's car alarm going off. And then, less than five minutes into her journey, the low thump of another set of footsteps behind her.

The second she heard them, Amy stopped and looked around. The street was empty. A little perturbed, but putting it down to her vivid imagination, she continued walking, mind already thinking ahead, plotting out a quick pee break for Huckleberry followed by a shower and bed.

The footsteps started again.

She told herself it was nothing, probably another pedestrian making their way home, but still she felt uneasy. Again, she glanced over her shoulder. About half a block back she could make out a shadowy figure standing motionless watching her. Although she couldn't make out the features, the build suggested it was a man.

Why had he stopped?

Amy weighed up her options. She could return to the Velvet Lounge, but in doing so she would have to pass the figure.

He was probably harmless and there was likely an innocent explanation for why he was out roaming the streets and had stopped at exactly the same time she did, but she didn't want to chance it. Option two was to carry on towards her apartment. This was the sensible plan, but the roads were becoming quieter and less built up. If she found herself in trouble she would be screwed.

Weighing up her options and not fancying either of them, she continued on shaky legs, repeatedly glancing over her shoulder to see if the man followed.

He did.

Reaching in her jeans pocket, Amy grabbed her door key, holding it as a weapon in her closed fist. She glanced around again. He was closer.

Heart jumping into her mouth she broke into a jog. Behind her came the footsteps – louder, pounding the concrete.

He was running after her.

Biting down on the panic that was clawing its way up her throat, Amy sped up. Pizza Paradise was up ahead. It was only a small takeaway business and usually dead at night, but it was a safe haven between here and her apartment. Reaching the door, she yanked it open and almost fell inside.

The young assistant behind the counter looked up from the magazine he was reading and eyed her with concern.

'I'm being followed,' Amy told him, glancing out of the window, trying to catch her breath.

The man who had been pursuing her had disappeared. Either that or he was hiding somewhere, waiting for her to emerge.

She turned back to the counter assistant, who was avoiding eye contact, clearly uncomfortable with conversing with the crazy lady who had burst into his shop. Amy drew in a shaky breath, unsure what to do. Although she couldn't see the man, she wasn't brave enough to go back outside, especially when her apartment was ten blocks away. She could call Gage, but he would still be locking up and didn't have a car, so would have to walk down to the takeaway. That would take time.

Another option came to mind. Pulling the card from her purse, she dialled the number on her cell phone. After six rings, her call was answered.

'Sullivan.'

He sounded tired and Amy guessed she had woken him. The detective might be a jerk, but he had told her to call if anything happened, so she swallowed her pride.

'It's Amy Gallaty. I'm sorry to be calling you so late, but there's a man following me.'

He was immediately alert. 'Where are you?'

'Pizza Paradise, the takeaway place on Main Street.'

'I know where it is. And the guy following you, where's he?'

Amy glanced out of the window again. 'I can't see him. He disappeared after I came in here.'

'Okay, stay in the pizza place. Don't go outside. I'm on my way.'

Before Amy could say anything else, he had hung up. She glanced over at the counter assistant who was eyeing her suspiciously and gave him an apologetic smile.

'I'll be gone in a bit.'

He didn't respond, instead buried his head back in his magazine. Amy wrung her hands together and paced the small room back and forth, feeling uncomfortable. While she waited, she perused the wall menu, going through the different combinations of pizza available, thinking the prices were a little inflated for the quality of pizza sold. She'd had takeaway from here once or twice, but it wouldn't be her first choice. Every now and again she glanced out of the shop front window, but could see no sign of the man.

She didn't have to wait long. Sullivan showed within ten minutes of her call, pulling to a halt outside the pizza takeaway. He wore jeans and a black T-shirt, probably thrown on in a rush, and a grim expression on his face.

'Any sign of him?' he asked Amy, by way of greeting.

She shook her head. 'Not since I came in here.'

He glanced briefly at the counter assistant, who was trying hard to look like he was concentrating on his magazine and not what they were saying.

'Okay, stay here.'

Sullivan disappeared outside the shop. He was gone for five long minutes, and when he returned Amy noticed the butt of a revolver poking out of the top of his jeans.

'Whoever he was, he's gone.'

'Okay.'

'Do you think it was someone who'd been in the bar?'

'I don't know. Maybe.'

'You get a good look at him?'

'Not really. It was dark and he wasn't close enough to see properly.'

'But you're sure he was following you?'

'Yes.' She was beginning to think calling Sullivan was a bad idea. 'I heard someone behind me. When I stopped, he stopped too. When I started running, he started running.'

Sullivan nodded, not looking overly convinced. He pulled out his badge and flashed it under the counter assistant's nose. 'The lady says she was being followed when she came in here. Did you see anything?'

'No! No! Nothing at all.'

Not that he would probably say if he had, Amy thought, but decided to keep it to herself. The counter assistant wasn't going to be any help.

Sullivan fired a few more questions at him before evidently coming to the same conclusion. He glanced at Amy; his expression unreadable. 'Come on. I'll take you home.'

With another quick apologetic glance at the counter assistant, Amy followed him out to the Audi.

'So, do you walk home from work after every shift?' he asked as she climbed in the passenger seat and closed the door.

'It's only twelve blocks. I've never had a problem before.'

'That wasn't what I asked.' He paused, hand on ignition, and looked at her, dark eyes questioning. 'Do you walk home after every shift?' he repeated.

Amy sighed, irritated at the pointless question. 'Yes... mostly. I don't see what relevance it has. I've never been followed before.'

'Not that you know about. Look, I'm trying to establish a pattern. If he was following you, he probably knows your routine.'

'If he *was* following me? You think I'm making it up? Being paranoid?'

'I never said you were making it up.'

'I know when I'm being followed.'

Annoyed he had doubted her, Amy crossed her arms and looked out of the passenger window.

She could feel his stare on her for a moment, maybe still questioning if she was telling the truth, perhaps frustrated that she was now sulking like a child, which she was, and yes, it was a little pathetic given the circumstances, but she couldn't help herself. Sullivan had a knack of rubbing her up the wrong way.

Eventually, she heard him give an exasperated sigh. He turned on the ignition and pulled away from the curb. They drove back to her apartment in silence. He was probably pissed at her for waking him up in the middle of the night; for making him leave his bed, probably his girlfriend, wife...

As subtly as possible she shifted her head, snuck a glance at his hand. No band on his ring finger. Regardless of whom he had left at home and whether he believed her, he had still turned out for her in the middle of the night. Amy felt a little guilty. As he pulled the car to a halt outside her apartment block, she gave him a quick smile.

'Well, thanks for the lift and sorry for dragging you out for nothing.'

To her surprise, he killed the ignition.

'I'll come up with you. If you were being followed, the guy might know where you live.'

Amy hadn't thought of it that way. What if she had been followed home before, but hadn't realised? What if the creep was waiting for her? The apartment block had a security buzzer, but the tenants were forever letting people in. She couldn't remember the last time a visitor had buzzed her to open the main door.

'Uh, okay,' she agreed, a little too freaked out to point out he had again questioned whether she had been followed.

He's making the effort to come upstairs. He wouldn't do that if he didn't believe you.

Sullivan followed her into the building and over to the elevators. While they waited, Amy was aware of his eyes sweeping the lobby. It was an old building that had been renovated; for the first time she realised there were plenty of places someone could hide. How often had she returned from her bar shift and stood here waiting alone? She had written six serial killer thrillers, yet never before noticed how many vulnerable situations she placed herself in.

You should know the rules better than anyone.

The elevator arrived and Amy stepped inside, Sullivan following. As she pressed the button for the fifth floor, she was acutely aware of his presence close behind her and the subtle spicy scent of his cologne. It was large enough to hold six people, but the space felt much smaller; almost suffocating. Being around Sullivan made her a little uncomfortable. She drew in a deep breath.

Stop freaking out, Amy. You're being paranoid because of what happened tonight.

She stole a glance at his profile. Straight nose, stubbled jaw, dark hair a shade too long and mussed, probably from where he'd been sleeping before she had woken him. Her attention focused on his mouth. And it hit her.

You're attracted to him.

The sudden realisation horrified her. This was Detective Jake Sullivan who had accused her of being involved in two murders. Though who, to be fair, had turned out tonight because she was being followed.

Stop making excuses. You are not attracted to him. It's one of those hero crush things. He helped you out of a bad situation and now you're being an idiot. It's nothing. He was doing his job.

She must have been looking at him a little goofily

because he was watching her, narrowing his eyes. 'What?'

'What?' Amy questioned back, defensively.

'You were staring at me.'

Heat coloured her cheeks. 'I was not.'

To her relief the elevator pinged, and the door opened, allowing her to escape from the uncomfortable situation and Sullivan's probing questions. The sound of muffled barking came from Amy's apartment.

Christ, Huckleberry. You're gonna get me evicted if you keep this up.

Sullivan followed her down the hallway as she fished for her keys in her purse.

'Are you planning on taking him out?'

Until this point, Amy had forgotten all about Huckleberry. She still hadn't gotten used to having a dog living with her. Sullivan wasn't going to be happy about her going out alone and, truth be told, Amy didn't much fancy it after the evening's events, but Huckleberry needed to pee.

'Umm...'

Sullivan shook his head, looking irritated that she wasn't heeding any of his advice about safety. 'Get me his leash. I'll do a quick check of your apartment, then take him round the block for you.'

'It's okay. You don't have to. You've already done...' Amy tapered off mid-sentence, as he fixed her with a pointed look.

Damn, he's bossy.

'Okay, I'll get the leash,' she conceded, opening the door to the apartment.

Huckleberry was delighted to see Sullivan, ignoring Amy as he showered the detective with licks.

You forget who feeds you, buddy.

Niggled by the dog's lack of loyalty, Amy waited patiently as Sullivan did a quick check of her apartment, Huckleberry in hot pursuit. As they returned from her bedroom, she reached for the leash, throwing it to Sullivan as Huckleberry went nuts.

'We'll be back in fifteen minutes,' Sullivan told her, clipping on the leash. 'Make sure you keep the door locked.'

Amy watched them go, saluting Sullivan behind his back.

Keep the door locked. Does he think I'm stupid?

After clicking the latch into place, she went into the kitchen and put on the coffee pot; it was late, but her mind was buzzing. Coffee and wine relaxed her, and she wasn't in the mood for the latter. While the machine whirred, she kicked off her shoes, opened the patio doors and stepped out onto the balcony. The evening was still warm and humid. Leaning on the railing, she watched as Sullivan and Huckleberry crossed the road and disappeared into the park.

Amy wasn't sure what it was about the man that was getting under her skin. Normally she was laid back and it took a lot to get a rise out of her. Sullivan seemed to manage it with little effort.

Perhaps it's because he never believes you.

Or maybe it was something else.

Pondering the question, Amy's glance wandered a little further up the street to the figure standing at the edge of the trees, watching her apartment. With a start she stepped back from the balcony railing, her skin going cold.

Was it him, the guy who had followed her? Did he know where she lived?

Quickly she stepped inside her apartment and locked the patio doors.

9

'You look like hell.'

Jake scowled at Rebecca's observation as he walked into the precinct. 'I had a late night.'

'Yeah?'

He narrowed his eyes at her suggestive tone. 'Not in that way.'

She pushed one of the two Starbucks cups she held in his direction. 'Good job I got you one of these, then.'

'Thanks.' Jake took the cup gratefully.

After the call from Amy, he'd managed to snatch about two hours' sleep, dozing through his alarm and having only enough time to shower, dress and let Roxy out for a quick pee, so coffee had been out, and he and

Rebecca had both learned a long time ago to avoid the acidic stuff sold in the vending machine at work.

'I bet my night can top yours,' Rebecca told him as he sipped the strong coffee. He noticed the slight frown on her face.

'Alan?'

Most of Rebecca's irritations tended to be directed at her dull boyfriend. Jake had lost count of the times he had questioned the point of their relationship. These days he mostly let her rant and tuned out.

'Not exactly. More like a pain in the ass from my past and it spells trouble for our investigation.'

'What do you mean?'

'You remember the case I was involved in when I was a rookie? The one where...' She trailed off, staring past Jake at the door, her frown intensifying.

'Morning, Angell.'

Jake turned at the cocksure voice, took a glance at the owner: a guy of about his own age, dark suit, unruly hair, slightly smug grin. The pain in the ass? He'd put money on it.

The man came to a halt beside Rebecca, helped himself to the coffee in her hand, took a large mouthful and almost choked, spitting it straight back in the cup.

Nice.

'Jeez, Angell, how much sugar did you put in this thing?' Ignoring the fuming look she gave him; he turned his attention to Jake. 'Sullivan, right?'

Jake shook the offered hand guardedly, while Rebecca looked on, seriously pissed off.

'I worked a case with your old partner, Frank Logan, down in Atlanta last year. Heard good things about you.'

Heard good things. Jake wondered briefly if his previous partner would've shared the same sentiment and quickly quashed the thought.

'Logan's a good cop,' he said instead.

The other man nodded.

'Special Agent Joel Hickok. Good to meet you.'

Hickok.

The name was familiar, and it only took a second to click into place.

The Alphabet Murders.

They had happened about six years ago. Jake had been serving with the Atlanta PD at the time, and hadn't moved to Oregon until a couple of years later. The case had been big and he'd heard the details time and again since joining Juniper PD. Hickok had been one of the FBI agents Rebecca had worked with and, on the occasions she had mentioned his name, it had been through gritted teeth. He had never questioned why before. Now he made a mental note to ask her about it later.

'Likewise,' he told Hickok, playing it carefully, remembering what Rebecca had said about it spelling trouble for their investigation.

The Feds were here because of the church murder, of that there was no doubt. Jake had worked with the Bureau before on a couple of homicides back home and didn't have a problem so long as everyone played ball. His partner's problem was more personal. Whether it was down to plain dislike or something more, he intended to find out.

'So, are we going to get down to business?' Rebecca asked tartly, still looking unimpressed. 'You said you brought your new partner, right?'

'Good to meet you, Detective Angell.'

She whirled round, surprised by the voice behind her.

The guy holding his hand out was late twenties, Jake estimated, lanky in build and baby-faced, wearing a navy suit that swamped him, and a syrupy smile.

'Special Agent Declan Rivers. I've read all about your work in the Alphabet Murders and been looking forward to meeting you.'

He pumped Rebecca's hand enthusiastically, then

Jake's, while Hickok looked on, his expression one of pure irritation.

'When you've finished your love fest, maybe we can get to work,' he snapped.

The four of them met with Captain Krigg before heading down to the office Jake and Rebecca shared with two other detectives.

'So, what have you got so far?' Hickok asked, taking a seat and getting straight to the point.

They talked Hickok and Rivers through the crime scene, told them about the book found in the car and its author, Amy Gallaty.

'So what's your take on her?' Hickok wanted to know. 'You think she's somehow involved?'

'Not directly involved,' Rebecca told him. 'She was working the night of the murder.'

'Doesn't mean she didn't get someone else to do it.'

'True. My instincts say otherwise.'

'Your instincts, eh?' Hickok grinned.

'Yes, Hickok, my instincts.'

'She has a new book to promote, doesn't she?' This was from Rivers, who had been scribbling notes furiously as if his life depended on it, oblivious to the fact his partner and Rebecca had been sniping at each other throughout the morning.

Definitely a rookie, Jake thought.

'The murder was taken from one of her old books,' he pointed out to the younger Fed. 'It wouldn't make sense she was killing for publicity, unless it was from the new one. Amy Gallaty is involved, but she's no killer. I think our perp specifically targeted her book, for what reason I don't know.'

'What makes you so sure her book wasn't picked at random?' Hickok asked. 'Maybe our guy read it, liked it and decided to re-enact it.'

'She said someone was following her last night.'

'She did?' Rebecca questioned, eyebrows slightly raised. 'How come I don't know about this?'

'Because I haven't had a chance to tell you until now,' Jake said levelly. 'She was being followed on the way home from the bar where she works, stopped off at a pizza place and called me, so I went and checked it out.'

'She called you?'

'She had my card.'

'You see who it was?' This was from Rivers.

'No. Whoever it was had gone by the time I got there.'

'So how do you know she wasn't making it up?' Rebecca asked, a little tightly.

'My instincts.' He could tell she was pissed at him for not sharing this snippet of information earlier, probably because she wanted to have the upper hand with Hickok. Truth was, Jake was still analysing the night's events himself. There had been no sign of anyone following Amy, but she had been genuinely unnerved and a little jumpy. If she had made up her stalker then she was one hell of an actress.

He believed her.

'Okay, so let's say someone is targeting her specifically,' Hickok theorised. 'Do we have any names: people she's pissed off, ex-boyfriends, husbands?'

'There was a woman, a fan, who had an altercation with her at a book signing a couple of days ago,' Rebecca told him. 'When Amy returned to her car, someone had written the word "bitch" across the windshield. The fan may have vandalised the car, but she has a solid alibi for the night of the murders.'

'Name?' Rivers was still scribbling away.

Jake figured they'd have a full transcript of their meeting by the end of it.

'Nadine Williams.'

'Got it.'

Hickok shot his partner an irritated look.

'Anyone else?' he questioned Rebecca and Jake.

'Not that we've come up with.'

'Seriously, Angell? That's all you've got for me?'

Rebecca glared at him.

'We've been eliminating suspects. Forgive me if you don't like where we're at. If we'd had some warning you were gonna show up out of the blue and muscle in on our investigation, perhaps we could have lined a few more up for you.'

Rivers had stopped writing to listen to their exchange and sat with his jaw agape.

'You're being a little unfair, Joel,' he chipped in, as Rebecca finished her outburst. 'Detective Angell is well respected.'

Hickok scowled at him.

'Shut up talking like an idiot, Rivers. When I want your opinion, I'll ask for it. Why don't you get back to writing your essay?'

The younger agent's face turned scarlet. 'You can't speak to me like that,' he spluttered.

'Sure I can.'

'You haven't changed,' Rebecca muttered. 'Obnoxious as ever.'

Hickok grinned at her and opened his mouth to retort. Exasperated by the route the meeting was taking, Jake stepped in.

'Our investigation has shifted to the dead kids. Maybe we should focus our attention on that,' he suggested, shooting a warning look at Rebecca to cool it. He didn't know what had happened between his partner and Hickok in the past, but it needed to stay there.

'Yeah?' Hickok looked interested. 'What have you got?'

'Kasey Miller had a jealous ex. Shawn Randall. He'd gotten into a couple of fights with Ben and didn't accept the relationship with Kasey was over. He claims to have been out in the campus bar, drinking alone. So far, we have no witnesses to verify that.'

'You think he could be our guy?'

'Possibly. According to other students he has a bad temper and he has the motivation, but nothing ties him to Amy.'

'Maybe her book was selected at random.'

'And her stalker?'

'Could be an unrelated incident,' Hickok mused. 'Or paranoia. Or perhaps she is making it up for attention. The ex-boyfriend is our priority right now.'

'So you're going to discount any connection?'

'For the moment.'

'You're making a mistake,' Jake disagreed, peeved by Hickok's high-handed manner. Amy was involved somehow. He'd bet his salary on it.

'Well, I guess we could send Rivers over to check up on her.' Hickok glanced at the younger agent's pile of notes and smirked. 'He'd probably like that. They could compare novels.'

Rivers immediately rose to the bait, dropping his pen in anger and glaring at his partner.

'I'm warning you, Joel. Stop—' He was interrupted by a knocking at the door.

It opened and Vic Boaz stuck his head in. He immediately clocked Hickok and a scowl formed on his face.

'What are you doing back here?'

Hickok's smirk widened to a grin.

'Officer Boaz. Long time no see. How's the family?'

Boaz muttered something unintelligible under his breath.

Jake knew the officer had worked with Hickok and Rebecca on the Alphabet Murders, which had been perpetrated by Boaz's older brother, Rodney Boone. He didn't particularly like Boaz, having found him to be a lazy cop looking for an easy ride through the job, but Jake figured that had to have stung.

Low blow, Hickok.

Ignoring Hickok and dismissing Rivers, Boaz focused his attention on Rebecca and Jake.

'We've had a call come in; figured you should know. A body has been found, out in the woods by Beaver Creek.'

'How is this relevant to us?' Hickok demanded. 'We're in the middle of another murder investigation here.'

Jake felt his heart sinking, already knowing what was coming. He glanced at Rebecca and knew she was thinking the same thing.

Boaz's scowl deepened as he finally addressed Hickok.

'I think you'll find it's relevant. Another paperback has been found with the victim.'

10

Amy paced back and forth across her apartment, raking her hands through her hair.

'Why is this happening?' she addressed no one in particular. 'Why has he picked my books?' She wasn't whining; more distraught that she had unwittingly written the death scene for another innocent victim.

'We're still trying to establish that,' Jake told her. He had been given the job of breaking the news to her that the killer had copycatted another of her novels. Rivers was with him; Hickok having chosen Rebecca to accompany him to the crime scene. Under normal circumstances Jake would've argued against the logic of splitting up from his partner, but Hickok and Rebecca had unresolved issues and it was creating a bad atmosphere. For the moment he was glad to be away from them.

Amy had been writing when they'd arrived. Her laptop was still lit up, sitting on the oak dining table, the words on the screen illegible from where he stood. Beside the laptop sat a coffee cup and a pair of reading glasses.

Her apartment was a mix of shabby and chic in muted shades of cream, green and soft grey. Cushions were scattered across the two couches and the pictures and ornaments in the room combined contemporary with antique. It had a feminine and homey feel. In the corner of the room, beside the open patio doors, Huckleberry watched them from his bed, where he had retired after enthusiastically greeting Jake and Rivers. The long curtains billowed gently, the much-needed breeze adding a little respite from another hot summer day.

'You know there are four more books in the series?' Amy looked at Jake, her eyes troubled.

Amber coloured eyes. He hadn't noticed them before. Almond in shape and framed by long lashes. They were the kind of eyes a man would fall for. Maybe a killer would fall for? She worked at the Velvet Lounge as a waitress. Perhaps she had attracted the wrong kind of attention. She had been followed from there. It would be worth checking out if Shawn Randall ever drank in her bar. Jake stored the idea away. Something to look into later.

'So the shooting death, it was from the second book?' Rivers questioned. He sat on the couch, pen poised, the cup of tea he'd insisted on Amy making when she had offered them a coffee from the pot she'd recently made, still untouched on the table beside him.

Jake shot him an irritated look.

The question was rhetorical. They already had the name of the book the first responding officers had found at the scene and bagged up as evidence.

'Yes, I thought you already knew that before you got here?' Amy said, echoing Jake's thoughts. She moved to sit back at the dining table, where she had been writing before their interruption, and scraped her hands back through her hair again, letting out a deep breath. She seemed drawn and nervous, with no sign of the feistiness from their previous meetings.

'We had been told that,' Rivers responded, his tone surly. 'But I like to be thorough. The information I put in here,' he continued, tapping his notebook with his pen in a patronising manner, 'it has to be orderly. I can't work with scribbles.'

Prick, Jake thought, keeping his temper reined in.

He pulled out a chair and sat down facing Amy, prompting Huckleberry to get up from his bed and mosey over. Rivers watched the dog guardedly, looking relieved when he settled against Jake's leg. The younger agent hadn't been impressed with Huckleberry's greeting when they'd arrived, and Jake had gotten the feeling Rivers didn't do slobbering tongues or dog hair on his suit pants.

Something he didn't get. He'd been around animals all his life; his parents owned a ranch back in Georgia and he had grown up surrounded by horses, dogs, cattle and chickens. Dogs had always featured in his life, and he couldn't imagine not having one.

'Why don't we ignore *thorough* for now,' he suggested, rubbing Huckleberry's soft ears, sounding calmer than he felt, 'and try and move things forward.' Out of the corner of his eye, he saw Rivers shoot him a look and he glared back at him, daring him, before refocusing his attention.

There was a vulnerability about Amy today and, for reasons he didn't care to define, he felt protective towards her, especially when Rivers was acting like an asshole.

'I need you to think,' he told her. 'I know we went over this before, but who in your life might have a problem with you? We already have Nadine Williams on the list, but I need you to think of other people. Anyone you may have inadvertently pissed off or who has a reason to spite you.'

'I don't think there is anyone; just Nadine.'

'Cast your mind back. No other fans or writers whose toes you've trodden on? Any of the employees in the Velvet you might have had a disagreement with? Friends or exes you've fallen out with?'

She did as asked, closing her eyes for a moment, her face pale as she struggled to come up with a name. Eventually she reopened them.

'I'm sorry, but I'm struggling. I guess I had a bit of a fight with Jocelyn, one of the waitresses I work with, a few weeks back, but it wasn't even a fight; just a stupid disagreement over tips. We were fine by the end of the shift. I try not to fall out with my friends; we're all good. And exes – I broke up with my last boyfriend nearly a year ago.'

Jake nodded. 'Was it amicable?'

'Is it ever amicable?'

'You broke up with him?'

'Yes, but it had been fizzling out for a while.'

'So you're saying he agreed with the decision.'

'Well, no.' Amy paused, a little flustered. 'He was peed off because he wasn't the one to end it.'

'So he was controlling?'

'Well... I guess he liked to have things his own way, but you can cross him off your list, he moved away six months ago.'

'Where did he move to?'

'Chicago, I heard. I didn't see him before he left. We'd already severed ties.'

'We're still gonna need to check him out, to be certain before we cross him off the list.'

Amy shrugged. 'I guess.'

'What's his name?'

'David. David Gavin.'

Jake glanced over at Rivers to make sure he was writing it down. They would definitely need to check the ex-boyfriend out. Exes often had a score to settle.

'How about work at the Velvet Lounge?' he asked. 'Have you noticed any customers paying you any extra attention?'

'No more than normal. It's a bar and I'm a cocktail waitress. Put men together with alcohol and there will always be situations where they try it on a little. It goes with the territory.'

'But no one has stood out as going a little too far?'

'No.'

'I know you've already told us you didn't know Ben Hogan or Kasey Miller. What about Shawn Randall? Does that name ring any bells?'

Amy thought for a moment. 'No, should it?'

'He was Kasey's ex-boyfriend.'

'Is he a suspect?'

'Everyone is a suspect at this point.'

'Including me.' It wasn't a question.

'You know that's not what I meant.'

'Of course you are the catalyst for all this,' Rivers piped up, far too cheerfully. 'You may not have *done the deed* shall we say, but three people would still be alive if you hadn't written those books.'

Jake wanted to punch him, tactless son of a bitch.

Amy paled further, but her tone had an edge when she spoke. 'I write fiction, Special Agent Rivers. I didn't expect some sicko to use my work as inspiration.'

'She's not to blame for this,' Jake added, scowling at Rivers. 'Our guy could have used anything for a trigger.'

'I realise that,' Rivers spluttered, his face reddening. 'I was only pointing out he used her books and if she hadn't written them—'

'The victims would still be dead. He would have found another way.'

'But—'

'But nothing,' Jake snapped. 'Only one person is to blame and that is whoever put Ben Hogan and Kasey Miller in the graves. And whoever strung our latest vic up in a tree. Our attention would be better focused finding out who did that, instead of casting the blame elsewhere.'

He turned to Amy, who was looking a little surprised at his outburst. As if she hadn't expected him to side with her. Thinking back to their previous encounters, he guessed she would have a point.

When did that change?

Deciding not to read into it, he got to his feet, throwing a scowl in Rivers' direction that it was time to go. As the young Fed scooped up his notes, Jake glanced down at Amy.

'Keep thinking of names. Remember, anyone who might be pissed at you, anyone showing a little bit too much interest or anyone acting at all oddly.'

Amy nodded. 'Okay.'

Jake hesitated, glancing briefly in Rivers' direction, before adding. 'And if you get any trouble at all, give me a call.'

* * *

'So what's the deal with Adam?' Hickok asked, as he and Rebecca made their way to the crime scene.

'Alan, Hickok. His name is Alan.'

'You guys serious?'

Rebecca gave him a stony look. 'Why do you care?'

This was like déja vu. Hickok beside her, driving like he was in a race, and knowing exactly what buttons to press to get her to bite.

And you do. Every time.

'Lighten up, Angell. I'm making conversation, being polite. We haven't seen each other in six years.'

And whose fault is that?

Rebecca thought the words but kept them to herself.

They were on their way to a murder scene, and she needed to have her full attention about her.

She wasn't the same wide-eyed, small-town rookie Hickok had once known. Six years was a long time, and she had worked hard to prove herself at work.

The Alphabet Murders case had raised her profile considerably. She had been injured in the line of duty, had helped to solve the case and been commended for her actions. Sure, she still liked to kick back with a few bourbons and, okay, the hot temper was still there simmering under the surface, but she had grown up a lot, earned her place in this town and put down roots. She now owned her own house, had made detective and was well respected among her colleagues. Hickok needed to understand and accept that she had changed, and he couldn't just roll the clock back.

'The guy's a douche, Angell.'

'The guy is my boyfriend, Hickok. You don't even know him, so please don't judge him.'

'Doesn't stop him from being a douche.'

'In your opinion.'

'In my opinion.'

Rebecca drew in a deep breath. 'Look, Hickok. We have to work together, and I think we both want the same result – to catch the son of a bitch doing these murders. So why don't we focus on that and not my personal life.' She expected a sarcastic response, so was surprised when he replied in an affable tone.

'Sure. If that is what you want. I was trying to show an interest, given our personal history, but we can keep it purely professional, no problem.'

Rebecca eyed him warily. This was not the Joel Hickok she knew. There had to be a 'but' coming. He would convince her he was doing as she had asked, then he would go back to being a jackass when she least expected it.

Except he didn't. He remained focused on the investigation for the rest of their journey, sticking only to questions and theories about the murders. Much to Rebecca's annoyance.

He's doing as you asked. Quit being an idiot.

Despite her little pep talk, it still pissed her off.

* * *

The crime scene was intact when they arrived.

Beaver Creek was a trail popular with hikers: a picturesque area of woodland backing on to farmland, and it was two hikers who had found the body as they made their way along one of the routes that eventually wound down to the coast.

The victim, female, maybe late thirties Rebecca guessed at first appearance, was suspended by her left foot, swinging from the branch of giant maple tree. She was blonde, may have been pretty before death, and wore a skirt suit, suggesting she'd come to the forest straight from work. Come to the forest on her own; perhaps been lured or tricked, or been brought here?

Her white blouse was shredded and bloody. Rebecca counted at least three bullet holes.

The responding officers, Peterson and Chalmers, had taped off the scene and led Rebecca and Hickok to where the hikers were waiting. They were young: a guy and a girl, and both nervous and eager to get away. The girl was particularly pale, and they later learned she had barfed her breakfast after finding the body. Aside from that, the couple were unable to help further, and Hickok cleared them to go home.

Wrong time, wrong place.

Rebecca guessed the same could be said for the victim. Unless she had been specifically targeted.

They would need to establish her identity first and see if this new murder yielded any further clues as to their killer's motive or identity.

As they waited for Greg Withers to arrive, Hickok glanced at the body and then at Rebecca.

'So, what are your thoughts, Angell?'

Rebecca shot him a look, still wary that this acting professional business was all a mask. For no other reason than she figured she would look an idiot calling his bluff, she decided to roll with it.

'Our killer is focused on Amy Gallaty,' she told him. 'Whether it is because he has a thing for her books, or has a more personal connection, we don't know. But it would make sense the victims aren't random.' She glanced at the woman suspended in the tree. 'She's wearing a suit. She wasn't hiking dressed like that, so our perp had to have brought her here. He could've picked off a hiker more easily. Why take the risk? I think this victim was intentional, which suggests she is somehow linked to Amy. We need to find out how.'

Hickok nodded, the ghost of a smile touching his lips. 'Ditto.'

11

He watched her walking the dog along the bank of the river. She was a creature of habit and had her routines. Although there were other people out and about, taking advantage of the warm June morning, he remained hidden within the safety of the trees. He couldn't risk her bumping into him, and that damn collie was too nosey, having already nearly sniffed him out and exposed his hiding place a couple of nights ago.

As she eventually turned and headed back towards him, he lifted the camera that hung around his neck and snapped off a couple of shots. Dressed casually in combats and a dark T-shirt that fitted snugly, showing off the shape of her small breasts, she threw a Frisbee for the dog. He took a couple of steps closer, certain she was too distracted to notice him as the dog caught the Frisbee and headed for the water.

'Huckleberry, don't you dare.'

He zoomed the lens in on her. She wore sunglasses, large round ones that swallowed her face. As she watched the dog, chewing on her full bottom lip – a trait of hers he recognised as anxiety – she lifted a hand and tucked strands of tawny brown hair behind her ear.

Click. Click.

The collie stopped and looked at her, orange Frisbee in his mouth, summing up the situation. After a long moment of hesitation, he dutifully returned to where she waited.

First time she hadn't had to go after him. Huckleberry was learning.

As she hooked the lead onto the collar, he slipped back into the bushes. She couldn't see him. That would ruin everything. A couple of nights ago, following her home from the Velvet Lounge, he'd taken a risk. She had realised she was being followed and instead of crossing the road, throwing her off track, he had pursued her to the pizza place. It had been foolish. She could have stopped at any point to confront him and his plans would have had to change, but she hadn't, and he had gotten off on scaring her. On the high of knowing she realised he had been following her.

Thinking back to how much he had enjoyed the feeling, he decided maybe it was time to up the ante.

An idea came into his head and he smiled. It was time to give Amy a scare.

* * *

Leaving an unhappy Huckleberry in her apartment Amy headed into town to run a few errands. After banking the latest cheque from her publisher and stocking up on groceries, she stopped at her favourite coffee shop for a latte and a chocolate chip cookie.

It was routine. She hated chores and the coffee shop treat was her motivation and reward for doing them.

When she returned to her apartment she would get stuck into the new book. No work at the Velvet Lounge tonight and so the opportunity was there to write as late as she wanted. Bearing this in mind, she had bought a pizza for dinner. Should she find her flow, she would not want to be interrupting it to prepare a laborious meal.

Mabel's was her coffee shop of choice. More personal than Starbucks and selling home-made baked goods. When she was in a rush, Amy would get her coffee and cookie to go; at other times she would settle herself into one of the booths and people watch out of the window.

Today she would people watch.

And think.

She had a lot to think about: the killer who had recreated murder scenes from two of her books; the man who had followed her when she left the Velvet Lounge on Wednesday night; Detective Jake Sullivan. All three things were unsettling her.

She felt guilty about the murders and more than a little helpless. The killer appeared to be using her Zack Maguire novels for inspiration and Amy was conscious there were four more books in the series. Was this lunatic going to kill again? The revelation of her connection to the church murders had been unnerving enough. Knowing the killer had taken it a step further and was targeting her writing specifically was a hell of a burden. She remembered Special Agent Rivers' words:

Three people would still be alive if you hadn't written those books.

Sullivan had tried to sugar-coat it, but Rivers was

right. She was responsible. Their blood was on her hands. Neatly bringing her on to Sullivan.

The man was bossy, blunt and to the point, and had initially given the impression he didn't particularly like her. Except he had turned out in the middle of the night when she had called him.

He was doing his job.

And he had defended her against Rivers yesterday.

He was reserving judgement. Maybe.

He had defended her. Had come to her aid when she'd called him. And she was attracted to him. Much to her annoyance. It had to be down to being followed. He had come to her rescue. She had been relieved and grateful, and it had somehow manifested itself into a silly crush. It wasn't real and she would get over it.

Choosing to believe she was right, Amy crossed the road to Mabel's and pushed open the door, charmed, as always, by the old-fashioned bell announcing her arrival.

She didn't recognise the girl behind the counter and guessed she must be new. Patiently, she waited in line behind an older couple, her attention drawn to the beautiful bouquets of flowers adorning one of the corner tables. Lilies, roses, irises and daisies in an array of colour. Some stood in vases, others were in wrappers. Amy's focus was drawn to the framed picture that sat in the centre. A young girl with dark hair and smiling eyes. The girl who usually served her.

A word, a name, drew her attention away from the table and back to the couple in front of her.

Kasey.

'Such a sad waste of a young life,' the gentleman in front of her was saying.

They were talking about the girl in the picture frame; the girl who had served latte and cookies to Amy on numerous occasions. And they were talking about her in the past tense.

Kasey Miller.

Realisation dawning, Amy turned and fled from the coffee shop, all appetite for latte and cookies gone, and crashed straight into a hard, masculine body.

Hands gripped her arms, strong, steadying, and for a brief moment she panicked.

'Amy?'

Heart thumping from the shock, she pulled back, relieved when they released her, and focused on the friendly, concerned face she immediately recognised. Troy. It was Nadine's boyfriend, Troy.

Warily she glanced around for Nadine, but he appeared to be alone.

'You okay?'

Amy ordered herself to breathe, to calm down. 'Yeah, sure, I'm sorry. I didn't mean to run into you.'

'It's fine.' He took another step back, realising he was crowding her space, but continued to look at her with concern. 'You're sure you're okay? You look white as a sheet.'

'I'm fine. I realised I'd forgotten something.'

Troy raised his brows slightly, waiting for her to elaborate. She didn't and instead changed the subject.

'You live around here?'

'No, I've just come from a meeting with a client.'

Nodding, Amy took in for the first time the suit he was wearing, the briefcase in his hand. On the previous occasions she'd seen him he'd been with Nadine and dressed more casually.

'I design security systems,' Troy elaborated. He hooked a thumb in the direction of the old brownstone building on the opposite side of the road to Mabel's. 'Just landed an account with Blake & Colman, the law firm, to update their system. Saw this place as I was leaving and thought I'd grab a coffee. Can I buy you a cup?'

'Sorry?'

'A coffee.'

Focus, Amy. Focus.

He was peering anxiously at her again and she

found herself looking at his eyes. They were a deep blue; the colour of midnight. They crinkled as he spoke again.

'I'd like to buy you a coffee as an apology for the other day. Nadine was out of line and I'm sorry. She gets passionate about things and she's a huge fan of your books, but she was wrong to confront you how she did.'

'I, um, it's okay.' It wasn't okay, but Amy's problem was with Nadine. Troy had done nothing wrong and had nothing to apologise for. 'It's kind of you to offer, but I need to get back home.'

She thanked him again, said goodbye and made her way back to her car, mind spinning.

She knew the victim.

Of course it had to be a coincidence, an awful, sick twist of fate, but it didn't make Amy feel any better. She hadn't known Kasey Miller by name, but she had by face. The girl had been serving her coffee for over a year and now she was dead. Murdered using one of the plots in Amy's books. She had to tell Sullivan. Correction. She had to tell the cops. Not specifically Sullivan.

He told you to call him if anything happened.

There was no reason she couldn't go to his partner, Detective Angell. She could drive to the police precinct right now. Tell them she knew the victim; that it had to be a coincidence. She only knew the girl by face, hadn't known her name or anything about her. She was just a girl working in a coffee shop and it happened to be a coffee shop Amy sometimes used. There was no way the killer would've made that connection. Could he? She forced herself to take another deep breath.

Take a moment, Amy. Pull yourself together and calm down.

Her skin was hot and clammy, her heart beating too fast. She needed to get a grip of herself, assess and evaluate the situation, and decide on the best course of action.

Drive home, take ten minutes to calm down then call Sullivan. You know it's the right thing to do.

The drive back to her apartment was a blur, her head still full of whats and whys and ifs; the picture of smiling Kasey Miller; the bouquets of flowers in Mabel's.

She pulled into her parking spot in the garage, grabbed the bag of groceries.

As she stepped inside the apartment building, Amy's attention was immediately drawn to the line of locker-style mailboxes.

Hers was hanging ajar. She hadn't left it that way.

Trepidation knotted her gut as she crossed the lobby, pulled the door open wide and let out a scream as she saw the rat hanging in front of her by its long, thin tail, grey-brown fur mottled with dry blood.

Stepping away from the lockers, she reached into her purse with shaking fingers for her cell phone, failing to spot that behind the rat sat an envelope with her name written across it in thick capital letters.

12

Amy sat on her couch; the glass of water on the table before her untouched. She looked pale, drawn, confused and a little scared.

Jake could understand why. She had just discovered she knew one of the murder victims; someone had left a dead rat in her mailbox and that same someone had been following her, taking pictures. The five photographs left in an envelope in her mailbox were laid out on the coffee table. Two showed Amy down at the river playing with Huckleberry; a third was a close-up of her face. It was a profile shot and she was wearing sunglasses. The others were from different occasions. One showed her leaving her apartment building, while the other had been taken as she left the book signing at Too Many Books. Which would suggest the photographer had been the one to graffiti Amy's car, but was he the same man who had followed her Wednesday night and could he be their killer?

Jake's hunch was yes.

'We're going to arrange for a police officer to stay here with you,' he told her.

'You think I'm in danger?'

Yes, he thought, but didn't say the word out loud.

'It's a precaution,' Rebecca answered smoothly. 'This may have nothing to do with the recent murders, but we're not prepared to take that risk.'

'Are you working at the Velvet Lounge tonight?'

Amy glanced at Jake. 'Not tonight. I was planning on staying here and catching up on some writing.'

'Okay.' He gave a quick nod to Rebecca who already had her cell phone out and was putting a call in to the department. As she stepped out onto the balcony and pulled the door closed behind her, he turned back to Amy.

'So you're fairly certain all of these pictures have been taken within the last week?' he asked, moving to sit beside her on the couch.

Amy studied the photographs again, leaning in close enough that he could smell the scent of co-

conut shampoo clinging to her hair. It was distracting.

Get a grip, Sullivan.

'The three by the river are from this morning.' She bit into her bottom lip, processing this bit of information. 'He must have been hiding in the woods. I would've seen if someone had a camera pointed at me otherwise. Wouldn't I?'

'You were distracted, playing with the dog. It's easy to miss stuff if you're not looking for it. What about the other two photographs?'

'One was after the book signing, as I left the bookstore. Just before I found the graffiti on my car.'

'That was Monday.'

'Yeah, and the other pic...' She took a moment. 'I think it must have been taken Wednesday, as I was leaving for work.'

'The night you were followed.' It wasn't a question.

They had a line of enquiry on the ex-boyfriend, David Gavin. He had moved to Chicago, but calls needed to be made to his current employers and landlord to verify he was still there.

When Amy's call had come in, they had been on their way to interview her publisher, something they would now do after leaving her apartment.

Jake thought back to the night he had first met

Amy in the park. How she had been down by the river with Huckleberry, unaware that she had attracted the interest of a stalker. Possibly even a murderer. Had she been watched that night?

It had been the same evening as the church murders, but they had happened earlier. Plenty of time for the killer to get to Amy's apartment block. What would have been the outcome had he and Roxy not been there?

'You think this guy is the killer, don't you?' she asked, reading his thoughts. 'He's using my book plots to commit murder and now he's following me and taking my picture.'

There was no edge to her voice. Her tone betrayed no nerves. She was simply stating facts.

She looked at him, amber eyes wide, and forced the smallest of smiles; it was in the smile he saw the faint tremor. Without thinking, he put his hand over hers and gave it a comforting squeeze.

The patio door opened, and Rebecca stepped inside. She gave a brief nod to Jake before her gaze dropped to their linked hands. Jake quickly removed his.

Fuck, Sullivan. What are you thinking?

Rebecca's eyes flashed with disapproval, but she kept her tone light as she spoke to Amy.

'Okay, it's all sorted. We have an officer on his way over. Detective Sullivan and I will stay until he arrives.' Again, she glared at Jake.

Irritated with himself, Jake got up from the couch. He dragged a hand back through his hair, wishing he hadn't quit smoking so he would have an excuse to go out to the balcony. What the hell was wrong with him? Amy Gallaty was at the centre of a murder investigation.

You know the rules. You do not go there, ever.

He wasn't short of female attention. Why the hell this one?

Fifteen long minutes passed before the buzzer rang.

Jake rolled his eyes when he opened the door to find Victor Boaz and Joel Hickok standing on the other side.

'You're leaving her with Boaz? Seriously?'

'Hey!' Boaz snapped, annoyed. 'I'm about as happy with this as you are.'

Hickok smirked at Jake before patting Boaz on the shoulder. 'Come on now, that's not the attitude, Officer Boaz. Think of the opportunity I've given you here. You could be out patrolling the street, but instead you get to watch a pretty lady.'

Despite Hickok's sarcastic tone, Jake noted Boaz

eyeing up Amy and felt his temper raise a notch. Reading him, Hickok signalled to the balcony, getting Jake to follow him outside.

'Before you say it, yes, I know the guy is lazy and yes, he's an idiot, but he will get the job done,' he said without preamble.

'You've got the lazy and the idiot part right,' Jake snapped. 'Seriously, Hickok? There was no one else available? No one?'

'He will get the job done. You have my word.'

'Really? I don't buy it.'

'You have my word,' Hickok repeated. As Jake started to walk back inside, he added, 'Wait up, Sullivan. There's something else you need to know.'

Jake stopped, turned, scowled at Hickok, not saying a word. 'We got an ID on the vic from Beaver Creek.'

'Go on.'

'Shannon Castle.'

'Go on,' Jake repeated.

Hickok gave a twisted smile. 'She was a secretary at a publishing firm. And guess which publishing firm she worked for.'

13

The babysitting gig wasn't so bad.

Vic had bitched like a baby when Hickok had first collared him. He was an officer of the law, not some dumbass bodyguard. Why the hell couldn't Peterson or Chalmers take the job? Sitting around in some lady's apartment all day was going to drag. No stopping off for snacks, no drive by of the elementary school where he knew Brooke Michaels worked, in the hope he might run into her, no chance of parking up somewhere quiet to listen to the baseball. Hickok had stitched him up. Vic knew the federal agent didn't like him, never had done. Give any shitty job to Vic Boaz.

His brief on the ride over was simple. Watch the

writer. Don't leave her apartment unless she does and stick with her at all times. Keep her safe.

Yeah, it was simple all right, and dull as fuck. But then he'd seen the writer. And it hadn't been so bad. Vic had always figured authors to be geeks. He wasn't much into books and imagined those who wrote them to be dowdy and academic.

Amy Gallaty was neither. Instead, she was slim and willowy with curves in all the right places and the kind of pokey out ass that, from where he sat on the couch watching her make coffee, begged to be grabbed. He wouldn't of course. He was a professional police officer, and on duty. But still, he could enjoy the view.

She sure didn't look like his idea of a writer.

Hickok had taken one of Amy's dining chairs and placed it by the front door, instructing Vic to stay there, keep his mouth shut and not disturb her. Initially he had tried not to, burying his head in his paper and doing his best not to be too obvious when he copped the odd sneaky look at her. Each time he did, he caught the dog, Huckleberry, looking at him from where he lay in his bed, as if to say, 'I clocked you, buddy.'

Amy had tried to get on with her writing, working

on her laptop at the dining table, but she seemed distracted. Probably thinking about the murders, and it had to be difficult focusing with someone else in the apartment. Vic tried his best to stay quiet, but he got in a muddle with the pages of the paper at one point and couldn't help clearing his throat a couple of times.

She'd looked over once or twice, but not said anything. Then after half an hour, decided to give up, closing down her laptop and glancing over again, this time her expression softer.

'I'm gonna put the coffee pot on,' she'd told him. 'You want one?'

Damn right he did.

From that point on Amy appeared to accept he was there doing her a favour and, although it might be disturbing her routine somewhat, it would work better if they could get along. That was how he came to be sitting on her couch, drinking a second cup of coffee, eating Oreos and watching reruns of *Cheers*.

The writer chick was okay. Hot to look at and not bad company either. No wonder Sullivan had been pissed off. Vic hadn't missed the look he'd given Amy before leaving and suspected he wanted to get into her pants. Sullivan hadn't wanted him here in the first place, fighting about it with Hickok out on the balcony. At the time Vic had assumed Sullivan hadn't thought him up to the job, but then he'd seen the look and realised why.

He was a threat.

It would no doubt annoy the hell out of Detective Dixie if he could see Vic and Amy settled in, enjoying each other's company. He would make sure Sullivan found out about it.

* * *

While Sullivan and Angell met with Amy's publisher, Joel and Rivers combed the lobby of her apartment block for clues, before interviewing the tenants in the hope someone may have seen whoever had left the rat and the photos.

There was a camera positioned above the main door, which they soon established hadn't worked in months, and the tenants didn't appear to give a damn about security, holding the door open for people on a daily basis. Their best hope was having someone re-member holding the door open for their perpetrator and being able to give a decent description.

Joel noted there were security cameras on each level and another in the lift. When they were done with the tenants, he would track down the super and see if any of them worked. As he rapped his knuckles on the door of 12B, he could hear Rivers further down the hallway, lecturing a young mother with a crying baby in her arms about the importance of not opening the door to strangers, and he rolled his eyes.

Damn you, Max Sutton, for retiring.

He hadn't been partnered with Rivers for long and so far, their relationship had been the exact opposite to the one he'd shared with Sutton. Joel's partnership with Max had been easy-going, trusting and mutually respectful; he doubted he would ever get to that with Rivers. The guy was a dope. The way he'd been sucking up to Angell had irritated him as well. He would prefer Rivers didn't look at, talk to or have any kind of interaction with Angell.

And why is that, Joel?

Six years had passed since they'd seen each other. Back then their investigation had ended, emotions had been running high after Angell was stabbed, and he had been fool enough to hang around. Their fling had been fun, but brief, and he'd cut it short, knowing it couldn't go anywhere. Commitment was never going to be on the cards and he had blasted his way through a dozen more women since Angell, keeping all of the liaisons short and sweet, not wanting to admit she was the only one he remembered with any fondness.

When they'd first pulled this case he had been apprehensive about crossing paths with her again, unsure how she would react to seeing him. What he hadn't counted on was the kick in the gut when he first saw her.

She was no longer a young wide-eyed rookie with a chip on her shoulder. She had matured into a smart, confident and sassy woman, and she was far prettier than he remembered. Much to his chagrin, and for the first time ever, Joel was finding himself wanting to go back. It pissed him off. He never went back. Annoyed with himself for even considering it, he refocused on the job at hand.

The tenant of 12B didn't appear to be home; he started to make a note for a call back – and was surprised when the door in front of him creaked open.

The face peering up at him with eyes magnified behind thick lenses and framed by silver, thinning hair, had to be one hundred years old. As the gap in the door widened he saw the walking frame.

'Can I help you?'

Joel doubted the lady standing before him would be any help at all. Regardless, he went through the motions, flashing his badge.

'Good afternoon, ma'am. My name is Special Agent Hickok. I'm with the FBI.'

'Sorry?' The lady cupped a hand to her ear. 'You're with the what?'

'I'm with the FBI.'

Giant eyes blinked at him, confused.

'The FBI,' he repeated loudly and waved his badge in front of her again. His voice was loud enough to have Rivers and the mother with the baby looking over. Rivers gave him a disapproving look and Joel scowled at him.

After studying the badge for what seemed like forever, a look of understanding crossed the old lady's face.

'Ah, the FBI.'

'Ma'am, I need to ask you some questions.'

'Say what?'

'Questions.'

'Would you like to come in for a coffee?'

Frustrated, Joel glanced at his partner again. 'Hey, Rivers? Come here.'

'Two minutes, Joel.' The younger agent held up his hand, the gesture patronising. 'I'm running through a few safety tips with Miss Nolan.'

Joel's shoulders tensed with irritation. 'Rivers, you idiot, focus on the damn case,' he snapped.

Red-faced, the younger agent apologised to the

young mother and hurried over. She was quick to shut the door after him, clearly glad to get away.

'I wish you wouldn't speak to me like that in front of people,' he hissed.

Ignoring his bleating, Joel nodded towards the old woman waiting expectantly in the doorway. 'I need you to speak to this lady.'

'Why can't you speak to her?'

'Because I need to go speak with the super about the cameras.'

'I can do that.'

'You can also talk to the lady.'

Joel gave the woman a wide grin. 'Special Agent Rivers here would love that cup of coffee.'

'But—'

He gave the younger agent a sharp prod in the back. 'Go on, Rivers. Don't be rude.'

'Ma'am.' Rivers nodded at the woman, before turning to Joel. 'What's her name?'

'Why don't you ask her?'

'Seriously, Joel, you haven't even got her name?'

'What? You want me to do your job for you too?' Joel gave Rivers another not so gentle shove. 'Now go, shoo.'

He waited for Rivers to step inside and the door to close before pulling out his cell.

He dialled Angell's number, heard it ring three times, then her voice on the line. 'Detective Angell.'

Joel smiled to himself. *Detective Angell*. He had to admit it suited her.

'It's Hickok.'

'What's up?'

All brisk and businesslike; she wasn't planning on cutting him any slack anytime soon. He would have to change that.

'Rivers is finishing up interviewing the tenants. I'm gonna speak with the super again about the camera situation. Dozens of the things up, but none of them appear to be working. What gives with the publisher?'

He listened as Angell updated him on the meeting, which, although necessary, hadn't thrown up anything they didn't already know. Shannon Castle had worked for the firm for six years. She had lived alone in the city and on the evening she had gone missing, she had been grocery shopping. Her car was still in the parking lot, implying she had been abducted from there.

This time round, Shawn Randall had a solid alibi, having been at a college football match with dozens of witnesses to verify, which left them with a short list of suspects.

It appeared the killer was targeting people Amy

knew, albeit loosely, so it had to be personal. First the girl who worked in the coffee shop she frequented, then – a victim with a slightly more personal connection – an assistant from her publishing firm. If the pattern continued, her friends and family would need to be on their guard.

14

When the buzzer rang Officer Boaz almost leapt off the couch, shoulders back and chest puffed out, fingers covered in Oreo crumbs hovering over his sidearm.

His reaction had Huckleberry standing in his bed and barking, hackles rising.

'It's probably the shift cover,' he told Amy in a tone she guessed was supposed to reassure her. 'Let me check it out.'

Glancing at her watch, Amy noted it was not yet seven-thirty. Boaz had told her earlier he was being relieved at eight. A little ball of apprehension knotted in her gut as she watched him approach the door like a coiled snake, as if he expected it to explode. Right hand clenching the door knob, his left pulling out his gun, he yanked the door wide, weapon pointed.

'What the fuck?'

'Oh, it's you.' Boaz didn't sound happy at the visitor.

'Don't point that thing at me. Jesus, man. Are you nuts?' Shaking his head in disbelief, Sullivan stepped inside. He looked beat, but his presence still ate up the room. Slamming the door behind him he glared at Boaz, who was clumsily holstering his weapon.

'You dumbass, what the hell are you doing pulling your gun?'

'I was told to watch the lady,' Boaz protested.

'Yeah, watch her, not shoot anyone who comes to the fucking door.'

'I didn't shoot you.'

'Guess I got lucky.'

'I was being cautious. How was I to know it was you standing the other side?'

Sullivan pointed to the peephole in the centre of the door. 'Ever think about using this?'

Boaz reddened. 'It was a gut reaction, okay?'

'Gut reaction, my ass. So aside from trying to put a bullet in me, any other problems I should know about, Officer Trigger Happy?'

'We're all good. Amy, I mean, uh, Ms Gallaty, has been looking after me fine.'

Sullivan's eyes narrowed. 'You're supposed to be looking after her.'

'Well, yeah, I have. I meant she made me coffee and stuff. We watched TV, but I was keeping an eye on her.' Boaz paused at Sullivan's scowl, before adding with a suggestive hint. 'I made sure I kept a real good eye on her.'

Although he didn't bite, Amy swore Sullivan's nostrils flared.

'There hasn't been any trouble,' she told him, not wanting him to get the wrong idea.

Sullivan nodded, continuing to glare at Boaz. 'I'll take it from here,' he said, his tone lighter than his expression.

'But I thought Peterson was—'

'Peterson isn't coming. I said I'll take it from here.'

'What do you mean he isn't—'

'I told you I'll take it from here.'

For the first time Sullivan looked over at Amy, his dark eyes intense and unreadable.

She busied herself while he saw Boaz out, clearing away cups and filling the kitchen sink with soapy water. Hearing the door close and lock, she glanced over. Sullivan's expression had softened, and he met her eyes with a lazy cat stare. Something stirred inside her.

He had traded his suit for jeans and a T-shirt, suggesting he wasn't punching the clock, but still had his sidearm resting snugly against his hip and a laptop bag under one arm.

'You didn't have to be so rude to him,' she pointed out. 'He was just doing his job.'

'The guy is an idiot.'

He closed the distance between them, setting the laptop bag down and leaning back against the work surface, watching her as she washed up. Huckleberry had followed him through and sat patiently at his side; they both looked far too comfortable in her kitchen.

Amy felt heat rise up her neck.

'So how come you're here?' she asked lightly.

'I'm watching you.'

'I'd have thought you'd have had more important things to do than watch me.'

'Not right now.'

'Okay. I thought there was supposed to be another officer. Peterson?'

Sullivan reached down, stroked Huckleberry's head.

'His kid had an epileptic episode earlier and he's at

the hospital. You were supposed to get Special Agent Rivers as a replacement. I took the shift instead.'

His lips curved slightly, but his eyes remained un-readable. Amy swallowed heavily, her kitchen feeling far too warm. She was pleased it wasn't Rivers. She didn't like him or want him back in her apartment. So instead, she got Sullivan, the detective she was at-tracted to. And who was looking at her now, sug-gesting the feeling was mutual.

He's here professionally. Stop being an idiot. Nothing is going to happen.

He was going to be in her apartment all night.

Why does that make you feel nervous? You've spent time alone with him before.

Because something had shifted. Amy wasn't sure what exactly. There was a tension between them that hadn't been there before.

I need a drink.

Pulling open the refrigerator door she reached for a beer. 'Want one?' she offered.

He hesitated for a brief moment. 'Sure.'

She took out a second, popped the tabs and handed him one.

His hand brushed hers briefly and, feeling the charge, she pulled away, taking a long drag.

Christ, Amy.

There had been no man in her life since David. He had been enough of a head fuck to make her want to take a break. Since him she had poured herself into her writing. Why was she now feeling this way?

You don't know if there's a wife at home.

No ring, she remembered.

That didn't mean anything. He could be married and not wearing a ring, and if no wife, there could be a girlfriend.

'Well, I hope I haven't messed up any plans you might have had. I wouldn't want to upset your wife... girlfriend?'

'You haven't. I'm not married.'

He gave her a measured look, and she suspected he knew exactly what was on her mind.

Her cheeks heated.

Subtle, Amy. Real subtle.

Feeling uncomfortably warm and needing breathing space, she excused herself to take a shower.

Bedroom door closed, she perched on the edge of the mattress and rubbed her hands over her face.

What the hell was going on?

The most turbulent thing in her life at the moment should have been the release of her new book.

Instead, she found herself centre stage in a murder investigation and attracted to the detective leading it.

Her thoughts remained on Sullivan as she soaped herself in the shower, the warm spray soothing and de-stressing her frazzled mind.

He was here to keep her safe, not get in her pants. She would get dressed, go back into the living room and nothing was going to happen.

But you want it to.

Ignoring the irritating voice in her head she took time drying her hair, tying it back into a low knot, moisturising and dressing, annoyed with herself for briefly questioning her outfit choice of sweats and a T-shirt.

He was on the couch working on his laptop when she emerged from the bedroom, beer bottle hooked in one hand while he used the other to type.

Amy padded through to the kitchen, collected her own bottle from the counter. Although she didn't have much appetite, she guessed she needed to eat. She opened the refrigerator and eyed the pizza she had bought earlier, before glancing back at Sullivan.

'You hungry?' she asked.

'Yeah.' He didn't look up. 'I already ordered Chinese.'

'Oh, okay.'

He was making himself at home.

'I ordered enough in case you hadn't eaten.' Now he looked up, meeting her eyes. 'You like Chinese, right?'

'Sure.'

Taking over her apartment, ordering Chinese; he was getting comfortable.

'What are you up to?' she asked, nodding at the computer for want of distraction.

'Running over stuff.'

'To do with the case?'

He shot her a look; didn't reply.

'If it's to do with the case, I have a right to know.'

There was an edge to her voice, and it irritated her. She didn't want to be one of those whiny self-pitying types she avoided writing about.

'Come here.' Sullivan patted the seat beside him.

Tentatively Amy ventured across and sat down.

Not too close.

But still close enough she could smell the faint scent of soap and cologne.

Focus, Amy.

Glancing at the computer screen, she recognised the website of her publishing firm, Maxwell Grey. The page was open on staff profiles.

'Anyone stand out?' Sullivan asked. 'They're a small firm, so I'm guessing they've all been involved in your books. Have any of them ever shown a little too much interest in you? No one there you've pissed off?'

Amy studied the pictures. She recognised most of their faces, knew some better than others. Her eyes dropped to the picture of Shannon Castle, her publisher's personal assistant. How many times had she made small talk with her? And now she was dead; the victim of a book she had helped to publish.

'They are all nice people. Professional, friendly, easy to work with. I honestly can't think of a single person there who would have a problem with me. Or want to hurt Shannon.'

'We met with the Maxwell Grey brothers today. They were genuinely shocked about Shannon Castle. She'd worked for them a while.'

'Yeah, she was there when my first book was published.'

'Did you know her well?'

'We weren't friends, but we would always chat when I saw her. She had a close family – have they...?'

'They've been told.'

'I should send flowers or a note. I met her mom once, bumped into them when they were shopping.

They'll be taking this hard. Shannon, she didn't deserve this.'

'No, she didn't.'

Amy's eyes went wide. 'Do they blame me? I wrote the book. It was my book that got her killed.'

'No, it was the person who shot her who got her killed,' Sullivan said firmly. 'Amy, look at me.'

Distracted, Amy continued to stare blankly at the picture of Shannon on the screen.

Sullivan clicked off the page, set the laptop down on the coffee table.

'Amy, look at me,' he repeated.

As his voice registered, she glanced up.

'Don't blame yourself for this. If it hadn't been your books, there would have been another trigger. People don't kill because they watch TV or read; they kill because they're sick. Whoever we're looking for would have done it anyway.'

'I guess.'

There was a pause.

'You ever get fan mail?'

'Some.'

'You keep it?'

'Sure. I mean, I've had emails I've deleted, but letters? I've kept those. It feels wrong to throw them out.'

'Can I see them?'

'Sure.'

She kept the letters in a shoebox, stashed away on one of the top shelves of her bedroom closet. Pulling the box down, she took it through to Sullivan, sitting back on the couch as he lifted the lid and pulled the letters out.

There were maybe thirty or forty, some yellowed with age, some typed, others handwritten. A few fans had written to her time and again; others had sent just the one letter.

Sullivan started rooting through them, reading each one. Scanning over a particularly flattering letter from a male fan, he grinned, and Amy's face flushed.

She drew her knees up to her chin, hugging her arms around her legs and watched him read, taking the opportunity to study him. What was his story, she wondered. What made him tick? He had a southern accent. What had brought him to Oregon? Did he have family here?

He picked up another letter, his brow furrowing as he started to read.

'Who sent this one?'

Amy glanced at the print. It was from one of her fans who aspired to be a writer, one of the few who always typed, never handwrote. She got a letter after the release of each book, and they were always signed 'X'.

'I don't know. There is never a name.'

'You've got more than one letter from this guy?'

'Yeah, there's usually one after each book. How do you know it's a guy?'

'What about a postmark?'

'Umm... local, I think. Why?'

Sullivan glanced over the letter again.

'Do the letters come here or to your publisher?'

'My publisher gets them and passes them on. Why?'

He read from the page.

'"We have a connection, Amy. We both have that darkness living inside us. You've channelled yours into your stories and brought them to life. I need to learn how to use mine before it spirals out of control. There are things I would like to do and the need inside me is growing. I must take my darkness and my desires and make things happen."'

Sullivan glanced up at Amy. 'You really believe he's talking about writing a book?'

'Isn't he?'

At Sullivan's raised eyebrows, she reddened, feeling stupid she'd never thought anything of the letters before. Her fans tended to say some weird stuff now and again. She honestly hadn't read anything into it. But now he had put a different spin on it, the words had taken on a sinister edge.

Sullivan picked up the shoebox, starting flicking through the remaining letters. He shot another glance at Amy, his lips twisting.

'Guess we'd better see what else Mr X has to say.'

15

The air around her was cool and damp, thick with a musty, earthy scent. Something else clung to it: another smell. Like copper or rust. As she took a further step down, her sense of foreboding grew. The stairs were steep and narrow; the only light was coming from an open door at the bottom. A faint bulb flickered, threatening to disappear altogether.

She should turn and go, before anything bad happened. Instead, she was compelled to continue; driven on by an overwhelming need to know what was in the room at the bottom of the stairs.

As she neared, her heart thumped uncomfortably in her chest. The only other noises were the sound of her own quiet footsteps, each one much louder in the silence than she wanted them to be and, as she got closer, the monotonous drip, she guessed from a tap.

The coppery smell was growing stronger, clogging her nose and her throat. She should go. Although her head instructed her to leave, her feet continued, and she couldn't stop them.

The light from the room flickered again and she heard the sound of shuffling and what she thought was a low moan.

Stop. Go back.

Her foot hit the final step and then she was standing on the stone floor, a few feet away from the room, its heavy wooden door wide open.

She paused, her shoulders tense, fists clenched by her sides. Her breathing was too loud, and she tried to steady it. She crept along the passage, her legs leaden, each step taking seconds, but feeling like minutes.

Readying herself, she peered through the door. And screamed.

* * *

Amy shot upright in bed.

Something – someone – grabbed hold of her by the shoulders.

Panicking in their firm grip she screamed again, thrashing out wildly with her fists.

'Hey! Stop it.' A male voice, one she recognised, sounded annoyed. 'It's Sullivan.'

He let go of her shoulders; caught hold of her wrists.

'Let me go.'

'Then quit hitting me.'

It was dark, but she could make out his silhouette in front of her. Taking a moment, she drew a deep breath, forced herself to relax. Her skin was hot and clammy; sweat beaded on her forehead and upper lip; droplets slid down her back and between her breasts.

It was okay. She was in her apartment, in her bed. The long curtains drawn across the open balcony door billowed in the breeze. She could hear the reassuring tick of her alarm clock, smell the familiar scents of her room: her perfumes and creams, the fabric conditioner on her sheets. On the floor beside the bed, Huckleberry let out a woof.

Sullivan let go of her wrists, leaned past her to switch on the night lamp. Amy caught the familiar scent of his cologne. It mingled with the feminine scents in the room, jangling her senses.

Soft light fell on the room. Sullivan sat back on her bed, a scowl on his face.

'What the hell was that about?' he demanded, dark eyes glaring.

Conscious she was only wearing a thin camisole Amy pulled the sheet higher. 'It was just a nightmare.'

'Just a nightmare?' He scrubbed his hand over his jaw, dragged it back through his hair. 'You were screaming like a banshee. Scared the crap out of me and the dog.'

'Umm... sorry?' She shrugged her shoulders. 'What do you want me to say? I have nightmares. I can't control what happens when I fall asleep.'

He studied her for a moment, drew in a deep breath. She had shaken him, Amy could see that now, and it made her feel foolish.

'You get these nightmares often?' Sullivan asked, his tone softening.

'Kind of.'

'Since the murders started?'

'Yeah. I mean, I used to get them all the time, then they stopped... until last week.'

He nodded. 'Do you remember them, the dreams?'

'Yeah.'

Her throat dry, the nightmare she had woken from still vivid and playing in her head, Amy pushed the sheet back, clambered from the bed. She didn't like her state of undress, but the need for water was more important.

She pushed open the bathroom door, leaving it ajar as she splashed cold water over her face and then drank greedily from the faucet. Her heart was pounding, her nerves jumpy, but she was calming down, slowly. Grabbing her robe, she tied it in place and stepped back into the bedroom.

Sullivan was still sat on the edge of her bed, one hand stroking Huckleberry as he watched her.

Amy gave him a twisted smile. 'I'm gonna put the coffee pot on. Don't think I'm ready for sleep again yet.'

* * *

As they sat at her dining table, she told him about the nightmare. About the stone steps leading down to the basement room, the sense of foreboding that something terrible was in the room, and how the dream ended as she entered and saw what was waiting for her. She always woke at that point and, although the rest of the dream was vividly clear, she could never remember what had been in the room.

Jake was no shrink, but it sounded like a repressed memory to him, and he told her so.

'So you think it's real? It's something that happened to me?' She sounded sceptical.

'It would make sense. I'm no expert on dreams, but if you have a recurring one, I'd figure it's going to change slightly each time. You say yours doesn't.'

'But I've never been in a situation where I've gone down into a basement. I mean, sure, my parents had a cellar at home, but it's not the same place.'

'If it's repressed, you're not going to remember it.'

Amy narrowed her eyes. 'I think I would remember something like that.'

'Would you?'

'Of course.'

'But the dream feels real?'

'Sure, but dreams do when you're having them. Then you wake up. They're make-believe. Remember, I'm a writer. I have an overactive imagination.'

'Don't you think it odd the nightmares have started up again since the murders?'

Amy shrugged, not buying whatever theory he was heading towards.

'It's a traumatic situation. I'm sure traumatic situations can bring on nightmares.'

She glanced over at the letters from her fan, Mr X, sitting in a pile at the other end of the table.

They had been talking about them before she'd

headed off to bed. Having read them all, Jake was convinced there was a connection to the murders. He had pretty much talked Amy round to the same conclusion. Finding out a murderer had been following her career, writing to her, would be enough to bring on a nightmare.

'How old are you? In the dream I mean.'

'I don't know. I'm just me.'

'But you've been having the same nightmare for years.'

'Yeah, since I was in my teens, maybe fourteen, fifteen. It stopped when I was in my early twenties and started again the other night.'

'You ever talk to anyone about it? Try to find out the trigger?'

Amy pulled a face. 'My parents knew I had bad dreams.'

'But they didn't know what caused them?'

'I guess they figured adolescence.' She gave him a wry smile. 'I'd ask them for you, but they're dead.'

Jake already knew that, but he didn't say so, instead he nodded. Amy had written the books a killer was copying, a killer he was trying to catch. He knew a lot about her. That her parents had been killed in an automobile accident when she was twenty-two, that she was an only child. He knew she had grown up in

Montana, attended Washington State University for a year before dropping out; that she had moved to Oregon after her parents died to stay with her college roomie, Heidi Pearce.

It had to be tough losing your only family at a young age.

He was lucky, he guessed, coming from a big southern family. He still had both his parents, one set of grandparents, plus aunts, uncles, an older brother, two sisters and a myriad of nieces and nephews. He might have moved to Oregon, but he held them close, making regular visits, speaking to his mom every week; he couldn't imagine the network not being there.

'You've never talked to anyone professionally?' he asked.

Amy's hazel eyes flashed angrily. 'What, you mean like a shrink?'

'A therapist.'

'It's the same thing. I don't need a head doctor. I'm not nuts. It's just a dumb nightmare.'

She got up from the table, took both their coffee cups into the kitchen and dumped them in the sink. She stood with her back to him, shoulders tense.

Jake wanted to go over to her, soothe out the knots.

Cut it out, Sullivan. Keep it professional.

He forced himself to stay seated.

'I'm not calling you nuts.' He kept his tone neutral. 'I think it would help to talk to someone. You're dealing with a lot right now, which is probably why you had the nightmare. I think it would help you to talk things through with someone.'

'Yeah? And what would you know?'

'More than you'd think.'

That had her turning, looking at him curiously.

He paused for a long moment, debating, clenched and unclenched his fist, wishing for a cigarette. He didn't talk about this stuff with anyone other than close family. Amy Gallaty was a person of interest in a crime he was investigating.

This is wrong, Sullivan.

'I saw a therapist for a while,' he told her, ignoring the nagging voice in his head telling him he was making a mistake. 'It was a work thing,' he added, a little abruptly, when her eyes widened.

'Okay.'

He wasn't prepared to give any more than that.

'There's a guy here in Juniper. Doctor Paul Shinnick. I think you should go talk to him.'

Amy's expression darkened from curious to pissed off. 'I told you I don't need to see any head doctor. I'm not nuts.'

'Neither was I. I needed to talk stuff through, get it clear in my head so I could move on. The guy is good, Amy. I think he can help you, even if it's how best to deal with everything going on.'

She stared at him, bottom lip pouting, as she wavered.

'Sometimes it helps to talk to someone who isn't involved. Someone who can look in with a clear perspective.'

'I don't know.'

Jake got up and, against his better judgement, went to her. 'Hey, look at me.'

She did, golden eyes calmer, but glittery green fireworks threatening beneath the surface.

Her mouth was still pouting, bottom lip full, and, feeling himself stir, he focused his attention back on her eyes.

You're on dangerous ground, Sullivan.

'One meeting, okay? Let me set you up an appointment with Doctor Shinnick. You go talk to him and if you still think it's a mistake you don't go again.'

She hesitated for a long moment, eyes still watching his, and he tried his best not to notice as she bit into that bottom lip. 'Okay. One session. Just the one and if I say no more, then you drop it. Deal?'

'Deal.'

Mustering every ounce of self-control, he took a step back. 'You should get to bed. I'll call Shinnick in the morning. Get you an appointment.'

Forcing himself to turn away, he headed back to the couch where he had been before she'd started screaming.

Following his cue, Amy disappeared back into her bedroom.

The door shut. Jake had a feeling it was going to be a long night.

16

'Another late night?' Rebecca questioned drily, as Jake wandered into the precinct forty minutes after their shift had begun, shirt loose and tie unknotted.

'Yes.' He narrowed his eyes. 'And not in the way you're thinking, before you ask.'

He glanced at the Starbucks cup waiting for him on the desk and, concluding it would be cold, headed over to the machine.

Rebecca followed.

'I wasn't thinking or going to ask anything, but you are late.'

'I had to wait for Boaz to relieve me before I could go home, shower and change. And Roxy needed walking.'

'Perhaps you should have let Rivers take the shift, like he was supposed to.'

Jake pumped quarters into the machine and slammed his fist against it when the last one jammed. The coin dropped and his cup began to fill. 'Rivers couldn't protect his own dick.'

'He wasn't being asked to protect his dick.'

'You know what I mean. He's a wet behind the ears rookie and his priorities are all screwed up.'

'Was it about him being a rookie, or was it more to do with you spending time with Amy Gallaty?' Rebecca asked, deciding to cut straight to the chase.

She had noted the subtle changes in Jake's behaviour towards the author during their last meeting, hadn't missed the exchanged looks or the fact Amy appeared to be reciprocating. Her partner was treading on dangerous ground.

You don't get personal with the case, Jake. You know better.

Jake took his cup, scowled at the foul-smelling liquid and then at Rebecca. 'Nothing happened.'

'Happened?'

'Nothing is going to happen,' he corrected.

Rebecca believed he believed that. She wasn't sure she did. 'I need your focus here with me. You want to

keep Amy safe? Help me catch this killer. Don't go getting distracted.'

'Distracted? You mean like you are with Hickok?'

Rebecca's cheeks heated as her temper rose a
notch. 'What the hell is that supposed to mean?'

'You think I haven't noticed there's something up
with you two? Hell, everyone has. It's no wonder we're
not making any progress with this case, what with you
constantly at each other's throats.'

'We are not.'

'Yes, Rebecca, you are. Don't give me this self-righteous bullshit about Amy when you've got your own
thing going on with Hickok.'

He glared at her, dark eyes flashing, but she saw
the spark of humour behind his anger. He was pissed
at her, but also amused. Rebecca guessed it had to do
with the colour of her burning cheeks.

Were she and Hickok that bad?

'Okay, so he brings out the worst in me,' she admitted, keeping her tone as light as possible.

Jake nodded, the amusement in his eyes now
stamping out the anger. 'Sure, he does.'

'He brings out the worst in a lot of people. But
there's nothing going on. Don't mistake the situation.'

'Okay, so how about a deal? Nothing has happened...' He stopped, made a point of correcting him-

self again. 'Nothing *is going to happen* with Amy, so you lay off me, and in return I'll lay off you about Hickok.'

'What about me?'

Rebecca and Jake turned to see Hickok standing behind them.

He raised his eyebrows expectantly.

Jake glanced at Rebecca, then Hickok, grin widening. 'Rebecca was telling me how much she's enjoying getting the chance to work with you again.'

Hickok narrowed his eyes suspiciously, his sole focus on Rebecca. 'Did she now?'

Her face now on fire, Rebecca pulled her best neutral expression and avoided looking at Jake, who she intended to kill later; instead, she met Hickok's gaze full on. 'Sure. It's been a real walk down memory lane,' she muttered sarcastically.

Hickok held her gaze for a moment longer, eyes narrowing further, before turning his attention to Jake. 'No trouble last night?' he asked.

He was the one who had agreed to Jake's request to take the nightshift instead of Rivers. Rebecca suspected it was mostly to piss the younger agent off. Hickok and Jake had had their disagreements, some of them heated, but both were united in the belief that Rivers didn't know his dick from his elbow.

'No trouble. It was an interesting evening.' Jake

shot Rebecca a look, daring her to make a sardonic comment as he pulled a plastic bag out of his jacket pocket.

She resisted, figuring she'd said her piece. Hopefully Jake would have the good sense to keep his personal life separate from his professional life. If not, well then, she'd deal with 'if not' when it happened.

'This may be evidence,' he said, handing the bag to Hickok.

'What is this? Letters?'

'They're from a fan. Read them and tell me Mr X isn't crazy.'

'Mr X?' Hickok grinned at Rebecca. 'Sounds kind of kinky, eh, Angell?'

Rebecca rolled her eyes, refusing to let him bait her. She turned her back on him, focusing her attention on Jake.

'We gonna take a look at the rest of these books?'

Amy's publisher had provided them with paperback copies of the remaining four novels in her Zack Maguire series.

The murders on which those of Ben Hogan and Kasey Miller had been based were a dominating part of Amy's first novel, *Grave Encounters*, but the death of Shannon Castle had been copied from a far less significant scene in her second book, *Deadly Vengeance*. It appeared the killer was being selective as to the death scenes he was recreating, and they needed to get a handle on what he might try next.

'I gotta make a call first. I want to get Amy an appointment with Paul Shinnick.'

'Shinnick? The psychologist guy? Why does she need a psychologist?' Rebecca shot a glance at Hickok. He didn't say anything but, like her, waited with interest to hear Jake's answer.

'She's having nightmares. I suggested she talk to someone.' When Rebecca continued to stare at him, Jake's eyes flashed dark with anger. 'What? You think by talking to a shrink she's gotta be crazy?'

'I never said that.' Rebecca kept her tone calm, despite feeling far from it. What the hell was her partner playing at? He was getting too involved. This was not good for him. Not good for the case.

'She had a nightmare last night, while you were there?'

This was from Hickok.

'Yeah, she did; scared the crap out of me. I thought someone was in the apartment trying to kill her.'

Hickok nodded, then to Rebecca's surprise agreed with Jake.

'Maybe it would be a good idea for her to talk to someone. Go ahead and set up the appointment.'

When Rebecca opened her mouth to argue, Hickok shot her a warning look to drop it.

'Come on, Angell, let's check out these letters, then we'll look at the rest of the books.'

* * *

Jake was right to be suspicious about the letters. While they could be the work of a slightly deluded fan, they carried a sinister edge. Hickok gave them to Chalmers to send to the lab for prints and then the three of them worked through the morning, Jake joining Hickok and Rebecca after calling Shinnick.

The third book in the series was a creepy little tale about a wannabe vampire serial killer, who drained his victims of blood. Would this be the fate of the next victim? Rebecca closed her eyes briefly, opened them again to find Hickok watching her.

He gave a half grin, his expression unreadable, and she felt something kick inside.

Breaking eye contact, she got to her feet; stretched again. Six years, she reminded herself. Six years with no contact. Besides, she was with Alan now. He was a good man; solid, honest and reliable. Whatever Hickok's game, she was not going to play it and ruin what she had.

'I need coffee,' she said, needing a break from the room. Actually, she needed a shot of bourbon, but that would have to wait until she was done with work. 'Who wants Starbucks?'

She noted down their orders and grabbed her purse, heading for the door and crashing straight into Rivers.

The younger agent had spent the morning with the janitor at Amy's apartment block, going through footage from the one camera in the building that did work. It was a shitty job and one they were sure would lead nowhere due to the camera's positioning, but Hickok had been hell-bent on making Rivers do it anyway. Judging from the excited grin on his face, maybe the long shot had paid off.

'Whoa, Detective Angell, you need to stay for this. I've got us a breakthrough.'

Hickok looked up, irritated. 'You've got us a break-through?' he questioned dubiously. Rebecca paused in the doorway, waiting to hear what Rivers had to say.

He didn't speak until Jake looked up, wanting his moment, wanting everyone's undivided attention.

'For chrissakes, Rivers, spit it out,' Hickok snapped impatiently.

'It's Amy Gallaty's ex-boyfriend – the one who moved to Chicago.'

'You saw him on the camera footage?' Rebecca asked, curious.

'Not on the camera. I made some calls while we were trawling through the footage. You know, multitasking? I'm good at that.' He grinned smugly at Hickok, who looked unimpressed. 'I checked out David Gavin's employers.'

It was a job on the list, but Rebecca would be the first to admit they hadn't gotten to it yet; hadn't figured it a priority.

'Go on,' Hickok said sharply.

'Well guess what? Gavin quit his job a couple of weeks back. I then spoke with his landlord and he's given up the lease on his apartment, said he was heading back to Oregon to take care of some business.'

All eyes were now on Rivers, who was loving the attention.

'And this is the best bit. You want to know when he left Chicago?' The smug grin widened as he gave a dramatic pause. 'Exactly one week before the first murders.'

17

Victor Boaz was beginning to think he had landed on his feet with this babysitting gig. He got to sit around all day, keeping an eye on a pretty lady and, to top it off, Hickok had let him lose the uniform. He still had to carry his gun, badge and cuffs, but that wasn't a problem. He usually kept them close to impress the ladies. Going plainclothes was a bonus as his work pants were getting a little snug around the waist. His own clothes were better.

Amy had made him a bagel with crispy bacon and cream cheese when he'd arrived, and set him up with a fresh pot of coffee and the TV remote, before disappearing into her bedroom, laptop under her arm.

Vic guessed she wanted to be alone for a bit and

didn't mind. He appreciated a lady who knew how to look after a man. Besides, she had looked stressed when he'd shown up to relieve Sullivan and he figured she'd probably spent most of the night trying to fight him off from getting in her pants. Sullivan had been in a bad mood, a scowl already on his face when he'd opened the door, but that was nothing new. He must have been unlucky in his quest and was still unhappy about Vic watching over Amy.

What a coup it would be if he could get Amy in the sack. That would sure give Sullivan something to be pissed about. Vic figured he would let her have her time alone and when she was ready for a little company he would lay on some of the Boaz moves. At forty-four he was a decade older than Sullivan. In Vic's book that gave him a decade's more experience; he still had his looks and knew how to the charm the ladies. Sure, the middle-age spread was catching up with him and he could do with putting a little more time in at the gym, but he was sure if he put his mind to it, he could win Amy over.

His mind was half on the cartoon he was watching, half on how he was going to make his move when the buzzer sounded. All thoughts of seducing Amy vanished the moment he laid his eyes on her best friend, Heidi Pearce.

Where Amy was pretty in a girl-next-door kind of way, Heidi was supermodel stunning: all legs, hair and cheekbones. Vic figured he might have died and gone to heaven.

'So, when were you planning on updating us?' Heidi was demanding of Amy, hands on hips, looking pissed off.

He liked a woman with fire, liked the way Heidi's cornflower eyes lit up with anger. Just a little anger, mind; not like Rebecca Angell who always tended to take it too far. Feisty was good, but women needed to know when to stop.

'I was going to tell you,' Amy protested. 'I was waiting for the right opportunity. You've been so busy with work and I know Gage and Fran have stuff going on. I didn't want to worry you.'

'You think *this* doesn't worry me?' Heidi waved a hand in the direction of Vic.

He immediately stood, clumsily knocking the TV remote and his empty coffee cup to the floor.

Way to go, Vic. Make a good first impression.

Hurriedly picking the cup and remote up and setting them on the coffee table, he crossed the room, hand held out. 'Officer Boaz, ma'am, nice to meet you. I can promise you I am doing everything possible to keep Amy, uh, Miss Gallaty, safe from harm.'

Heidi gave him an appraising look before shaking his hand. 'You better do.'

Vic imagined her lying on her back, legs spread, and grinned. 'You have my word I will protect her, ma'am.' He turned the grin up a notch, made a show of pulling up his shirt to reveal his sidearm, as he knew women were turned on by that shit. 'And of course, while you're in her company, I will keep you safe too.' He winked at her before returning to the couch, leaving the girls to talk.

Well, mainly it was Heidi doing the talking, still mad at Amy.

Vic tuned most of it out. He tended to lose focus when women whined about stuff. He watched his cartoons, casting the occasional glance at Heidi, smiling whenever their eyes made contact, until he heard Amy call him.

'Officer Boaz, we're gonna go out for a bit. I need some fresh air.'

Immediately he was back on his feet. 'You know you can't leave the apartment unless I come with you. Those are the rules.' He sounded defensive, which he guessed is why she smiled.

'I know. I meant you come with us.'

Vic relaxed, feeling stupid when the two girls exchanged a look. 'Uh, okay. Where do you want to go?'

'The coast would be good. We can take Huckleberry for a walk on the beach.'

Vic was dubious about having the dog in his car. He spent a lot of time polishing his Camaro and didn't want dog hairs, mud and saliva on the back seat. He weighed it up against a walk on the beach with two pretty girls and figured it was worth the sacrifice.

'Okay,' he agreed, puffing out his chest. 'I need to go out first, make sure the coast is clear and secure the route down to the garage. You ladies follow when I tell you it's safe.'

He waited for Amy to get her things together and leash Huckleberry before taking out his sidearm and signalling for them to get in line behind him.

'Is this necessary?' Heidi complained. 'We're only going from the apartment to the garage.'

Vic shot her a look. He was beginning to think Amy's best friend was another Rebecca Angell, but she was super pretty so he would persevere.

It will all be worth the effort when you get her in the sack, Vic, buddy.

'We have to be prepared for every situation. You never know when danger can strike. Stay behind me and I will keep you safe.'

He heard Heidi sigh, wouldn't have been at all surprised if she wasn't rolling her eyes at the back of his head, and gritted his teeth. Easing open the door, he raised his weapon, peered out and took a couple of steps onto the landing. Without looking back, he signalled the girls to follow.

Huckleberry let out a loud woof, startling him, and the gun slipped from his fingers, landing with a thud against the carpet.

Vic swore, stooping to get the gun. Behind him, Heidi muttered. 'Jeez, Amy, does Barney Fife here know what he's doing?'

He swung around, cheeks colouring. 'Hey, I'm an officer of the law, and I'd appreciate you don't speak about me that way.' This time he saw Heidi did indeed roll her eyes and his temper boiled.

Sensing trouble, Amy intervened. Vic was beginning to swing back in her favour. Heidi was too mouthy. At least Amy was nice to him.

'Come on, Heidi, it was an accident. Huckleberry made him jump. No harm done. Let's get out of here. I really need that walk.'

Heidi glowered, but kept her mouth shut. Beginning to regret she was tagging along, Vic lead the way.

* * *

Amy was glad to be out of her apartment; the sea air helped to clear her mind and ease the nagging headache that had been plaguing her since she had woken. The situation wasn't ideal. She liked to drive out to the coast alone, spend hours walking the beach, lost in the fictitious world of her characters as she plotted the next twists and turns in their lives, and she couldn't do that with company.

At least out in a wide-open space she could take those few extra steps away, let the noise of the surf drown out the voices as she stared out across the ocean, collecting her own thoughts.

Officer Boaz didn't let her stray far. Not that Amy believed she was in any danger as there were other people on the beach, but she appreciated the concern. And Heidi let her be for a while, walking alongside her in companionable silence, understanding she needed the space.

Normally, she drove to a deserted spot a few miles south, but Officer Boaz felt it safer they stick to a more populated area. Between the sand and the backdrop of pine trees sat a row of houses varying in size and structure, but all affording their owners a spectacular view. She guessed he figured if anything happened, they would be nearer to help.

Huckleberry was enjoying his trip out to the

beach. Amy watched him splashing in the waves, chasing the pebbles she and Heidi threw for him, and thought she should bring him to the coast more often. Ryan wasn't back for six weeks. Would her life be back to normal by then?

The idea of having officers camping out in her apartment for the foreseeable future wasn't an appealing one. But then again, she didn't favour being alone knowing a killer had her in his sights.

Despite the warmth of the sun, a cold shiver of fear ran through her as she thought back to the photographs she'd received. Rubbing goose-pimpled arms, she cautiously glanced around. Was she being watched right now? Was her picture being taken as she walked along the beach?

The thought was unnerving, and she decided the sacrifice of giving up her alone time was worth it for the feeling of being safe.

Despite Heidi's opinion of him, Officer Boaz meant well. Sure, he had some annoying habits and he liked making himself at home in her apartment, but she believed he wanted to keep her safe.

As for Sullivan... well, she wasn't sure about Sullivan. He had stepped in as replacement cover last night, so she would probably get the other officer, Peterson, tonight. While that should have relieved her, it left her disappointed.

Because you like him.

Amy slapped the annoying voice down.

Last night had caught her off guard. She hadn't been expecting him and then he had been there, all brooding and intense with his dark eyes and stubbled jaw, asking her too many questions about the murders and her personal life, which her flustered brain had tried to process while she kept reminding herself her little crush on him was inappropriate given the circumstances under which they had met.

And all the time a nagging little voice in her head kept asking the question, *I wonder what he kisses like?*

He had remained professional, stayed focused on the job, which left her disappointed, relieved, and feeling kind of stupid for thinking he might try anything in the first place. It was best he wasn't there tonight. She wasn't a kid, and the crush was nothing short of embarrassing.

Thoughts still on Sullivan, Amy glanced along the beach. There were still a few people about. A couple of sunbathers, in the distance a jogger. Heading towards them she spotted an older couple walking a poodle. She glanced back at Huckleberry hoping he hadn't seen. The crazy collie had a thing for poodles, tending to want to hump them or fight them, depending on their sex.

He was off his lead, still playing in the edge of the water. Nudging Heidi, Amy pointed to the poodle. They both knew the deal with Ryan's dog.

Sneaking up behind him, Heidi to the left, Amy to the right, both girls attempted to grab his collar. They didn't succeed; the dog was wily and heard them coming. As he darted away, he caught sight of the poodle and let out an excited bark. Officer Boaz, who was a few yards ahead, glanced round.

'Can you grab him?' Amy called. 'He doesn't do poodles.'

'Uh, sure.'

Immediately alert and ready for duty, Boaz lurched for the dog as he ran past him, catching his collar. Huckleberry wasn't amused at being stopped in his tracks and yanked hard. As Boaz tightened his grip, the dog tried to pull forward and, like a scene playing out in slow motion, the officer lost his footing and, taking Huckleberry with him, tumbled face down into the surf.

'Oh God, no.'

Mortified, Amy rushed forward to help Boaz. Beside her, Heidi giggled, clearly amused by the situation.

Boaz wasn't impressed, muttering under his breath, a scowl on his face. Amy almost had him back on his feet when he lost his footing again and fell on his butt. She ignored the splash of water that soaked her sundress. Boaz was drenched. And he looked pissed off.

'I am so sorry,' she apologised, helping him to his feet.

Behind her, Huckleberry woofed. He had run out of the sea ahead of them and Heidi had caught hold of him, trying to avoid a soaking as he shook off the excess water. Fortunately, the poodle had passed.

Boaz started emptying his pockets, his wallet, badge, his cell, unclipped his gun.

'If anything is damaged, I will pay for it,' Amy told him, not sure how to compensate. It was a fifteen-minute drive back to her apartment. She would get him some towels, dry his clothes for him.

'Is everything okay here?'

Amy glanced round. It was the jogger from further up the beach. For a moment she didn't recognise him, maybe because of the bandana around his head. Troy.

He clocked it was her about the same time. Smiled. 'Amy? I didn't expect to run into you here.' He glanced at Boaz, dripping wet. 'You look like you need a towel.'

Boaz scowled at him. 'Very funny.'

'No, I'm being serious. I live right over there.' Troy nodded in the direction of the beach houses.

'Umm...' Amy looked at the puzzled looks on Heidi's and Boaz's faces, realised she hadn't made any introductions. 'This is Troy.' She left it at that, not sure how to say she knew him. That he was the boyfriend of her stalker fan wasn't appropriate. 'Troy, this is my friend Heidi and Officer Boaz.'

Troy nodded a hello to them both, looking mildly curious at Boaz, but questioning nothing.

'I can get you a towel,' he said. 'Lend you some sweats.' He smiled at Amy. 'I'm guessing if not he has to ride back into the city wet?'

'Well, okay, thanks. A towel and sweats would be good.' Boaz shot a wary look at Huckleberry, now on his leash and sitting grinning, resting against Heidi's leg.

'This way.'

Without preamble, Troy led the way across the sand towards his house, Boaz close behind him.

Heidi gave Amy an intrigued look and mouthed, 'And who is he?'

Trouble, Amy thought, but didn't say it out loud. She didn't want to go to Troy's house. What if Nadine was there? After their last encounter she hoped never to see the woman again, but Officer Boaz was wet and it was her fault.

Brushing past Heidi and Huckleberry, she muttered, 'Come on,' and grudgingly followed the men up some wooden steps and onto a decked veranda. The set-up was nice: a bamboo-and-glass table and chairs, plumped-up cream cushions, and, in the corner of the decking, a hot tub. Amy remembered Troy saying he worked designing security systems, a job that paid well. The patio door was open, suggesting someone was already home.

Nadine.

'Come on in,' Troy beckoned them, entering the house.

'I'd better stay out here with the dog.'

Troy glanced back, smiled at Amy. 'He's fine; all hard floors inside. Besides, the place needs a clean, so it's not a problem.'

Out of excuses, Amy reluctantly stepped inside.

The living room she found herself in was simply furnished and she was surprised by the minimalist modern style. Not her taste, but better than the kind of place she had imagined Nadine to live. In her head she had pictured the woman to have fanciful tastes: lots of ornaments, flowers, painted plates and dolls.

This was the complete opposite: all black, white and chrome with uncluttered surfaces.

'Come with me, Officer Boaz. Let's go find you a towel and some dry clothes.'

As Amy watched Boaz follow Troy, her attention was drawn to the metal bookcase next to the door they disappeared through. Flanked by large silver A and Z bookends, the titles of her Zack Maguire series – all six novels – sat in pride of place on the centre shelf.

She stepped closer, and noted there were no other titles, just her books. On the shelf below sat two expensive looking picture frames. One held a shot of Troy and Nadine; the other was a picture of Amy and Nadine, taken at one of the launches.

'Who is she?'

Heidi's voice made Amy jump. She glanced carefully around the room before answering, keeping her voice down in case Nadine overheard.

'She's the lady from the bookstore, the fan.'

'You mean crazy lady?'

'Yeah.'

Heidi's eyes widened. 'We're in crazy lady's house?'

'Keep your voice down. I don't want her to know we're here.'

'If she's home, I'd imagine she's already heard us.

Anyway, I'd like to meet her. Have a word with her about what she did at your signing, and to your car.'

'We don't know for sure she did anything to the car.'

'Who the hell else could it have been?'

Amy hadn't mentioned the photographs or the dead rat, or the fact she had been followed. Heidi was already upset about the murders. If she knew her friend was being specifically targeted it would only cause more worry. Amy had to trust the cops would keep her safe.

'Drop it, Heidi. Troy is being nice helping Officer Boaz out. I think he's embarrassed about what happened. I don't want another scene.'

'That still doesn't excuse what she did.'

'I don't care. Please, drop it. I'm asking you nicely.'

Heidi gave her a measured look, shaking her head.

'Okay, if I have to, but I'm not happy about it.'

'Thank you.'

They waited patiently, but Boaz and Troy didn't reappear. Fortunately, neither did Nadine. The patio doors had been open, but maybe she wasn't home. Amy was sure if she was, she'd have made an appearance by now. Unless she was embarrassed about what happened at their last meeting. It was possible, though unlikely.

Beside Heidi, Huckleberry started to whine. He had been sitting patiently, a puddle of seawater forming around him on the floor.

'I think he needs to pee,' Heidi said, tightening her grip on the leash of the agitated dog. 'I'd better take him outside.'

'And leave me here alone?'

That sounded really lame, Amy.

'You'll be fine. Go find Barney Fife and tell him to hurry his ass up.'

'How about I take Huckleberry outside and you go find him?'

'Okay,' Heidi agreed. 'But if I run into crazy lady, don't expect me to hold my tongue.'

Amy deliberated.

Grow some balls you idiot.

'No, it's fine. You take Huckleberry. I'll go find Officer Boaz.'

She watched Heidi walk the dog out of the house, listened to the pattering of his paws on the decking as she led him down to the beach.

In that instant the atmosphere within the house changed and her sense of foreboding grew.

She was being stupid. There was nothing here to be afraid of.

Well, okay, perhaps she was a little scared of Na-

dine. The woman had a presence about her that unnerved Amy. But other than that, there was nothing
for her to fear.

Go get Boaz and you can get out of here.

Sucking in a breath, she stepped into the centre of
the house, finding herself in a long, narrow central
hallway with several doorways leading off. She paused
for a moment as she heard the faint murmur of voices
coming from the end of the house. The air held a
scent of lemon, some kind of household spray or dis-
infectant.

Feeling like she was trespassing, despite Troy
having invited her in, she made her way towards the
sound, pausing as she passed a cluster of pictures in
frames along the hall wall. More photographs. Troy or
Nadine appeared in most of them: in some together; in
others with family members, she guessed.

She spotted another picture from one of her
launches: again, she stood with Nadine, the woman
proudly holding a signed book. She wavered for a moment, feeling uncomfortable. The woman barely knew
Amy, yet had photographs of her in the house. It
wasn't right.

Get Boaz. Get out.

She took another step forward, her gaze drawn
towards an open door. The room had the curtains

drawn and the light on. Amy could see more pictures and, although her brain told her not to, curiosity had her stepping inside.

It was filled with more photographs, some on shelves, others hung on the wall. Most appeared to be family shots, but among them she spotted a couple more pictures taken at her launches. It was as if Nadine had deluded herself into thinking they were friends.

One frame hung empty, the glass cracked.

Amy stared at it for a moment before finding her eyes drawn to the bureau, to the damaged photograph lying on the desktop. Again, it was of her with Nadine, except someone had tried to erase her image with a red marker pen.

What the hell is this?

Her mouth was dry. Something tickled at the little ball of unease knotting in her belly.

Fear.

She took a shaky step back, wanting to get out of the house, and now.

A hand touched her shoulder, making her jump. Swinging around, she found herself staring into cool eyes. Scarlet lips curved as Nadine blocked the doorway.

'Well, hello, Amy.'

18

Jake got the call from Paul Shinnick early afternoon. He had left the doctor a message on his cell that morning, knowing he was unlikely to be working on a Saturday but hoping he could schedule an appointment for Amy the following week.

As luck would have it, Shinnick had finished a round of golf and was stopping by his office on the way home to write up a couple of files. If Amy could make it over at short notice he would spare her an hour late afternoon. Jake thanked him, hung up and called Amy's cell.

It rang continuously.

He tried Boaz, irritated when it went straight to voicemail.

'Problem?' Rebecca questioned.

'No answer from Amy or Boaz.'

'Perhaps they went out.'

'Boaz knows to keep his phone with him, and on.'

At least Jake hoped he did. The officer was an idiot, but he wanted to give him a little credit. It bothered him he couldn't get an answer.

'Maybe he's in the john,' Hickok suggested. 'Give him five minutes and try again.'

Jake did. Still there was no answer.

He dug out Amy's landline. As with Boaz's cell, it went to voicemail.

'I'm going over there.'

Rebecca threw her pen down, looking annoyed.

'You're overreacting, Jake. Why the hell are you so convinced something's wrong?'

'Because Boaz is in charge and he's a fuck-up. That's why.' Jake shot Hickok a look, making sure he knew the barb was directed at him.

The agent didn't react, which pissed him off. He grabbed his car keys and his cell phone.

'Hickok! You're gonna let him go?'

Hickok glanced at Rebecca, then at Jake, and shrugged.

'If he wants to check it out, let him. It wouldn't hurt with Gavin back in town.'

Hickok and Rivers were trying to get a line on Amy's ex-boyfriend's exact whereabouts, but had so far drawn blanks.

Jake could see Rebecca biting down on her anger. He nodded a quick thank you to Hickok. Although they'd had their differences, he appreciated the support. Out in the parking lot, he tried both cells again. Boaz's continued to go to voicemail. Amy's rang a dozen times before it was answered.

'Hello?'

It wasn't her voice.

'Can you put Amy on the phone?'

There was a pause. He heard muttering in the background 'Listen, Detective Sullivan, right?' The voice seemed to know who he was. Amy must have stored his number in her phone. 'You might want to come out here. We're at the beach and there's been an incident.'

'What do you mean an incident? Who is this?'

'Heidi Pearce. I'm Amy's friend. Look, get here as soon as you can.' She gave him an address before hanging up.

Jake recognised it. It was where he'd been to interview Nadine Williams. What the hell was going on and why was Amy in the woman's house?

And Heidi, what the fuck did she mean by an *incident*?

Where was Boaz? Was he with them? Had something happened to him?

Had something happened to Amy?

Jake gunned the car out of the parking lot. Once on the highway heading out to the beach, he put a call in to Rebecca and updated her on what he knew.

'You want me to send backup?' she asked immediately.

'I don't think it's necessary. Heidi Pearce didn't sound in any danger. I'll call you when I find out what's going on.'

He didn't believe there was any danger, but still he broke the speed limit. Heidi hadn't put Amy on the phone, and his gut wouldn't settle until he knew she was okay.

When he pulled up outside the house Nadine Williams shared with her boyfriend, Troy Cunningham, he found Amy, Heidi and Huckleberry on the porch, waiting for him. Huckleberry was the most pleased to see him, barking in delight, while both Heidi and Amy wore scowls. It wasn't until he'd exited the car and stepped up onto the porch that he noticed Amy's face, the bloody scratches down her left cheek.

'What the hell happened?'

'Crazy super bitch, that's what happened,' Heidi told him, eyes flashing angrily.

'Why are you here, and in her house?'

Heidi quickly explained Boaz falling in the surf, running into Troy. Amy stayed silent, her gaze focused straight ahead, annoyed.

'How did this happen?' Jake directed the question at Amy, his tone softer, resisting the urge to stroke her bloody cheek. It looked like it had been cleaned up some, but the wound was still raw.

For the first time, she turned to meet his eyes. Her own were flecked with green, cooling the amber, and she looked a little embarrassed.

'Nadine took objection to me being in her home.'

'So she scratched you?' Jake swallowed down the anger he could feel rising. 'Where is she now?'

'Officer Boaz arrested her. They're inside. She's been going nuts. Huckleberry bit her.'

Amy reached down, hugged an arm around the collie.

Jake muttered a curse, stepped into the house without knocking. He found Boaz with Troy and Nadine in the kitchen. Nadine was sitting at the table, eyes tearful and make-up running down her face. She had a bloody dish towel wrapped around her right hand and her left wrist was cuffed to the table leg.

Boaz and Troy were talking heatedly, but both hushed as he entered the room. Jake immediately clocked the Hawaiian shirt and checked shorts Boaz had on.

'What the fuck are you wearing, man?'

Boaz coloured.

'Mr Cunningham here lent me some clothes while mine dried.' He pointed to the wet pile on the table in front of Nadine.

'Detective Sullivan, may I get you a drink: juice, coffee, water?' Troy offered, suddenly all manners.

'No,' Jake said sharply. 'What I want is someone to explain what the hell happened here.'

'The damn dog bit me,' Nadine snapped, speaking for the first time. She waved her bloody hand at Jake, red lips scowling. 'I want him put down and I want this cuff off me now.'

'And did he bite you before or after you attacked Miss Gallaty?'

'It was all a misunderstanding,' Troy said, stepping in smoothly.

'A misunderstanding?' Jake repeated. This guy was starting to tick him off.

'Yes, it was my fault. I should never have invited Officer Boaz and Amy back here without Nadine knowing.' Troy looked sympathetically at his girlfriend. 'She's had a migraine all day and had been sleeping. When she woke up and found Amy in the house, well, she's still a little upset with Amy, and she didn't react well.'

'She scratched her face. I think "not reacting well" is something of an understatement.'

Troy at least had the good grace to look embarrassed by his comment.

'The dog was protecting Amy, we understand that, but to arrest Nadine is ridiculous. Obviously if you agree to let her go, we won't be reporting it or taking it further.'

'What?' Nadine looked furious. 'He's a dangerous animal. I may need stitches.'

'Shut up, Nadine.'

For a moment the façade slipped, and Jake saw the cold anger beneath Troy's mask. There was something he didn't like about this guy, and he wanted to check him out further.

'As I said, we won't take action against the dog if Amy doesn't press charges against Nadine.'

'That's for her to decide,' Jake said coolly.

There was no way this pair would get away with doing anything to Huckleberry.

He turned to Boaz. 'Dare I ask where you were while all this was playing out?'

Boaz shuffled his feet, looking uncomfortable.

'I was with Mr Cunningham. We were finding some clothes that fit. I went to help as soon as I heard the screaming and arrested the lady for what she did to Amy.'

'I tried your cell. It's switched off.'

'Uh, I think it's broken from where it got wet.'

Jake shook his head. The man was a walking liability. He sucked in a breath, held it, counted. Losing his temper wouldn't help anyone.

'Okay, come on, Officer Magnum. I need you to take Heidi and Huckleberry home.' Somewhat reluctantly he took out his cuff key and released Nadine from the table.

'You're letting her go after what she did?' Boaz demanded angrily.

'For now, yes.' Jake glanced at Troy and then Nadine. 'I'll talk to Amy about whether she wants to press charges. If she does, I'll be in touch. But don't think about pulling any shit with her dog. If you do, you'll come off worse.'

Nadine's red lips trembled, her steely eyes glaring at him. She didn't say a word.

Troy gushed his thanks and apologies, the mask he habitually wore now back in place.

'What about Amy?' Boaz wanted to know. 'I'm supposed to be watching her.'

'I've got Amy. I have an appointment to get her to.'

* * *

'I don't think this is a good idea,' Amy protested as Sullivan opened the passenger door of his car. He put his hand on her head and pushed her down into the seat when she made no attempt to get in.

'I can't go like this, with these cuts on my face. It's too short notice. Besides, I've been giving it some thought and I don't think—'

He shut the door, cutting off her complaint, so Amy paused, waited until he got in the driver's side, before continuing.

'Seeing this guy isn't a good idea. I don't need to see a shrink because of a stupid nightmare. I'm perfectly fine. I just have a stressful situation going on at the moment. A shrink is not going to be able to help me. I already know what's wrong. See, I diagnosed myself.'

Sullivan sat patiently through her argument, a neutral expression on his face.

'You done?' he asked when she finally paused for breath.

'Yes. No... Maybe.'

'Which is it?' His eyebrows lifted, dark eyes questioning, the slightest hint of amusement in them.

'Yes. I guess.'

'Good.' He cranked the ignition, pulled away from the beach house. 'You'll be fine. Shinnick is a nice guy. He doesn't bite.'

'You're still making me go? I said I didn't want to.'

'I know.' He glanced over at her. 'Put your seat belt on.'

Amy huffed, annoyed he had changed the subject, but put the belt on anyway.

She had never been much of a rebellious type.

'So what possessed you to go into Nadine's house? You had to know it would spell trouble,' Sullivan asked, tone casual, eyes on the road.

Keeping the subject away from Doctor Shinnick, Amy noted.

'I already told you. Officer Boaz fell in the sea. Troy happened to be passing and offered him a towel and a change of clothes.'

'You could have waited outside.'

'Troy told us to go inside.'

'So you do everything you're told?' Sullivan glanced across at her again. This time there was definitely amusement in his eyes.

'No. Well, um, I guess maybe some of the time.'

He grinned. 'I thought so.'

'What's that supposed to mean? I was told not to go anywhere without Officer Boaz. I was following your rules.'

'See, you're doing it again.'

'Doing what again?'

'Doing as you're told.'

'Sure. Whatever.' Amy rolled her eyes.

He was teasing her, she realised, but she didn't mind. After what had happened with Nadine, it was a welcome relief. She didn't like arguments and would avoid them unless necessary, and she had never been involved in a physical fight, until today. Nadine had scared the crap out of her if she was honest, sneaking up behind her, blocking the doorway. Amy had tried to defuse the situation, firstly with words, then by trying to leave the room, but the woman was furious with rage at finding her in the house and had caught hold of her by the hair, raking long nails across her face.

Huckleberry had been first on the scene, barking at Nadine and sinking his teeth into the wrist she tried to swipe him away with. That was how Heidi, Troy and Officer Boaz had found them: Nadine clinging on to Amy's hair with one hand, the other trapped in

Huckleberry's mouth. Boaz had taken charge, tackling Nadine to the floor and arresting her, much to Troy's annoyance.

You were such a wimp you didn't even try to fight back.

It all happened so fast Amy hadn't had a chance. She thought back to the room she had found, to the destroyed photograph.

'I didn't like that Nadine had my picture up in her house. We're not friends. I don't even really know the woman. Why would she have my picture up?'

'Because she's your number one fan?' Sullivan suggested drily.

'It was weird, creepy-weird. She'd crossed me out in one of the pictures.'

He glanced over, raised his eyebrows.

'With a marker pen,' Amy elaborated. 'It was creepy.'

'Yeah, it is. Listen, Amy. I want you stay away from these people. No more trips to the beach. No more house visits. I'm going to check them out some more.'

'Sure, I have no problem with that.'

'That goes for Troy, as well as Nadine.'

'You think there's something up with Troy?'

'I get a vibe from the guy. It isn't good.'

'Okay.'

Troy had always been polite, friendly and nice to

her. But if Sullivan had seen something else, she had to trust him. 'You think he has something to do with the murders?'

'Probably not,' Sullivan admitted. 'They both have an alibi for the murders. I don't trust either of them though. Something is off.' He glanced over, held her gaze for a moment, his eyes warm.

Amy felt something inside her melt. She liked his eyes. 'Stay away from them, okay?'

19

Doctor Paul Shinnick occupied an office on the second floor of a converted brownstone in part of Juniper's older district. The quiet street with its wide pavements and verges lined with blossoming trees reminded Amy of the place her grandparents had lived. She fondly remembered summers visiting them before they passed away.

She stood by Sullivan's car, still unsure about the meeting with Shinnick and part of her wary about talking with a stranger about personal stuff. She had lost her grandparents in her teens, her parents in her twenties. Her friends were now her family, but there was only so much you could share with your friends.

As if sensing her unease, Sullivan offered his hand.

Amy hesitated for a moment before taking it. His grip was warm and firm.

He's the detective looking after you. Is this right?

It felt right. It also felt personal, and while that messed with her head, she liked it.

'Come on. You can do this.' He gave her hand a comforting squeeze, before leading her into the brownstone, up to the first floor.

Shinnick's office door was open. Hearing their footsteps, the doctor came out to meet them.

'Jake, how are you?'

Sullivan released Amy's hand, shook Shinnick's.

'I'm good, doc. Thanks for agreeing to see us on short notice.'

The doctor turned to Amy. He had kind eyes, that was the first thing she noticed about him: middle-aged, average height and build, brown hair slightly greying with a neatly clipped moustache and kind grey-blue eyes. There was nothing threatening about him.

Still, she was wary.

'You must be Amy.' Shinnick held out a hand.

She shook it tentatively. Sullivan trusted this guy. She had promised she would give it a go.

'It's nice to meet you, Doctor Shinnick.'

He smiled, a kind smile, like the eyes, and Amy felt her unease lifting.

'Shall we?' Shinnick indicated his office.

You're really gonna do this?

Sullivan touched her arm. 'I'll wait right here for you.'

When she hesitated, he lightly ran his fingertips down to the soft flesh of her wrist. 'Go on, you'll be fine.'

Taking a deep breath, she broke the contact and stepped into Shinnick's office, closed the door.

'Why don't you take a seat, Amy?'

The office was comfortably furnished. Sunlight streamed through the large window, bouncing off the mahogany desk. Potted plants, and scattered cushions on the two dark leather couches gave the room a homely feel.

Amy chose one of the two chairs in front of his desk, drumming her fingers together and giving the doctor a polite smile as he sat down opposite her. He put his hands in his lap mirroring her pose and leant slightly forward.

'Jake filled me in a little. I understand you're going through a difficult time at the moment. How would you describe your feelings with what has happened?'

He had a calming voice; his tone was low and mellow. She appreciated he hadn't drawn attention to the scratches on her cheek, asked questions about it.

'I don't know. Anxious, I guess, and nervous. I'm worried about what is going to happen next; who is going to be hurt next.'

'Those are normal reactions. It's the uncertainty, the not knowing. I imagine you feel like you are not in control of the situation. Would you agree with that, Amy?'

'Yeah, I guess.'

'I understand the killer has been mimicking the plots from your books. What kind of feelings does this arouse?'

'I don't understand why he chose my books. It's hard knowing I thought up death scenes for fictitious characters and now they're being made real. These people would be alive if I hadn't written the books.'

Shinnick shook his head. 'No, Amy. Don't be fooled into thinking that. Do you honestly believe the murders are about your books? People don't kill because they've read a story or watched a movie; they will already have deep-rooted psychological problems.'

'I guess.'

'The person the police are looking for, he – or indeed, she – would still kill if you hadn't written your books. They would be using a different reason. The feelings of guilt you are experiencing are perfectly normal, but in time you will realise they are not your responsibility.'

'It feels like it's because of me.'

'Why does it feel like it's because of you?'

'The killer is targeting me. He sent me a dead rat.' Amy was aware she was still fidgeting with her hands. She made a conscious effort to stop, knotting her fingers together. 'And he's been following me, taking my photograph.'

If Shinnick was surprised by her revelation, he didn't show it. She didn't know how much Sullivan had told him. Instead, he focused on her body language.

'I notice you have a tendency to fidget, but keep trying to stop yourself. Why does the fidgeting make you feel uncomfortable?'

'I don't know.'

Shinnick nodded. 'Well, it does sound like the killer is fixated on you rather than your books. If it wasn't you, he was copying, what do you think he would do?'

'I don't know. Umm, find someone else to target, I guess.'

'Exactly. You are not responsible for any deaths,

despite what your emotions are telling you. I understand the police have provided you with protection.'

'Yes.'

'That's wise.' Shinnick smiled sympathetically. 'I
know Jake well. He's a good cop and will look after you.'

A good cop who'd also had reason to see a therapist, Amy thought, but didn't say the words out loud.
She was curious to know what Sullivan's deal was, but
this wasn't the time or place to try and find out.

He did make her feel safe. There was no denying
that.

Yeah, he makes you feel safe, among other things.

She ignored the taunting voice in her head, trying
to keep her face carefully blank. Shinnick had already
picked up on her fidgeting. She sure as hell didn't
want him to home in on her embarrassing little crush
on Sullivan.

'Are you comfortable if we talk a little about your
background, Amy?'

No. I'm not comfortable with that at all.

'Sure, of course,' she lied.

Shinnick probed her gently about her childhood,
her relationship with her parents and how their
deaths had affected her. It had to be hard, he sympa-
thised, finding yourself alone at twenty-two.

Amy answered his questions as lightly as she could. Despite his relaxed approach, she just wasn't comfortable talking about this stuff. It was personal, some of it buried deep where it wouldn't cause pain. She had worked hard to reach her goals, to build a life for herself, and she had been careful to surround herself with a close circle of friends. Raking over the past wasn't going to help her, as far as she was concerned. Her parents had been good people and she missed them, as she did her grandparents, but they were all gone now and focusing on the gaping hole they had left was only making her feel shitty.

'When did your nightmares first start?' Shinnick asked.

He had this easy conversational way of shifting between topics. It was what made him a good therapist, Amy guessed. Shame she wasn't good at being a patient.

'I was fifteen,' she told him. 'I was involved in a car accident. The dreams started shortly afterwards.'

'You were involved in a car accident too?' Shinnick shifted slightly. Amy watched him make a note in the leather-bound book on his lap.

'Yeah, guess they run in the family,' she said, her tone more bitter than she'd intended.

Shinnick didn't react; he simply waited for her to continue.

'I wasn't in a car. I was hit by one. I was in a coma for three days, swelling on the brain. You know how it is.' She screwed up her nose, trying to make light of the situation. 'Then I woke up and everything was okay.'

'I can't imagine how that feels.'

'It wasn't great. Lots of bumps and bruises, but otherwise I was okay.'

'Except for the nightmares,' Shinnick said gently.

'Yeah, except for the nightmares.'

'How long after the accident did they start up?'

Amy thought back. Fifteen had been a long time ago. Back then she'd had her whole life ahead of her. Had thought her dad would one day get to walk her down the aisle, her mom get to hold grandchildren. How innocent fifteen had been.

'I dunno. I guess maybe a few weeks, a month later.'

'Are you comfortable talking about the nightmare? It's the same dream each time I believe.'

'Yeah, it is.' *And no I'm not.* 'I guess.'

As she had done with Sullivan the previous night, she talked Shinnick through the dream. The stone steps leading down, the sense of dread as she neared the bottom and the room she entered, where the dream always finished.

Shinnick was nodding slowly, looking thoughtful.

'And you have no idea where this staircase is or what this dream might mean?'

Amy shrugged. 'It's a dream; it's not real. I used to think it was to do with being in a coma. Maybe the stairs were me finding my way back to consciousness.'

'Possibly,' Shinnick agreed, but he didn't look convinced. 'You said you were hit by a car. What were the circumstances leading to your accident?'

Amy wrung her hands together, biting into her bottom lip. 'I don't know.'

'You don't know? Is that a realistic statement?' Shinnick raised his eyebrows. He had so far been good at masking his reactions, but this time his surprise was evident.

'I don't know,' she repeated, offering him the ghost of a smile. 'I suffered memory loss with the car accident. I had been staying with friends, and we had dinner; I remember lying on my bed reading. After that I woke up in hospital. The doctors said it was temporary amnesia and I would likely remember what had happened within a few days. I never did.'

'You said you were staying with friends? These were friends of your parents?'

'Yes. Deanna was my mom's best friend from high school. Her daughters were the same age as me and if my folks were ever away, I would go stay with them.'

'Was this in your home town in Montana?'

'No, they lived here in Oregon. In a town called Melford; it's an hour or so east of here.'

'Do they not know what happened leading up to the accident?'

'No.' Amy shook her head. 'Deanna and Pete, that's her husband, they thought I'd gone to bed. They were as shocked as hell when they got a call from the hospital. That kind of killed my mom's friendship with them. She never trusted them to look after me again and I haven't seen them since it happened.'

'So you were in your bedroom, then you were hit by a car, and no one knows how it happened, how you got there?'

'That's right.' Amy shrugged her shoulders. 'Guess I always figured I was sleepwalking.'

'Sleepwalking? You've done that before?'

'Well... no. It could've happened as a one off, right?'

Shinnick was silent for a long moment as he made further notes. Eventually he looked up.

'Have you ever considered hypnotherapy?'

Amy's guard immediately went up. 'No, and before you ask, I don't want to.'

'It's not as you see on TV,' Shinnick told her, tone calm despite her heated reaction. 'You would be in control and conscious the whole time. We would work it in gradually over several sessions and I think it would benefit you.'

'I'm not interested.'

Flustered, Amy grabbed her purse, got to her feet. She should never have let Sullivan bring her here. This therapy shit was a bad idea. 'Thank you for agreeing to see me, Doctor Shinnick, but this isn't going to work.'

Shinnick remained seated.

'Are you sure you want to leave, Amy? If you walk out of this door, you may never discover the cause of your nightmares.'

When she faltered, he continued. 'I understand you're apprehensive, nervous even, but don't you want to know what is causing them? It's possible your sub-conscious mind suppressed the trauma because it was too difficult to deal with at the time, but it might be ready to release the repressed memory, and you can get back the missing piece of the puzzle before the car accident.'

'I'm not being hypnotised.' She looked him

squarely in the eye, her tone firm, mind already made up.

'Of course, it's entirely up to you. If you do change your mind, and I hope you do, my door will be open.'

Amy gave him a quick smile, relief flooding through her as she opened the door and stepped back out into the waiting area.

Sullivan glanced up from the magazine he'd been flicking through.

'Come on,' she said tightly. 'I want to go home.'

* * *

Amy was quiet on the drive back to her apartment. Between the look on Shinnick's face as they'd left and the terse 'Fine' he'd received when asking if she was okay, Jake knew well enough to leave her alone.

He had sisters.

Something had rattled her while she'd been in with the doc and he would give her time to process her thoughts before trying to figure out what it was.

He hadn't told her about the latest developments with David Gavin. After the incident at the beach then the visit to the therapist, she was dealing with enough. Gavin being back in town could wait.

Amy excused herself to her bedroom as soon as

they arrived back. Jake left her to it, putting on the coffee pot and settling down on the couch with the papers, when he heard the shower start running. A warm body pressed against his leg and a wet nose against his hand as Huckleberry shoved his head under the paper and whined.

Scratching the collie's ears he felt a pang of guilt for his own dog. This case had kept him busy, and Roxy had been suffering as a result. He'd spent limited time with her over the past week, being there only for the obligatory walks and feeding. He would rectify that tonight and take her for a long walk.

When Amy emerged from the bedroom twenty minutes later, she was wrapped in a bathrobe and towel drying her damp hair. She headed straight into the kitchen.

'There's coffee in the pot,' Jake told her, turning his attention back to the sports pages.

'I'm fine.'

He heard her rummaging in the refrigerator; a few seconds later there was the sound of a cork popping, and he looked up to see her filling a large glass of wine.

She shot him a defensive look.

'What? I'm not allowed to have a drink in my own home now?'

Putting the paper down, he nudged Huckleberry to one side. 'So, are you gonna talk about it?'

When she didn't answer, instead taking a long sip of her wine, he went to her, noticing for the first time the redness around her eyes. 'Amy.'

When he touched her arm, she pulled away.

'I'm fine,' she repeated for the third time since they'd left Shinnick's office.

She took her glass, went over to the patio doors, opened them and stepped out onto the balcony.

Jake followed, went to stand beside her where she leant against the wall, looking out over the park.

'What happened?' he asked quietly.

'Nothing happened. We talked. He wanted to hypnotise me. I said no.'

'Okay.' Jake knew the doctor wouldn't have suggested hypnotherapy unless there was good reason. At the moment, Amy was hostile to the idea and needed time to calm down, think rationally. 'So is that what upset you, the thought of being hypnotised?'

'I'm not upset. I'm fine.'

That damn word again. It was beginning to irritate him.

'Okay, you're not upset. But something has pissed you off.'

Her hands tensed around the wine glass. 'I told

you it was a bad idea. I'm not comfortable talking about stuff with people. I don't like dredging up the past.' She took another long drink of her wine, set the glass down on the balcony wall. 'It's difficult being reminded of what I've lost, knowing I can't get it back. It brought up a few painful memories is all.'

She shrugged, trying to make light of it.

But finally, he understood and felt guilty. The family he took for granted that she no longer had. By making her see Shinnick, he had forced her to relive the past.

'I'm sorry.'

'It's fine.'

'Come here.' He caught hold of her as she made to walk past him.

'I have to get ready for work.'

'I know. Come here.'

Giving into the urge, he pulled her into his arms.

Surprised, her breath hitched and she stiffened, but only for a brief moment before she relaxed into him.

The warm musky scents from her shower filled his senses.

Careful, Sullivan.

The rational part of his brain fought to gain control, knowing he had to stay professional, could not go down this route. He wouldn't kiss her. He would not let it go that far. But he continued to hold her, convincing himself he was only offering comfort and not doing anything wrong.

* * *

In the street below, hidden in the shadows of the trees, a lone figure watched, a ball of anger building in his gut.

Bitch.

He raised the camera, zoomed in the lens.

Click. Click.

She would pay for this. He was going to make sure she paid.

It was Saturday night – Alan was out of town at a plastics convention and Rebecca had a hot date with a takeaway pizza, the Tarantino double-bill playing on cable and a six-pack of beer. When did her life become so rock 'n' roll?

Showered, hair tied back and dressed in a pair of old sweats, she fed the cats, watered her plants and played through her answerphone messages.

Two from her mother, blabbering on about coming into town, something about wanting help to plan a party; one from Alan telling her he'd arrived in Denver and when he got back they had some stuff they needed to talk about; and one cold-caller trying to sell her life insurance. She hit delete, erased the lot.

Her mother she would deal with in the morning. Why on earth she thought Rebecca would have the first clue about planning parties, she didn't know. Surely that was more Wendy's area of expertise. Besides, she sure as hell couldn't cope with a Sarah Angell mom-daughter chat after a full day in the office. The Storybook Killer, as they had informally named him, was no closer to being caught and they had a growing pool of suspects.

Shawn Randall was no longer a suspect given his airtight alibi for the night of the second murder.

David Gavin was allegedly in town, but they had not yet been able to verify his whereabouts to confirm this. His break-up with Amy had been bitter, but was it enough to make him want to kill?

Nadine Williams and her boyfriend, Troy Cunningham, had provided each other with alibis for the murders and initially been crossed from the list. Following Nadine's aggressive behaviour towards Amy at the beach house, Jake wanted them looked into further.

Then there were the fan letters. They hoped to have the lab results back in a couple of days. Had the killer written the letters? Had he been obsessed with Amy all this time and building up to the kills?

Popping the tab on a bottle of beer, Rebecca took a long cool sip, savouring the mouthful, and clicked the remote for the TV.

The doorbell rang and she glanced at her watch. The pizza delivery was early. Grabbing her purse, beer bottle still in the other hand, she went to the front door and threw it open, expecting to be hit with the waft of melted cheese and onions.

Instead, her jaw dropped.

'You've gotta be fucking kidding me!'

Joel Hickok grinned back at her.

'You've got such a dirty mouth, Angell.'

He pushed his way past her into the house, quick to locate the kitchen.

Rebecca slammed the front door shut and followed behind him.

He already had the refrigerator door open.

'What are you doing, Hickok?'

'Getting a beer, what does it look like I'm doing?'

'You know what I mean. Why are you here, in my house?'

He emerged with a bottle, spent a moment rummaging in her kitchen drawers looking for the opener. Finding it, he popped the tab, took a swig of beer and finally looked at her.

'You're not very hospitable, Angell. What's wrong with an old friend dropping by?'

'An old friend?' Rebecca repeated, seething. Six weeks of sex, six years of nothing and that made them old friends? She didn't think so.

Okay, so the sex had been good, really good, but that was irrelevant.

He grinned, walked over and clinked his bottle against hers. 'Here's to old friends.'

Then he was gone, off into the heart of the house, checking out the rest of her pad.

Rebecca followed him, flustered. If it was any other guy she would be in control, calling the shots. Why did Hickok always manage to get the upper hand?

'Where the hell are you going?' she demanded, as he made his way into the living room. She found him holding the photo frame that sat on the mantle, the picture of her parents on their ruby wedding anniversary.

'How is your mom?' he asked, conversationally.

Sarah Angell had initially been impressed by the young FBI agent who had stayed close to her daughter's bedside while she recovered from a stab wound in hospital. She wanted Rebecca to meet a nice man, settle down, and he had good credentials.

Her opinion had changed a couple of weeks later when she'd unexpectedly visited Rebecca's apartment, and walked in on the two of them naked on the couch.

Rebecca's cheeks flamed even now as she recalled the incident.

She hadn't been able to look her mom in the eye for months afterwards and Hickok had gone from being referred to as potential boyfriend material to 'that FBI agent'.

'She's fine. I'm sure she would be thrilled to know you're back in town.'

Hickok grinned, clearly thinking about the same incident.

'Not our finest moment, eh?' His eyes wandered over to the couch she had brought with her from the apartment, then back to her face, and his grin widened. 'Keeping it for old time's sake?'

Rebecca, mid-sip, nearly choked on her beer. Before she could recover and respond, he'd already moved on and changed the subject.

'So, where's Adam? You guys live here together, right?'

'Alan is at a plastics convention in Denver.' She made a point of pronouncing his name, as she couldn't be bothered to correct Hickok's mistake, yet again. It was one she was certain he kept making on purpose. 'And no, we don't live together.'

Maybe that's what he wants to talk about when he gets back: moving in together.

Something was definitely up with Alan. He had been acting really cagily around her recently. Either that or he was still pissed at her about the fight. Maybe he wanted to end things. Rebecca wasn't sure how she felt about that, so she pushed the thought away.

'A plastics convention; are you serious? So what is that; a bunch of dorks meeting up to discuss spoons and Tupperware pots?'

'You're unbelievable. You walk into my home, and you insult my boyfriend? You've crossed the line, Hickok.'

'And there I was thinking my timing was perfect, showing up when you're at a loose end.'

When Rebecca shook her head, lost for words, he took a step closer, eyes not leaving her face.

'You know, I've missed this. Sparring with you.'

'You mean insulting me,' Rebecca corrected, this time wise enough to not to get suckered in.

The doorbell sounded and Hickok raised his eyebrows.

'Pizza,' Rebecca told him.

'I should've guessed.' When she made to push past him, he stopped her. 'I got it.'

'No, I—' He'd already left the room. 'I'm not sharing my dinner with you, Hickok!' she yelled at his back. She could see he had his wallet out and was paying the guy.

Kicking the door closed, he carried the pizza back through into the living room.

'Jeez, Angell. You eat like a horse. How much food have you got here?'

Rebecca made a grab for the box.

'Give me my pizza.'

'Technically it's my pizza. I paid for it,' Hickok pointed out, grinning, holding the box at arm's length.

'You are such an asshole.'

Rebecca launched herself at him, catching hold of his arm as she reached for the pizza box.

Hickok's grin widened as he held it out of her reach and instinctively she slipped her foot behind his, tripping him as he took a step back. His free hand locked around her arm as he stumbled and they both went down, Hickok landing on his back on the couch, Rebecca on top of him. The pizza box crashed to the floor behind them.

Oh shit.

Keeping her distance was one thing, but now, lying

here on top of him and on the same damn couch where they had once been at it like rabbits, old feelings resurfaced.

Hickok grinned, realising, and lifted his hand to her face, brushing his fingers down her cheek.

Everything inside Rebecca tingled and, caught up in the moment, her mouth inched towards his.

What are you doing you idiot?

Rationality kicked in at the last second.

Before he could stop her, she pushed herself back and got up from the couch.

Hickok lay there for a second, watching her as she busied herself picking pizza up from the floor. A couple of slices were ruined, but most of it was still in the box.

What the hell had she been thinking? Her thoughts went to Alan, and she immediately felt guilty.

'You know you want it as much as I do.' Hickok's words cut through her thoughts.

'Excuse me?'

'You, me.' He slowly sat up, patted the couch and grinned. 'Here, for old time's sake.'

'I have a boyfriend,' she said tightly.

'Yeah, we'll see.'

'I mean it, Hickok. I'm not here to be your plaything whenever you decide to roll into town.'

When he continued to stare at her, that cocky grin on his face, Rebecca shook her head. 'I'll get plates.'

From now on she had to keep things strictly professional with Hickok, focus purely on the case. He was an idiot coming here, but he was here, and she would take the higher road, share her dinner with him, after which she would politely ask him to leave.

She could do that.

* * *

The room was gloomy, the single overhead light flickering annoyingly and he briefly considered changing the bulb. He had enough light for what he needed to do, though, and decided it would probably enhance the atmosphere once his victim was in place. The room had been perfect for the job. The bathtub was positioned beneath a sturdy wooden beam, which would securely hold the rope he had hooked over it. On the floor lay his tools: more rope, cuffs, duct tape, a plastic overall and gloves, his butcher's knife and a taser. Beside them was a copy of Amy Gallaty's third novel, *Blood Crime*.

He glanced at his watch, noted it was nearly nine-thirty. The next victim would soon be in place, ready for him to make his move. Carefully he selected the tools he needed, placed them in his sports bag. Casting a final glance over the room, he allowed himself a small smile. Everything was perfect, everything in place.

He grabbed his bag, killed the light and stepped out of the room.

21

Jake walked Roxy by the river, enjoying the time spent alone with his thoughts. She seemed delighted to have him to herself and, although he'd let her off the leash, she mostly stayed close.

Dusk had settled; the street lights were already on and there were maybe another fifteen minutes left before night took hold. As he made his way along the riverbank his thoughts were on Amy.

Away from her he could be rational, understood he was crossing boundaries. This wasn't his style. He had always been a cop who'd been able to keep work life and personal life in separate boxes. Why was Amy Gallaty different? Subconsciously he found himself wandering the route through the park leading out opposite her apartment building.

Damn it, Jake. Focus.

Although a faint glow of light came from the patio window, he knew she wasn't home. He had left her with Hal Peterson, a level-headed patrol officer from the precinct. Peterson was no Boaz and Jake trusted him to keep Amy safe. She had a bar shift tonight and the officer would be blending discreetly with the clientele, while watching her every move.

Which leaves you with some free time.

The thought made him restless. It was Saturday night, and he should be enjoying some downtime.

His neighbour, Natalie, was having a party. She'd invited him weeks ago and it had slipped his mind. He'd seen her as he'd been heading out with Roxy, dressed in a little black number, and she'd asked him if he was coming. Maybe he should go.

Either that or he could call up Brad Kramer; grab a beer down at Mahoney's. It tended to be the local cop hangout and there would be a dozen of their other colleagues in there. Musing on the idea, he bent down to clip the leash on Roxy before they reached the roadside, attention drawn to the dozen or so cigarette butts on the ground. Perhaps it was nothing, but it was dead opposite Amy's apartment and an odd place for someone to stand and smoke.

He thought of Amy's ex-boyfriend, David Gavin, allegedly back in town. Was he watching her, with a score to settle? Then there was Nadine Williams and Troy Cunningham. Nadine seemed too hot-headed to lurk around in bushes, but what about Troy? There was something off about the guy.

Out of habit he kept a couple of evidence bags in his wallet. Careful to use the plastic of the bag, he picked up the butts, secured them and stuffed them in his pocket.

It wouldn't hurt to check them out.

* * *

'So where is Robin tonight?' Angell asked through a mouthful of pizza.

'What was that?' Although he'd gotten the gist of it, Joel shook his head. 'I can't tell what you're saying with all that bread stuffed in your mouth.'

She scowled at him, this time finishing her mouthful before speaking. 'I asked where Robin was.'

'Robin?'

'Yeah, I figure you'd want to be Batman. Your ego couldn't handle being Robin.'

They'd settled into an uneasy truce following the earlier incident on her couch, Angell having grudgingly allowed him to stay and share her pizza.

She'd nearly kissed him. They both knew that. He also knew it pissed her off.

He wasn't honestly sure how it made him feel.

It irritated the hell out of him she was dating a douche like Alan. He'd forgotten how feisty she was, how much he enjoyed sparring with her, and he was still attracted to her.

She hadn't changed a whole lot. Maybe there was the odd line on her face, but she still wore her dark hair long and her feline eyes sparked when she was angry. She was definitely more confident, sexier.

Six years ago, they had both rushed in without thinking about it. Joel didn't do relationships and, even if he did, how the hell was it supposed to work when they lived on opposite sides of the country? And so he had made sure it stayed short and sweet.

Why was now any different?

'If we're talking about Rivers then he'd never handle being Batman,' he told her, pushing the problem out of his mind. 'To be honest, he makes a pretty lame Robin too.'

'So you ditched him to come annoy me?'

'I didn't ditch him, Angell. I don't hang out with

him period.' When she raised her eyebrows, he pulled a face. 'What? I'm not his babysitter for crying out loud. Besides, he's got the whole rich kid thing going on. His daddy is well connected and hooks him up with a lot of freebies to benefits and big sports games. He mentioned something about driving up to Portland to watch the Trail Blazers.'

'He's a rich kid, eh?'

'How else do you think he got into the Bureau? It wasn't because he passed his field agent training with flying colours.'

Joel had heard rumours Rivers should have flunked out at Quantico. His daddy, Chuck Rivers, was pals with the assistant director and had called in a favour. Declan wanted to be an FBI field agent so Declan would be an FBI field agent, no matter what strings needed to be pulled.

The politics of it stank, and now Joel was stuck looking after him.

'Trust me, we're safer if he keeps himself occupied with ball games and stays away from the case.'

'He didn't do bad work today,' Angell pointed out, dropping a crust back in the pizza box. She'd ordered extra-large and between them they'd eaten it all.

Joel wondered how the hell she had planned on

putting away the whole pizza herself. But then the woman did have the appetite of a pig.

'Yeah, he did okay today,' he admitted grudgingly. 'Still doesn't excuse all the other times he's been a complete fuck-up. I don't trust him to have my back in the field.'

'Not like Max.'

'No, not like Max at all.' Joel shoved the last mouthful of pizza into his mouth, wiped his hands on a serviette and threw it in the box. 'So, Angell, what say you and I go for a drink?'

His suggestion had her frowning.

'No, Hickok. I thought I made myself clear. I'm in a relationship. I'm not going for a drink with you.'

'Chill out. I'm not asking you out on a date. I said let's go for a drink.'

'Theoretically, they are the same thing. Besides, I remember the last time we went for a drink you got yourself punched in the face and it ended up being my fault.'

'It was your fault.'

'You needed quicker reactions.'

'My reactions are just fine.' He grinned at her, remembering. 'That bar still there?'

'You mean the Blue Moose? Yeah, though I haven't been there in years. I mostly drink at Mahoney's these days.' Rebecca screwed up her nose. 'Bourbon's not so good, but it's the local cop hangout.'

'I was thinking we should go visit the Velvet Lounge. Our cocktail-serving mystery writer is working tonight. Peterson is with her, but wouldn't hurt to have extra eyes in the bar.'

'Okay.'

'Okay, yes?'

Angell narrowed her eyes. 'Okay, I'm considering your suggestion.'

Joel glanced at his watch. 'Well consider faster. If we're gonna go, we need to leave pretty sharpish.' He glanced at her sweats. 'And you're gonna need to change first. I'm not walking in with you looking like a bag lady.' He grinned when her eyes flashed angrily. 'Maybe you can wear the red number you had on the other night.'

The red number that had hugged her curves in all the right places.

The red number she had worn for Alan.

Angell smiled tightly. 'I'll go put on my jeans.'

Joel cleared away the pizza box and plates while he waited.

So Alan the douche got the red dress and he got jeans. Go figure.

The jeans did look good on her, he had to admit,

when she emerged ten minutes later. They hugged her ass and fit to her curves like glue. Yeah, the jeans were good. And whatever perfume she was wearing, that smelt good too.

She looked a little distracted, as she emptied the contents of her purse onto the couch.

'What's up?'

'I can't find my ring.'

'So? You don't normally wear a ring.'

'Not for work. It's one my folks gave me. My mom will kill me if I've lost it.'

Joel glanced at his watch. It was getting late.

'You want to stay here and hunt for it now? We need to get going, Angell.'

'Okay.' She snapped her purse shut, gave him a tight smile. 'I'll look for it tomorrow.'

* * *

Nadine sipped a large Martini while she waited for Troy to finish getting ready.

She was restless after the day's events; still couldn't believe he had let Amy Gallaty into her house. And to then have that bonehead officer try to arrest her. Troy owed her big time. She had talked him into buying her dinner. A new Vietnamese restaurant had opened in town and by some kind of miracle they had managed to secure a last-minute reservation. Nadine would have pho and a nice bottle of wine on Troy.

He had suggested they then take in a movie. There was a remake of *The Italian Job* playing he wanted to see.

Nadine had smiled, but remained non-committal. She was still seething about earlier and had her own plans in mind. The Velvet Lounge was only a block away from the movie theatre. Maybe she would get her own back on Amy and pay her a surprise visit.

* * *

Jake opted for Natalie's party, showering and throwing on clean jeans and a shirt before digging out a bottle of Jameson's he had lying around in a cupboard.

Natalie opened the door, pleased to see him. They had been neighbours for a couple of years, and she had a key to his place, taking Roxy out if he ever had to work late.

He recognised a few other tenants, Natalie's current boyfriend, Dan, and one or two of her friends who had visited before. She pushed him in the direction of three girls who were standing in the kitchen caught up in conversation.

'Jake, I want you to meet some good friends of mine: Kim, Melissa and Haley. Girls, this is my neighbour, Jake, who I was telling you about.'

Jake caught the knowing look the girls exchanged, understood now Natalie's intention of getting him to the party had been to set him up. On the occasions they ran into each other, she would rag him about his love life, telling him he worked too hard and needed to meet a nice girl.

He swore she was in cahoots with his mother.

'It's good to meet you, Jake. Natalie has told us all about you.' This was from Haley, easily the prettiest of the three, with dark hair and a toothpaste smile.

'Has she now.' Jake shot Natalie a look, letting her know he was onto her. While her interference mildly irritated him, he was also figuring what was the harm? They seemed nice enough girls. A couple of drinks and conversation would take his mind off Amy.

Natalie poured him some of the Jameson's before leaving him with her friends, looking mighty pleased with her cupid effort.

For the next hour, Jake found himself trapped in the kitchen as the three girls vied for his attention. Kim was the pushiest, using every opportunity to make physical contact and already proposing he take her out, while Melissa and Haley hung on his every word. They were three pleasant, attractive girls and any guy in his position would have been lapping up the attention, so why did he find himself bored, restless, his mind wandering?

Because you're an idiot, Sullivan.

He stole a glance at his watch, disappointed it wasn't as late as he thought.

'You got somewhere else you need to be?' Kim asked, running a finger down the front of his shirt.

Jake thought of Amy, working in the Velvet Lounge. Peterson was with her and he was a good cop. He would keep her safe. Still, it wouldn't hurt to have a second pair of eyes. If the place was busy, it would be harder to keep tabs on her. He finished his whiskey, set the glass down and eased himself away from the counter.

'There's a work situation I have to check in on.'

All three girls looked disappointed. They knew he was a cop and in his line of work things cropped up.

'Will you be coming back?' That was from Kim again.

When he told her it was unlikely, she practically pouted, so he softened it to a maybe.

Coward. You know you're not coming back.

Ignoring the unsubtle attempts to get his cell number, he excused himself, found Natalie to say goodbye and left the party.

He returned briefly to his apartment to grab his service revolver and car keys, then locked up and made his way downstairs, convincing himself his visit to the Velvet Lounge was going to be purely for professional reasons.

* * *

He watched the bar from a lot across the street. Although the Velvet Lounge had its own parking he couldn't risk waiting there. The cops had already put a protection detail on Amy Gallaty and there was every possibility they would be watching this place tonight.

He appreciated it more when the stakes were high; it made pulling off the kill risky, but the results and the buzz were worth it.

He waited patiently, watched the patrons come and go, the bouncer guarding the door, one of the cocktail waitresses step outside on her break for a quick smoke. Glancing at his wristwatch he knew it would soon be time to make his move.

Just a short while longer.

He leaned forward, forearms resting on the steering wheel and continued to watch. The thrill was steadily building inside him, but he had to be patient.

Not long now.

22

The Velvet Lounge drew a good crowd on Saturdays and tonight was no exception.

Amy's shift began at seven and she found it a blessed relief to throw her head into work, appreciating the return to normality after what had been an unsettling day. She was working the shift with two other waitresses, Fran, and one of the new girls, Chloe. As the three of them collected orders and served drinks, Gage and Tom mixed up cocktails.

No one had commented on Amy's scratches. She had spent half an hour working with make-up to disguise them and wore her tawny brown hair loose around her face. If anyone did comment, she figured she'd blame Huckleberry.

Her bodyguard for the night was Hal Peterson, an older officer with sharp eyes and a serious disposition. He was a man of few words, which suited Amy fine. At least she didn't feel obligated to make small talk with him.

While she waited tables, he sat at the bar sipping soda water and lime and watched her, watched everyone around her, his foot tapping against the bar stool in time to the in-house jazz band.

He took his job seriously, which made her feel safe.

She had just finished serving a table of regulars when she recognised Detective Angell and Special Agent Hickok entering the bar. Amy's heartbeat quickened. Had there been another murder? She couldn't think of any other reason why the two of them would be here. Ignoring the table of frat boys who were trying to catch her attention, she went over.

'Is everything okay?'

Angell gave her a reassuring smile immediately picking up on her unease.

'Yes, don't worry. We figured Saturday night is busy, so it wouldn't hurt to have a couple of extra pairs of eyes.'

'Okay.' It made sense and Amy did feel safer with a larger police presence.

'How's your cheek?' Hickok asked, blatantly staring at where Nadine had scratched her.

So much for my make-up job.

'Um, it's okay. I put antiseptic cream on it to take out the sting.'

'You can press charges, you know.'

'Yeah, I know.' Amy didn't want the hassle. She had the impression pressing charges against Nadine would only provoke the woman. 'I'd rather just forget about it.'

'Your call.' Hickok shrugged, nodding to Hal Peterson who was sliding off his bar stool and making his way over.

'Detective Angell. Special Agent Hickok. There a problem?'

'No problem. Figured it wouldn't hurt to have a few extra bodies down here tonight. Everything okay so far?'

'Yeah, no trouble; I've been keeping a close eye on the lady.'

'Do you want drinks?' Amy offered. 'If you get a table, I'll bring them over.'

She took their order of two beers to the bar.

'More cops?' Gage asked, raising his eyebrows. At Amy's neutral expression, he added, 'I remember the woman from your apartment, Ames.'

Amy glanced around.

'Okay, well don't publicise it. They're here to keep an eye on things.' She smiled sweetly at him as he fetched the bottles of beer, placed them on the tray. 'Any chance these can go on the house?'

'Okay,' Gage agreed after a long moment, before pulling a face. 'The things I do to keep you safe.'

Amy blew him a kiss of thanks and took the beers over to Angell and Hickok.

'You notice anyone acting suspicious tonight?' Hickok wanted to know.

'No.' Amy shook her head. She'd been keeping an eye out for suspicious behaviour. Nothing had struck her as out of the ordinary.

She took her tray back to the bar, caught Fran's eye to let her know she was taking a bathroom break.

The restroom was down a corridor at the back of the bar and Amy made her way along the passage, noting for about the fifth time the overhead bulb was still flickering and needed replacing. She passed the fire escape, headed downstairs and through the door next to the cellar that led to the restroom, taking one of the two open stalls.

As she sat waiting to pee, the door creaked opened. Hearing footsteps, she waited for the sound of the other stall door to close.

It didn't.

It's probably someone touching up their lipstick, she rationalised, but it bothered her she didn't hear them enter the stall, didn't hear the sound of the faucet running or the click of a lipstick tube.

She held her pee, her breath; waited silently.

There was no noise coming from the other side of the stall, yet she'd heard the footsteps enter the bathroom. And they hadn't left.

Who is there?

She was tempted to call out a 'hello' but stopped herself. People did shit like that in the movies and it usually got them killed.

This isn't a movie, Amy. It's real life.

Several long seconds passed. Amy could feel her bladder ache. This was stupid. She couldn't stay in here until someone came looking for her.

Yes, you can.

Angell, Hickok or Peterson would soon notice she was missing.

But what if they don't? You need to see who is there.

More seconds ticked by, the sound of the band in the bar was muted, reminding her how far away help was. The only close sound was the thump, thump of her heart.

Look under the door.

Amy glanced at the floor, wondered how many times it had been pissed on or barfed over, then at the gap at the bottom of the stall door. The idea of putting her head down there was gross, but she had to know. Slowly she eased herself forward, holding her hair back with one hand so it didn't brush the floor. She was low enough to be able to see the row of washbasins.

A shriek had her losing her balance and she fell forward, the palm of her free hand smacking the sticky floor.

The door creaked again and two sets of feet entered the bathroom, both wearing stiletto heels. The owners were giggling and chatting excitedly about a couple of guys they'd hooked up with.

Feeling stupid, Amy picked herself up, quickly peed and got out of the cubicle before they left.

She glanced around the bathroom, looking for the source of the original footsteps, but it was only the three of them.

The two women who'd entered were in no hurry. They were still applying make-up and swapping details, barely affording her a glance, as she rinsed and dried her hands.

Still shaken, she left them to it, pushing open the

restroom door and walking headlong into Officer Peterson, who was waiting outside.

'You should've told me you were going to the bathroom,' he scolded. 'I'm not supposed to let you out of my sight.'

'Someone came into the restroom. I heard footsteps.'

'It was just me, Miss Gallaty. Checking everything was okay.'

'Oh, okay.' Now Amy felt stupid. She had overreacted.

Get a grip.

Forcing a smile for Peterson, she hurried back to the bar.

* * *

Seeing Amy return, Fran deposited her tray on the counter and leant over to retrieve her cigarettes and lighter.

'I'm taking my break,' she called to Gage.

He nodded, not bothering to look up as he filled two glasses with margarita.

She snuck an arm around Amy as her friend approached for her own tray, noticing the distracted look on her face. 'You okay, honey?'

'Yeah, sure, I just...' Amy hesitated before having a change of heart. 'It was nothing.'

'I'm going out for a smoke. You okay to watch my tables?'

'Yeah, sure.'

As Fran made her way to the door, it opened and she recognised the man who stepped inside. He was the other detective who had been at Amy's apartment. The cute one: Sullivan, she remembered. She glanced back at her friend, noticed her clock Sullivan, didn't miss the slightly flustered look on her face, and made a note to question her later. Smiling sweetly at the detective, Fran slipped through the door he held open for her, almost regretting going out for a cigarette. Things looked like they could be getting interesting.

Leon was on the door and, as things were quiet with most of the customers already inside, he joined her for a smoke. As they usually did, the two of them discussed music. They were both fans of hard rock and spent a lot of time debating the best bands and recommending new artists to each other.

'You heard the Deftones new album?'

'Not yet.' Leon rubbed a hand over his bald head. 'It's on my list.'

'I've got it in my car if you want to borrow it for a listen.'

'Yeah, okay. Thanks.'

Fran stubbed out her cigarette, reached for her car keys in the back pocket of her jeans.

'Be right back.'

The parking lot was well lit and packed out. Saturday nights were busy and the staff made sure they parked the furthest away from the bar, leaving the better spaces for the patrons. Fran's Buick was at the end of the row, sheltered by overhanging trees. She unlocked and opened the passenger door. Sitting down, she started rummaging in the glovebox for the CD.

So much crap in here, Fran.

She found the case, swore when she discovered it was empty. As she started the hunt for the disc, a clicking sound and a rustle from the bushes startled her and she dropped the case. She glanced around and saw no one.

'Is that you, Leon?'

Telling herself to stop being an idiot, she picked up the case and continued to hunt for the disc.

* * *

Nadine ditched Troy at the movie theatre.

After leaving the restaurant she had voiced her

intent to visit the Velvet Lounge. Troy had tried to talk her out of it, telling her it was a stupid idea, and their disagreement had resulted in a fight.

It had been Nadine doing most of the shouting. Well, okay, all the shouting. Troy was more controlled than her, which she found irritating. There was heat behind his eyes and she wanted him to snap, to fight back. Eventually her voice had grown hoarse and she had become weary from shouting. She had sulked as he had dragged her to the movie theatre then, on a whim, ditched him while he queued for the tickets. She figured he knew where she was heading and would come after her.

Except he didn't.

Nadine found herself approaching the Velvet Lounge, her bravado disappearing by the second, knowing she had no backup and would be entering a place where Amy was surrounded by work colleagues and friends. She entered the parking lot, noting the bouncer on the door and, instead of approaching him, made her way around the side of the building.

Perhaps there was a back entrance she could sneak in through.

* * *

He watched and he waited.

Confident the time was right to make his move, he started the engine, pulled out of the parking lot across the street and into the one belonging to the Velvet Lounge.

The place was rammed and there were no spots by the entrance. But that was good. He would pull up around the back of the building, leave the van with the engine running and the door open, ready to move in quick and make his getaway. Finding a suitable spot, he pulled to a halt, exited the van.

It was time to go fetch the next victim.

* * *

After checking through half a dozen loose discs and coming to the conclusion her car was a mess, Fran finally found the one she was looking for and slotted it back into the case.

As she got out of the car there was another rustle from the bushes. A dark shape launched itself at her; she dropped both the CD and her car keys and screamed.

* * *

Nadine skirted the building, realising the only other entrance was a fire door which was locked.

She debated for a moment. Was she going to enter the bar through the main door and cause a scene or slink back to the movie theatre with her tail between her legs? Option B would mean Troy had won; she drew a deep breath and made her way back to the front of the bar. She'd had enough of hanging around outside. Although the parking lot was well lit, it was still dark and there was hardly anyone about. Plus, there were all these creepy bushes. Anyone could be lurking in them.

Pondering the thought as she took a step back towards the front of the building, she was startled as a firm hand grabbed her by the shoulder.

* * *

'Bruno.'

The shape had paws on Fran's shoulders and a wet slobbery tongue. Her hands felt fur.

'Bruno!' The voice came again, sharper, and the shape was pulled off her.

It's just a freaking dog.

She picked herself up, heart racing, and found herself looking into the soulful eyes of a St Bernard. The owner, a woman who looked far too frail to be walking such a giant dog, started apologising profusely.

'I'm so sorry. He's normally so well behaved.'

'It's okay. Honestly, it's okay.'

A little shaken from the encounter, but wanting to draw a line under it, Fran retrieved her CD and car keys, locked the car and made her way back to Leon.

* * *

Nadine swung around, startled.

'What the hell are you doing here?' she demanded.

'No, Nadine. What the hell are you doing here?' Troy looked angry, really angry. 'I told you to leave it. Not to come here tonight.' He grabbed his head with both hands, frustrated. 'I can't believe you would do this after today.' He was almost shouting now.

This is what Nadine had wanted, wasn't it; to get him involved in a real fight? She hadn't expected him to be so mad.

'Is there a problem?'

It was the bald-headed bouncer from the door. Troy glared at him, eyes flashing angrily. Nadine could see him fighting for control.

'No problem. We were just leaving.'

* * *

Leon watched the fighting couple cross the parking lot, head down the street where they were no longer his problem, before returning to the door.

As he did, a low whistle came from the other side of the bar. He glanced towards the dark bushes, debating for a moment whether it came from within the premises or out on the street – maybe another dog walker.

The whistle came again.

Low, a little taunting and not the kind of whistle anyone made to a dog. Curiosity getting the better of him, he left his post and made his way round the side of the building towards where the noise had come from. There was no one there, just the dark outline of bushes, the silhouettes of the few cars parked round the back of the building. He could hear the faint of hum of an engine running.

Leon took a couple of steps further into the blackness, allowing his eyes a moment to adjust in case there was someone hiding in the bushes. Satisfied he was alone, and figuring the whistling had to have come from the road, he turned to walk back to the main door.

Someone grabbed him from behind, gripping him in a headlock.

Leon grunted, surprised by the strength of the arm around his neck, and lurched forward, attempting to throw his attacker over his shoulder. Something hard pressed into his side, below his ribcage. It zapped into him, pulsating into his body, and he stiffened like a board.

Fuck, no, stop. Dear God, no, please stop, please!

He thought he'd said the words aloud, but realised they were in his head.

After what seemed like minutes, but was probably only seconds, the zapping stopped. The arm eased around his neck and, although he remained coherent, Leon felt his body give out as he fell to the floor.

Unable to defend himself; he stared up into the face of his attacker, noting the cold smile and the dead eyes, and a shiver ran down his spine.

23

Leon Pruitt's body was discovered Tuesday morning by a jogger, and Jake was being bored senseless by Declan Rivers about the Trail Blazers' game when the call came in. He didn't hate basketball, but Rivers hadn't stopped talking about the damn game since the weekend. Jake understood the kid was enthusiastic, but he needed to quit being such a geek and go get laid or something.

He's not the only one, Sullivan.

His thoughts briefly turned to Amy. He'd last seen her working in the Velvet Lounge on Saturday night, and had made an effort to stay away from her since. It had been stupid going to the bar. Deep down he knew he hadn't gone there as backup for Peterson, and so did Rebecca.

She'd been decidedly frosty with him, annoyed he wasn't heeding her warnings about getting personally involved.

Jake knew she was right, and it pissed him off. He also knew she was irritated he'd caught her out with Hickok. There was something going on with the two of them; she just wasn't admitting it. He didn't miss the exchanged look between them when Hickok came into the office with the announcement that another body had been found.

'We've got a call about another vic.'

'What do we know?' Rebecca asked.

'Male, late twenties, body dumped in the woods.'

'You think it's our guy?'

'I'd say so. Throat has been slit. That and the location would match book three.' Hickok scowled at Rivers, who already had his notebook open, scribbling. 'Hey, Boy Wonder, there's not gonna be a test.'

Rivers glanced up, cheeks reddening, as Hickok shook his head.

'Come on, people, let's get moving. Withers is gonna meet us at the crime scene.' He glanced briefly at Jake. 'You're gonna love where that is.'

Jake narrowed his eyes. 'Go on.'

'Our unsub has played things closer to home this time.'

Hickok gave a twisted smile. 'He dumped the body in the woods across the road from Amy Gallaty's apartment.'

* * *

Vic fetched Amy's mail in the mornings, figuring it was safer she stay in her apartment. He always insisted she lock the door behind him and, since Sullivan had pointed it out to him, always check the peephole before letting him back in. They couldn't afford to take any risks.

He knew he was taking on the protector role, but that was fine because he knew women ate that shit up and he still harboured desires of getting Amy into bed, even if Sullivan was giving him a bit of competition.

Play it slow, Vic, buddy. Keep looking after her, lay on the charm and reel her in.

She was in her bedroom when he went down for the mail. Over the past couple of days she had taken to locking herself away for a few hours. Vic guessed she needed her own space, probably in order to write, and the TV disturbed her.

He knocked twice on her bedroom door before

quickly pushing it open, half wishing, and a little dis-appointed when he didn't, catch her in some state of undress. Instead, she sat on her bed, cross-legged, hunched over her laptop, reading glasses on and a frown on her face as she studied the screen.

She looked kind of geeky, but there was still some-thing sexy about her, even with the glasses. He coughed loudly and she glanced up, startled.

'I'm heading down to get the mail,' he told her.

'Okay.' She looked a little annoyed he'd disturbed her and Vic guessed he'd interrupted her mid-flow.

'You need to come and lock the door behind me,' he reminded.

Amy sighed, looked like she was going to object, but stopped. She pushed her glasses onto her head and gave a tight smile. 'Sure.'

Vic instructed her, as he always did, not to unlock the door when he rang the buzzer until she was sure it was him on the other side.

'It's okay, I've got it.'

She closed the door behind him, and he hesitated for a moment. Amy was being a little testy today. It was unlike her, as she was normally easy-going. Hoping it would be a brief thing, Vic headed down to the lobby to collect her mail.

No more dead rats he was pleased to note. Amy had a couple of letters – bills by the look of them – and a package. It felt squishy – some mail-order clothing no doubt. Maybe underwear, Vic thought hopefully, picturing what she would look like in a matching black silky bra and panties set.

He felt himself harden as the elevator door started to close.

'Hold the elevator. Hold the elevator.'

Peering out, he saw the crazy lady from 12B heading furiously towards him on her walking frame.

Oh crap, no.

He hit the button for the top floor again, willing the doors to close.

Vic didn't do old people at the best of times; they tended to spook him, especially ones who stunk of lavender and mothballs and wore thick lenses that magnified their eyes. This lady had the glasses and the lavender smell thing going on. She was also hard of hearing and crazy as a coot. He knew because he'd been stuck in the elevator with her a couple of days back and, as well as having to attempt a conversation with her on the ride up, he'd then been tricked into helping her back to her apartment.

He guessed it was his own fault for playing up the

fact he was a cop. Once she knew, she'd told him all about her daughter's missing poodle, Ringo, asking him to open an investigation.

'Officer Bozo?'

Vic cringed. He'd told the dumb old broad his name half a dozen times and she was still getting it wrong. Glancing at the floor, he pretended he hadn't seen or heard her, relieved when the door finally slid shut, and made a mental note to fetch the mail at a different time in future.

Amy was in a better mood when he returned to the apartment. He pressed the buzzer, waited patiently while she unlocked the door and walked back in to the aroma of freshly brewed coffee.

Huckleberry sat on the rug in the living room, a rope toy in his mouth and she went and sat on the floor beside him, grabbing the end of the toy for a game of tug of war.

'I made coffee. I've left you a cup on the counter and there are some doughnuts Officer Peterson left if you want them.'

'Great, thanks.' Vic watched the dog going nuts rolling on his back as he tried to wrestle the rope toy away from her, before dumping the mail on the table and heading into the kitchen. He had spied the doughnuts when he'd arrived and been wondering when she was going to offer him one. Pulling a sugared ring out of the bag, he took a bite.

'So what have you been up to all morning?' he asked through his mouthful, as he walked back into the living room. 'Working on your next book?'

'Yeah, I'm trying to.' Amy pulled a face. 'It's not easy to concentrate with everything going on.'

Sensing her frustration, Huckleberry dropped the rope and laid his chin on her thigh. She reached down, stroking his head and rubbing his ears.

'I guess so. So what's the new one about?'

Vic wasn't a reader and not really interested in what Amy was writing, but he needed to get her talking. No chance of hitting the jackpot if she locked herself away in her bedroom again.

'It's supernatural, a follow-up to the book I've just released. No murder. I'm not sure I could write about death after what has happened.'

'What, like ghosts and stuff?' Vic snorted. 'You know that shit isn't real.'

'You don't know for sure.'

'I know dead is dead. People don't come back and haunt you.'

'No, you don't know that. How can you?' Amy seemed amused he was challenging her. 'So you're a non-believer then, Officer Boaz?'

'It's Vic.'

'Okay, Vic, so you've never had a supernatural experience?'

'No.'

'Not even an odd experience or sensation you can't explain. Like you've never put something down in one place, yet found it in another; or heard a weird sound or a whisper; caught sight of something out of the corner of your eye; felt the temperature of the room you're in dip for no reason?'

'Nope.' Although it was another warm day, Vic was aware he had goosebumps on his arms. He didn't believe in ghosts, but the idea of them still scared the crap out of him. He'd had to leave the light on all night after watching that Bruce Willis film with the kid who saw dead people.

'What about when you're asleep? Have you never woken up convinced there is someone in the room with you watching you while you sleep?'

'Okay, enough.' Feeling unnerved, he walked back into the kitchen, grabbed his coffee. Damn woman, spooking him like that. He wouldn't sleep tonight now. He drew a deep breath, realising he looked a fool.

So much for winning her over with your big strong hero act, Vic, you idiot.

'So, you believe, then?' he asked, trying to play down his outburst.

Amy shrugged. 'Not necessarily. I'm not sure what I believe, to be honest, but I find it fascinating.'

She left Huckleberry with his rope toy, eyeing the mail on the table.

'But you must believe if you're writing about ghosts?' Vic pushed.

'I guess, maybe a little.'

She sounded distracted as she opened the two envelopes, pulled out what looked like bills and cast them to one side. She turned her attention to the package.

'I don't remember ordering anything.'

Vic watched as she tore open the bag, hoping to see something lacy or maybe silky come out. Maybe she'd ordered underwear and forgotten about it.

Instead, Amy pulled out a chain. A large pendant hung on the end and she held it up, a confused look on her face.

'What have you got?'

Amy didn't answer; her face had gone pale. Vic put down his cup and went to her.

'Amy?'

It was then he noticed the deep red of the pendant.

'It's a vial.' She turned to him, her expression calm,

but her golden eyes betraying her with a brief flicker of fear. 'It's someone's blood.'

Realising what she was holding, she put the pendant down on the table, took a step back from it.

Vic stared at the pendant. Was this for real? Had someone sent her a blood necklace?

Taking charge, he told her, 'I need a rubber glove or a plastic bag.'

Without saying a word, Amy disappeared into the kitchen, returning seconds later with a pair of yellow rubber gloves. Vic glanced at them disdainfully before slipping one on. He picked up the package, holding it by one corner so as not to destroy any evidence. The postmark was local and the bag heavy: something still inside.

He shook it and a paperback and an envelope fell onto the table, both stained in blood. The cover of the book was barely visible, but he could tell it was another of Amy's novels, *Blood Crime*.

He glanced at her briefly. She stood by, watching, clenching her hands and biting nervously on her bottom lip.

'He's killed again, hasn't he?'

Vic didn't answer her, instead turning his attention to the envelope. It wasn't sealed and he carefully removed the card inside, laying it on the table. Typed words stared up at him from the bloody paper.

To Amy
  A gift
  Until we meet again

He shook his head grimly and tore off the glove. 'I need to call this in.'

24

Amy had just poured herself a glass of wine when the buzzer sounded, making her jump. She wasn't a daytime drinker, but the package had shaken her, and she needed something to calm her nerves.

She glanced at Boaz, already on his way to the door, checking the peephole before letting Sullivan and Rivers in. They'd arrived sooner than she'd expected.

She hadn't seen Sullivan since Saturday night, and it had crossed her mind he was avoiding her. Stupid, she'd told herself. He was working a murder case and had more important things to do than checking in on her. His interest in her was purely professional.

He'd held her. That hadn't felt professional. It had

felt personal. And it was still messing with her head a little.

She glanced at him now and he briefly made eye contact, his expression unreadable, before turning his attention back to the package.

What the hell do you expect, Amy? It's what he should be focusing on. There's a killer on the loose, people are dying and you're acting like a lovesick teenager. Get over yourself.

She stayed in the kitchen, sipping her wine, as Boaz showed them the pendant, the bloodstained book and the note, and talked them through what had happened.

In his bed, Huckleberry thumped his tail and whined a little, disappointed at the lack of attention.

Sullivan read the card, his expression tightening.

Rivers took out his notebook and started scribbling.

'This puts a new spin on things,' she heard him mutter to Sullivan.

They took photos, bagged all three items. Amy watched them, anxiously, until eventually their focus shifted to her.

'Do you have any idea who sent this?' Rivers asked patronisingly.

'No, I honestly don't know.'

'Well, it's someone who knows you.'

'I see that from the card, but I don't know who it is.' She took another sip of her wine, noted Rivers' disapproving glance and set the glass on the counter, feeling guilty.

'I need you to think, Miss Gallaty. People are dying around you; you need to try a little harder to help us here. Focus and take some responsibility.'

His words stung. Was she responsible?

'I don't know,' she repeated, heat creeping into her tone.

'Ease up, Rivers,' Sullivan warned, a scowl on his face.

'Yeah,' Boaz agreed. 'I was with her. She had no idea who sent the package.'

Amy smiled gratefully at him, thankful for the support.

Rivers glared at Sullivan and Boaz. 'You two need to stop going soft on the lady. It's time she gave us something to work with. She's responsible for a lot of deaths here.'

'And I told you, you need to ease up,' Sullivan repeated, tone mildly threatening. 'I know you carry that fancy FBI badge, but it doesn't mean jack shit to me if you don't have the experience or integrity to back it up.'

Rivers spluttered. 'You can't talk to me that way.'

When Sullivan merely hooked a brow in response, Rivers looked to Boaz to back him up.

Boaz shrugged and pulled a face. 'You want me to take these in?' he asked Sullivan, turning his back dismissively on Rivers.

'What is wrong with you people?' Rivers snapped. 'We've got another dead body on our hands; another victim *she* knows. The pressure is on, and we need answers. Hickok will back me on this. I'm trying to do my job, for chrissakes.'

'You've found another body?' Amy felt her blood run cold. All three men looked at her.

'Another body?' Boaz repeated; his own expression confused as he played catch up.

Amy had learned over the days they'd spent together that he wasn't the brightest cop, but his heart was in the right place, most of the time.

Sullivan gave Rivers a heated look.

'You pick your moments,' he muttered, before finally fully acknowledging Amy and closing the distance between them with easy strides. 'We've just come from the crime scene. Victim was found this morning.'

Amy stiffened. 'Who?'

'ID in his pocket says Leon Pruitt. He's a doorman at your bar, right?'

She closed her eyes for a moment as a mixture of emotions bubbled; sadness, guilt, anger, frustration. Leon was one of the regular doormen at the Velvet Lounge and although she only knew him through work, she knew him well enough. He didn't deserve this; none of the victims deserved this.

'Saturday night he took off. He's recently separated from his wife and been going through a tough time. She'd come to the bar a few times and they'd argued. We figured same thing had happened again and that was why he'd disappeared. We should have known it was out of character.'

Without thinking, she reached out for physical contact, and took hold of Sullivan's hand. His eyes narrowed, but he didn't pull away.

'His wife is going to wonder why he hasn't been in touch. They have a little girl.' Her grip tightened. 'Oh Jesus, his little girl; and Fran – she doesn't know. She's gonna take this hard. They were close.'

'We'll speak to his wife.'

'How did it happen? How did he die?'

Sullivan hesitated.

'I want to know, please? I need to know.'

'The vampire killer book,' Rivers told her. 'Throat was slit and body drained of blood.'

'Oh God.' Amy drew in a shaky breath.

'That's enough, Rivers.'

'The pathologist is at the scene now, which happens to be across the road from your apartment. I expect we'll find he was strung up like the victims in your book and left to bleed out; it would have been a slow and cruel way to go.'

It happened quickly. One moment Sullivan was in the kitchen with Amy, the next he had hold of Rivers by the collar and was dragging him to the door.

Huckleberry was on his feet, emitting a low growl at the federal agent.

'I told you, enough.'

'Hey, get your damn hands off me.'

Sullivan threw open the door, pushed Rivers out into the hallway and followed. The door slammed shut behind them. Amy sucked in a breath, her mind reeling. She looked at Boaz. He was watching her warily, awaiting her reaction.

'Uh, you okay?' he asked, looking half afraid her answer would be no.

She guessed he didn't want her to fall apart on him. He didn't seem the type of man who was good at dealing with emotional women.

Pull it together, Amy.

She drew another breath, clenched her hands together tightly and forced a smile.

'Yeah, I'm okay. It's a lot to take in.'

His shoulders dropped slightly and his face relaxed. He looked more comfortable now he knew she wasn't going to have a breakdown on him.

'Special Agent Rivers was out of line. He shouldn't have spoken to you like that.'

'It's okay.'

'Dumb federal agents, they're all the same. Think they're better than the rest of us.'

Amy hadn't realised Boaz had such a strong opinion about the FBI.

'Damn Feds.' He stared at her thoughtfully and she expected him to elaborate. Instead, his gaze shifted to the counter behind her. 'There's still a doughnut left, right?'

'Doughnut? Uh, yeah, why? Do you want it?'

'Yeah, stressful situations give me an appetite.'

She handed him the bag, amazed the guy could be thinking about his belly after what they'd learned.

She thought of the doorman, the occasions she'd chatted with him on her break. He was a good man, a kind man, and still young. Tears pricked again at the back of her throat, and she forced them down. Crying for Leon wouldn't help him, wouldn't help his little girl, who would now grow up without a father. She picked up the wine glass, took another long sip.

Rivers was right. She was responsible. The killer was focusing on her, on people she knew. The package she'd received indicated he knew her personally and she searched her brain trying to think how. There had to be a clue somewhere in her past.

She thought back to the nightmare, to her visit with Doctor Shinnick. He had wanted to use hypnotherapy, and she had refused. If she had agreed, would she have remembered something? Would it have given the police clues that led to the killer? Would Leon still be alive?

When Sullivan returned a few minutes later, he was alone. This time Huckleberry went to him, pressing his nose against his hand and looking up at him adoringly.

Boaz had just crammed the last bite of doughnut into his mouth.

'Where's Special Agent Big Mouth?' he asked, spitting sugary crumbs into the air.

Sullivan glanced at him briefly. 'Cooling off.' He went to Amy. 'I'm sorry; he was out of order.'

'No, he wasn't.' She gave a twisted smile. 'Let's face it, he had a point. I am the reason this is happening.'

'Amy—'

'You think whoever sent the blood necklace is the same person who's been writing me the fan letters?' She paused. 'Mr X?'

'I think it's probable.'

'And you think this person is responsible for killing Kasey and Ben, Shannon and...' She swallowed. 'And Leon?'

'Yeah, I do.'

'But you don't know who he is. And I might do.'

'Where's this going, Amy?'

She was silent for a moment, glancing at Boaz, wiping his sugar-covered hands on his pants, then back at Sullivan. His dark eyes were intent, waiting for her answer.

These feelings she had for him, would they be there if he'd come into her life under different circumstances?

Her gaze dropped to his stubbled jaw, lips pulled in a half scowl.

She wanted to touch him, draw in his scent, feel him against her. But she didn't, knowing it was wrong. She felt guilty for wanting that. People were dying around her.

'Amy?'

Sullivan's voice brought her back. Her skin tingled

at the touch of his hand on her arm and her cheeks heated.

Focus, Amy.

She knew what she had to do.

'I want to go back and see Doctor Shinnick, undergo hypnosis.'

Sullivan's scowl intensified. 'You sure? You were dead set against it before.'

'Yeah, I'm sure.' She forced a smile. 'It's the right thing to do.'

* * *

Shinnick rescheduled a couple of appointments and was able to fit Amy in at short notice. As before, Sullivan drove her. This time she was subdued, still nervous, but determined. When they pulled up outside Shinnick's brownstone office, she looked at Sullivan for a moment.

'You okay?'

'Yeah.' Amy nodded. 'Did you do this? Did you have hypnotherapy when you saw Doctor Shinnick?'

'No.'

'Why? Why did you need to see him?'

Sullivan was silent for a long moment. A muscle twitched in his jaw and something, maybe irritation, passed over his face. 'This isn't the time, Amy. Shinnick is waiting.'

He was out of the car before she could protest. Quashing down the feeling of annoyance, her determination starting to waver, she followed him into the brownstone.

* * *

Shinnick was there to greet them. He smiled at Amy and asked her if she would mind waiting for a moment, before signalling Jake to follow him into the office.

Jake glanced at her as she took a seat. Although it had been her decision this time to undergo hypnotherapy, he suspected now they were here she was having second thoughts. She looked nervous and ready to bolt. Hesitantly he followed the doctor inside.

'This isn't going to be a quick fix, Jake.' Shinnick clicked the door closed, keeping his tone low so Amy wouldn't hear them. 'I know you want answers, but I'm going to need more than one session with her, maybe several.'

'We don't have time, doc.'

'You have to understand this is a delicate area. If

the memory is buried deep, it's unlikely I will be able to reach it in one session.'

This wasn't what Jake needed to hear. Their killer had picked up pace and could strike again at any time. Amy was the key and if they didn't get answers out of her today, he doubted he would be able to persuade her to come back.

'I need you to try, please. I know it isn't standard practice, but at the moment she is our only hope of catching this son of a bitch before he kills again.'

Shinnick leant back against his desk and studied him for a long moment. Eventually he nodded. 'Okay, I will try. But it's going to be a long shot, Jake, and you have to understand it may not work.'

'Thank you.' Jake opened the door before the doc could change his mind, and nodded to Amy.

'You okay?'

He could see she wasn't. Her face was drained of colour and she was drumming her fingers together nervously. They needed to get her into Shinnick's office before she backed out, and fast.

'Would you like to come inside, Amy?' Doctor Shinnick held his office door open wide.

* * *

Amy got to her feet nervously, trading places with Sullivan. Her heart was thumping and her mouth dry.

Leave now, before it's too late.

She couldn't leave. She had to do this for the victims.

Hesitating in the doorway she glanced back at Sullivan. He met her eyes; gave a reassuring smile.

'Can he come in?'

Shinnick looked at her, surprised. 'It's not advisable, Amy.'

'I'll feel more comfortable if he is here.' She locked eyes with Sullivan again. 'You okay with that?'

He paused for a second, before throwing down the magazine he'd picked up. 'Sure. If it's what you want.'

Shinnick shook his head, but didn't argue. He directed Amy to a leather chair in the corner of the room. As she sat, Sullivan dropped onto one of the leather couches. He leaned forward, fingers laced, watching her as Shinnick spent a few minutes talking through the procedure, explaining he would use a progressive relaxation method.

She heard the doctor's voice, but the words weren't registering, the walls closing in.

I need to get out of here.

'I'm sorry. I can't do this. I have to go.'

Sullivan started to get up, stopping when Shinnick calmly raised a hand. His focus remained on Amy.

'It is going to be okay, Amy. We'll take it slow and steady, in your own time.' When she paused and sucked in a breath, held it, he smiled reassuringly at her. 'Why don't you lie back and try to relax?'

Come on, Amy. You can do this.

'I'll try.'

She leant back in the chair, ordered herself to get a grip and bit her bottom lip anxiously as Shinnick spoke to her in that clear, calm voice of his, telling her to take a long deep breath and close her eyes.

She glanced one last time at Sullivan. His expression was impassive as he watched her. Following the doctor's suggestion, she let her eyes shut, listened as he told her to relax her body, breathe deeply and feel her muscles loosen.

This time the words were registering but, despite breathing deeply, she found it hard to relax.

He told her to think of a place where she felt happy, safe; that he was going to count down from ten and with each number she would take a step closer to that place.

Amy thought of her childhood home, as Shinnick counted down, the wooden swing in the backyard. Although her limbs were growing heavy, she was conscious that she was trembling, could still hear her heart thumping. She wasn't going under.

'Seven, six, five, four, three—'

'This isn't working.' Amy opened her eyes. 'I'm still awake.'

'Being under hypnotherapy isn't the same as being unconscious,' Shinnick explained patiently. 'You will still be awake. Now, why don't we try again?'

Amy closed her eyes, told herself to think back to the swing, to the backyard. This was stupid. Thinking about this stuff wasn't going to help her remember anything. Maybe she couldn't be hypnotised.

More like you don't want to be hypnotised.

This time she allowed Shinnick to finish counting down.

'I want you to use your powerful subconscious mind to imagine yourself in a long corridor. A corridor lined with doors. Each door has a number on it, a number referring to each year of your life. Imagine walking down the corridor.'

'I can't. I'm sorry. There's just too much going on in my head. I'm sorry, it's just not working.'

This time Amy started to get up. This was a stupid idea. She should never have come back here.

'Please, Amy.' Shinnick exchanged a look with Sullivan. Although he tried to mask it, she could see the frustration starting to show. 'I need you to focus. Please try for me one more time.'

'What's the point? It's not going to work.'

'You don't know that. Please try for me one more time.'

Reluctantly Amy lay back in the chair.

'We will take it slower this time,' Shinnick told her as she closed her eyes. 'Let's focus on your place where you feel safe and happy. I want you to really visualise it, Amy. Think back to when you were last there and of the happy memories. How does it feel? What sounds can you hear? What smells are in the air?'

Amy forced herself to concentrate, tried to remember the scent of forest, feel the warmth of the spring air on her skin. It was a quiet, peaceful place, with only the occasional chatter of birds in the trees.

'Spend some time in this place. Familiarise yourself with how happy and safe you feel here.'

She thought back to sunny afternoons following school, playing on the swing, the branches of trees gathering overhead to form a leafy ceiling. Her mother was often busy in the kitchen, cooking dinner or a fruit pie, while she played outside, and the smell would waft across the yard, invading her nostrils and stirring her taste buds.

This time, as Shinnick began to slowly count

down, she enjoyed the moment of being back in her childhood, unaware the trembling had stopped and her breathing was now deep and even.

He gave her a moment before leading her back to the corridor. This time Amy could see it, the backyard replaced with a long, dark hallway.

'Each door has a number on it, a number referring to each year of your life. Imagine walking down the corridor until you find the door with number fifteen on it.' Shinnick then instructed Amy to open the door and go through it. 'You are now fifteen years old, Amy, and you are staying with family friends.'

She stepped through the door and suddenly she was back there. It was summer vacation and she was staying with the Rooneys while her parents were away. The weather was warm and the days stretched out, long and light with simple childhood pleasures.

'I'm at Deanna and Pete's,' she confirmed.

'You've had dinner and you've gone to your room.'

'We had blueberry pie for dessert. It's my favourite.'

'What happens after you go to your room, Amy?'

'Deanna thinks I've gone to bed. She doesn't know.'

'Doesn't know what, Amy?'

'Tonight, we're gonna sneak out.'

'Who are you going to sneak out with?'

'The twins, of course.' Amy shook her head at his stupid question. Who else would she be sneaking out with?

'Where are you and the twins going to sneak out to, Amy?'

'Leslie wants us to go to the house in the woods. We're gonna see if it's really haunted.'

'What happens next, Amy?'

'I'm not sure I really want to go. Leslie says we have to. Crystal is just going along with what she says. She always does that. I am staying with them. If I don't go, they'll be mean to me.'

'Go on, Amy.'

'But Danielle isn't supposed to come with us. It isn't part of the plan.'

'Who is Danielle?'

'She's new in town and the twins don't like her. They say she is a dork. That she isn't cool. She seems okay. I feel sorry for her. She just wants to be friends.'

'She is with you?'

'She's seen us sneaking out and wants to come along. Leslie has told her no, but Danielle says she's gonna tell Deanna. If she tells Deanna we'll all be grounded. Deanna might tell my mom too. I don't want her to tell my mom. She gets really mad at me when I break the rules. I tell Leslie that I want to go back.'

'And what does Leslie say?'

'She says we have to go, that Danielle can come along. I can tell she is mad about it, though.'

'So Danielle is going with you. Where are you now?'

'We're in the woods at the house. It's really creepy out here in the dark. I'm sure there is someone or something hiding in the trees. I don't like it and want to go back. Leslie wants to play a game first, a dare for Danielle.'

'What is the dare?'

'She says Danielle has to go inside the house. I think she's really mad at her for blackmailing us into bringing her along.'

'Tell me about this house. It's in the woods, you say?'

Amy drew a breath.

'Yeah. Some guy lives here. Leslie says he is creepy. I've never seen him.'

'And Danielle goes into his house?'

'She doesn't want to. I can tell she's scared.' Amy shook her head, the sense of foreboding growing. 'Leslie is making her do it. She wants her to steal something personal from him, to prove she's been inside. A trophy, she says. It's like an initiation. Then Danielle can hang with us.'

'So, what happens?'

Amy was silent for a moment. 'Danielle is inside. She has snuck in through the back door, but she hasn't come out.'

It's been too long. Where is she?

'She hasn't come out?' Shinnick repeated, his tone still calm. 'What happens next, Amy?'

'The twins, they want to go, but we can't leave her. They say I should go find her.'

'And?'

'I don't want to, but we can't go. I am scared, really scared, but we can't leave her.'

'Go on.'

Amy's heart was thudding as she crossed the yard, heading towards the door Danielle had disappeared through. She glanced back at the twins and saw Leslie smirk.

You can do this. Find Danielle and then you can go home.

She twisted the doorknob, caught her breath at the squeak it made as she eased it open.

'I'm in the kitchen. It's silent, no one is about. It's really messy in here and the sink is full of dirty stuff. Oh yuck, there are flies buzzing around and it smells gross. I don't know where Danielle is. I have to stay quiet. We have broken in. What if he calls the police on us?'

'Where are you now, Amy?'

'In the hall. It smells funny; really dusty and old. There are pictures on the wall and they're covered in cobwebs. I don't want to be here. I want to go home. I can see his boots. They're just lying on the floor and caked in mud and I can hear the TV playing, but I don't think he's watching it. Where is he?'

Amy started trembling. 'This is wrong. Something is wrong.'

'It's okay. You're in the hall. What do you do now?'

'There's a door ajar. I think it leads to the basement. I shouldn't go down there.'

Amy pulled it open, her heart catching when it creaked. The staircase was dark, the steps narrow, and the damp coolness of the air hit her. A single flickering bulb from somewhere at the bottom of the stairs gave the only light. Something bad was waiting at the bottom.

'I don't want to go down there. It smells funny. Please, I don't want to do this. I just want to go home.'

'Where are you, Amy?'

'I'm on the stairs leading into the basement.

There's a room at the bottom. Something is in there. I don't want to go down there. Please don't make me.'

'What is in the room, Amy?'

'No. I don't want to look. Please. I don't want to.'

She could smell the coppery scent of blood before she got to the room and peered inside. The feeling of dread was overwhelming.

And then she saw.

Oh my God! Oh my God!

No!

Instinct had her turning to run back up the stairs. She slammed into a hard body, smelt the stench of stale sweat and urine.

She screamed, and continued to scream, even as the calm voice of Doctor Shinnick spoke to her.

'You're in your safe place, Amy. Everything is okay and no one can hurt you. I'm going to bring you back now by counting down from ten to one. Ten, nine, eight... Do you want to remember what happened?'

'Yes. I have to.'

'Seven, six, five... Focus on your safe place, Amy. When I get to one you will wake up. Four, three, two, one.'

Amy opened her eyes: she found Sullivan pinning her thrashing arms down as Shinnick looked on concerned.

'What the hell happened, Amy?' Sullivan demanded.

'Give her a moment,' the doctor urged.

She tried to control her breathing and failed. Everything was too clear and bright in her head.

It didn't happen. It couldn't have happened. She'd have remembered it.

A wave of nausea washed over her. Pulling herself free from Sullivan's grip, she pushed herself off the chair, crossed the room to the wastepaper basket by Shinnick's desk, and threw up.

25

He had been unable to watch Amy's apartment from his usual spot due to the number of cops swarming on the riverbank, so had parked further along the street. It wasn't ideal as he didn't have such a clear view, but it still helped him keep tabs on her, and he'd felt his temper rise when he saw her leave the building with the dark-haired cop and they had both got into his Audi.

Although he wore a suit instead of a uniform, he knew he was a cop because he'd noticed the bulge of his holster.

The cop from the balcony who'd had his arms around her.

He glanced down at the picture he had taken, lying

on the seat beside him, fighting the urge to pick it up and tear it to shreds.

Calm down. Be smart. You can use this.

He had been tempted to follow them, but knew his time would be better spent here. Slipping the picture into his briefcase he exited the car, locked the door and crossed the road. As he strolled along to the apartment block, he figured anyone passing would assume he was another tenant. He'd entered Amy's building before with ease. It was all about having confidence and acting like you belonged. People only doubted or questioned you if you acted suspiciously.

One eye on the path leading down to the river and certain no one was paying attention to him, he slipped into the stairwell that led to the garage below her building. He recognised her Beetle parked at the far end of the row: cream in colour and battered with age. She had owned it a long time and it suited her personality. The windshield was clean and there was no trace of the offending word he'd left. The incident had rattled her; he knew because he'd watched from across the street. He only wished he could have enjoyed her reaction when she'd found the other gifts in her mailbox. Knowing she was spooked and aware she was being watched would have to be enough for him.

He opened his briefcase and retrieved the photograph; glancing around casually to ensure he was alone, he slipped it beneath her wiper blade. Satisfied it was secure he took out the lipstick from his pocket, the same tube of red he had used on her car before.

This time he left a different word.

WHORE.

That would get her thinking.

He took a moment to admire his handiwork, then, whistling to himself, he slipped out of the garage and headed back down the street to his car. As he crossed the road, he passed one of the police officers – a youngish man with russet hair and a cowlick. He recognised him as the other cop who'd entered Amy's building earlier, the one who'd exited the building ahead of his partner looking pissed off, smoking a cigarette and cursing at himself, before heading down to the river to join his colleagues.

He kept it casual, confident: a passer-by in the street, going about his business. The cop was looking at his cell phone, but hearing footsteps glanced up; their eyes met briefly. He gave an easy smile. The cop didn't smile back, immediately returning his attention to his phone. No sign of suspicion; none the wiser. His smile widening, he made his way back to his car.

* * *

Rebecca and Hickok spent the afternoon canvassing Amy's neighbourhood in the hope that someone might have seen something that would lead them to Leon Pruitt's killer. The crime scene was free of blood, Pruitt having been murdered in a different location and dumped by the river, probably in the early hours of the morning. Two tiny marks on the back of his neck indicated he had been subdued, probably with some kind of stun gun and most likely while he was still on duty at the Velvet Lounge. He had then been taken to wherever he had been killed.

It would have been messy, Withers told them. Ligature marks suggested the doorman had been strung upside down and the killer had slit his jugular, leaving him to bleed out. There would have been a lot of blood and the spray would have gotten everywhere, making it unlikely the kill had taken place in someone's house. Whoever had carried out the deed had been thoughtful enough to fill a vial with Pruitt's blood and post it to Amy, along with the copy of her book, *Blood Crime*. It seemed the killer wanted to make it clear to her that she was the catalyst for his murder spree.

Jake was with her right now, as Amy had agreed to undergo hypnotherapy. It might lead to nothing, but they needed to understand what had happened to

Amy before her car accident; retrieve the missing piece of memory to complete that part of the puzzle.

Rebecca didn't think it was a wise idea, the two of them spending time together, but it made sense Jake be the one to take her to Shinnick's office given his relationship with the doctor. She knew a little about his past in Atlanta and what had happened. Jake didn't like to talk about it, but he'd opened up a couple of times, and she knew the doctor had helped him.

Rivers, meanwhile, was over at the Velvet Lounge. The staff who had been working Saturday night had all been asked to come in and give statements.

Rebecca rubbed at her temples, feeling the dull throb of a headache starting. It had been a long day, and she would give anything for a soak in the tub and a cold bottle of beer. They had several more tenants to question before she would get either. At the moment their prime suspect was Amy's ex-boyfriend, David Gavin. It was too coincidental he had returned to Juniper a week before the murders started.

She glanced at the photograph in her hand. Gavin was a good-looking man: wide eyes, strong jawline, thick wavy brown hair. He appeared pleasant enough in the picture Amy had provided them with, but Rebecca knew looks could be deceiving. Information they had uncovered suggested Gavin was a controlling man with a temper. He had been arrested before, once for a bar fight and another time for road rage after smashing the windshield of a car he'd claimed had cut him up. Amy insisted he had never been physically violent towards her, but as their relationship progressed, he had become jealous and possessive, and he liked to play mind games. It was for those reasons she had ended the relationship, and Gavin wouldn't be the type to react well to being dumped.

The fact he hadn't surfaced also added suspicion. The only confirmation they had he was back in town were the three withdrawals he had made from various ATMs, all for large amounts, suggesting he was keeping low and paying with cash to avoid leaving any electronic trace. The cigarette butts Jake had found were also a match, so they knew Gavin was watching Amy. Watching her and also committing murder because of her?

They had his cell phone number, but it was going to voicemail and there was no signal trace, indicating he was no longer using it. Rebecca suspected he'd switched to a disposable phone they wouldn't be able to link to him.

All too coincidental, but maybe a bit too convenient; Gavin had a hot temper, whereas the murders had taken considerable planning and staging. They seemed too controlled for a man of his nature. Then there were the fan letters. Amy had received them before and during her relationship with Gavin. Had he sent stalker fan mail to his own girlfriend? Rebecca suspected the letters were sent by someone else but, as forensics had been unable to pull any prints, they had no way of confirming who was responsible and it was proving to be another dead end.

A lot of clues for them to work with, but none of them adding up.

'You want to grab a beer?' Hickok asked, as they finally finished early evening.

No one had seen anything. It had been a long and futile day.

Stopping off for a beer was tempting and there was no intimation he meant anything other than a drink, but still Rebecca hesitated. This was dangerous ground and, after Saturday, she wasn't sure she trusted herself around Hickok.

You nearly kissed him.

She thought back to Alan. Good, solid, trusting Alan. She hadn't kissed Hickok, but the temptation had been there. Alan did not deserve that.

'I'll pass, thanks. I just want to get home and soak in the tub.' At Hickok's raised brow and widening grin, she added, 'Alone.'

'No plans with Adam tonight?'

'We're both busy with work.' She'd given up correcting him. He only did it to annoy her, so it was best to ignore him.

'Guess the plastic spoon industry calls for some late nights.'

'Something like that.'

Truth was, she'd been avoiding Alan over the last few days. He wanted to talk, and Alan only ever wanted to talk if it was about something serious. She suspected it was to give her an ultimatum or call time on their relationship. If it was the latter, she guessed she couldn't really blame him. After all, she hadn't been the best of girlfriends. Regardless of what it was, Rebecca didn't have the time to deal with it right now. And she sure as hell didn't need Hickok on the scene if she was about to get dumped.

'So what's the plan with you two? You gonna get married, squeeze out a couple of kids?'

Don't bite.

'You realise if you have kids with him there's a 50 per cent chance they'll turn out to be dorks?'

Too late.

Rebecca wheeled on him, hands on hips.

'We're dating. There is no marriage on the cards and no kids, but if there was it wouldn't be any of your damn business. You and I were six years ago. You have no right to walk back into my life and expect to pick up where we left off.' She paused for breath. 'And don't insult him. Adam is not a dork.'

'Alan.' Hickok's smug look had her fists balling.

Fuck.

'Alan,' Rebecca repeated, her tone icy.

'You'd think you'd know your own boyfriend's name.'

Cursing herself for being drawn into Hickok's little game, she put up her hand, took a step back.

'Stay away from me, Hickok.'

As he opened his mouth to retort, a woman stepped out of the driveway that led up from the garage of Amy's building. She collided with Rebecca, making both of them jump.

'Shit, jeez, sorry.' Rebecca steadied herself, recognising the woman from when they had questioned her earlier. As with everyone else, they had left her with their card in case she remembered something later. 'You okay, ma'am?'

'Detective Angell, sorry to bother you, but there's something you should see.' The woman's lips were drawn in a tight line, her face pale.

'Is it something you have remembered?'

'Not exactly; it's easier if I show you.'

Rebecca glanced at Hickok; his expression was un-readable as he stepped into line beside her and they followed the woman back down into the garage.

She pointed to Amy's Beetle, but Rebecca had al-ready clocked it, her eyes immediately drawn to the crude red lettering. There was something hooked under the wiper blade.

'I don't know if this is connected to your questions earlier,' the woman was saying, 'but I thought you should know.'

Rebecca murmured her thanks, already strolling over to the car.

She snatched up the picture under the wiper blade, feeling her insides knot. Another photograph of Amy, but this time with Jake, and he had his arms around her.

No, Sullivan, you damn idiot.

What the hell was he thinking?

She bit down on a curse as Hickok took the photo-graph and spent a moment studying it.

'Well, no one can accuse your partner of not get-ting involved with his cases.'

Although his tone was light and joking, Rebecca recognised the edge beneath it. Jake had crossed a line. And with the people Amy knew dropping like flies, he could have also unwittingly made himself a target for the killer.

* * *

Things had remained tense between Troy and Nadine since Saturday night.

After arriving home from the Velvet Lounge they'd had a huge fight; for once Troy had stood his ground. Voices had been raised, doors slammed, and picture frames and vases smashed.

Nadine was furious he hadn't supported her in her quest to take down Amy, while Troy was pissed Nadine had disobeyed him when he'd made it clear she was to stay away from the Velvet Lounge. They'd paused their fighting for hot, urgent sex, Troy throwing Nadine down and taking her hard and fast amidst the shards of broken pottery and feathers from ripped cushions, while she tore blood red nails over his back.

It wasn't make-up sex and when it was over Troy had gone to sleep in the spare room. He'd remained there since and the atmosphere was frigid, with barely a word spoken between them. As the previous evening, Troy stayed at Blake & Colman, working late on their security design and ordering takeout. He didn't return to the beach house until close to midnight, knowing Nadine would be in bed.

Things couldn't continue this way, he understood that, but it was hard knowing it had to come to an end. He had a special connection with Nadine and always would, but she was too headstrong, too stubborn.

Maybe he could try one last time to talk to her, somehow make her understand, before it was too late. Or was it already too late? He walked down the hallway to the bedrooms. The door to the master suite was shut. He paused briefly outside, raised his hand and contemplated knocking.

It was late and he was tired. Maybe he would try tomorrow.

He backed into the spare room, hit the light and placed his briefcase on the floor. Wearily, he dropped down on the bed, kicked off his shoes and lay back on the mattress. It felt good under the aching muscles of his back.

His jacket pocket vibrated, and he reached for his cell, frowning at the number that flashed up and clicking open the text. He read the words on the screen, felt his mouth dry up. A small ball of dread knotted and snaked its way up his belly.

Sitting up straight and wide awake now, he read the words again.

I'm going to kill your girlfriend.

26

The summer of 1983 was one Troy Cunningham would never forget.

It began when his parents decided to uproot and move to Melford – which Troy soon learned was a tiny pissant town at the back end of nowhere.

For a twelve-year-old boy it sucked leaving his friends behind. His parents told him the move was for a better life; the city was dangerous and full of bad influences. Melford was better and they would be able to spend quality time together as a family.

Troy wasn't so sure. Melford, as far as he could see, had no mall, just one lousy movie theatre that only opened at weekends, and the kids at his new school weren't cool.

He was an only child, and his parents had just ruined his childhood.

For the first few weeks he sulked around the house, reading comics in his room or watching television, but then his mom started roping him into chores. It wasn't healthy to laze around; if he had nothing better to do, he could help her around the house or give his father a hand outside.

Troy knew it was a ploy to get him outside and it worked. Not wanting to help with chores, he took his bike and explored the four corners of the town: the open fields, the railway track, the thick surrounding forest.

Before, he had been a sociable kid with plenty of friends, but now he chose to keep to himself, cycling the forest paths and trying to net the fish in the creek.

And that was where he first saw her, hiking in the woods with the Rooney twins, her long brown hair scraped into a braid, wearing a baggy white T-shirt tucked into chino shorts, her eyes gold and full of excitement.

Amy Gallaty.

He learned her name from following the girls; listening to their conversations. The twins went to his school, were a couple of years older. Amy was older too and visiting for a week or so while her parents were on vacation. And she had the most beautiful smile Troy had ever seen. That summer he fell in love.

And so moving to Melford became not so bad.

The girls were out most days, hiking and exploring, paddling in the creek and climbing trees. Troy followed. He kept a distance, always out of sight but close enough to hear their conversation.

On one occasion, while in town, he had run into Amy as she was leaving the grocery store. For a moment he had been close enough to smell the fresh, peachy scent of soap or shampoo and, as he had blustered out an apology, tripping over his words, she had smiled that smile at him, told him not to worry, and his heart had melted. He was too young for her, too young for love, he knew. How he wished to be fifteen, sixteen even, so maybe she would take notice.

But age was irrelevant; she was leaving in a few days, going back home to Montana, to her family.

The thought of being stuck here in this hick town without her was almost more than Troy could bear. It was the following day while tracking them down to the creek he heard them talk about the old Johnson house. Leslie Rooney claimed the place to be haunted.

Troy knew it belonged to Tucker Johnson, but he'd only seen the man once. Tucker was a loner. He was friendly enough from what Troy had heard. Came into town every once in a while to stock up on his groceries, tipped generously, and was solicitous to everyone whose path he crossed. But other than that, he kept to himself. His wife and child had died, Troy had learned. Shortly after moving into the house in the woods, Mrs Johnson had fed their young daughter a lethal dose of sleeping pills before running herself a bath and slitting her wrists. Word around town was she had suffered with depression. That was the reason Tucker wasn't big on company; he preferred to stay home and grieve for his lost family.

Leslie Rooney was convinced the house was haunted by the spirits of Tucker's dead wife and child, and for Amy's last night in town she proposed an adventure: a trip to check out the Johnson residence. Amy had seemed dubious; maybe even a little afraid, but Leslie wasn't one to take no for an answer. She had a stronger personality than Amy and Troy had noticed that she was often quick to put her down. She had begged, bribed, badgered and bullied until she got her way, and plans had been made to slip out of the house once the twins' parents went to bed.

Troy was watching from the bushes when the three girls clambered down the oak tree outside of Crystal Rooney's bedroom window: the twins with their blonde Debbie Harry styled bobs, dressed identically in jeans, sneakers and off the shoulder T-shirts; Amy behind them, also in jeans, with her long hair tied back through a baseball cap. They carried flashlights, but the evening was clear, dusk not long settled, and they wouldn't need them yet. They had almost reached the end of the street when Leslie stopped.

'What was that?'

'What was what?' Crystal wanted to know.

'I heard footsteps.'

'They're ours.'

'No, stupid, not ours. It's someone else.'

Troy paused, his heart thumping as he watched the three girls looking around. He had kept his distance, tried to be as quiet as possible. Had he been rumbled?

Leslie turned on her flashlight; she shone it in his direction, then across the street.

'Who's there?'

For a moment there was nothing, but then a figure emerged from the shadows. As she came into sight, Troy recognised her. Danielle Colton. She was seventeen and had moved to town around the same time as the Cunninghams, but while Troy preferred his own company, Danielle was desperate to fit in.

She was kind of geeky-looking, with frizzy brown hair and a brace, and she dressed like a dork, wearing frumpy dresses that looked like they'd been handed down from her grandma. Troy knew her family were poor and lived in one of the clapboard houses on the edge of town. Their front yard was overgrown with weeds and Danielle's stepdad drove a beat-up pick-up that was forever breaking down.

Danielle was desperate to fit in, but no one wanted to hang out with her. The other seniors ignored her and even the younger kids wanted nothing to do with her. Right now, she was wringing her hands together looking like a frightened deer caught in the beam of Leslie's flashlight.

'Were you following us?'

'I don't mean any trouble. I saw y'all sneaking out and wondered if I could maybe come with you.' Danielle smiled hopefully, but it was lost on Leslie.

'We don't need a fourth,' she sneered, dismissively.

'But please, I won't be any trouble.'

'You're not wanted; go home.'

'Yeah, loser. We don't want you hanging out with us.' Crystal moved to stand beside her sister, arms folded.

Danielle looked like she was gonna tear up.

Amy shuffled her feet, clearly uncomfortable. 'Why don't you let her tag along, Leslie? There's no harm.'

'Because we don't want her with us, ruining our plans.'

'Please let me come.'

'No, go home. And don't you dare tell anyone you saw us, or you'll regret it.'

'Leslie.' That was Amy again, protesting. She looked embarrassed and Troy guessed she felt sorry for the girl.

'Shut up, Amy. I'm not interested in anything you have to say.'

'I'll tell.'

Leslie's head shot back. She glared at Danielle. 'What did you say?'

'I'll tell.' For the first time Danielle stuck her chin out defiantly. 'I know you snuck out. I saw you climb down the tree. If you don't let me go with you, I'm gonna go wake your parents up and tell them.'

'You wouldn't dare.'

'Maybe we should let her come, Les.' Crystal was backing down, looking uncertainly at Amy.

'Or perhaps none of us should go,' Amy added, her tone hopeful. 'This was a bad idea. Let's go back.'

'I said shut up, Amy,' Leslie snapped. 'Quit being such a wuss. We're going, so stop trying to get out of it.' She was silent, weighing up the situation as she stared at Danielle, probably trying to determine how serious the girl was about telling on them. 'Okay,' she agreed eventually. 'You can come with us, but I promise if you cause any trouble or if you don't do exactly as I say, you will regret it.'

* * *

The Johnson house was a fifteen-minute hike along a dirt trail into the woods. Troy had walked it often and had passed the house on several occasions, but never at night.

The thick trees and bushes took on a life of their own at night, their dark mass engulfing the path from both sides, and the sound of every twig snapped and leaf rustled was magnified. Overhead an owl hooted, and the noise sounded spooky. Although he would never admit it, he was glad the girls were there for company, even if they didn't realise he was there. Eventually the path turned a corner and there in the clearing stood the house.

The white brickwork had faded with age, and the front yard was empty apart from a child's swing, the wooden seat hanging from chains that creaked gently in the light breeze. The dark windows of the house were like black eyes staring out, making the house more creepy than normal.

The girls walked the perimeter. Leslie noted there was a single light on in one of the downstairs rooms. Tucker Johnson was home and probably watching television, she concluded.

She recounted the tale of how she had heard the ghostly screams, taking delight in how spooked Amy and Danielle were.

'It's getting late. We should start heading back.'

'Not yet.' Leslie smiled wickedly at Amy. 'We have a dare for Danielle to do first.'

'A dare?' Danielle sounded unsure. There was a tremor in her voice.

'Yes, a dare. You want to hang with us, right?'

'Well, yes.'

'Then we need to know you're cool, so you have to pass an initiation.'

'What do I have to do?'

'You have to sneak into the house.'

'No way.' Danielle was backing up, shaking her head.

'Don't be crazy, Leslie.'

'Shut up, Amy. Danielle will do this because she wants to be our friend.'

'I'm not going in there.'

'Yes, you are.' Leslie's lips twisted. 'If you go in the

house we will let you hang out with us. If you don't, we're all gonna run off and leave you.'

'You wouldn't do that.'

'Try me.'

Danielle looked uncertainly at the house. 'How about if I just go into the yard?'

'No, you go into the house, and I want you to bring back something from inside; that is the initiation.'

'But what if the door is locked? How do I get in?'

I saw a window open round back. 'If the door isn't open, go through there.'

'What do you want me to get?'

'I dunno. Surprise us: maybe a book or an ornament, or even a piece of clothing.'

There was a moment of silence while Danielle contemplated. Crystal, who had said nothing throughout the exchange, stood by her sister shuffling her feet, while Amy looked like she wished she could be somewhere else.

'Okay, I'll do it.'

'Good girl. I knew you wouldn't let us down, Danielle.'

'Danielle, you don't have to do this.'

'Damn it! Shut the hell up, Amy.'

'No, I'm serious. This is a stupid idea. I won't leave

you, Danielle. I won't run off if you don't want to go inside.'

'Amy! Goddammit.'

'It's okay.' Danielle still looked unsure. 'I'll do it.'

'Good girl,' Leslie smirked. 'Now off you go.'

* * *

Five minutes passed, rolling into ten, then fifteen.

They knew Danielle was in the house; the back door had been unlocked, and she'd given them the thumbs up before gently pulling it closed behind her.

Troy watched and waited, his heart beating anxiously. She should be out by now.

Then came the scream: one long bloodcurdling scream, followed by silence.

The twins and Amy looked uncertainly at each other.

'We should go.' Leslie Rooney wasn't sounding so confident any more.

'And leave Danielle?'

'She's messing with us, Amy. I'll bet she screamed to scare us and she's probably on her way back to town.'

'It came from inside the house.'

'You don't know that for sure.'

The girls continued to argue. Crystal was complaining she was tired and wanted her bed, while Leslie tried to convince them all it was a trick.

Amy was insistent they couldn't leave without Danielle and after much heated whispering Leslie came up with a compromise.

'If you're so sure she's still inside, Amy, why don't you go and find her?'

'What?'

'You heard me. You go find Danielle.'

Leaving the girls to fight, Troy snuck his way through the trees round to the back of the house. He was curious to find out what had happened to Danielle. It was odd she hadn't reappeared. The backyard was open, leading straight into the woods. Maybe Leslie was right, and she had managed to sneak out, ditching the other girls.

He spied the one open window Leslie had talked about. It would have been easy for her to get out and make a run for the woods. Light came from another window towards the end of the house. The curtains were open and the flickering shadows dancing across the yard suggested a television was playing. Curious, Troy approached. Although he was a little afraid, he had an urge to know what the Johnson place looked like inside. Was it homey or as creepy as it looked from the woods?

He crossed the backyard and felt his way along the wall to the window, peering inside. The living room was sparse, with two old-fashioned chairs, a thread-bare rug and a television set, lit by a large table lamp on the floor beside the door. There was no sign of Mr Johnson. Perhaps the man was in the kitchen making snacks. Troy liked snacks when he watched TV. Pop-corn mostly and it had to be the sweet kind. He passed the window, made his way round to the side of the house and nearly tripped over the hatchway door rising up out of the overgrown grass. Drawing a deep breath, he steadied himself, studied the door, won-dering where it led. A cellar maybe?

And then he did something crazy. He tried the door to see if it opened.

For a moment it stuck. The way the grass had grown over the door, it probably wasn't used much. He yanked again, harder, nearly falling over when the door sprang back. He glanced into the hatch, saw three stone steps; the rest disappeared into darkness. This was stupid. He wasn't gonna go down there.

He toyed with going to find the girls, tell them what he'd found, but knew Leslie Rooney would kick his ass if she realised he had followed them. Reluctant, but scared to go into the hatch alone, he started to close the door. Perhaps he should try it with some of the other kids; come back with safety in numbers. He did want to know where the door led to. It was about to drop shut when he heard the whimper.

Troy froze, catching his breath.

The sound came again: low, guttural and terrifying. And it came from below the hatch.

His heart raced as he tried to think clearly. He should go find the girls, run home and call the police. But what if it was nothing? What if it was something stupid, maybe a cat or a dog, or his imagination? He would be made to look a fool.

Slowly, he eased the door back open. Down in the darkness he thought he could hear sobbing.

What if it's Danielle? What if she has fallen and is hurt?

He should close the hatchway, go back home and pretend tonight had never happened.

Coward.

He wasn't a coward. He was a twelve-year-old kid. What was he supposed to do?

Just check it out. You have to know. If you don't find out, you will always wonder.

Tentatively he eased one foot onto the top stone step.

Go on; you can do this.

The other foot followed.

The door is open and you can leave at any time.

Darkness swallowed him as he made his way down the steps, feeling his way with the toes of his sneakers and holding on to the cold stone wall for support.

When he was halfway down, he glanced behind him, saw the clear night sky scattered with stars and imagined the door closing, trapping him inside. For a moment he nearly lost his bottle and ran.

The door isn't gonna close. Don't be an idiot. The quicker you find out what is in the basement, the quicker you can leave.

As he continued down the steps, the air grew musty, stale, and he recognised another scent but couldn't quite place it. It roiled his stomach; gave him a bad feeling.

He reached the bottom of the steps and a faint beam of light showed he was in a narrow corridor. The light came from a doorway. As he edged towards it the whimper came again. This time it was louder and chilled him to the bone.

Go, now. You shouldn't be here.

Ignoring the voice in his head, Troy peered through the crack in the door. What he saw had his hand flying to his mouth to stop the scream escaping, stop the contents of his dinner spilling up onto the floor.

The room was like a prison: grey brick walls, a hardback wooden kitchen chair and table. Someone was on the table but not moving, and, from the amount of blood and the way the head was twisted at an unnatural angle, dead.

Beyond the table stood Danielle, her arms pulled overhead and her wrists secured with chains that hung from the ceiling. Blood bubbled from her mouth, smearing her face and dripping down the frumpy blue dress she wore.

Troy stared, horrified, his brain unable to process what he was seeing. Before he could react there was another sound: footsteps approaching the door at the far end of the room.

Both Danielle and Troy watched as Amy stumbled into the room, taking in the scene before her. Seeing Danielle, then the body on the table, she screamed. Danielle started whimpering again, the sound becoming more frantic as she looked beyond Amy. Troy saw the dark shadow fall on the room as Amy turned to run, slamming into the man behind her. She tried to duck, but he was too quick for her, grabbing hold of her shoulder and pushing her hard to the floor. He slammed the door closed behind him, cutting off any escape.

Amy was screaming, Danielle whimpering, and Troy watching wide-eyed through the crack of the doorway, rooted to the spot. As the man turned to Danielle, Troy caught a look at his face.

Tucker Johnson.

'So, you little snoop.' He caught hold of Danielle by the frizz of her hair, glanced over at Amy. 'I see you've brought a friend.'

27

Amy was scheduled to work at the Velvet Lounge on Wednesday night, but a call to Gage had him reorganising staff, and the two of them sat in her apartment, along with Heidi, Fran, Officer Peterson and Huckleberry, while she tried to deal with what had happened in Doctor Shinnick's office.

She had spent much of the day with Sullivan, Angell and the two FBI agents down at the police department, going over details from yesterday's session with Shinnick, plus more time with the doctor who had insisted she have follow-up sessions to help her deal with the trauma she had uncovered, and her mind was tired, her body exhausted. She knew she wouldn't sleep tonight, just as she hadn't slept a wink last night.

Fran had cooked a chilli, urged her to eat a bowl, but Amy had no appetite. Instead, she nursed her second glass of wine, hand trembling on the glass despite the warmth of the evening.

Since uncovering the memory of Danielle she had been under a microscope, probed by the police and by Doctor Shinnick. She knew they only wanted to help her, but Amy just wanted to be left alone. The nightmare she had suffered over the years was real; how was she supposed to come to terms with it?

'So, is this Johnson guy the one doing the murders?' Gage wanted to know.

Her friends were both shocked and intrigued by the latest turn of events and still upset at Leon's murder. They'd all known him, liked him, and now he was dead.

Amy took another sip from her glass. It was a good Rioja and under normal circumstances she would have enjoyed it. Tonight, she barely tasted the wine as it went down. She drank anyway in the hope it would eventually numb her senses.

'I think they're looking at a few people, but they need to check it out. Even if the murders aren't related, they need to arrest Johnson for what he did, for how he hurt... for Danielle.' Her voice cracked and she paused. 'God, how did I forget?'

She felt Heidi's arm tighten around her. Huckleberry, who had been nestled against her leg, turned slightly and put his head on her lap, big brown eyes staring up at her.

'It was the trauma,' Fran reminded her gently. 'Something terrible happened and then you were hit by the car. It's no surprise your mind couldn't deal with it all. You were only fifteen.'

'Maybe it's Johnson who has been sending you the fan mail,' Gage suggested.

The thought had Amy shuddering. Had the man been stalking her? If he was following her, why hadn't he tried to kill her? She remembered back to the night she'd been followed home. Had it been Johnson? Had he planned to kill her that night? And had he been taking pictures of her?

Angell and Hickok had shown her the latest photograph, left on her Beetle: her with Sullivan on the balcony. Sullivan had been mad as hell, disappearing into one of the offices with Hickok where the two of them had engaged in a heated exchange. She had caught Rivers' smirk and Angell's disapproving look and felt the need to defend herself.

'It's not what it looks like. Nothing happened.'

'Of course not,' Rivers had agreed, patronisingly.

He probably loved this, after what had happened in her apartment earlier the previous day.

Angell had been kind, saying she understood how feelings could become complicated in these situations, but Sullivan needed to keep his focus on the case and couldn't if he was distracted. Amy had flushed with embarrassment. Had her stupid crush been that obvious?

'Nothing happened and nothing is going to happen,' she promised Angell.

Her friends didn't know about the latest photograph, and she had no intention of telling them. She only hoped Sullivan wasn't mad at her and she hadn't gotten him into trouble.

They left just after ten; Amy turned down Heidi's offer for one of them to stay the night with her. She had her police guard and wanted to be alone, have time to process her thoughts and feelings about everything. Leaving Peterson on guard duty in the living room, she took the rest of the Rioja and retired to her bedroom.

* * *

He glanced at the address on the piece of paper one

more time before folding it up and shoving it in his pocket.

The place wouldn't be difficult to find.

Grabbing his cell phone and his keys, he killed the light in the motel room, stepped outside and locked the door. As he walked to his car he thought about Amy.

Had she found the photograph he had left for her yet? He smiled, imagining her reaction and wishing he could have seen it. Unfortunately, he had other places to be, other business to take care of.

He started the engine, pulled the car out of the parking lot and indicated at the first exit, heading out towards the beach.

Things were about to get interesting.

* * *

'You should head home.'

Jake glanced up from the computer screen he had been studying. He looked tired and frustrated. 'In a bit.'

Rebecca knew he was still pissed off about the photograph, but wasn't sure if he was annoyed he had put himself in the situation in the first place or because he had been caught out.

'Go home, Jake. There's nothing more you can do here tonight. We have Amy's statement, the sheriff's office in Melford have been notified, and we'll pay Troy Cunningham and Nadine Williams a visit tomorrow.'

Following Rivers' interviews, a member of staff from the Velvet Lounge had come forward, recalling seeing a man and a woman fighting outside on the night Leon Pruitt had disappeared; the description sounded similar to Amy's number one fan and her boyfriend. It was a lead worth following up.

Jake sat back in his chair, stretched and yawned, before switching off the monitor. He glanced at Rebecca. 'Nothing happened.'

'Yeah, you said.' Rebecca kept her tone light. It was too late for arguments.

'She was upset and I was there. You'd have done the same.'

'Okay.'

'I won't lie; I like her, and under different circumstances...' He exhaled, trailing off, and raked both hands back through his hair. 'I gave you my word nothing would happen. It didn't and I want to be clear you know that.'

Rebecca let out a sigh. 'It's okay, Jake. I believe you.'

She did believe him. He was her partner, and they were close enough she knew he wouldn't go to pains to stress it if it wasn't the truth. So nothing had happened, but it didn't mean it wouldn't. There was something between the two of them and he had admitted he was attracted to her. It just hadn't reached boiling point yet. Would Jake be prepared to stop it when it eventually did? Rebecca hoped so.

The killer had re-enacted murders from three of Amy's books and they were no closer to catching him. With three more books to go and the killer's vendetta against Amy stepping up, she needed her partner to be focused more than ever.

* * *

Sleep took a while.

Amy tossed and turned, unable to relax and switch off. The evening was warm, her open window offering little relief, and when she eventually drifted off it was in a mess of tangled sheets.

Almost immediately she dropped into the nightmare, finding herself on the stone steps leading down into the basement. The steep stone steps leading down, the flickering light, the cold damp in the air and the ominous coppery smell warning something bad awaited.

Then eventually the point where the nightmare ended, when she stepped into the room at the bottom of the stairs and screamed, waking herself up and then blocking what she saw from her mind. Except this time she didn't scream out loud, didn't wake herself up.

She was in the basement room at the bottom of the stairs, screaming in her head, wanting someone to hear, someone to help, as she took in the horror before her. Danielle chained up, the body on the table and the blood. There was so much blood.

She had to get out and she turned, with the intention of running, instead slamming straight into the man. He caught hold of her, throwing her to the ground, and her elbow cracked as it hit concrete.

Blood dripped from the body on the table, pooling on the floor beside her, and she scooted away huddling herself against the wall. Danielle was mumbling incoherently, probably because of all the blood in her mouth.

Why is there so much blood in her mouth?

Her gaze drifted past Danielle to the tools hanging from the hooks on the wall: the axes, the knives, pliers, rope and chain.

Oh, dear God.

She started to scream again, trying to push herself further back into the wall, when the man crossed the room, caught hold of her ponytail and pulled her head viciously back. He covered her mouth with his free hand, and she smelt blood and dirt. It made her gag and she struggled to breathe.

'Your friend screamed so I cut out her tongue. You have one warning to stop or I'll do the same to you.' He yanked her hair hard. 'Do you understand?'

Amy nodded, her heart thumping as his words registered. She glanced again at Danielle, at her bloody mouth and realised. As the man let go of her she covered her mouth with her own hand to prevent any scream escaping.

Oh my God! Oh my God! He's going to kill us.

She watched him go to the wall of tools, selecting a length of chain.

Amy glanced at the door.

He had shut it when he'd entered the room, but it wasn't locked. But how was she supposed to get to the door, get it open and make her escape without him catching her?

He was going to chain her up like Danielle. If he did, she wouldn't be able to escape. She doubted the twins would come looking for her and, even if they did, they were in the middle of the woods. By the time help arrived it would be too late. Her only chance of escape was now.

Frantically glancing around the basement, her eyes fell on the dead body on the table; the woman lying with her head twisted. On the table beside her lay a screwdriver. Amy looked at the man. He was still busy with the chain. In front of him Danielle hung pathetically, barely conscious, blood still dribbling from her mouth.

She had to get out of here, had to get help, and quick.

She eased herself off the floor, back to the wall, all of the time watching the man. Slowly, carefully, she took a step towards the body, pausing when she heard him sigh, her heart in her mouth as he scratched his head, started to turn round.

She froze to the spot, waited, letting out the breath she hadn't realised she was holding when he turned back to the wall. In one fluid move she reached for the screwdriver and clenching it tightly in her hand stepped back and slipped down to the floor.

When the man turned round a few seconds later she was in exactly the same place he had left her, cowering against the wall. The chain in one hand, he crossed the room to her, a perverse grin on his face.

'So, are you gonna behave yourself or are you gonna struggle like your friend?' he asked, before adding with a wiggle of his brow, 'I like it when they struggle.'

He yanked Amy to her feet and she yelped, tightening her grip on the screwdriver as he dragged her across to where Danielle stood. As he held her in an arm lock, her eyes connected with the door on the far side of the room, shrouded in dark shadows, and she swore it creaked open slightly, that someone was watching.

The man roughly caught hold of her wrist and in an automatic reaction she brought the screwdriver forward, stabbing him hard in the belly.

He yelped in surprise, took a step back, and Amy took the split-second chance, running at the door, praying for it to be open. Her hand slipped on the door knob and she tried again, this time succeeding.

She heard him behind her as she ran up the stairs, through the kitchen, knocking over the chair, into the hall, again begging for the front door to be unlocked. His fingers skimmed her hair as she yanked the door open, ran down the steps, across the front yard and into the woods.

He was behind her, so close behind her, but as she ran she put a little distance between them. Then she stumbled down the bank. A moment of respite before he returned and then she was on her feet, limping to get away. She heard the sound of the car and ran towards it.

Down the bank, into the path of bright headlights.

Then nothing.

* * *

Amy jerked awake. This time she hadn't woken herself screaming and had lived through the entirety of the nightmare. She shuddered, panting heavily, sweat rolling down her forehead, down the back of her neck and back.

Do not throw up. Do not throw up.

How could she have forgotten?

Every detail was now etched in her memory as clear as if it had been yesterday.

The basement, finding Danielle, the body on the table and the man threatening to cut out her tongue. She had stabbed him with a screwdriver, had managed to escape, and she remembered it all now with such clarity.

Except the eyes; they remained in her subconscious. She didn't remember the watching eyes.

28

Troy was working late again, much to Nadine's annoyance. Things had not been good between them since Saturday, after he had found her at the Velvet Lounge. Usually when they fought, she could win Troy over. He might sulk or disagree, but he always came round. This time was different, and he was still so angry with her for defying him and going to the bar.

Nadine Williams liked to be in control. This time she wasn't and it unsettled her. It occurred to her perhaps Troy was no longer in love with her. Maybe it wasn't to do with the fight. Had he met someone else? Did he want to end things? She couldn't bear that. She might be confrontational, but it was her nature. She loved the man and couldn't stand to lose him.

As the previous two evenings, she cooked him dinner, set it out on the table along with a bottle of wine opened to breathe, waiting for him to return. Again, he didn't come home, she picked at the steak she had grilled, mostly pushing it round her plate, refilling her glass until the bottle of wine was empty.

A little drunk, she glanced at her phone, tapped her red talons against the glass table and toyed with calling him. A call would be an apology; she would have to grovel. Nadine didn't do grovelling. Why couldn't he understand? Why couldn't he see how upset she had been?

Irritated she cleared away her half-eaten steak and Troy's untouched plate, dropped the contents into the trash and dumped both plates onto the counter. Taking her glass of wine, she walked through to the living room and the open patio doors; spent a few minutes staring out across the beach, watching the rise and fall of the surf. Despite the warmth of the evening, the sea was unsettled, the almost full moon casting a shimmering glow across the water and the frothy waves rolling over the sand.

Leaving the door open, she went back into the house, down the long hallway into her bedroom, stripping off as she went. A shower would relax her, ease the knots of tension out of her shoulders. She would let the spray soothe her mind and body and hopefully Troy would be home by the time she was finished. If he wasn't, well, maybe she would call him.

As she pinned up her hair, stepped into the bathroom and turned on the faucet, she was oblivious to the figure who stood watching her from the shadows in the hallway.

* * *

Stepping out into the warm steamy bathroom, the first thing Nadine was aware of was the sound of Marvin Gaye playing low in the background.

She smiled to herself.

Troy was home.

Wrapping herself in a large white fluffy bath sheet, she padded into the bedroom, spent a couple of minutes drying and dressing in a skimpy negligee. She checked her reflection in the free-standing mirror: her cheeks flushed from the warmth of the shower, tanned body silhouetted beneath the sheer red silk. She squirted perfume around her head and shoulders, pulled the pins from her hair, gave herself a final appraising look in the mirror and left the bedroom.

She walked towards the sound of Marvin singing 'Let's get it on' and smiled. Troy was in a romantic mood. A good sign. Practising her pout, rehearsing how this was going to play out, she stepped into the living room – and frowned.

It was empty.

She glanced around for a sign of Troy. No discarded jacket or briefcase. No sign of his cell phone or car keys on the coffee table where he frequently, much to her irritation, left them.

She went back into the hallway, glanced through the window into the drive.

His car wasn't there.

Realisation dawning, Nadine's shoulders tensed.

Who had put the music on?

She glanced towards the bedroom and then back at the living room. Gingerly she took a step back into the room, eyes suspiciously on the CD player. The sound of the waves thrashing against the sand drew her attention to the open balcony door.

Oh jeez. Had someone come in while she was in the shower? Turned on the music?

It was a dumb idea, she scolded herself. Still, she quickly crossed to the patio door, closing and locking it, before going to the CD player and killing the song. She sucked in a breath.

Pull yourself together, Nadine.

She was being an idiot. Okay, so there was no rational explanation for why the music had come on, but it was stupid thinking an intruder had broken in to use the CD player.

Calm down, get your cell phone and give Troy a call.

Glancing around for her cell phone she remembered she'd left it on the kitchen table and she padded back down the hallway to fetch it, warily passing the open dark doorways to the den and the spare bedroom.

Stop being paranoid.

Drawing a deep breath, she forced herself to go back and flick on the light for both rooms. No one was hiding inside. She turned off the lights and closed both doors.

Grabbing her cell phone from the kitchen table she speed-dialled Troy's number. It went straight to voicemail.

Was he ignoring her?

She hung up, hesitated, then redialled, this time leaving a voicemail. 'Hey baby, it's me. I'm a little creeped out. Something happened. Will you give me a call? Or come home? Just come home please.' Ending the call, she rubbed her goose-pimpled arms, feeling a little exposed in her negligee, again thinking about the CD player, not wanting to admit she was a little shaken up.

Perhaps she should call the police.

And tell them what, Nadine? Please come help me. Someone turned my CD player on while I was in the shower.

She cursed, disgusted with herself for playing into the paranoia, but nonetheless grabbed her largest knife before leaving the kitchen. She had barely stepped foot into the hall when the music started again.

I've been really trying baby...

Nadine froze; the knife gripped tightly in her hand.

What the fuck?

Someone was screwing with her.

Maybe it was Troy, trying to teach her a lesson. Or what if it was that bitch, Amy, or one of her friends? They knew where she lived, and the open balcony door would have made it easy to slip inside. The idea was irrational, but then listening to a CD playing by itself in an empty house would do that to you.

Gripping the knife tightly in one hand, her cell phone in the other, she again made her way down the hallway to the living room, heart pounding, not sure if she was more scared or relieved when she saw the room was empty. Marvin was still wailing into the room.

Let's get it on...

Let's get it on...

Nadine drew a shaky breath.

Before she could release it, an arm caught her from behind, gripping tightly around her throat.

Surprised, she let her cell phone slip from her grasp, clattering against the wooden floor. As the arm tightened she struggled, waving the kitchen knife frantically.

Can't breathe, can't breathe.

Nausea took over and a feeling of light-headedness, and she started to drift. Blackness washed over her as she collapsed into her attacker's arms.

* * *

She awoke to find herself sitting at the kitchen table.

Her throat was sore and for a moment she had trouble lifting her head. As the room swam into focus, she remembered being attacked and immediately glanced around.

Her head was throbbing and she tried to move; found she couldn't.

She was stuck to the chair.

Panic set in as she struggled to get up. Her wrists were taped to the arms of the chair, her feet to the front legs. She screamed, but the noise coming was muffled. Something was covering her mouth.

The man strolled into the kitchen, smiled at her.

'I see you're awake at last,' he said conversationally.

I know you.

She shook her head from side to side, trying to talk to him, ask him why he had done this to her.

'I'm sorry. I have no idea what you're saying.'

He smiled again, looking amused, before stepping behind her and busying himself looking through her cupboards, pulling open drawers.

Nadine cranked her neck, trying to see behind her.

What was he up to? What did he plan to do to her? Whatever it was it couldn't be good or he wouldn't have tied her to the chair.

God, Troy. Please come home. Please come home now before he hurts me. I promise if you come home now, I'll never fight with you again.

Returning to the table, he set down a metal funnel, pulled a glass bottle from his pocket. It was filled with liquid and he placed it beside the funnel. He pulled out a chair and sat down facing her.

Nadine glanced at the two items, her heart pounding. Her mind went to Amy Gallaty's book: *Murder Games*, the story of a husband and wife trying to kill each other, the husband eventually succeeding by forcing his wife to drink acid.

She looked at the man again, noticing for the first time he wore gloves. Surgical gloves, she guessed, so he didn't leave fingerprints. Why wear gloves when he had left his face uncovered and she would be able to identify him to the police.

She looked again at the bottle, her blood running cold as realisation kicked in. It didn't matter if she saw his face because he didn't plan on leaving her alive to tell anyone who he was.

Frantically she started to struggle against the tape holding her to the chair, finally understanding the man's intentions.

God, Troy, come home, please. Come home now.

Calmly the man uncapped the bottle.

He lent over her, pulled the tape from her mouth.

She sucked in a breath.

'God, no, please don't do this this. Please, no.'

In an almost tender gesture, he smoothed her hair back from her forehead before grabbing hold of the funnel.

Nadine thrashed in the chair. 'No, please!'

'I'm sorry, Nadine. I didn't want it to come to this. You left me no choice.'

No choice? What the hell was he talking about?

'Whatever it is, whatever you want me to do, I'll do it. Please don't this to me, please. No—'

She screamed as he pulled her head back by her hair, forcing the end of the funnel into her mouth.

He reached for the bottle.

'Don't struggle. It will be quick, I promise.'

Nadine tried to spit the funnel out, but his grip was firm and she choked as he pushed it further into her mouth.

Dear God, no. Please don't let it end like this.

But then she felt the burning acid in her mouth and throat, and she knew it was too late.

* * *

Once she was dead, he went to her library of books. It was only fitting he leave Nadine's copy of *Murder Games* as the calling card. He arranged the book neatly in front of her, picked up the kitchen knife she had been holding when he attacked her and replaced it in the knife drawer, before sparing her a final glance. She hadn't been part of the plan, but the damn woman had gotten in the way. She wouldn't let things drop.

Shaking his head in pity for the way she'd had to die, he made his way into the living room. Marvin Gaye was still playing, and he stopped by the CD player, set the track back to 'Let's Get It On' and put it on loop. He liked the song and felt it was a fitting tribute to Nadine.

Behind him, a male voice coughed.

He turned to face the figure standing by the patio door he had unlocked after Nadine had lost consciousness, before he had tied her to the chair and poured acid down her throat, and smiled.

'Good, you're here at last.'

29

Nadine Williams was found in the early hours of Thursday morning.

Troy was the one to make the gruesome discovery, returning to the beach house around three-thirty, having put in another late-night shift at Blake & Colman. He dialled 911 and the first responders found him twenty minutes later sat on the kitchen floor, weeping over his girlfriend's body.

Joel got a call around four-forty, and by six was in the beach house kitchen with Rivers, Angell and Sullivan, waiting on the pathologist to arrive.

'He's picked up his pace,' Angell commented, taking in the scene. 'Only four days between kills. The others have been around the week mark.'

She was right and the development was worrying, with only two books to go, one of their suspects dead and another an inconsolable mess on the floor.

Had Troy Cunningham killed his girlfriend or was his grief genuine? And if it was, where did that leave things? The print results had come back from the Mr X letters and revealed nothing. Whoever had sent them had been careful to avoid detection. David Gavin was still the prime suspect and the only other one they had, unless the lead from Amy's nightmare panned out.

Gavin's behaviour since arriving back in Juniper was suspicious, but did that make him a killer?

The only motive to link him to the murders was his broken relationship with Amy. Had he emerged so bitter he was willing to kill to get back at her?

The photographs suggested a spurned ex, as did the words BITCH and WHORE, crudely written across her windshield, but there was a big jump from taking pictures and vandalising property to committing murder.

'That had to have hurt.' Rivers spared a pitying glance at Nadine. He had his notepad out and was scribbling as usual, but Joel noted the lack of colour in his face and had thought he was gonna puke when they'd first arrived. This was the worst kill Rivers had seen to date and from what Joel knew of his partner, he wasn't the type to get his hands dirty.

'Acid would have eaten her from the inside out,' Greg Withers told him matter-of-factly, not noticing when Rivers visibly retched. 'Probably sulfuric; I'll have to run some tests to be sure. Wouldn't have been a pleasant way to go.'

Behind him, Troy sobbed loudly.

Joel nudged Rivers. 'Get him out of here, will you?'

Rivers didn't argue, looking glad to be asked. He took Troy by the arm. 'Come on, Mr Cunningham. Let's move through into the living room.'

Angell watched them go.

'He seems genuinely cut up about her.' She glanced at Sullivan, then Joel. 'You think he's for real?'

'That's what I was wondering,' Joel agreed.

'He would have to be one cold bastard to do that to his own girlfriend.'

'Hell of a way to throw suspicion off of yourself.'

Joel looked at Sullivan; the man had a point.

'Those tears were Oscar-worthy.'

'What's his alibi?' Angell asked.

'All we've managed to get out of him so far is that he was at work. We'll have to see if his story checks out.'

'Funny how he happened to be working so late on

the night his girlfriend was killed,' Sullivan muttered, clearly not buying it. 'The whole thing seems too convenient.'

'Except for Nadine,' Angell pointed out. 'She wasn't expecting this.'

Joel glanced at the dead woman: the bluish grey tint to her skin, the blood congealed around her mouth and down the front of her negligee and her eyes still wide open in horror.

They were dealing with a sadistic son of a bitch and time was running out to catch him. He'd also shifted the time frame on them, suggesting another kill could happen imminently.

'Okay, people, we have a lot of work to do. Sullivan, speak with the sheriff's office in Melford and see what they have turned up. Angell, I want you with Amy. Go over everything from yesterday; make sure there is nothing we have missed.'

Joel caught the look Sullivan shot him and chose to ignore it. Now wasn't the time for another argument about Amy Gallaty, and hanging around her apartment was not a good place for the man to be. Both detectives needed to be fully focused.

'I'll get Rivers back checking out motels and hotels for Gavin. We need to know what part he plays in all of this. Meanwhile, I'll see what sense I can get out of

Troy and check out this alibi of his.' He glanced at both Angell and Sullivan. 'You both got all that?'

Angell nodded, eager to get on, while Sullivan hesitated for a moment, seeming vaguely annoyed, before agreeing.

'Sure.'

Joel's temper spiked, annoyed to have to be spelling it out. 'We've got two books left to catch this son of a bitch. The next on the list is about a cop killer. Since you decided to cosy up with the lady our killer has a hard-on for, you need to be watching your back.'

'He's right, Jake,' Angell agreed.

'I can look after myself,' Sullivan scowled, eyes darkening.

Joel smiled thinly. 'Good. Make sure you do.'

* * *

Amy didn't take the news of Nadine's murder well.

Rebecca knew she hadn't liked the woman, had even been a little afraid of her, but that hadn't been enough to want her dead and it was another death she now had to feel guilty about.

Vic Boaz had just taken over the day shift from Peterson and immediately returned to his coffee and Danish pastry after letting Rebecca in. She noted he was making himself at home in Amy's apartment, feet up on the couch, television on.

He had been instructed to keep a close eye on Amy following her hypnotherapy session with Paul Shinnick. The doctor had been providing her with aftercare, but wanted the officers watching her to keep a close eye on her mental state. Both Boaz and Peterson had his number should they need it, but Rebecca suspected the only one who might make that call would be Peterson. As usual, Boaz's number-one priority was himself.

She understood Jake's reservations about having him watch Amy. For some reason, Hickok had faith Boaz could be trusted to do the job. Either that or he wanted to piss off Jake. Rebecca wasn't sure Boaz would have been her choice for the job, but having partnered him for two years, she would grudgingly admit he had always come through for her in the end, albeit usually by the skin of the teeth.

He let her talk with Amy, seeming glad to stay out of the way.

That was Boaz all over, anything for an easy life.

'Do you want some more coffee?' Amy offered, getting up from the table where they been sitting.

'Sure.' It seemed to calm Amy to be doing things, and Rebecca understood her frustration, cooped up in her apartment under police watch, waiting and unable to do anything as a killer struck again and again – one who seemed to have a personal vendetta against her.

Events were taking their toll on her. Dark shadows were smudged around her eyes and her complexion was pale and drawn. Rebecca noticed how she kept nervously fidgeting with her hands, tucking the long strands of hair that had escaped her ponytail behind her ears and biting at her nails.

Over the course of the morning they'd gone over the murder of Danielle, Amy talking through the details she could remember. Jake's name cropped up once and Rebecca didn't miss the look in Amy's eyes, noticed the way she bit into her bottom lip. She understood she wanted to ask after him but, to her credit, she didn't.

'We have the local police going over to Tucker Johnson's house to bring him in for questioning,' she explained now. 'We will find out what happened to Danielle and also if he has any part of this. You said he was maybe late thirties, early forties when he attacked you?'

'Yeah, around that age.'

'That would put him in his fifties or sixties now. He could be our guy.'

Amy poured coffee into cups, added milk and sugar before handing one to Rebecca and taking another over to Boaz. 'Do you really think it could be him after all these years?' she asked, returning to the kitchen.

'I think it's possible. We will know more later on today. Of course we haven't been able to rule out your ex-boyfriend yet.'

'David?' Amy paled. 'Why do you think he's involved?'

So far they had been careful how much information they had told Amy about Gavin's involvement, but Hickok had given Rebecca the go-ahead to fill her in.

'He's back in Juniper and we picked up a number of cigarette butts across from the road from your apartment. He's been watching you, Amy.'

'Shit. Are you serious?' Amy closed her eyes, rubbed her hands over them. 'My car, the pictures. You think it's him?'

'Yes, I think it's likely.'

'Oh, jeez. It never rains, but it pours, right?' She was silent for a moment as realisation dawned. 'Oh crap, you think he could have killed these people?'

'Maybe.' Rebecca paused. 'Was he ever violent towards you, Amy?'

'No. He was controlling, but not violent. He was big on mind games.'

'What kind of mind games?'

'He was possessive and didn't trust me, and he would often turn up when I wasn't expecting him, convinced he was going to catch me cheating on him. Sometimes he would get paranoid and go hunting around my apartment looking for signs.'

'So he had jealousy issues, then?' Rebecca pressed.

'You could say that. He liked things done his way and on his terms and was good at trying to break down my confidence, make out things were my fault. He could be a real Jekyll and Hyde; one minute he'd be showering me with gifts and flowers, the next trying to make me feel worthless, telling me I should be lucky to have him in my life.' Amy paused, a little embarrassed. 'He did control me for a while, knocked my confidence too, but I eventually wised up to his games, realised he was never going to change, and I managed to get him out of my life.'

Rebecca knew Gavin's type, understood how they operated. 'I'm guessing he didn't take the break-up well?'

'You could say that.' Amy smiled tightly, but didn't elaborate. 'I got him out of my life, that's all that mattered. Or at least I thought I did.'

'Controlling would fit our subject's MO. He's calm and methodical, and doesn't act in the heat of the moment. He plans things. He wants them done a certain way and knows how to achieve that.'

'Jeez, I slept with the man. I was in a long-term relationship with him.' Amy started to pace nervously. 'Are you saying I had sex with a serial killer?'

Boaz chose that moment to bring his cup back for a refill, catching the tail end of the conversation.

'I have experience with this stuff, Amy. You wouldn't know this, but I found out I personally knew someone who was a serial killer.'

Amy looked at him, waiting for him to elaborate, while Rebecca rolled her eyes behind Boaz's head. All they needed were a few of his pearls of wisdom.

'When I was struggling to cope and deal with things, I found the church helped me.'

'The church?'

'Yeah, Pastor Ralph is a real good guy. Maybe you could pay him a visit.'

'I'm an atheist.'

'So was I before. Pastor Ralph helped me see things clearly. I think he could help you if you wanted to talk to him.'

'I think the last thing Amy needs is the church, Vic.'

'And what would you know?' Vic snapped defensively.

Rebecca crossed her arms, steadily losing patience.

'Enough to know it won't help her at this moment in time.' She didn't bother to remind Boaz her own father was minister of the parish church back in her home town of Swallow Falls.

'I appreciate the sentiment, Officer Boaz, but I think Detective Angell is right.'

'Well… if you change your mind.'

'Then I will let you know. Thank you; I do appreciate the thought.'

Boaz pulled his sulky face, topped up his cup and headed back to the couch.

'What about Mr X?' Amy asked, turning back to Rebecca.

'Sorry?'

'Mr X, the guy who wrote me the fan letters. You think the killer is the same person who wrote me the letters, right?'

'We strongly suspect a connection.'

'It doesn't make sense that David would write them.'

'No, it doesn't,' Rebecca agreed. She gave a twisted smile. 'But then, how well can you say you really knew your boyfriend?'

* * *

He stopped at McDonald's before heading out of town, and ordered a Big Mac meal to go. The storage unit he had rented was a few miles out. There were closer ones he could have used, but this one offered more privacy.

Leaving his car, he took the paper bag of food, unlocked the door to the unit and slid it open. Although it was quiet and no one was about, once inside he closed the door before turning on the light.

He had hidden the car here, knowing he couldn't afford for the police to trace it, and had left the camera sitting on the front seat, along with the photographs of Amy Gallaty. He spent a moment flicking through them again, looking at the shots of her playing in the park with her dog, with the cop on the balcony of the apartment; all copies of the pictures sent to her.

Things were working in his favour, better than he could have hoped. With the photographs and the murders, he had her scared and was enjoying feeding on her fear. Same as he'd enjoyed slitting the throat of the doorman from her bar, and, although he'd regretted having to do it, same as he'd enjoyed pouring the acid down Nadine's throat.

Setting the photographs to one side, he took the

bag of food round to the trunk. He was aware of the muffled sounds coming from inside before he popped it open. This one was going to be a struggler, but he couldn't kill yet. It wasn't time.

Smiling down at the blinking face, he waved the bag. 'Play nice. I brought you lunch.'

30

Five summers passed before Troy Cunningham returned to the house in the woods, and this time he wasn't alone.

Sure, he had biked past the place on numerous occasions. Had even paused at times, drawn to the house and the memories of what had happened there, staring at the dirty, dark windows, and wondering if Johnson had any more victims locked up inside.

He had never told anyone.

After Amy had made her escape he'd run all the way home. The twins were gone. He suspected they had left after sending her into the house.

His plan while running home was to wake his parents, tell them what had happened and get them to call the police. But then he'd started thinking about the consequences. They would be mad at him for sneaking out and would probably ground him for a year. And if they did call the police he could end up being arrested for breaking into Tucker Johnson's house. Worse still, if Tucker wasn't arrested and he knew Troy had seen what he did, he might come after him.

He was best to stay quiet. The twins would raise the alarm. No one ever had to know he was there.

Except the twins didn't raise the alarm; they said nothing.

Word around town the following day was that Amy was in hospital, having been hit by a car. There was no mention of Danielle, and no one seemed able to fathom why Amy had been out on the wooded road so late at night.

There were murmurs she had been sleepwalking, others said she'd had a fight with Deanna Rooney and had been running away. Her parents cut short their trip and came to the hospital, spending three anxious days waiting by her bedside. Eventually she was well enough to be released and returned home to Montana.

She never returned to Melford and Troy's last

memory of her was watching her flee from Tucker Johnson and his basement of horror.

It was a full twenty-four hours before Danielle was reported missing. Her mom and stepdad both worked long shifts, and it wasn't unusual for Danielle to take herself off for the day. The police investigated her disappearance, asking questions around town. Leslie and Crystal Rooney kept quiet, never coming forward to say they had been with Danielle or that they had dared her to go into Tucker Johnson's house.

Unsure what to do, Troy stayed quiet as well.

Over the years he often thought about Amy, wondering what she was doing and why she had never told anyone about that night. He was seventeen now and she would be twenty, and she was likely at college somewhere, probably had a boyfriend. Troy wasn't too bothered about girls. Sure, he dated, but none of the girls at his school compared to Amy. He had a few friends, but preferred to keep to himself, alone with his thoughts and secrets.

That changed the summer that Cap came to town. He was a couple of years younger than Troy, but full of the same anger and frustration at being shunted off to Hicksville, and the two of them formed a bond.

Cap, like Troy, was a city boy, and furious with his parents at dumping him on his elderly aunt for the summer while they fought out the terms of their divorce. Melford was dull and he wanted to be home with his friends, hanging out at the mall, going to ball games, movies and parties, not stuck in the back end of nowhere.

At first, they had sized each other up warily. Cap might be a city kid, but he was new in town. He was also younger and petulant – spoilt, even. Troy preferred his own company. Did he want this kid hanging on his coat-tails? Likewise, Cap had reservations, at first seeing Troy as another kid from the sticks. If he caved and formed a friendship, it would go against his stance to hate everything in Melford.

They walked the same forest trails, fished in the same stretch of the river, continually running into each other. Wariness became grudging acceptance which in turn thawed into friendship.

As the warm summer days rolled on, Troy realised he had found his first true friend since moving to town, which sucked as only a couple of weeks remained before Cap would return to his life in the city, leaving him once again alone.

It was during an evening of fishing that Troy shared the secret he had kept to himself for five long summers. The two of them were sitting on the bank, sipping beer Cap had taken from his aunt's refrigerator. Virginia Martin had a cupboard full of cans and it was easy for Cap to replace the ones he had taken.

They had hooked a few fish between them. Troy photographed his before releasing them back into the river, while Cap preferred to watch his squirm and flip about as they suffocated to death on the bank.

'Why do you do that?' Troy had wanted to know as he watched his friend's latest catch wriggle on the end of the line. 'It's cruel.'

Cap had shrugged. 'It's just a dumb fish. Don't you like having power over something, knowing you're in control of whether it lives or dies?'

'I dunno. I guess I never thought about it.'

'I can put the fish back or I can make it suffer. It's my decision, my choice. I get to decide what happens.' He hauled the line in, unhooked the fish and threw it back into the river. 'There you go; this one got lucky.'

They fished in silence for a while longer, finishing their beers as the sun set over the trees and dusk started to take hold.

'I love the woods at night,' Cap commented. 'When the darkness falls and everything comes alive. Some people find it creepy. I don't get that.'

'It can be creepy. You never know what is lurking about in the dark.'

'You scared of the dark then, are you?'

Although there was a teasing glint in Cap's eye, the question had Troy's back up. 'Of course not. There's plenty things scarier than the dark.'

'Like what?'

Troy shrugged. 'Nothing much.'

'There must be something.' Cap was silent for a moment, thinking. 'Come on, let's trade creepy stories. I'll tell you the scariest thing that has ever happened to me and you tell me yours. What do you say?'

When Troy didn't answer, Cap began his story anyway, telling him about the time he and his friends had decided to mess with a Ouija board. He claimed a glass had smashed and the board had caught fire. Troy wasn't sure he believed him, but he didn't say so. No need to go pissing his friend off.

'So what about you? What's your creepiest thing?' Cap asked, story finished. 'Bet you can't beat mine.'

Troy was silent for a long moment. He could tell Cap about the murder house. He didn't have to give him all the details.

'There's a house in the woods here that is really creepy.'

'You mean that spooky looking place down the road?'

'That's the one.'

'So what about it? What's so creepy? Has something happened there?'

'Someone was murdered in the basement.'

'No shit. Is the place haunted or something?'

'Not haunted, I don't think.' Troy shook his head. 'But bad stuff happened there.'

'A long time ago?'

'A few years back.'

'How do you know that?' Cap's eyes were narrowed, filled with disbelief. 'You can't just pretend that because a house looks creepy that bad shit happened there. This has to be a true story, Troy, that's the deal.'

Troy's temper flared. He was sure Cap's tale about the Ouija board was bullshit. How dare he suggest the Johnson house story wasn't true? 'I'm not making it up. It honestly happened.'

'Sure it did. Why should I believe you? I mean, how would you know?'

'Because I saw it happen.'

The words were out before he could take them back. Cap's jaw dropped, his eyes widened, but there was still a hint of disbelief in them. 'You what?'

Somehow the story came tumbling out. Troy didn't mean to tell him everything, but over the next hour Cap learned about perfect Amy Gallaty, the bitchy twins, and poor nerdy Danielle. How Troy had followed them into the woods, that Danielle had gone into the Johnson house as part of a dare and had never come out. How Troy had found the hatchway door, gone into the basement and seen the dead body on the table, Danielle chained up and covered in blood, and how Amy had entered the room, been caught by Johnson, but had managed to escape.

When he was done, Cap was looking at him in amazement. 'That happened?'

'Yeah.' Troy could tell from the look on Cap's face that he believed him. He would have had to have been a hell of a storyteller to make it all up.

'And you never told anyone?'

'I was twelve. I should've told, but I was afraid of getting in trouble. I thought the twins would tell.'

'But they didn't.'

'No, they pretended like it hadn't happened.'

'And Amy never told either.'

'She went home after the accident.'

Cap was silent for a long moment. 'Have you ever been back to the house?'

'Yeah, I ride past it all the time.'

'I mean inside. Have you ever been back inside?' Cap paused. 'Back into the basement?'

'No, hell no.'

'I would love to see it.' Cap's lips curved. 'We should go.'

'Shit, are you crazy? I never want to go back down there.'

'Why not? Are you afraid? We can go in by the hatchway door again. He won't know we're there.'

'I'm not afraid. It's a stupid idea. A really stupid idea.'

'Aren't you curious to know if there's anyone else down there? He could have done this kind of thing again. Unlikely it was a one-off.'

'No, I'm not curious.'

It was a lie. Troy was, and had thought about the murder house a lot over the past few years, wondering what was happening in the basement and if there had been other victims. He had been tempted to return, but had never been able to pluck up the courage.

'Come on, Troy, we have to go,' Cap pleaded. 'You can't tell me this and expect me to forget about it. I really want to see inside.'

Troy hesitated. With two of them they had safety in numbers. He was curious, but also reluctant to put himself back into a bad situation.

'I dunno. I don't think it's a good idea.'

'We can go now. Be in and out in ten minutes.'

When Troy continued to ponder, Cap added slyly, 'Or of course I could go by myself.'

'You wouldn't.'

'Sure I would. I'm not afraid of an old basement.'

'It's not just an old basement. It's what happened there.'

'I'm not afraid of that either.'

'You're nuts. Why do you want to go there so badly?'

'Because I like creepy shit.'

'No kidding.'

'So what's it gonna be, Troy? You gonna make me go on my own or are you gonna come and be my wingman?'

Troy pulled in his rod, set it to one side.

Cap wasn't going to drop this. He should never have told him. 'Okay, but in and out in ten minutes. That's it.'

* * *

It was fully dark by the time they reached the house, and creeping around back, seeing the same window lit and the television playing, had Troy reliving the past and feeling the butterflies fluttering in his belly. He felt twelve again and more afraid than he would ever let on to Cap.

The hatchway door was hard to get open. Age had stiffened and swelled the wood and it took the full strength of both of them to yank it open. The door squeaked as they pulled it back and both boys paused. Troy's heart thumped, terrified in case it had disturbed Johnson. They waited a full ten seconds before descending the stairs. This time round there was no moonlight to help guide their way down the stone steps and Cap lit a match so they could be sure not to trip.

Troy guided him to the door, the one he had stood behind five years earlier and watched as Amy and Danielle were attacked by Johnson. There was no light coming from the other side and Cap lit another match, casting a faint shadowy glow on the room. The door on the far side of the room, the one Amy had made her escape through, was closed. Probably locked.

Cap pushed the door open, ignoring Troy's hesitant grip on his arm. The dying match showed him where the one bare bulb hung centre of the room and he went to it, pulled the cord. Weak light bathed the room and Troy glanced around, recognising the table on which the body had lain, the chains hanging from the ceiling that had held Danielle prisoner, and the wall of tools Johnson had used to torture her.

'Wow. This shit did happen.' Cap's voice was a whisper, but the excitement in his tone was unmistakable. With no sense of fear he was already over at the table, running the palm of his hand over the wooden surface. 'You can see the blood markings in the wood.' His attention turned to the chains. 'That's where he had Danielle, right?'

'Yeah, that's right.' Troy shuffled his feet uncomfortably, staying by the door. 'We should get going before he finds us.'

Cap wasn't listening. He was already over at the wall, running his finger along the blade of a saw. 'This is insane, man. This guy is like a serial killer.'

'We don't know that. No one else has gone missing from town.'

'Not that you know of. Look around, man. This room wasn't geared up for a one-off kill. This shit has all the markings of a serial killer's den. I've read books on this stuff. I know how it works.'

Cap wandered back over to where the chains hung, crouched to the floor and dabbed his finger in something. 'See, I told you I was right.' He held up his finger to show Troy the dark tip and grinned broadly. 'Fresh blood. Someone has died here recently.'

31

Troy Cunningham hadn't killed Nadine Williams.

Much as Jake wanted to find a way to tie him to the murder, had a gut feeling he was somehow involved, the facts didn't lie, and his alibi was airtight. Hickok shared the news as Jake came off a call with Sheriff Wagner over in Melford, explaining Cunningham had been in the office of Blake & Colman with two other employees until gone one. Computer records said he logged off their system around two-thirty and these were backed up by the security cameras showing him exiting the parking lot just before three.

Jake swore, balled up a sheet of paper on his desk and aimed it at the trashcan. He kicked back his chair in frustration.

'He's not our guy, Sullivan.' Hickok shrugged out of his jacket, threw it across his own desk, loosening his tie and rolling up his shirtsleeves. He looked equally frustrated, having spent the day at the beach house trying to make sense of things. 'I agree something doesn't add up about him, but the facts don't lie. He didn't kill his girlfriend.'

'Did you ask him about the Velvet Lounge on Saturday night?'

'Yeah, and he fully admits to being there. He claims Nadine was planning to confront Amy and he followed, stopped her before she went inside. I don't like it any more than you do, but we have no evidence to suggest he's not telling the truth.'

Damn it, the woman had had a bug up her ass about Amy. Jake regretted she was dead, felt pity for the way she had died, but somewhere mixed in with regret was a relief Nadine could no longer harass Amy.

'So what did our sheriff friend over in Melford have to report?' Hickok asked, leaning back against his desk.

'House is owned by Tucker Johnson, sixty-two. He's a carpenter, lives there alone. Bought the place back in seventy-nine; moved in with his wife and kid. Wife suffered with depression, killed the kid and herself shortly after. Wagner says the guy is a recluse, only comes into town when he needs stuff. Since he's been able to buy stuff online and get it delivered, they rarely see him.'

'Okay.' Hickok leaned forward, resting his elbows on the desk and linking his fingers together. 'Sixty-two would have made him early forties when he attacked Amy.'

'Wagner went to the house last night, but there was no answer. They got a search warrant this morning and went back. There's no trace of the guy even living there. Sure, his clothes are hanging in the closet, but the stuff in his refrigerator is out of date, the mail piling up.'

'Maybe he thought he was gonna get caught so he ran.'

'They checked the basement.' Jake swallowed down the anger. 'It was exactly as Amy described. Johnson was using it as some kind of torture room. Forensics is getting blood samples.'

'No bodies?'

'Not in the basement. He's gotten rid of them somewhere, but we'll find them. It's gonna be bad, Hickok. Wagner thinks we are talking double numbers.'

He thought of Amy wandering into that hellhole at

fifteen years old. No wonder she had suppressed the memory.

Hickok nodded, taking in the information.

'So, we have a fifteen-year-old girl who stumbles across a serial killer, one who has been operating for possibly decades. And now she's grown up, she's become the focus of another serial killer. What are the chances of that?'

'Slim to none.'

'Unless the two sets of murders are somehow connected.'

Jake narrowed his eyes. 'You think Johnson would be targeting Amy after all this time?'

'He's missing from his hometown and she's the one who got away.' Hickok gave a twisted smile. 'I would say it's very possible.'

* * *

Rebecca had just finished up when her cell phone buzzed. She pulled it out of her pocket, glanced at the screen before answering, expecting it to be Hickok or Jake; frowned when Alan's name flashed up on the screen.

Not now, dammit.

She let it ring another couple of times before killing the call.

'I can give you some privacy if you need to take that.'

'It's fine. It's nothing that can't wait.' Scooping up her notes, she smiled at Amy. 'I think we're done here for today. If I think of anything else, or if there are any more developments, I'll give you a call. Officers Boaz and Peterson will keep you safe, but if you need anything at all, get in touch.' Rebecca shot a look in Boaz's direction. He was totally absorbed in the show he was watching.

God, Hickok. I hope you know what you're doing.

Her pocket started buzzing again. Irritated she pulled her phone out. Alan knew she was working. What the hell was so damn important? She smiled apologetically at Amy.

'I'm sorry, I'd better take this.'

Nodding, Amy gathered the coffee cups, disappearing discreetly into the kitchen.

Rebecca wandered off to the corner of the room, distancing herself from Boaz.

'What?' she hissed into the phone.

'Becky? It's Alan.'

'Yes, I know it's you. What do you want? You know I'm working.'

'Is everything okay? You sound a little... testy.'

Rebecca drew in a breath, counted to three and released it slowly.

Don't bite.

'I'm fine, just very busy.'

'I guess I shouldn't be surprised.'

The buzzer sounded, distracting her. 'Hold on a second, Alan.'

She was aware of him still blabbering on as she signalled to Boaz, who had nearly fallen off the couch at the noise. He was already fumbling with his sidearm. A relief to see he'd remembered he was on duty.

Amy stepped out of the kitchen, watching nervously as Boaz approached the door as if it was about to attack him. He glanced through the peephole before holstering his weapon and unbolting the latch.

'Oh, it's you,' he muttered unenthusiastically as Heidi Pearce entered the apartment.

She gave him a disdainful look and headed straight over to Amy.

Boaz locked the door, pulled a face behind her back and returned to the couch.

No love lost there, then.

Rebecca nodded a greeting to Heidi, and returned

her attention to Alan. 'I'm sorry, I didn't catch what you said.'

'I said I'm going to have to make another trip out of town tomorrow.' Alan sounded annoyed at having to repeat himself. 'I won't be back until Sunday.'

'Another conference?'

'No, nothing like that. An old friend has been in touch. He wants to discuss a business proposal.'

'Okay.'

'I'm sorry to do this to you a second week running, Becky. Do you forgive me?'

'Sure.' Rebecca glanced around, distracted. Heidi was in the kitchen with Amy and they were having a heated discussion. 'Listen, Alan. I need to go.'

'There's one more thing. I have a delivery scheduled for tomorrow, some new samples. I won't be around to collect them. Are you okay if I give them your address instead?'

'I'll be working, but if you give me a time, I'll try and be around.'

'Okay, I'll speak with the warehouse, let you know. I must get these samples so it's very important you are home at the time I tell you to be there to collect them for me.'

'I said okay.'

'And your mother has been trying to get hold of

you. She says can you please call her. It's important. She wants to speak with you about this weekend.'

Damn it, Mom. You've got Alan hounding me now too?

'Listen, Alan, I really have to go.'

'Are you listening to me, Becky? I said this is important.'

'Yes, fine. I'll call her.'

'Okay, well I love—'

Rebecca killed the call, slipping her cell phone back into her pocket.

'Is everything okay in here?' she asked, stepping into the kitchen.

Heidi whirled around, surprised. 'Everything is fine, thank you, Officer.'

'Detective,' Rebecca corrected.

'It's not exactly fine, Heidi.' Amy scowled at her friend. 'You should have told me.'

'And give you another thing to worry about? It's no big deal.'

'Are you kidding? It's a huge deal.'

'What's going on?' Rebecca snapped, losing patience.

Amy turned to her. 'It's our friend, Ryan. The one whose dog I'm looking after. He's travelling around Europe and no one can get hold of him.'

'You know what he's like, Amy. He's pretty crap when it comes to phones and keeping in touch. He's fine.'

'How do you know that, Heidi? You've been trying to get hold of him for nearly two weeks and nothing.' Amy closed her eyes, rubbed her palms over her temples. 'God, I didn't know. I hadn't even thought about him or tried to get in touch. I am such a shitty friend.'

'I think you can be forgiven,' Rebecca told her sympathetically. 'You've had a lot on your plate.'

'That still doesn't make it right.'

'See, I knew we shouldn't have told you,' Heidi huffed sulkily. 'Gage was all, like, we should tell her, we should tell her, but I knew you'd get stressed out and start blaming yourself.' She shook her head, annoyed.

'Give me his details,' Rebecca suggested, stepping in as mediator. 'I'm sure your friend is fine, but I'll see what I can find out.'

Heidi scribbled down Ryan's name, address and cell phone number for her, and Rebecca left the two girls to clear the air, under the watch of Boaz.

Walking out to her car she glanced at the paper. Ryan Caparelli, 860 Lombard Street. She recognised the road name. It was on the other side of town. She folded the paper, slipping it into her pocket, thinking Ryan Caparelli was probably better off in Europe staying as far away from Amy Gallaty as possible.

32

Victor Boaz went down sick on Thursday night, a few hours after eating curry from his favourite takeout, and called in early Friday morning to say he wouldn't be able to make it over to Amy's to relieve Peterson.

'Jesus, are you kidding me? Can't he hug the toilet bowl over at Amy's?' Joel grumbled when he got the message, and swore about Boaz under his breath. They were short on staff and time, and this wasn't a good time to be a man down. He needed everyone following leads, but with the killer closing in he could not afford to leave Amy alone either. He debated who to send.

Sullivan was a bad idea for more reasons than one. Besides, Joel needed him following up the lead in

Melford. Same with Angell. Both detectives were too valuable to the case to waste time on babysitting duties.

Rivers ambled into the office, preoccupied texting, a stupid grin plastered across his face. The idiot spent far too much time attached to his phone, talking with his buddies back home. Over the past couple of days he had been checking on hotel accommodation in the area, trying to get a tab on David Gavin, and had so far turned up nothing. A job Joel would have to get Angell to finish.

'I need you over at Amy Gallaty's. Boaz has called in sick.'

Rivers glanced up from his phone, irritated. 'You seriously expect me to sit around in her apartment all day? I'm not a babysitter.'

'Today you are.'

'Come on, Joel. This isn't fair. I'm an FBI agent. Surely someone else can go. I'm working on the Gavin lead.'

'Which Angell can take over. Today you watch Amy.'

'This isn't fair.'

'And?' Joel felt his temper fraying. Rivers had a knack of irritating him. 'This isn't kindergarten. It's part of the job and I don't give a shit whether you like it or not. Today you watch Amy.'

Rivers pouted, but didn't argue. He was still a rookie and knew Joel could pull rank. That didn't mean he had to like it, and he stomped from the room like a spoilt child, punching the keys of his cell phone furiously, no doubt telling his friends what a jerk of a partner he'd been saddled with.

Joel watched him go, the feeling mutual. Maybe Rivers would surprise him and get his shit together, but he wouldn't hold his breath.

* * *

Amy's heart sank when Peterson opened the door and Special Agent Rivers smugly stepped inside.

He glanced disdainfully at her before briefing Peterson that he would be taking over and she listened as he explained Boaz had gone down sick. Peterson nodded, collected his things from the couch and waved a goodbye to Amy, telling her he would see her later in the evening. As the door closed after him, Rivers dropped the paper bag he'd brought with him on her coffee table, clapped his hands together, and turned to face her.

In his bed, Huckleberry growled, ears pricked back. He wasn't a fan of Rivers either.

'So, looks like we're stuck together for the day.'

Amy pulled a face. 'Yeah,' was all she could muster.

The guy was a rude, pompous little idiot. She knew he didn't like her; he had made it clear from day one, accusing her of having blood on her hands. She suspected that after their last encounter, when Sullivan had dragged him from her apartment, he liked her even less. Still, she had to make an effort; try and make the situation more bearable. Her natural good manners automatically kicked in.

'Do you want coffee? There's some in the pot.'

'No, but I'll have tea, with milk and two sugars. And I'll need your laptop. I wasn't expecting to come here today, so I don't have mine with me.'

'What? But I need it to write.'

'I think federal business is more important than your silly little stories, Miss Gallaty. Besides, when you write people seem to die. I'd give it a break if I were you.'

'I—'

'You can set it up over there while I use your bathroom.' He nodded towards the couch. 'Which way?'

Amy directed him, her blood boiling.

Obnoxious little prick.

She made his tea, slamming the cup down and dumping in the teabag, milk and sugar, resisting the urge to spit in it.

Who the hell did he think he was, coming into her apartment and taking over?

She put the laptop on the coffee table, set his tea beside it, and was sat at the dining table reading a magazine when he emerged. He glanced at her and went to sit on the couch. Seeing him approach, Huckleberry got out of his bed and slunk over to Amy.

Rivers watched him warily as he fired up the laptop and took a sip of his tea. He set the cup down on the table and clicked his fingers, not bothering to look round.

'Can you get me some more sugar? You didn't make it sweet enough.'

'What did your last slave die of?' Amy muttered, getting to her feet.

'What was that?'

'Nothing.' She gave him her best sickly-sweet smile when he glanced round.

Fetching the sugar bowl from the kitchen, she took it over to the coffee table, dumped it down. 'Here, knock yourself out.'

She went back to her magazine, and tried to ignore

the fact he was there in the room. She glanced up occasionally to seeing him tapping away either online or on his cell phone. A couple of times he looked up and caught her watching. Eyeing her suspiciously, he angled the laptop away so she couldn't see the screen.

Amy rolled her eyes. Like she gave a shit what super important FBI stuff he was working on. The paper bag he'd brought contained a selection of goods from the local bakery, which he ploughed his way through as he worked. His appetite amazed her; the man was a pig. He ate at least six or seven pastries and didn't even offer her one. Not that she was bothered. The last thing she wanted was to share food with Special Agent Rivers.

The sooner today was over, the better.

* * *

The first thing Wes Peterson was aware of when he woke up was the blistering pain in his head. The second was the feeling of something wrapped snugly around his throat.

He tried to move, groaning as he raised his head slightly, banging into something.

Christ, his head hurt.

He tried to open his eyes, found them stuck.

What the fuck?

And tried again, aware something was covering them.

What was it? Tape?

And it wasn't just on his eyes. As feeling came back, he realised it was covering his mouth too. And his body; when he tried to move a second time, he found his arms were strapped tightly against his torso. He attempted to roll to the side, and felt whatever was around his throat starting to tighten.

A noose.

Where the hell was he? What had happened?

Resisting the urge to panic, he forced himself to breathe through his nose. He couldn't get stressed if he wanted to get himself out of this situation. Slowly his last memories came back: saying goodbye to Amy, leaving her with Special Agent Rivers. He had made his way down to the garage, was about to get in his car. Something, someone, had attacked him from behind, by hitting him over the head.

So where was he?

Start with the basics.

He was lying flat on his back, possibly outside, but where he wasn't sure. He listened for any give-away sounds. In the distance he heard a car. His torso was taped up, but his legs weren't. He wriggled them, aware of something around his ankles, holding them together. He tested the bond again, felt metal cutting into his skin. His cuffs, he suspected.

Peterson weighed up the situation. This wasn't good. He was completely immobilised, couldn't see or shout for help. That left his brain and he needed to use it, to think of a way out of this situation fast, before whoever had left him here came back.

* * *

Amy finished reading her magazine, bored and frustrated that she couldn't write. Picking up her cell phone she checked it for missed calls or messages. She'd left a couple for Ryan, but had heard nothing back. She sent him another text.

AMY

Please call or text me when you get this. I want to know you're safe. Xx

Where was he? Why wasn't he returning any of their calls?

She set the phone down, glanced at Rivers again. He had yet to remove his suit jacket, even though it had to be ninety degrees outside, and he sat there all prim on her couch, back ramrod straight and not a hair out of place, not a crease in his clothing.

No wonder she couldn't relax around him. He was so stuffy. And he kept making an irritating popping noise, sucking in his cheek. It crossed Amy's mind he was doing it on purpose to annoy her.

She picked up her phone again, bored. Still nothing from Ryan. She knew because it hadn't beeped, but she checked anyway.

Her thoughts wandered to Sullivan and she wondered what he was up to. Was he still looking into Danielle's murder? She hadn't seen him since Special Agent Hickok had shown them the photograph of the two of them on her balcony. From what Detective Angell had said, she suspected Hickok was intentionally keeping them apart. It was stupid. Nothing had happened.

Playing with her phone, she clicked open a new message, started to type.

AMY

I can't believe I got stuck with Rivers. He's driving me nuts.

She tapped her finger against the side of the phone, debating for a moment before entering Sullivan's name and clicking send.

Immediately she regretted sending the text. Sullivan was busy working the case and he didn't have time to read or respond to stupid messages. Besides, like him or loathe him, Rivers was here looking after her. It was ungrateful of her to complain when she'd been provided with police protection.

Amy got up from the table, took her cup into the kitchen and filled the coffee pot. She glanced over at Rivers again, who was totally engrossed with something on the screen. He had better be using her laptop for work purposes and not looking at porn. Not that he seemed the type to look at porn. He was too squeaky clean. Still, you never could tell. She'd thought David was a choirboy the first six months they'd dated.

The coffee pot boiled and she poured her drink, not bothering to offer Rivers a refill on his tea. She was sure he would soon inform her if he wanted another cup, probably by clicking his fingers at her again, as if she was his maid.

Although it irritated her being in the same room as him, she was loath to go through to the bedroom and let him take over her living room. Instead, she returned to the table, set down her cup, and noticed she had a message flashing on her phone.

It was from Sullivan.

JAKE SULLIVAN

I can imagine. Lock him out in the
hall.

She smiled. It was such a little thing, but she felt
stupidly happy he'd texted her back.

'What are you grinning at?'

Amy glanced up to find Rivers watching her, his
eyes narrowed suspiciously.

It's none of your damn business. 'Nothing. Just a text.'

Rivers gave an irritated sigh, set the laptop down
on the coffee table and glanced at his watch. 'It's getting close to lunch. Do you have anything to eat
around here?'

Seriously? He'd sat and stuffed half a dozen pastries and now he wanted her to feed him?

'How can you be hungry? You didn't eat long ago.'

'It was a couple of hours and yes, I am hungry. Can
you make me a sandwich?'

Balling her fists, Amy got up from the table, went
through to the kitchen and opened her refrigerator.

'I have cheddar.'

'I'm allergic to cheese.'

'Egg?'

'I like meat. Ham or beef. Chicken if not.'

Amy shook her head, closed the door.

'Well, sorry, you're out of luck. Cheese or egg is all I have.'

'Are you serious?' Rivers huffed.

'What?'

'You have people here watching over you, keeping you safe, and you can't be bothered to feed them?'

Amy's temper boiled over. He had crossed a line.

'You ungrateful little shit. I offered to make you a sandwich. It's not my fault if you don't like what I've got in the refrigerator. Besides, I wasn't aware I was supposed to be providing room service for you.'

'It's not that you're supposed to be providing anything, it's just plain good manners.' Rivers glared at her, his words clipped. 'I'll have to go out and get some lunch from somewhere. I can't go all afternoon hungry.'

'Fine, go. I don't really care.'

'You'll to have to come with me. I can't leave you here alone.' He got up shaking his head, closed the lid of the laptop. 'This is such an inconvenience.'

'Seriously? We have to go out just to get you food?' Rivers scowled at her.

'I'm not getting in trouble with Hickok for leaving you here alone, and I'm hungry, so yes, we have to go out to get me food.'

Annoyed, Amy disappeared into her bedroom to

fetch her purse. She returned a couple of seconds later, picking her cell phone up and slipping it in her pocket. Seeing her getting ready to go out, Huckleberry sat up and fixed her with a pitiful look. 'We might as well take him with us. He's gonna need a walk soon. We can coincide going out with taking him over the park.'

'I don't want him in my car.'

'Why not?'

'I don't like dogs.'

'Oh, for crying out loud. We'll be five minutes.'

'I don't care.' Rivers pulled a petulant face. 'The dog stays here. If we have to, we'll take him out when we get back.'

Amy held her tongue. It wasn't worth arguing.

'Sorry, buddy,' she muttered under her breath to Huckleberry as she followed Rivers out of the door.

* * *

Peterson was aware of approaching footsteps.

Was it his attacker?

He had no idea of the time and had gone through a number of emotions – anger, confusion, frustration, fear – as his mind ticked overtime. Although he continually tested his bonds, he knew he wasn't going to get free, and that left him to wait. And God the waiting was awful.

He thought of his wife and his kid, and he thought about what was going to happen to him. It was the not knowing that was the worst bit.

The footsteps came closer and he mumbled against the tape, knowing he couldn't call out but hoping it would be enough to attract attention. Above him came a click, then some kind of vibration disturbing the noose around his neck. He attempted to call out again. It sounded loud in his head, but he knew it was barely a mumble.

A door slammed directly overhead. A car door. And he understood where he was.

Oh jeez. Oh dear God, no.

The click of the ignition, the roar of the engine, the smell of the fumes.

Realising the full implications of what was about to happen, Peterson attempted again to roll to the side. He felt the car move forward, the brief second when it was no longer above him, then the noose around his neck choked him as it tightened sharply, dragging the weight of his body, and he lost consciousness.

* * *

'There's something wrong with my car.'

Rivers was scrutinising the dashboard as he drove up the ramp and out of the garage, looking like a man who didn't have the first clue about how machinery worked.

Amy wished he would keep his eyes on the road. The damn idiot would crash if he didn't pay attention.

He was right; the ride wasn't smooth. It felt like the suspension. Gawking at the dashboard wasn't going to help.

'Don't you feel it?'

'Yeah, I do. Why don't you pull over?' she suggested.

On the sidewalk a passing woman screamed, drawing their attention.

What the heck?

She had dropped her shopping bags, was pointing to the car. As they passed her, Amy turned in her seat to see what she had been pointing at.

'Oh my God, oh my God, stop the car.'

Rivers slammed on the brakes, looking annoyed. 'What the hell?'

Amy opened the door, almost falling onto the road.

Jesus. Oh, dear God, no.

She stared at the body they had been dragging along the street, her legs going weak.

The woman had rushed over to the victim and was already joined by other passers-by. Rivers came around the side of the car; his face drained of colour, his expression shocked.

Dropping to his knees beside Amy he started puking into the gutter.

33

By the time Rebecca and Jake arrived on the scene the street had been cordoned off with patrol cars positioned either end and cleared of pedestrians. Hickok arrived seconds later, pulling up behind Jake's Audi, and the three of them approached the scene together.

Peterson was lying in the street, the noose that that had strangled him still attached to the car Rivers had been driving.

Rebecca clenched her fists, drew in a deep breath, as a wave of emotion hit.

Keep it together, Angell.

She had worked with Wes Peterson for six years and, while they had not always seen eye to eye, he was a good cop and a family man. He had been looking after Amy, doing his job, and he didn't deserve for his life to end this way.

Niggling at the back of the sadness and anger was another little ball of emotion. Relief it hadn't been Jake. And that brought with it feelings of guilt.

Jake's life wasn't more important than Peterson's, but he was her partner, and they had a bond. She tried to quash the feeling; it was a natural reaction, and she had no need to feel guilty.

She spotted Rivers sitting on the side of the road, head in his hands. He looked pretty shook up.

Rebecca guessed killing someone would do that to you.

Amy was in the back of a patrol car, face pale and hands clenched nervously. She looked to be in shock. If the killer's aim was to break her down, he was succeeding. This time she hadn't just written about the crime, she had witnessed the murder first-hand.

Seeing Jake approach, she got up, went straight to him and into his arms. Holding her close, he shot Rebecca a look, daring her to say anything.

'Leave it, Angell,' Hickok warned. 'Now is not the time.'

Rebecca got that and understood Amy's turmoil. It didn't stop her worrying for the safety of her partner. The closer he got to Amy, the more worried she became that his guard would slip. Like her, he had worked with Peterson on numerous occasions, had shared a beer with him down at Mahoney's. She knew the anger flashing in his eyes wasn't directed at her, but at the person who had murdered one of their own.

Just be careful, Jake.

This murder came from Amy's book about the cop killer, but it didn't mean any of them were out of the woods yet. The killer was still on the loose and there was one final novel in the series. They were all connected to Amy, making every one of them a target. Jake had gotten closest, and the killer knew that. He was going to want to end on a high, and her partner needed to watch his back.

Hickok headed over to Rivers. Rebecca could tell he was reining in his temper, trying to cut the younger agent some slack.

'So, what happened, Declan?'

Rivers wasn't sobbing, but he was close to tears and the cockiness had gone. Peterson was dead and he had been the man to end his life.

'I don't know. One minute we were going out for food, the next he was in the road behind us. There was something wrong with my engine, I could feel it. I didn't know he was under the car.' He glanced up at Hickok, face distraught, his eyes huge and glassy. 'I swear to God, I didn't know. Oh jeez, I killed him. I killed a cop.' He leant forward, throwing up fresh puke on the pile of sick already dripping into the gutter.

Rebecca screwed up her nose, waited until he had finished.

'When did you last see Peterson? He was in Amy's apartment when you arrived, right?'

'Yeah, I told him about Boaz going sick and that I would be stepping in.' Rivers caught a shaky breath. 'He left. Told Amy he would see her tonight. I thought he'd gone home.'

The killer had to have been waiting for Peterson when he'd left Amy's apartment building. They hadn't yet checked, but Rebecca suspected they would find the officer's car still in the garage.

She hadn't anticipated this murder scenario. Amy Gallaty's fifth book had been about a cop killer who used various methods of dispatch. The car scene had only been described in the story as a threat; the murder hadn't been carried out.

It seemed their killer was improvising and trying to make the deaths more sadistic. And he was speeding up the time frame, having gone from a week to four days and now two between murders, which meant he could strike again as soon as tomorrow.

'You can ride back with me and we'll get your

statement,' Hickok told Rivers. He glanced around, seeing Greg Withers pull up at the scene. 'I need to speak with the pathologist. Clean yourself up and go wait in the car.'

Rivers nodded, didn't attempt to argue.

As they headed over to Withers, Jake stepped into Hickok's path. 'I've got Amy tonight.'

It wasn't a question or a request. Rebecca recognised her partner's tone; knew the matter wasn't open to debate.

Hickok glanced around, saw Amy already sitting in the passenger seat of Jake's car.

'Okay,' he agreed after a moment of hesitation. 'You want her, you've got her.'

Nodding, Jake started to walk back to his car.

'Sullivan?'

He stopped, glanced back at Hickok. 'Yeah?'

'There's one book left.' Hickok gave a twisted smile. 'Keep her safe.'

* * *

Sullivan wanted to swing by his apartment to feed his dog and grab an overnight bag, before going back to Amy's.

She followed him up the communal stairs in a

building not dissimilar to her own, mind tired from trying to analyse the day's events, but also curious to see where he lived. Officer Peterson's murder was playing on a loop in her head. She wished she could make it stop, that she could block out the image of his body lying in the middle of the road. One moment he had been in her apartment drinking coffee and talking to his wife on the phone; the next he had been under the car, powerless to stop them as they drove out of the garage, dragging him behind, the noose tightening around his neck.

Peterson was dead and it was her fault. She had created the method of execution, had put the idea into the killer's head and an innocent man was dead because of her.

She thought about his last moments, knowing how terrified he would have been waiting for the inevitable.

How could another human being do something so horrific?

It was your sick idea in the first place. You might as well have handed the killer a loaded gun.

Amy shivered, wrapping her arms around her body.

Sullivan unlocked the door to his apartment, and she followed him inside.

The narrow entrance hallway led into an open-plan living area, about the same size as hers. Neutral walls were offset by stainless steel and walnut furnishings and a large picture window overlooked the same park Amy's apartment did, but from a different angle.

She heard the tap of nails on the hardwood floor, saw the golden retriever who'd been with him the night they'd met mosey over to greet him. He dropped down to her level and fussed her for a moment before glancing at Amy.

'Grab a seat. I'll just be a couple of minutes.'

She watched him disappear, went to sit on one of the two large leather couches, not unhappy when the dog followed, leaning up against her leg as Huckleberry often did. She stroked her soft velvety ears, felt herself relax slightly.

So this was where Sullivan lived.

The place had a comfortable, homey feel about it. Two framed photographs sat on a bookshelf filled with paperbacks. The titles were mostly biographies, but Amy recognised a couple of James Patterson and Michael Connelly novels among the mix.

Curious, she got up and went to view the photos. Were they of his family?

One she guessed to be a family shot: Sullivan was in it, younger, maybe mid-twenties, with an older couple she guessed to be his parents, another guy and two girls. All shared the same dark hair and eyes. It looked like it had been taken at a party, maybe a barbecue, the dad wearing a cowboy hat and all of them holding bottles of beer.

The other photo was of the two girls in the picture: one wore a wedding dress and they were hugging and smiling for the camera. Had to be sisters. Amy recognised the smile.

'That's Julianne and Peyton.'

Amy jumped, hearing him behind her, feeling a little guilty snooping at his stuff.

'Sisters?' she asked.

'Yeah, it was taken on Julianne's wedding day. Peyton, she's the baby of the family, she was her maid of honour.'

'Is that your mom and dad in the other pic?'

Sullivan nodded, picked up the frame.

'And the bozo on the end is my brother, Kenny. That picture was taken back home at a family barbecue.'

Amy looked at the picture, at the smiling faces. As an only child she couldn't imagine what it was like to have one sibling, let alone three.

'Where's home?' she asked.

'Arden, Georgia. It's just south of Atlanta.'

Ah, that explains the accent.

'They look like nice people. You're lucky. And I like your dad's cowboy hat.' She turned to face him, a half-smile on her face. 'Have you got one of those?'

'Yeah.' His lips curved. 'I've got one around somewhere.'

For a moment he was silent as he studied her. Amy's heartbeat quickened and the loop of Peterson's murder stopped playing in her head.

'Is all of your family back in Georgia?' she asked quietly.

'Yeah, my parents have a farm and my brother and sisters all live nearby.'

'You're close to them?'

'Very.'

'So why did you move away? What brought you to Oregon?' She wanted to understand him, know why he had left a home he clearly loved. Immediately she felt him backing off.

'Work; I got a transfer.'

'How come?'

He was still looking at her, but the smile had gone, replaced with a look of irritation.

'It's not important.' And then he was stepping away, the moment broken. 'Give me a couple more minutes. I need to feed Roxy, see if my neighbour will take her out, then we can go.'

Amy watched him disappear into the kitchen, the dog hot on his heels, feeling a mixture of disappointment and frustration.

What was his story, she wondered, and why was he so damn cagey about his past?

* * *

The mood within Juniper Police Department was sombre. Peterson had been a popular cop and his fellow officers were in shock over his death, particularly the cruel manner in which he had been killed. A few of his colleagues had approached Joel, asking if they could help, making it clear they would be prepared to put in unpaid overtime to help catch the cop killer.

After taking his statement, Joel gave Rivers the rest of the day off, telling him to lie low at the hotel and avoid any reporters who might come snooping around. Word spread quickly that a cop had been murdered and the last thing Joel needed was for them to find out the driver had been an FBI agent who'd been brought in to help work a murder case. They would have a field day.

Until Leon Pruitt, the case had been flying fairly low on the press radar. Sure, there had been a few reporters at each of the murder scenes, but they hadn't made any connection, until Pruitt – probably due to the differing styles of death.

Although Sullivan was watching Amy, he was still working the case from her apartment and liaising with them over any developments. The Melford police had been unable to locate Tucker Johnson; the man seemed to have vanished into thin air. And they had yet to speak with Leslie and Crystal Rooney, though they had managed to talk with the twins' parents.

Deanna and Pete Rooney were shocked at the developments and unwilling at first to believe either of their daughters had been involved. They clearly remembered the night of Amy's car accident, had assumed she had been sleepwalking when it happened. They hadn't seen her after she'd been released from hospital. Amy's parents had held them responsible for what had happened and severed ties. Hopefully their daughters would be able to provide more information.

Leslie Rooney worked as a teaching aide and was away on a school skiing trip in Colorado. She was due back at the weekend, while Crystal lived a few miles out of town but hadn't returned their calls. A drive out to the house, where she lived alone following her divorce, suggested she was also away, but no one was sure where.

Danielle Colton's stepfather still lived locally; her mother having passed away a few years back. He had been of little help: a daytime drinker with vague memories of the night in question and still firmly of the belief Danielle had run away and the police were wasting his time. It was unlikely they would get anything useful from him.

Angell had taken over the search for Gavin from Rivers and spent much of the afternoon trailing round hotels showing Amy's ex-boyfriend's picture, but to no avail. She met Joel back at headquarters early evening, looking despondent and frustrated. He understood how she was feeling.

When were they going to catch a break?

She was in the middle of updating him when her cell phone starting buzzing in her pocket. Pulling it out, she glanced, annoyed, at the screen and killed the call.

'Where was I?' she asked, slipping the phone back into her pocket, gathering her train of thought.

'Who was that?'

'No one.' She still looked irritated. 'So, I've covered all of the hotels and motels on the east side of—'

Her phone buzzed again; she pulled it roughly from her pocket, put it to her ear.

'What do you want, Alan? I'm kind of busy here.'

Joel stifled the smirk. She had no idea quite how exasperated she looked or sounded. Alan wasn't right for her. She just couldn't see it. He listened in on her side of the conversation, able to make out that she was supposed to have done something for her boyfriend and had forgotten. Rather than apologise, she tried to turn the situation around.

'Okay, okay. I will drop everything and head home now. Your samples are clearly more important than a murdered police officer.' Another long pause. She had twisted the argument, making Alan the bad guy. 'I'm on my way.'

Without saying goodbye, Angell killed the call and threw a furious glance at Hickok, as she realised he had heard everything.

'What the hell are you smirking at?'

'Trouble in paradise?'

'Fuck you.'

'Okay.' He broke out into a broad grin at the flustered look on her face. 'Whenever you're ready.'

She shook her head, looking annoyed at herself for biting. 'I need to get home. He's got a delivery arriving I need to be there to collect.'

'At this time of night?'

'It's a friend of his dropping off some samples he needs.' Angell shrugged. 'I guess they might have called by earlier, but I wasn't there so they're coming back. Hell knows why it's so important I have to be there.'

'Why's he out of town again? How many of these plastic spoon conventions do they have a month? If I were you, I'd start questioning if maybe Alan is fooling around on you.'

'He's not fooling around. Don't be stupid.'

'Why wouldn't he be? He never seems to be at home. You not considered it?'

He could see from the look on her face that she hadn't but now was.

'Can you give me a ride?' she asked, ignoring the question.

Joel's grin widened further.

'A ride home, Hickok. A ride home,' she snapped, cheeks reddening at his deliberate misinterpretation of her question.

She had ridden in with Sullivan and used a patrol car to visit the hotels in her hunt for Gavin.

Joel was tempted to tease her some more, but it was getting late and he was hungry. Besides, Angell was going to be home alone, and he was thinking about picking up takeout and then working his way through her front door. If Alan was going to keep being out of town, he might as well take advantage of it.

'Sure. Let me shut down the computer.'

Angell slipped on her jacket and was standing by the door waiting for him when Louise Barton, one of the younger officers in the department, appeared.

'Hey, Detective Angell. I checked out that guy you asked me to.'

Joel frowned, looking up.

What guy?

'Yeah?' Angell was looking interested. 'You turn anything up?'

'I did. I checked the cell phone number you gave me with the phone company and got them to trace the signal. You said this guy was in Europe, right?'

'That's where he's supposed to be, yeah.'

'Well, he's not.' Barton looked pleased with herself. 'They triangulated the signal and it was last used right here in Juniper.'

'No shit.'

'Who are we talking about?' Joel asked, irritated he wasn't in on the loop.

Angell turned to face him, her green eyes glittering

with excitement. She had something; had caught a break. He remembered that look fondly.

'Ryan Caparelli, the friend Amy is dog-sitting for.'

'What about him?'

'Amy and her friends think he's in Europe. They haven't been able to contact him, so I said I'd look into it. Turns out he's right here in Juniper. Now what are the chances of that?'

34

Jake worked from his laptop at the dining table throughout the afternoon, doing research and making calls, trying his best not to disturb Amy who had crashed and burned on the couch, the coffee she had made untouched on the table in front of her.

She was exhausted – the case now taking its toll on her – and he had slipped a cushion beneath her head, smoothed tawny brown locks of hair from her cheek and left her to it.

When she awoke just after eight-thirty, glancing around sleepily, she seemed surprised that dusk was already settling outside.

'You sleep okay?'

'Yeah, thanks.' She glanced at her watch. 'Wow, sorry, I didn't realise I'd been out so long. I didn't mean to doze off.'

'You needed the rest. Besides I've been busy.'

Amy glanced at his laptop, at the pile of notes beside it.

'It really happened, didn't it? Officer Peterson is dead.'

'Yeah, he is.'

She looked thoughtful for a moment before getting up, padding into the kitchen. He heard her rummaging in the refrigerator. 'You want a glass of wine?'

Jake glanced at the cup of coffee he'd recently made. Although wine was tempting, he needed to keep his mind alert and active. 'No thanks.' He looked over at Huckleberry who was lying patiently in his bed considering he hadn't peed in hours. 'We should probably take the dog out before it gets dark.'

Amy sat the wine bottle and glass down on the counter. 'Damn, Huckleberry. Sorry, buddy, I forgot about you.'

'I'd take him myself, but I don't think leaving you here alone is a good idea.'

'It's fine. I could do with the fresh air.' She smiled tightly and Jake knew she was thinking about the implication of his words: that she was no longer safe in her own home. 'I'll go get his lead.'

While he didn't want to scare her, she had to be prepared. They would keep her safe as best as they could, but she needed to stay on her guard. He thought back to the last conversation he'd had with Rebecca, before Amy had woken up. The developments with Ryan Caparelli were worrying and it was difficult to believe he wasn't somehow involved. Until they found out how, they had made the decision to keep the news from Amy. She would find out sooner or later, but right now it would be something else she didn't need to deal with.

* * *

As they walked along the riverbank he broached the subject of therapy.

'Paul Shinnick called me this morning.'

'Okay.'

'He says he's been trying to get hold of you and you're not returning his calls.'

'I know.' Amy kicked at a pebble, rolling it down the bank and into the water. 'He's left me a couple of voicemails.'

'And?'

'And I think I've had enough sessions. What's done is done. I don't want to rehash it any more.'

Jake had expected this reaction.

'It's standard stuff, Amy. He's trying to help you come to terms with the memories you've uncovered.'

'I am coming to terms with them: in my own way.'

'Are you? Because it seems to me you're still reeling from what happened.'

Amy stopped walking, turned on him angrily. 'What are you now, a therapist too?'

It was good to see some fire back in her eyes.

'Just someone trying to help,' Jake told her calmly.

'I don't need your help, and I don't need any more help from Doctor Shinnick. Yes, I'm reeling from what happened. And even more from the fact that some sick psycho is out there using my books as an excuse to kill people I know. But I'll deal with it in my own way.'

'If it doesn't break you first,' Jake muttered, taking a quick step back when Amy looked like she was going to take a swipe at him.

'Stick to the detective stuff, okay?' she snapped. 'And keep the psychoanalytical bullshit to yourself – unless of course you're prepared to share. You want to know all my secrets, but I notice you're not so willing to tell me your own.'

Jake's temper prickled. 'I don't have secrets. I have a past that has nothing to do with this case. Yours does.'

'But I never asked for it. I never asked for any of this. You want me to trust you, you want me to put my faith in you, believe you will keep me safe and catch this asshole. Why should I?'

'Don't make this personal. I'm just doing my job, Amy.'

'Are you?' She held his gaze for a moment, and he saw the frustration and disappointment in her eyes. 'Are you really *just* doing your job?'

When he didn't answer, she shook her head, stormed past him back in the direction of her apartment building.

'Amy!'

'I'm going back. You've got Huckleberry.'

'Amy! Dammit. Come back here.'

Irritated when she ignored him, Jake whistled to the dog. Huckleberry came to him obediently and stood patiently while he clipped on his leash, before hurrying after her.

They walked back up to her apartment in silence.

Back inside, Amy stormed off to her bedroom,

slamming the door hard enough for Jake to know she was pissed. He went to the kitchen, made a fresh pot of coffee, deciding to let her simmer.

It was his own damn fault; he should never have told her he'd seen Shinnick professionally. Now she knew, she was never going to let it drop. As far as he was concerned, the past was the past and he intended for his to stay there.

Amy hasn't had that luxury. Hers has come back to haunt her.

And she would deal with it. Get past it. Telling her about his own problems and why he had seen Shinnick wasn't going to help her.

But she wants to trust you. Let her in.

Annoyed, he took his coffee to the couch and grabbed the TV remote. He was channel hopping when Amy emerged some twenty minutes later. She still looked sulky, but the initial hot wave of anger had evaporated.

'I'm hungry. Do you want something to eat?'

'Sure.'

He watched her as she searched the contents of the refrigerator. 'I have some leftover chilli I can heat up. That okay?'

'Sure,' he repeated.

She warmed up the food and they ate in silence,

Amy accompanying her chilli with a large glass of wine. Jake watched her drain it empty, refill the glass again, and bit his tongue to resist pointing out that alcohol was not the way forward. Amy wasn't in the mood for any more of his advice. He sighed in frustration, realising he was going to have to open up if he wanted to get her back into Shinnick's office.

'Why do you want to know about my past so badly?' he asked. She looked up, surprised by the question.

'I told you. You know everything about me. I want to know something about you.'

'You already know stuff about me,' he pointed out lightly. 'You know I have a dog called Roxy. You know I come from Arden, Georgia, that I have two sisters and a brother. What else do you want to know? I'm a big Falcons fan? I have a thing for Mexican food? I almost quit the force a few years back to buy a horse ranch?'

'Really, you nearly quit?'

'I thought about it for a while. I love horses; used to work with them back on my parents' farm.'

'Is that why you saw Shinnick, because you nearly quit?'

Damn it, Amy. You won't let it drop.

He sat back in his seat and studied her.

'Okay, I will tell you why I saw Shinnick, but if I do

I want you to promise me you'll go back and finish your sessions. Deal?'

She was silent, and he could see the conflict as she wavered between wanting to know about his past and not wanting to go back to the doctor. Eventually she caved.

'Okay, deal.'

Jake drew in a breath. He would tell her what had happened, but only hoped he wouldn't live to regret it.

* * *

Rebecca sat in the passenger seat of Hickok's car, the giant pizza box on her lap and the aroma of melted cheese and pepperoni attacking her nostrils.

He had insisted on stopping for a takeaway and then made her hold the damn thing, and she knew it was all part of a ploy to get inside her front door. The pizza was huge. No way was he planning to eat the whole thing himself. No, he knew Alan was out of town again and was banking on inviting himself in for dinner.

She told herself when the time came, she would summon up the willpower to send him on his way. His dirty little pizza trick wasn't going to work.

And neither were his continual digs about Alan

and insinuations that he might be cheating on her, which he had stepped up now he had her trapped in his car. Alan wouldn't cheat on her. He wasn't the type. Was he?

'Has your mom met him yet? I'll bet your mom loves him, doesn't she?'

'Yes, and yes.' Rebecca rolled her eyes.

'Guess he ticks all of the boxes for her: safe, stable, inoffensive; able to cater to all her picnicking needs.'

'You're not funny.'

'I'll bet she's already planning your big day. Alan will probably want a picnic theme – sandwiches and blankets in the backyard. You can have your own monogrammed plastic forks and spoons.'

'Sure, whatever you say, Hickok.'

'Alan and Rebecca. No, it would be Alan and Becky, wouldn't it? That's what he likes to call you, right?'

Don't bite.

'In fact, Becky and Alan would work better, cos you're the one wearing the balls in your relationship.'

Rebecca scowled at him, her temper simmering. 'You don't even know him. You have no idea what kind of man he is.'

'One you have wrapped around your finger. Or so you think.'

'What?'

Hickok grinned at her, nodding.

'I heard your conversation earlier, chewing the guy out because you forgot to collect his delivery, making it out to be his fault.'

'I did not.'

'Sure you did, Angell. I'll bet he's constantly walking on eggshells around you, trying to keep you happy. No wonder he's probably straying.'

'Too far, Hickok. You've gone too far.'

'Well why else would he keep disappearing at the weekend? If he spends it with you, he has to leave his balls at the front door.'

'Stop the car.'

They were only a couple of blocks from her townhouse. She would walk it.

'Stop the car, Hickok,' she repeated when he failed to slow. 'Do it now before I punch you in the face.'

He grinned at her threat.

'And to think I was gonna share my pizza with you.'

'You are not coming in my house.'

'Why not? You haven't got any other plans.'

'I don't need to have other plans. You're not setting foot inside my house.'

'Come on, Angell. I have pizza. I know you're a cheap date.'

'You'll have pizza on your face if you don't shut up.'

Deciding to ignore him, she glanced out of the window, furious with Hickok, but more so with herself for biting.

Every time, Rebecca. He gets you every time.

And the stuff he said about Alan, about how she had him wrapped around her finger and he had to leave his balls at the front door. It wasn't true.

Was it?

She thought back to their earlier conversation. Had she turned the tables on him, making him out to be the bad guy? And was he seeing someone else behind her back? He'd said he was meeting with someone, but it had all been rather sudden that he had to go away this weekend. Maybe he was hooking up with another woman behind her back. Perhaps that was why he wanted to talk to her, to call time on things because he had met someone else.

She quashed the concerns as Hickok pulled up outside her house.

The porch light was on. That was odd. She was certain she'd turned it off before she'd left that morning. She must have forgotten.

Without a word she dumped the pizza box on

Hickok's lap, grabbed her purse and got out of the car, slamming the door behind her.

Before she had even stepped off the sidewalk, she heard his door open and close, and his footsteps close behind as she walked up the steps.

'I said no, Hickok.'

He held the pizza box under one arm and the grin on his face was full of pure cocky confidence. Why would he never take her seriously? Why did he think she would always give in?

'Come on, Angell. I got your favourite toppings.'

'You are not gonna win me over with pizza this time.'

He nodded, set the box down.

'Okay, well how about this?'

Without warning he cupped his hand behind her head, pulled her to him and kissed her hard. Momentarily shocked, Rebecca tried to push him away, but then she yielded, her body reacting to his automatically. He deepened the kiss, pulling her close as his hands slid down her back to grab her ass. Rebecca moaned as everything melted inside her.

What the hell are you doing? You have a boyfriend.

Coming to her senses, she shoved him hard.

Hickok let go of her, took a step back, and smiled smugly.

'What the hell was that?' Rebecca demanded.

'*That*? That was hot.'

When the smile widened to a grin, she slapped him hard across the face.

Jesus, Rebecca. What were you thinking?

What about Alan? How could she do this to him?

Alan doesn't kiss like that. Alan has never kissed you like that. Fuck it.

Giving in to the urge she grabbed hold of Hickok, pulled him close again, slamming her mouth against his, need immediately building.

As they groped like a couple of horny teenagers on her doorstep, she reached for her keys, fishing them out of her purse and dropping it to the floor. While Hickok nibbled at her ear, she fumbled with the lock, finally getting the door open, and they stumbled inside.

Rebecca managed to hook her purse with her foot, pull it into the hall before the door slammed shut and Hickok had her pressed hard against it. Preoccupied, she failed to notice the mail from the mat had been stacked neatly on the hall table.

Greedily she reached down, ripping the buttons off his shirt, feeling the familiar warm flesh against her palms. 'Upstairs.'

'No, the living room.' She felt his lips curve against hers. 'Let's do it on the couch for old time's sake.'

Rebecca was already tugging at his belt as they made their way into the dark room.

'Hurry up and get your pants off,' she demanded as he slipped his hands under her blouse, worked the straps of her bra.

Light spilled onto the room, and she drew her head up from Hickok's neck.

What the hell?

She stopped sharp, taking in the shocked faces watching the two of them.

Alan; her sisters, Wendy and Jess; Wendy's husband, Keith; her mom and dad; Alan's mom.

Why were they all here? What was going on?

A little dazed she pulled back from Hickok, turned to her family. 'What the fuck? What are you all doing here?'

Her mother's face was a picture, while the expressions of those around her were either stony or shocked. Only Jess appeared to find the situation amusing.

The silence seemed to drag on forever, before eventually Sarah Angell found her voice.

'I think the more appropriate question is, what are you doing, Rebecca?' She scowled at her daughter, threw a filthy look at Hickok, her gaze dropping to Rebecca's blouse, hanging undone, her bra on show.

Self-consciously Rebecca covered herself up. She glanced at Alan who had so far remained quiet. The expression on his face was one of humiliation. He had something clenched in his fist, she noted.

'Alan.' Lost for words she took a step towards him, flinched when his hand came up and he threw a tiny box at her. As it dropped to the floor he pushed past her, storming out of the room. His mom followed, giving Rebecca a scathing look. Rebecca glanced at the box on the floor: a ring box.

Oh, dear God. He was going to propose. Shit.

She glanced briefly at Hickok, who for once had the decency to look contrite as he discreetly did up his fly.

Her dad and Wendy were shaking their heads, Jess sniggering behind her hand, while Keith looked on embarrassed. Sarah Angell stepped forward; her disappointment clear.

'Mom?'

'Save it, Rebecca. *Hurry up and get your pants off*? Is this how I raised you? What kind of lady are you?' She turned to Hickok. 'And you, stay away from my daughter.'

Without another word she stormed from the room.

Rebecca started to go after her. This was on the same level as the couch incident. No, scrub that. This was worse, much worse.

'Mom!'

A hand grabbed her shoulder.

'Leave it a while. Let her blow off steam.'

Rebecca turned to her older sister.

'I can't believe you're all here, Jess. Oh my God, how did I not see this coming?'

'It was Alan and Mom. They've been in cahoots for weeks. Alan even stole your ring so he could get it measured.' Jessica Angell grinned, seeming to find the whole situation highly amusing. 'I told them this was a bad idea.' She turned to Hickok, gave him a sly smile. 'So, I'm guessing you're the FBI guy, right? I've heard a lot about you.'

'Jess!' Rebecca felt her cheeks flame. Discretion had never been her sister's strongest quality.

She glanced at Wendy, her middle sister, who was eyeing Hickok with disapproval. She was the good daughter of the family, and the shining example her sisters were supposed to follow. If Sarah Angell had her way, all three of her daughters would be married baby machines, living down the road from each other in Swallow Falls.

'Well, I hope you're happy with what you've done,' Wendy snapped.

Hickok turned to Rebecca, ignoring the remark. He looked somewhere between amused and embarrassed.

'You know what, Angell. Maybe I should just go. Let you catch up with your family.'

'Catch up with them?' Rebecca shook her head flustered. He was right, though. It was better if he left. 'Yes. Just go, Hickok. I'll see you in the morning.'

As he left the room, she looked over to her father who'd remained quiet through the whole episode. His lips were pulled in a tight line, his jaw twitching, a sign Rebecca knew meant he was irritated. Unlike her mom, he tended to shy away from drama, preferring a quiet life. The way he was looking at her made Rebecca feel as though she was sixteen again.

'Um, Dad, I'm sorry I...'

'I don't want to hear it, Rebecca. Alan is the one you should be apologising to. You should go find him. I'll get your mother to give you a call tomorrow when she has cooled down.'

He paused by her, as he started to walk out of the room, touched her arm and started to say something, before changing his mind. Instead, he just shook his head and left. Wendy was hot on his heels with Keith trotting after her. She always had been the goody two shoes and deep down probably loved that this would earn her extra brownie points with their parents.

Jess caught Rebecca's hand, squeezed it. 'It'll blow over. Give it a few days. I told Mom this was a really stupid idea.'

That was her older sister, so laid-back and optimistic. Rebecca just hoped she was right.

* * *

He whistled cheerfully as he made his way to the storage unit. Everything was going to plan; the pieces all falling into place. Once inside, and certain he hadn't been seen, he hit the light and closed the door, before popping the lid on the trunk.

He went about feeding the man inside. It was McDonalds again; a little repetitive and not good for a regular diet, but in this case it was of no consequence. Fast food burgers wouldn't be the death of him.

The man ate and drank greedily. The first time he had struggled, trying to escape. Now he realised it was futile and, as his strength waned and his body cramped in the small trunk, he was reliant upon the one meal a day, knowing he needed it to keep him alive.

Not that being alive was a mercy. The trunk was beginning to stink, filled with the pungent odours of sweat, urine and faeces. With the warm June weather, it must be hell being locked up all day in such a confined space, but he couldn't risk taking the man outside to go to the bathroom. Besides, it wouldn't be for much longer. Soon it would be time to move this player into position. The years of careful planning all came down to this.

The game was about to move to a new level.

35

'I killed someone.'

Amy wasn't expecting that. She took a large sip of wine, studied Sullivan's face, expecting him to smirk, tell her he was kidding, but he didn't.

'Okay, but you're a cop. You killed a bad guy, right?' When he didn't answer, she reached out, grabbed hold of his hand. 'What happened?'

'I was a rookie, couple of years into the job, and my partner and I were first responders to a domestic. It was an address we were familiar with. Bruce Corbin and his wife, Loretta, lived there. Bruce worked construction. He was an okay guy when he was sober, but he had a temper, and a jealous streak. Add alcohol to the mix and he became paranoid, violent.

'We'd gone to his address before. He would have a few beers, use Loretta as a punching bag, we'd get a call from the neighbours, show up, arrest him and he'd sleep it off in the cells. Next morning Loretta always turned up begging us to release him. She'd claim she'd fallen or walked into a door. We tried to get her to press charges, but she wouldn't consider it.'

Amy knew the type. She'd had a friend at college who'd been beaten up by her boyfriend, had refused to accept his actions, preferring to blame herself every time he hit her. She understood Sullivan's frustration, but also the woman's perspective. David had never been physically violent towards her, but he had been mentally abusive, slowly wearing her down. She had been strong enough to tell him to leave, but she'd had to build the strength up to do it. It hadn't been an overnight decision.

'So what happened? Bruce Corbin – he's the one you killed, right?'

Sullivan didn't answer her; instead, he gave her hand a slight squeeze before continuing.

'So, Christmas Eve '97, dispatch gets a call. It's Corbin's neighbour. Bruce has been drinking and there are screams coming from inside the house. I'm on patrol with my partner and we're closest, so we take the call. We pull up out front and as we're getting out of the car there's a gunshot.

'We radio for backup. They tell us to wait, say another car is on its way. But then there's a scream and my partner, Denny, he doesn't think there's time to wait. Corbin has a couple of young kids. If he's drunk and waving a gun around the situation could turn bad fast. I was with him all the way. Back then I was reckless, too cocksure. I wanted to be the hero, take him down and save the day.'

He smiled bitterly, looking annoyed at himself for who he had once been.

Huckleberry brushed past Amy's leg. He stopped by Sullivan, settling down by his feet.

'So you went in the house? I don't think that was stupid. You put yourself in a dangerous situation to try and help someone. I think you were both very brave.'

'Okay then, brave and stupid. We'd been told to wait. They tell you that for a reason. We should have followed procedure.'

'What happened when you went inside?'

'Denny knew Corbin. He took the front door, saying he'd try and reason with him, while I went round back. We figured if he tried anything stupid, I'd have the element of surprise. I came in through the kitchen, could hear Denny and Corbin arguing.

Denny was trying to persuade him to put down the gun, but Bruce was a mean drunk, and he wasn't listening. Loretta was screaming and then there was another gunshot. Bruce was yelling, sobbing, and Loretta had gone quiet. As I turned the corner I could see Loretta lying on the floor in a pool of blood.

'Denny was reaching for his sidearm, still trying to reason with him, pull him away from the body, when Bruce turned and punched him in the face. The gun went flying. I had my weapon drawn; I told him to drop the gun. He moved quickly, had Denny in a headlock and the gun pointed at his temple.'

Amy was no fool. She knew the police dealt with dangerous situations on a daily basis. She'd written about a fictitious cop. But hearing this first-hand drove it home how dangerous the job was.

'What happened?'

'I made a split-second decision, pulled the trigger. I don't know if he sensed I was going to, but Corbin moved. The bullet hit Denny in the chest. I killed my partner.'

'Jesus.' Amy hadn't been expecting that. She'd forced Sullivan to tell her and now she understood why he hadn't wanted to. 'It wasn't your fault. It was an accident.'

'Yeah, so a dozen sessions with the police shrink

told me. I've dealt with it, but it doesn't stop it being wrong. If we'd followed procedure, it wouldn't have happened in the first place.'

'What happened to Corbin?'

'After I put a bullet in Denny, I put one in him. He still had his weapon and was about to take me down. The wound wasn't fatal, and he stood trial for Loretta's murder. He was found guilty and is serving time. I got a rap on the knuckles, had to face a disciplinary hearing, but they let me stay on the job. It was around that time I started thinking about a career change and maybe buying the ranch.'

'You didn't, though.'

'No, I didn't. I love the job. It was hard for a while, and I had a lot of guilt riding on my shoulders. I worked with the shrink, used the guilt to try and make myself a better cop. I made detective, worked a couple of big homicide cases, but it was still hard to shake off the memories of Denny. That's why I put in for the transfer, so I could make a fresh start. I moved here with my girlfriend, Lara, and the shrink back in Atlanta referred me to Shinnick, said if I ever wanted to talk through stuff, he was the man. I did a few times in the first year. If I hit a rough patch, felt I'd made a bad decision, he helped me get past it. We kept in touch.'

'And what happened to Lara?' Amy kept the question light.

Sullivan had told her he wasn't married, but he'd never said he wasn't in a relationship. She'd seen no trace of the woman in his apartment, and this was the first time he'd ever mentioned her, but still, she couldn't be certain.

The way he looked at her, dark eyes narrowing, had her squirming a little. She was being nosy and for personal reasons, and he understood that. Her cheeks started to burn.

You can't help yourself, can you, Amy?

'We broke up.' He left it at that, letting go of her hand and sitting back in the chair. 'Okay, Amy. So now you know everything there is to know about me and why I saw Shinnick. I've held up my part of the bargain. Tomorrow, you go back to see the doc. Deal?'

She wasn't happy about it, but he was right, he had held up his end of the deal and she felt pretty crappy for making him relive what had happened. She would have to go.

'Sure, deal.'

She got up, set about clearing the table, taking their plates and her wine glass through to the kitchen. While she ran hot soapy water in the sink, Sullivan went out through the patio doors, Huckleberry at his side.

She guessed he wanted a moment alone. Okay, so she shouldn't have asked, she knew that, but she couldn't bring herself to regret it either. Now she knew and she felt she understood him a little better. Turning off the faucet, she dumped the plates and glass in the sink, left them there to soak and went out to join him.

He had his back to her, shoulders broad, the light breeze playing with his hair as he leant against the balcony wall, looking out over the parkland where the trees were silhouetted by the moonlight. Stars littered the clear night sky. It was pretty, it was peaceful and it was a brief lull in the storm they were riding.

Tentatively she touched his shoulder. He still wore his work suit but had discarded the jacket and tie, and the warmth of his skin heated the thin material of his shirt. This was wrong and she had promised Detective Angell nothing was going to happen, but at this moment in time Amy didn't care. She ran her hand over his collar, her fingers into his hair, felt him stiffen slightly.

He straightened, turning to face her, and her hand fell away.

'We can't do this, Amy.'

By way of response she took hold of both his hands, stepped forward and lightly brushed her lips against his. When he stilled, she edged back an inch and smiled. 'We just did.'

Sullivan was silent for a moment, dark eyes locked on hers, the air charged with tension, then without warning he had hold of her, crushing his mouth against hers. Amy hugged him to her, her hands working their way back up his neck and into his hair as he kissed her deeply, held her hard against him so she was left in no doubt how much he wanted her.

She caught her breath, laced her arms around his neck as he cupped his hands over her ass, lifting her slightly, pinning her against the wall. Wrapping her legs around him, she held on tight.

God, she wanted this. She wanted him so bad.

Yes, it was wrong, but everything happening around them was wrong. She'd had her cut of bad luck recently. Why shouldn't she have this one little thing?

Sullivan pulled back, looked at her. He was breathing hard. And then she saw the change in his expression, saw him take the control back. He eased her down; still kept his arms linked around her and leant his forehead against hers.

'We can't do this.'

'Why?' She hadn't meant the word to sound sharp, but it did. It was the frustration.

Gently he cupped her face in his hands, kissed her again, soft and passionate, before pulling back.

'Because it's wrong: I'm a cop and you're at the centre of this investigation. Yes, I want you, you know that, but we can't.'

Looking vexed with himself at his lack of restraint, he stepped back, shaking his head before going back inside her apartment.

Amy closed her eyes, drew in a deep shaky breath. He was right, she did know that, but it didn't make it any easier to swallow.

Damn you, Jake Sullivan.

* * *

Down below, in the safety of the trees, he watched, noted they were at it again. This time they couldn't pretend nothing was going on, that it was an innocent embrace.

Amy was now alone on the balcony. She looked annoyed, unhappy. Lovers' tiff? He slipped back into the shadows, made his way down to where he had parked his car.

It wouldn't be much longer before Amy Gallaty realised there was more in life to worry about than having a broken heart.

36

There were two breaks in the case on Saturday, both providing answers but throwing up several more questions in the process.

Boaz had recovered from his bout of food poisoning and was back looking after Amy. Jake was glad when he showed up, keen to get out of Amy's apartment and clear his head. Things had been tense between them after the kiss. Amy didn't understand, or want to understand, the implications, and he'd been a fool to lead her on.

He had spent a restless night on the couch, the scents of her shampoo, her perfume, of her, clogging his senses, making it hard to focus on anything other than kissing her, needing again the taste of her mouth and the feel of her body against his.

He was a damn idiot. Rebecca had warned him, but he hadn't listened, had thought he had it under control. Hard as it would be, he needed to stay away from Amy for a while. She was messing with his head.

When he walked into the precinct, he hoped his transgressions weren't too obvious for his partner to notice. Rebecca could be annoyingly intuitive at times.

She seemed rather subdued, not her usual self, and he noted the sudden change in atmosphere when Hickok walked into the room a couple of minutes later. It felt a little like the frigid one he'd left in Amy's apartment, and he immediately picked up that the two of them were avoiding eye contact.

What had he missed yesterday?

Rivers followed contritely after Hickok, his tail still between his legs.

Jake had a certain amount of sympathy for him. There was no denying the guy was an idiot, but he'd been set up and now had to live with the consequences of killing a police officer.

He knew how that part felt.

With several hotels still to check for David Gavin, Rebecca and Rivers both worked that angle, while Hickok and Jake headed over to Ryan Caparelli's place for clues to his whereabouts. It was his apartment that threw up the first revelation.

Jake and Hickok met with the super, who was affable enough to let them have a quick look inside for any sign of Caparelli. From his shifting eyes, the way he bent over backwards to accommodate them, Jake suspected he wanted them out of his hair. An ex-criminal who didn't want attention drawn to his rap sheet; he would bet good money on it.

Caparelli lived on the first floor; patio doors led out to the communal grounds, which included a swimming pool and tennis court. While there was no sign of anyone being home, the refrigerator empty and the super vouching he hadn't seen Caparelli in over two weeks, the mail had been piled up onto a side table. If he was away, who had done that?

Without a warrant they couldn't search the place, so they did a quick sweep of each room, looking for cause to need one. It was the bathroom that gave them the cause: a speck of blood on the back of the door. Jake noticed it as he was about to leave the room.

Maybe Caparelli had cut himself shaving, but the blood was nowhere near the sink. There could be a logical explanation, but it still needed checking out.

They thanked the super and Hickok made a call. They had the warrant signed and were back in Caparelli's apartment by lunchtime, this time with Withers and his bloodstain pattern analyst, a smart young redhead named Hannah. While Withers and Hannah worked in the bathroom, Hickok and Jake conducted a thorough search of the rest of the apartment.

The discovery of Caparelli's passport in a desk drawer in the bedroom verified he was in the country, while the screwed-up ticket in the trash can for a Portland to Paris flight confirmed he had never made it to Europe. His clothes were hanging in the closet and the suitcase they found under the bed was empty.

So, where the hell was Ryan Caparelli and what part did he play in all of this? Was it his blood in the bathroom or did it belong to someone else?

A further clue to his involvement was found in a bag stashed in a cupboard under the kitchen sink: plastic sheeting, towels, rope and reams of used duct tape, all of it soaked in blood. Seconds after Jake made the discovery, Withers called them through, stepping out of the bathroom and pulling the door closed after him, leaving Hannah to work the scene.

'Gentlemen, we have ourselves a crime scene.' He smiled grimly. 'Lucky for us, you spotted the blood – and also lucky for us, our killer missed it when cleaning up. We sprayed luminol on the walls and in the tub to see what he did clean up. Someone turned that bathroom into an abattoir.'

'Which ties in with the bag we've found,' Jake muttered, glancing at Hickok.

The Fed nodded his head, as he thought things over. 'How quickly do you think you can get a match?' he asked Withers.

'We'll get it over to the lab now. Start working on it straightaway.'

'Good.' Hickok looked at Jake. 'In the meantime, we'd better get another warrant – for the arrest of Ryan Caparelli.'

* * *

Rebecca struck gold with David Gavin late Saturday afternoon. She had been glad to get out on the road, to have some time alone with her thoughts so she could process what had happened the previous evening. Damn it! How had she not seen Alan's proposal coming? She was a police detective, for chrissakes.

Because you weren't interested. You've been too preoccupied with the case, and with Hickok.

She had kissed him. Hell, had they not been interrupted she would have done a lot more than just kiss him. What had she been thinking? But she couldn't bring herself to regret it.

Kissing Hickok had knocked it home that she didn't feel the same passion for Alan. Yes, Alan might be kind and grounded and reliable, and the perfect choice for her mother, but without passion, was he the right choice for her?

'Give it time,' Sarah Angell had told her, when she had finally calmed down enough to have a rational conversation with her daughter. 'The passion might not be there now, but you can grow to love him. Marriage isn't just about attraction; it's about companionship and having someone steady and supportive by your side.'

Rebecca wasn't sure she agreed, but she kept her opinions to herself, figuring enough damage had been done. She had yet to speak with Alan; knew she had to have the conversation, but hadn't been able to face up to it. For now, it was easier to throw herself into her work.

She was down to a final four places to check and beginning to think they were wasting their time, that perhaps Gavin was holed up with a friend and they had been approaching this from the wrong angle, when she pulled into the parking lot of the Marine Bay Motel, a cheap looking establishment a few miles west on the coastal road and on the periphery of their search area.

A young girl, no older than eighteen, manned the reception, cowboy boots on the desk and popping gum as she read a magazine. She barely glanced up as Rebecca entered. From the number of keys hanging on the hooks behind the desk, not many of the rooms were let. No real surprise as the place was rundown and unappealing.

'Good afternoon, my name is Detective Angell with the Juniper Police Department.' Rebecca flashed her badge, stifling a laugh when the girl nearly fell off her chair trying to get her feet down from the desk. She looked up at Rebecca, giving her full attention, expression anxious and expectant.

'How can I help you?'

Rebecca passed her the picture of Gavin.

'We're looking for this man and believe he may be staying in the area. Have you seen him at all?'

She didn't expect the girl to recognise Gavin. This place was further out of the city than the others she had checked, and she had almost scrubbed it from the list, believing it to be a waste of time. So she was surprised when the girl nodded her head.

'Yeah, I know him. He's the guy in room twenty-six.' She glanced at the register. 'David Gavin.'

Rebecca's heartbeat quickened. They were desperate for a lead. Was this the one they needed? 'When did Mr Gavin check in?'

'A couple of weeks back.' The girl pulled a face. 'Most people stop for the night, passing through on their way to someplace, but not him. Guess he's new in town or something and needing a place to stay. He keeps himself to himself, paid to have the room for a month and in cash. My old man liked that. So how come you're looking for him? Is he like, a fugitive or something?'

'Can you show me his room please?' Rebecca asked, ignoring the question.

The girl shrugged. 'I guess so.'

She pulled a ring of keys from a drawer in the desk, led Rebecca outside to the row of motel rooms. 'He wanted one giving him privacy. Weird guy, didn't even want maid service, but as I say, he paid cash a month up front, so we didn't argue.'

They stopped outside the end room. Rebecca noted the cheap floral curtains were drawn.

'I'd better knock in case he's in there,' the girl told her. 'I doubt he is; he goes out a lot.'

She rapped her knuckles on the door, waited a moment before finding the key she needed. As she eased open the door, Rebecca smelt the stale odour of male sweat. The girl flicked on the switch, throwing light onto the unmade bed, the open suitcase with clothes piled high. Several empty bottles of beer sat on the floor and a half bottle of vodka was on the dresser, next to a fancy camera.

Rebecca entered the room, went to the camera and turned it on. It was digital and she flicked through the various shots, recognising the ones of Amy playing with her dog, the picture of Jake holding her.

So Gavin was their photographer. Was he also their killer?

At best he was a jealous ex-boyfriend with a grudge against Amy. At worst he was a vicious killer claiming the lives of people she knew. Neither option boded well for her partner.

* * *

This time there was no food for the man in the trunk of the car in the storage unit. He would require feeding again before he died, but it would have to wait. There were more important things to take care of first.

He went about business quickly, performing a per-functory glance in the trunk to check the man was still breathing and hadn't managed to loosen his bonds, before pulling the car out of the unit and replacing it with his own. This one needed to stay alive. He couldn't die too early.

He smiled to himself, musing how easy it had been to fool him into coming to the beach house the night Nadine had died. He had shown up, believing they could be partners in taking Amy Gallaty down and, with the element of surprise and the taser, he had been quickly overpowered. The man hadn't expected that and certainly hadn't expected to find himself spending the next week bound and gagged in the trunk of a car.

Life could be cruel, and it was regrettable he'd been taken so soon, but the police were closing in on him. If they had found him and arrested him, he would not be able to play out his role in the game. And it was a very important role.

Pulling out of the storage facility, he indicated left and pulled out onto the highway, careful to adhere to the speed limit. He couldn't risk drawing undue attention to the vehicle and they had a long journey ahead of them.

* * *

Angell had just arrived back at the precinct when Joel got the call from Withers.

Sullivan was still over at Ryan Caparelli's apartment and had spent the remainder of the afternoon questioning his neighbours, hoping to find someone who had seen him. Rivers was already back, having been called off the search after Angell had located David Gavin's motel room.

He was still subdued following Peterson's death. Maybe he was re-evaluating his career choice, realising the FBI wasn't the right path for him.

Joel doubted it, but he could hope. He met Angell's eyes briefly, as he answered the call, grinning at her when she scowled at him.

She had been quick to shunt him out of the door the night before, keen to try and explain things to her family. He wasn't sure quite how she'd planned on doing that, given she'd been caught trying to get his pants off.

While he was sorry about how things had turned out, felt a little bad for Alan, even though the guy was a douche, he didn't regret what had happened. It had been on the cards with Angell and brewing for a while. She might want to pretend she didn't feel anything, but he knew she did. Last night had proved it.

Watching her walk over to her desk, his gaze dropped to her rear, and he wondered when he would get another chance to have his hands on it. Distracted, he almost missed what Withers had said.

'Repeat that. What did you say?'

'I said we got a match on the blood,' Withers told him. 'It's not Caparelli's. It's Leon Pruitt's. Caparelli's bathroom is where our doorman friend was murdered.'

* * *

He arrived in Melford just before dark, had time to park the car in a location he knew wouldn't be discovered, before making his way down the street to Leslie Rooney's house.

She had been out of town and was due to return home later in the evening. Like her sister, she lived alone. Love hadn't been kind to the Rooney twins. Crystal had sworn off men after a soulless marriage to her college sweetheart ended when she caught him in bed with her best friend, while Leslie had remained single, having flings with numerous married men and never managing to persuade any of them to leave their wives.

He broke into the house easily, knowing exactly how to gain entry through the back patio door. That was the thing with the inhabitants of small towns.

They believed they were safe, and their security was usually lax.

While he waited for her return, he took the time to familiarise himself with what she had done to the house. It was typically girly with ditzy prints and a lot of bright colour. The bathroom contained several flowery creams and lotions in pretty bottles and a childhood doll sat on the comforter at the end of her bed. There was no sign of any man here, he thought, catching a glimpse of himself in her free-standing mirror. Except him, of course.

Leslie was a voracious reader, and she had a large collection of books. He looked for titles by Amy Gallaty, but she was a romantic at heart and all her novels were fluffy love stories.

He had been waiting at home for just over an hour when she returned, and he moved to hide behind the door in her bedroom. He heard her downstairs, dumping her stuff and locking the door. The aroma of Chinese food drifted up the stairs, reminding him he hadn't had time to eat. He heard her gathering plates and cutlery, the pop of a wine cork and then the sound of the television.

As he had hoped, she came upstairs before sitting down to eat. Hearing her approach the bedroom, he clenched his fists, readying.

She entered the room, kicked off her shoes and unhooked her earrings. Raising her head, she glanced in the mirror and he caught sight of her shocked expression as he approached from behind, covering her mouth with a gloved hand as she tried to scream. As she kicked and thrashed, he put his free hand round her throat and squeezed, raising her from the floor and watching her reflection in the mirror as she tried to pull his fingers away, her stockinged feet pummelling his knees as she fought to free herself.

He choked her harder, watching the light fade in her eyes, eventually felt her legs go still and her body limp. Laying her on the bed, he checked for a pulse, before going downstairs and making himself at home in front of the television.

He picked up the plate of Chinese food, tasted it, and sipped at the wine. No need to waste good food. He was hungry and a little nostalgic. He deserved a half-hour break before finishing the rest of the night's tasks.

37

After Cap left town, Troy withdrew, upset at losing the one friend he could connect with.

He worked hard at school, knowing the only way he would escape Melford would be to excel academically, and he did so, graduating and getting accepted at Cornell University in New York to study for a degree in computer science.

It was during the first summer break back home in Melford that he met Nadine Williams, a sullen girl with a bad attitude who had been kicked out of her parents' house and taken in by her sympathetic aunt.

Nadine was a couple of years older than Troy, hard work to be around and acted as if the world owed her a favour. She wasn't soft and pretty in a natural way like Amy, but there was still a connection and something special about her.

His parents disagreed. Nadine Williams was trash. She had a criminal record for shoplifting, had dropped out of high school and drifted aimlessly through an array of dead-end jobs before moving to Melford. Her aunt had pulled some strings, persuaded the owner of the local diner to take her on, but did their hard-working son really want to hook up with a waitress?

Troy didn't listen to them. He was already fixated on Nadine and spent the first two weeks of his summer vacation sitting in a booth in the diner, sipping coffee, and watching her as she worked. At first, she seemed irritated by the attention, but eventually she relented and agreed to go out with him; he went to pains to make her feel special, knowing he had to win her over. By the end of summer, she was putty in his hands.

This was good. He needed this one. This one was special.

And so, their relationship blossomed, much to the Cunninghams' chagrin. Troy had at least been a positive influence on Nadine, who kept her head down and, although still sullen, toed the line and held on to her job in the diner, living for the promise that once he graduated, he would take her away from Melford and they would start a life together.

It was during his third year at Cornell that Troy ran into Cap. His old friend had not long graduated high school and was in New York staying at his father's plush apartment. It was good to see him and the years apart melted away as they settled straight back into the easy friendship they had once shared.

It was after watching a ball game at Cap's dad's place that the subject of Tucker Johnson came up.

'I wish I had been there with you the night it had happened.'

'What night?' Troy asked, knowing full well what his friend was referring to.

'The night in the basement with the girl. I'm guessing you never told anyone else?'

Troy was silent for a moment. Cap was the only one who knew he'd been there. 'No, no one else knows.'

'I would have liked to have been there; to see it happen.'

'Why?'

'You know, to see what he did to her.'

'That's sick, man.'

'Is it?' Cap grinned and Troy was unsure if he was

fooling around or not. 'Is it sick? Did it not turn you on just a bit, seeing her all chained up?'

'I was just a kid.'

'But old enough to have a crush on a girl. What was her name, the one who got away?'

'Amy.'

'You ever hear any more about her?'

'Not since she got out of hospital and went back home.'

'I bet she still thinks about that night and what would have happened if she hadn't gotten away. I wonder why she never told the police.'

Troy shrugged and took a sip of his beer. 'I dunno. I guess she had her reasons.'

'You didn't tell.'

'No.'

'I bet it's because you liked what you saw.'

'I did not.' Colour heated Troy's cheeks as anger bubbled inside. 'I didn't tell because I didn't want to get into trouble.'

'Liar.'

'I am not.'

'You couldn't wait to tell me about the basement, show me where it was. Admit it: you've thought about that night a lot.'

Troy had, but he wasn't going to admit anything.

'What if you knew you couldn't get caught?' Cap continued. 'If you knew you were safe, and no one would ever find out. Wouldn't you like to know what it felt like to have that power over someone?'

'You mean kill them?'

'I mean have some fun with them, do whatever you want to them, and then of course you would have to kill them so they couldn't tell.'

'Why would you want to do that?' Troy gripped the neck of his beer bottle. His heart was thudding in his chest, and he was appalled by what his friend was saying, though also slightly fascinated. 'It's sick.'

'It's not sick. It's taking what you want. People kill animals for sport or fun. How is it any different? Some people say it's cruel; well, how is taking a human life any different?'

'Because humans don't kill other humans. It's wrong.'

'And who decided on that rule? If you have the courage to do it, why shouldn't you take what you want? Take your friend, Amy. I bet she never gave you a second glance. Imagine having power over her, to be able to do anything you wanted to her, to hold her life in your hands. She would notice you then.'

'You're talking about murder.'

'It's not murder if you get away with it.'

'This is a stupid conversation.' Troy necked the rest of his beer, placed the empty bottle on the table and got up. 'I need to use the bathroom.'

He made his way down the long hallway, taking in the expensive prints and furnishings and thinking Cap's dad must be loaded, and shut the bathroom door, glad to have a moment away from the conversation. The direction it had taken had made him feel uncomfortable. Was Cap screwing around with him or was he implying he wanted to kill someone for real?

He used the john, washed his hands and splashed cold water over his face, the imprint of Danielle in the basement firmly on his mind.

Cap was waiting for him in the living room, a smile on his lips. 'Do you have any plans this weekend?'

'Studying.' Troy shrugged his shoulders. 'But aside from that, I guess not.'

'Good. My dad has a log cabin upstate. I was thinking we could head up there Friday night, spend the weekend fishing, hunting, having a few beers. What do you reckon?'

Troy was relieved the whole murder conversation had been dropped. Cap must have been dicking with him. 'Yeah, sounds good.'

'I was hoping you would say that. How about I pick you up after class on Friday?'

'Okay.'

Cap's smile widened. 'It'll be a lot of fun.'

* * *

The cabin was a couple of hours north of the city, situated off a dirt track on the edge of a lake, and surrounded by thick forest. The nearest neighbour, Cap informed Troy, was a good three miles away, which meant they could party and go crazy as much as they wanted.

'Are you sure your dad won't mind us being here?'

Cap shook his head. 'He rarely uses the place these days. Busy with his girlfriend. We used to come up here a lot when I was a kid. Spend the day fishing on the lake. I sometimes drive up at the weekend. You're the first friend I've brought here.'

'Well, thanks for the invite.'

Cap grinned, pulling Troy's weekend bag from the back seat and throwing it to him, before scooping up the bag of groceries he'd brought with him. He unlocked the cabin door, nudged it open with the toe of his sneaker, and led the way inside.

Troy whistled, taking in the place. This was no regular log cabin, and, like the New York apartment, the place reeked of money with leather couches and expensive looking furnishings, a huge television set and a wide-open fireplace.

'This place is amazing, Cap; is your dad Steven Spielberg or something?'

Cap laughed. 'Ha, that'd be pretty cool. No, he just has a lot of investments in different things. Come check this out.'

Troy sucked in a breath as Cap unlocked a cabinet to reveal an arsenal of hunting rifles.

'Wow. Your dad doesn't do things by half measures.'

'He has a big knife collection too. As I say, we used to spend a lot of time up here. Anyway, put your stuff down. I have something to show you.'

Troy dumped his bag, followed Cap back out to the car.

This place was amazing: the cabin, the huge lake, the acres of forest. Cap had said they had boats and plenty of fishing equipment, and he couldn't wait to get out on the water.

'Check this out.'

'What is—' Troy turned, stopping short as he stared at the girl trussed up in the trunk of the car, and took a step back, hands flying to his head. 'Jesus, Cap, what the fuck have you done?'

'Troy, meet Melanie. Melanie, meet Troy.'

'Seriously, Cap. What the fuck is going on?'

Melanie stared up at them both, eyes wet as she struggled against the ropes holding her. She whimpered against the tape covering her mouth.

Troy stared at her, trying to comprehend that they had driven all the way up here from New York and she had been in the trunk of the car the whole time. Now it made sense why Cap had got him to dump his stuff on the back seat, saying there was no room in the trunk. He had lost his mind.

'Let her go, Cap.'

'I don't think so. And I know you don't want me to.'

'Yes, I do. This is wrong. Let her go now before this goes too far and we get into trouble.'

'We're not going to get into trouble, Troy. We're not going to get caught. She's a hooker. No one will care she's missing. And even if they do, they won't ever find her.'

In the trunk, Melanie struggled violently and let out a strangled sob.

Looking peeved, Cap slammed the trunk shut. 'Listen to me, Troy. You might pretend, but I know what you're like. You're the same as me. You want this; you just don't realise it yet. I'm going to show you how easy it is to take what you want and not get caught.'

'You've done this before?'

'Once before, about six months ago. It was easy, it was an adrenaline rush and you're going to enjoy it.'

'Sick bastard. Give me the keys.'

'No way. Look around you, Troy. It's just us here and we have the whole weekend to do exactly what we want to her. Now help me get her inside.' Cap popped the trunk open again and grinned down at Melanie. 'Are you ready, sweetheart? We've got big plans for you.'

* * *

Troy thought back to that afternoon with Cap and Melanie. Things had changed then and would never be the same. Downing the full glass of Jack Daniel's he had poured, he got up from the couch, stepped over to the shelf where the framed picture of Nadine and Amy stood. He had snapped it at one of Amy's early book launches and both girls were smiling, happy. He had introduced Nadine to Amy's books, encouraged her to read them and driven her to the book signings, wanting a connection to Amy but not realising how obsessed his girlfriend would become. And now it had led to this. Picking the frame up, he skimmed his thumb across both of their faces.

I'm sorry.

He didn't hear footsteps but felt the presence behind him and, as he turned, looked at the familiar face. He glimpsed the flash of the blade, and was only quick enough to grimace as it plunged into his side.

Searing pain soared through him and he cried out, dropping the frame and automatically putting his hands to the wound. Hot wet blood seeped through his fingers, dripping onto the broken shards of glass. As his legs went weak, he stumbled forward, catching hold of the arm of the couch, cold sweat beading on his forehead as he dropped to his knees.

A dark haze threatened to envelop him.

Fight it. You have to fight it.

But even as he thought the words, a surge of pain rushed through him, knocking him backwards. He felt his limbs go heavy, heard the thud as his head hit the floor; and then the grip of the hand on his collar, yanking him forward.

He stared into those cold eyes he knew so well and listened to the words as they registered in his foggy brain.

'Wake up. We're not done yet.'

38

'But why do I have to go?'

'Because I said so,' Joel snapped, irritated that in less than two days Rivers had gone back to whining like a child. He had cut his partner some slack, understanding he would need time to come to terms with Peterson's death, and for a while there he had seemed contrite, genuinely knocked for six by what had happened. How quickly that had changed.

'I am an FBI agent. I should be here where the crime scenes are. Not in some stupid town in the back end of nowhere.'

'You should be wherever the hell I tell you to be.'

Sending Rivers with Sullivan was a smart idea. Regardless of the attitude, the man had accidentally killed a police officer. Getting away from Juniper, away from the thick of things, was exactly what he needed.

Ryan Caparelli was top of their agenda, with Gavin now a close second, but that didn't mean Melford was off the radar. Tucker Johnson had committed murder, and the local police hadn't been able to locate him. Add to that the connection to Amy, plus the fact the Rooney twins had decided to go AWOL, it needed checking out, and sooner rather than later. Rivers and Sullivan were the right people for the job. That it would leave Joel alone with Angell was purely a coincidence, albeit a convenient one.

Things had been uncomfortable between them since Friday night. It was now Sunday; time to clear the air. So far, they hadn't had a chance to talk, as Sullivan and Rivers had been hanging around. Get them out of the picture and he and Angell would be able to cut straight to the chase.

* * *

Victor Boaz liked Amy Gallaty.

She was smart and sweet, she was really pretty, and she didn't cop him any attitude. So far, looking after her had been a walk in the park. He got to watch TV, she was a good host, looking after him with coffee and snacks, and she was definitely easy to look at. But over the past couple of days, she had become a real pain in the ass.

He had heard a rumour she'd had a thing going on with Sullivan and it had turned sour. Vic hoped it wasn't the case, wanted to respect her enough to think she wouldn't stoop low enough to sleeping with Detective Dixie. Whatever it was, she was sullen and more irritable than usual, restless too, and it was starting to tick him off. Where she went, he had to go, and out to the grocery store, walking the dog and paying visits to her friends was a little too much effort when he had gotten quite used to spending his days on the couch. He had started getting into all the daytime soaps too, and being dragged out to have coffee with her stuck-up friend, Heidi, listening to the two of them talk about Heidi's latest diet and dating dilemmas, meant he was going to miss the outcome of a couple of crucial cliff hangers. Vic wasn't impressed.

Of course they talked about the murders a lot. Heidi was annoyed they were no closer to arresting any suspects and kept shooting daggers in Vic's direction as if it was personally his fault, which pissed him off, as he was only trying to keep her friend safe.

She mentioned Sullivan too and he noted Amy gave nothing away.

On the drive back to her apartment Vic decided to broach the subject of church again. The first time Amy had been dismissive of the idea, but then Angell had been with them, being her usual overly opinionated and sarcastic self, and had probably influenced Amy's answer. Meeting with Pastor Ralph would give her a fresh perspective; probably help her deal with what was happening. And, of course, the pastor would no doubt sing Vic's praises, earning him brownie points, which he could certainly do with if the rumours about Sullivan were true. Word might even get back to Brooke Michaels that he was guarding a pretty lady and his attentions were focused elsewhere. As far as he could see it, getting Amy to meet with the pastor was a win–win situation.

She was looking distracted, staring out of the passenger window. Vic glanced in the rear-view mirror at the dog who sat on the back seat, smiling back, his tongue hanging out and a dopey look on his face.

Dumb animal. It was one thing giving Amy a ride around town, but she insisted on bringing Huckleberry with her everywhere they went. Vic had spread a blanket out on the back seat, but the dog kept managing to knock it off, and his car was starting to smell of the damn mutt.

'Do you need to go anywhere else, or can we go back to the apartment?'

'Sorry, what did you say?' Amy glanced around, pulled back to reality from her daydream. No doubt about Sullivan.

'I said do you need to go anywhere else?' Vic repeated, a little irritably.

'No, I guess back home.' She turned to look out of the window again.

'I know you said you don't do churchy type stuff,' Vic started, not quite as subtly as he had hoped.

'I'm an atheist.' Amy narrowed her eyes, gave him a quick sharp smile. 'I don't do church, period.'

'But that doesn't matter.'

'What doesn't matter?'

'That you don't believe in God. Sometimes it helps to talk to someone. Pastor Ralph is good to talk to.'

'I already talked to Doctor Shinnick. I'm done talking.'

'But Pastor Ralph is different. He helped me by explaining stuff.'

'And now you believe in God?'

'Umm, well, yeah, I guess.'

'So, he took advantage of your situation and used it to push religion down your throat?'

She was tying him up in knots; not exactly the way Vic had seen this panning out.

'Well, no, I... He didn't force me or anything.'

'But he conveniently led you to that conclusion?'

'He helped me, okay?' Vic's hands tightened on the wheel as frustration bubbled into anger. He didn't like Amy being difficult like this. It reminded him of having to deal with Angell and her smart mouth, which always pissed him off. 'He helped me, like I'm trying to help you. There's no hidden agenda. I thought it would help to have someone to talk to who wouldn't judge you or try to analyse you.' He stopped, realising Amy was staring at him, looking surprised. He had never gotten angry around her before.

'You're really passionate about this, aren't you?'

'Well, yeah.' Vic wasn't sure using religion to try and get into a girl's pants was passionate, but if it was going to work then he'd go with it. 'As I say, Pastor Ralph helped me, and I honestly believe he can help you too. Plus, his wife, Mrs Michaels, is a great cook. The pastor normally has a tin of cookies or muffins with him.'

Amy shook her head. 'I'm not sure I want to talk, and I have big reservations about talking to a pastor, but if it will shut you up, I'll think about it, okay? No promises, but I will think about it. Deal?'

It was as good as he was going to get for now.

'Okay, deal.'

He didn't have her persuaded yet, but it was a start, so he would drop the subject for now and attempt to work on her again later.

* * *

Jake and Rivers arrived in Melford mid-afternoon and headed to the Sheriff's office. They were met by Deputy Wayne Rawlins, a lanky man in his late forties, who greeted them enthusiastically before taking them back to meet Sheriff Buck Wagner and Deputy Emily Benson, a self-assured young brunette who couldn't have been more than mid-twenties.

Wagner pumped Jake's hand, offered them both a seat, before proceeding to update them on the case.

'We've got an APB out on Tucker Johnson. Man seems to have disappeared without a trace. We're thinking he knew we were onto him and has either skipped town or is hiding out in the woods. If he is, we will find him. I have people combing through his house as we speak.'

'Does he have any relatives in town?' Rivers was already busy scribbling. He had sulked most of the journey after forgetting to bring his dumb notebooks with him and when Jake had refused to turn the car around so he could go back for them, he had insisted they stop off along the way so he could pick up a new one. Jake was beginning to wonder what the hell the kid wrote in them.

'No one in Melford, not since his wife and kid died. We've located his mother. She's in a nursing home in Boise. She hasn't seen or heard from him in years. Aside from that he has no other living relatives, which is probably why he has been able to get away killing for so long undetected.'

'There's a well on the property,' Benson piped up. 'We suspect it may be where he hid the victims. We've got a couple of guys down there now looking for bodies.'

'If the blood spatter in the basement is anything to go by, we're looking for at least fifteen victims, including Danielle Colton,' Wagner added. 'We've been going over missing persons reports from the last twenty years, got a handful of hitchhikers, another girl it was assumed had skipped town. Those are just the ones we know about.'

Jake nodded, mind working overtime. Tucker Johnson was a killer, but it was a stretch for a man with a history of abducting hitchhikers to change his routine. Whoever was killing from Amy's books was smart, inventive and wanted the world to see. That was a different type of psychopath. Yet there was no denying the connection between Amy Gallaty and Tucker Johnson. She had nearly been one of his victims.

'Have you managed to locate Leslie or Crystal Rooney yet?' he asked, hoping the twins might provide a missing clue.

'Not yet.' Wagner's expression was grim. 'We still haven't been able to get hold of Crystal Rooney. It's been nearly a week and her mother, Deanna, says it's out of character. She let us in the house, but there's no sign of her. Leslie returned home from a school trip yesterday, but has also pulled a disappearing act. We don't know if they think they're in trouble and have skipped town or...' He trailed off, not needing to spell out the alternative.

'Can you show us Leslie Rooney's place?'

Wagner nodded at Jake. 'Sure. I can have a word with Deanna. She'll let us in.'

'She lives in town, right?' Rivers asked.

'Yeah, just down the road from her parents, in the old Cunningham house.'

The what?

The name registered in Jake's brain as Benson

glanced at Wagner before continuing. 'Want me to go give Deanna a ring, boss?'

'Whoa... wait up a minute.'

Wagner and his two deputies looked at Jake curious, while Rivers seemed oblivious.

How the hell did this guy make the cut with the FBI?

'The old Cunningham house?'

'Yeah, George and Mary Cunningham's place. What about it?' Wagner asked.

Rivers' eyes narrowed. Jake could see he had cottoned on.

'The Cunninghams. They wouldn't have happened to have a son?'

'Yeah, odd kid.' Rawlins was shaking his head. 'Bit of a loner. Trent or Clay, it's something like that.'

'Troy.'

'Yeah, that's the one.'

Jake glanced at Rivers. 'Things just got interesting.'

* * *

Two things were certain. Ryan Caparelli had never left Oregon, and one of the murder victims had been killed in his apartment. His cell phone had been found. It hadn't been used in over a week and the battery was dead, but they had been able to triangulate the signal to the last used point and after a brief search it was located lying in undergrowth near a farmer's field on the outskirts of town. Either Caparelli had lost it, or he was no longer around to need it.

Or maybe he wanted it to appear that way. At this stage it was too early to come to conclusions.

Further clues came when the phone was charged. The last call had been to Heidi Pearce; the last text message to Ben Caparelli, Ryan's brother, thanking him for wishing him a safe trip. It was the message stored in draft that caught Rebecca and Hickok's attention.

Destined for Amy, it read, 'Don't want to alarm you, but I saw Dav'.

It hadn't been finished; had never been sent.

Was 'Dav' David Gavin?

The message had been typed on the morning Ryan Caparelli was supposed to depart on his flight to Paris. Four hours later he had lost or dropped his phone in the location where it had been found.

Rebecca and Hickok spent Sunday afternoon trying to retrace his steps. It was just the two of them working the Caparelli lead, with Jake and Rivers conveniently dispatched to Melford to follow up on the still missing Tucker Johnson.

Rebecca had gone from confused to contrite following Friday night's incident. She had plucked up courage to contact Alan the previous evening, but he was refusing to take her calls; added to that she had received a further dressing down from her mother before her family had left town, while Wendy and her father had looked on in disapproval, nodding in agreement at every word said. Jess – her only ally – had rolled her eyes, having heard it all before.

It was perhaps a good thing she hadn't been able to reach Alan. She'd left him a voicemail apologising, but while she was truly sorry for what he had witnessed, she had come to realise one thing.

She wasn't in love with him. And that was a concern given he was thinking about marriage. While she wanted to make things right *for* him, she wasn't sure she wanted to make things right *with* him.

Her family had returned to Swallow Falls earlier that morning, her mother trying to force her into making promises that she would work hard to win Alan back, and the second she had gone Rebecca had headed straight into work, preferring to throw herself back into the case than deal with the aftermath of her love life.

Of course that meant facing Hickok, but him she could deal with, even if he had pulled his sly little stunt of getting rid of Jake and Rivers so they were alone.

They traced Caparelli's footsteps, questioning his friends and neighbours, careful not to pass on too much information to Amy and Heidi at this early stage. The news one of her best friends might in some way be involved in the murders would probably push Amy over the edge. She didn't need to know until they were sure.

Caparelli belonged to a city gym and the receptionist was able to confirm he had attended his usual early morning session on the day he was supposed to depart for Paris. She pulled up the security camera tape for them to watch and, as they sat in the back office alone, the lights dimmed, Rebecca was conscious of Hickok having one eye on the footage and one eye on her.

'Quit staring at me and watch the tape,' she snapped, irked, as she wound the cassette forward.

'Have you dumped Alan yet?'

'No.'

'Seriously?'

'He won't return my calls.'

'So?'

'So the man has feelings, Hickok. He wanted to marry me.'

'Yeah, I kind of got that from our Friday night audience. How is your mom by the way?'

'Your name is mud.'

'She'll come around.'

Rebecca scowled when he smirked. 'Don't count on it. And anyway, who says I've come around? Don't think I'm not wise to your little set up here. Jake and Rivers conveniently out of town.'

'Well, you seemed as if you had pretty much come around when you were trying to rip my pants off Friday night.' When her scowl deepened, he added, 'But don't flatter yourself, Angell. This is about the case, not you.'

'Sure it is, Hickok. And when we're done with this case, we need to talk – about us.'

When she shot him a knowing look, he merely grinned again, running his knuckles down her arm.

Rebecca pulled away, not wanting to be distracted. 'Okay, enough. Cool it, Romeo, and watch the tape. Here he is.'

They watched the footage of Caparelli arriving at the gym, signing in. Rebecca fast forwarded an hour and a half before they found him again in the reception area, getting ready to leave. He was talking with someone: another guy. As they headed out into the parking lot, Rebecca glimpsed his face.

'Holy shit, you see who that is?'

Hickok had and was already leaning forward, had his finger on the rewind button. He paused and zoomed in the camera, before glancing at Rebecca, the expression on his face satisfied and a little smug.

The net was closing in.

'So, what are the chances of that?' he muttered, shaking his head. 'Ryan Caparelli is pals with Troy Cunningham.'

39

Tucker Johnson lived like a slob.

The furniture in his house, at least what little there was of it, was threadbare and covered in a film of dust. Dozens of empty beer cans lay on the floor beside the couch and the ashtrays on the coffee and side table were full to spilling over.

Declan Rivers screwed up his nose in disgust when he opened the refrigerator door and was hit by the stench of long-expired milk and gone-off fruit. Dirty dishes lined the counter and filled the sink, and the dish towels were filthy. The man was a pig. There was no order or efficiency, no method, just mess. How had he managed to kill undetected for so long when his life was in such a state of disarray?

The basement was a different story. There were blood stains on the floor and the walls, but the room itself was the most orderly in the house: neat and devoid of mess, the tools he had used to torture and kill his victims hanging neatly from hooks in the wall, all meticulously clean and sharp. The man had taken pride in his tools.

Declan noticed Sullivan went quiet when they entered the basement, taking in the room and probably thinking about Amy and how she had once been in here. How she had managed a lucky escape. Personally, he wasn't sure he believed the bullshit that she hadn't remembered that night. No, Declan was convinced Amy Gallaty knew more than she was letting on. It would be interesting to find out how much she remembered.

Wagner was convinced the bodies of the victims, Danielle Colton included, were hidden in the well on the property. Fifteen victims he had predicted. Declan figured it would be interesting to see if he was right.

So far Johnson's place had given the sheriff's office no clue as to his whereabouts and it was assumed he had somehow become alerted to the investigation and fled into the woods. Declan was the one to produce the big find of the morning. After what had happened with Peterson, he needed the vote of confidence to show he was up to the job.

Wagner and his deputies had already been combing the house for evidence of victims, and while they had uncovered plenty, nothing had led to Johnson. The letter Declan found in the foot of one of the man's boots sitting in the bottom of his closet wasn't exactly a map to his whereabouts, but it did offer up an important link and was the biggest clue they had found so far.

It was addressed to Johnson, giving details of the night of Danielle Colton's murder. In exchange for silence, the blackmailer wanted Johnson to help him get revenge on Amy Gallaty.

It was written a week before the murders started and came from David Gavin.

Sullivan was dubious at first. If the contents were true, Amy must have told Gavin what had happened to her, which meant she had lied about that night, about not remembering. The letter implied Johnson and Gavin were partners, or at least that was Gavin's intention.

Declan watched the flicker of doubt in the detective's expression, knew he wanted to believe Amy, but also that the evidence didn't lie.

* * *

Sullivan was subdued as they drove back into town and Declan couldn't resist a smug smile of satisfaction as the man's face revealed his shock and doubts about Amy; that he had maybe fallen for the wrong girl.

Emily Benson was waiting for them as they arrived back at the sheriff's office.

Declan was already finding her annoying. The petite but plump deputy was bright-eyed and fresh-faced, with breasts too large for her frame and a toothpaste smile. She was the kind of overly enthusiastic goody-two-shoes girl he couldn't stand. Still, he masked his distaste with a smile.

'Rawlins radioed ahead and said about the letter. Nice find.' She gave Declan a mock punch on the arm, cranking his irritation level higher.

'Yeah, I can't believe your people missed it,' he pointed out, smoothing the sleeve of his jacket where she'd touched him.

The comment rolled off Benson. She appeared to be a girl without an irritation threshold.

'It's a big house. Sure they would have come across it sooner or later. Luckily you were on hand to save them a job. You guys want coffee? We just made a fresh pot.'

'We're gonna head over to the motel,' Sullivan told her. 'Get checked in, but thanks.'

'Good idea. Sheriff Wagner has booked you rooms at the Pine Lodge. Marcie knows you boys are law enforcement and she will look after you fine. Before you go, I do have a quick question.'

'Sure.'

Sullivan was all ears, giving Benson his full attention, and Declan swore he could see a blush creeping up the girl's neck and onto her cheeks. Take away the uniform and she was no different to all the other women.

'While you were over at Tucker's place I was reading through your reports on the victims in Juniper.'

'Okay.'

'I think I picked something up.'

Declan rolled his eyes. Great, Deputy Benson here thought she was Nancy Drew.

'We're here to focus on Tucker Johnson,' he pointed out, his tone sarcastic. 'He needs to have our full attention right now.'

Sullivan shot him a glare. 'Let her talk, Rivers.'

'The girl who was killed with the acid,' Benson continued in her perky tone, either unfazed or just not picking up on Declan's sarcasm. 'Nadine Williams, right?'

'That's correct,' Sullivan confirmed.

'And she was Troy Cunningham's girlfriend?'

'She was.'

'Well, assuming she is the same Nadine Williams, cos I'm guessing there are not many of them around in Oregon, and chances Troy Cunningham would date two girls with identical names has got to be almost zero—'

'For chrissakes, spit it out.'

Benson stared at Declan for a long moment, and he saw something in her expression change. Her eyes narrowed and she looked like she was going to challenge him, but then she seemed to change her mind, instead flashing him a big smile and refusing to bite.

'Nadine was Danielle Colton's cousin.'

'She lived here in Melford, too?' That was from Sullivan.

'Yes, but she didn't move here until a few years after Danielle went missing. Had trouble with her folks and they kicked her out. She lived with her aunt, Danielle's mom, and worked in the town diner. She was dating Troy while he was away at college and then they both moved out of town.'

'You're sure about this?'

'Uh, of course, Special Agent Rivers; it's not the kind of thing I'd get wrong. I knew her.'

Benson was being sarcastic with him now and it was pissing him off.

How he would like to wipe that jaunty smile off her face.

'Nice spot, Deputy Benson.' Sullivan locked the car door, glanced at Declan. 'We'd better touch base with Hickok and Rebecca.'

* * *

The clues were there, but the dots weren't quite linking.

Joel had spoken with Sullivan and Rivers, and they had exchanged information. They now knew Ryan Caparelli and Troy Cunningham knew each other. They also knew Troy had lived in Melford during the time Danielle Colton was murdered, that he may have known Amy. And Nadine Williams had also lived in Melford, had been Danielle's cousin.

It had become clear Amy's ex-boyfriend had been in contact with Tucker Johnson, the man who had killed Danielle, and that Gavin, Johnson and Caparelli had all vanished without a trace, as had the twins, Leslie and Crystal Rooney.

And in order for Gavin to know about Danielle's murder, Amy had to have told him.

Why had she lied about what had happened to Danielle, gone through the ruse of hypnotherapy, and why hadn't she come forward sooner? It didn't make sense.

And at the centre of everything sat Troy Cunningham – yet what part did he play in all of this?

He was the first port of call on Monday morning after Joel picked up Angell from her home, where he hadn't expected to see Alan come storming out as he went to knock on the door. The man barely glanced his way as he pushed past him, walking stiltedly to his car. The expression on his face suggested he'd just been dumped.

Joel felt a little bad. The man was a nerd, but he was harmless and hadn't deserved to be humiliated. Regardless, he couldn't bring himself to regret what had happened. Alan hadn't been right for Angell, and she needed a good shake for even indulging the notion he could have been.

So who is right for her, Joel?

He ignored the nagging question, telling himself

he'd done her a favour. There was no need to justify his actions.

Angell stomped out of the front door seconds after Alan, her expression not much happier.

'Stop gawping, Hickok. This isn't a sideshow.'

'No, but it's just as entertaining.'

She had already brushed past him and was getting into the passenger seat of his car; he went to join her, ignoring her insistence that she didn't want to talk about it. By the time they had reached Cunningham's beach house, he had wheedled out of her that Alan was history, a revelation that brightened his morning more than he cared to admit.

Troy wasn't home. Or at least he didn't appear to be. A quick check of the perimeter of the property revealed the patio door was ajar and Joel eased it open, stepping inside and calling out.

'Mr Cunningham, this is the FBI. Are you home?'

It was while glancing around the room when there was no answer that he saw the blood: a pool of it congealing on the wooden floor of the living room. There were three red handprints leading towards the couch, a fourth on the arm of the couch itself and a final partial print on the wall behind. Joel drew his sidearm, pointed to the prints and signalled for Angell to do the same. Together they conducted a search of the beach house, and came up empty.

'What are you thinking?' she asked when they reconvened in the living room a few minutes later. 'Troy Cunningham's blood?'

'No sign of forced entry, the door was already open, too much blood to be an accident, but no body, which pretty much rules out suicide. There are a few more drops of blood leading through in the front hall and out on the front step, but his car is still here.' He glanced at Angell, mulling the possibilities over in his mind. 'I think we'd better get Withers over here as soon as. We need to get a match on this blood.'

* * *

Deputy Wayne Rawlins was the one to find David Gavin's car, while out on patrol in the early hours of Monday morning.

At first no one realised it was Gavin's car. A vehicle had crashed off the road heading out of town and was found floating upside down in a ditch. The driver appeared to have escaped, and it wasn't until later in the morning the gruesome discovery was made of two bodies in the trunk of the car.

They would need to make an official identification, but the remains appeared to be those of Leslie and Crystal Rooney, while a trace on the car showed it belonged to a rental company back in Juniper and the man who had paid cash for it was none other than David Gavin, though he had used a false name. A copy of Amy's sixth and final book had been found sealed in a plastic bag in the trunk with the dead girls.

With the car registered to Gavin, all evidence seemed to point to him being the killer. A spurned lover out for revenge, as Sheriff Wagner put it, and Rivers was quick to agree. To Jake, it all seemed too convenient. Sure, Gavin had done a vague cover-up job by paying cash for the car and giving a fake name, but he had to have known they would quickly uncover his true identity. It didn't fit the pattern of a killer who had so far proven creative, smart and elusive, always staying one step ahead. And Gavin being the killer brought Jake back to the question that had been eating at him much of the day. How had he known about the basement and what had happened to Danielle Colton, unless Amy had told him?

If Amy had been lying, then she was a damn good actress. He had been with her in Paul Shinnick's office, had known her reservations about the hypnotherapy and had woken her from her nightmare. It made no sense, and what would she have to gain from the lie anyway?

You're blinded because you've fallen for her.

Jake pushed the voice down. He couldn't overthink this. Amy, he would deal with when he returned to Juniper. For now, they had to figure out where Gavin was.

The book series was finished, which would suggest it was game over. Was the plan for Gavin to disappear now he had exacted revenge? And why had there been no big finale? The killer had been flashy with his previous murder scenes; surely, he would want to finish on a bang. The murder of the twins had been low-key and staged as an accident. It was almost as if the killer had grown bored and run out of steam.

There were more questions than answers and they still hadn't managed to figure where Troy Cunningham and Ryan Caparelli, who was still missing, fitted into all of this. And then, of course, there was Tucker Johnson. The remains of eight bodies had so far been recovered from the well on his property. Even if Gavin was responsible for the recent murders in Juniper, Johnson was still at large and needed to be apprehended.

Something about the whole situation didn't ring true and Jake was determined to find out what it was.

* * *

While Withers worked the scene at Troy Cunningham's house, Rebecca and Hickok paid Amy a visit.

Vic opened the door to them looking vexed when he saw who it was. As Amy got up from her dining table to greet them, he returned to his spot on the couch and Rebecca rolled her eyes. How could the man be so content watching TV all day? He remained engrossed in his soaps while they spoke with Amy, not seeming particularly interested in the case or why they were there, and only glancing over when Amy raised her voice, clearly upset when Hickok intimated she had lied about not remembering being in Tucker Johnson's basement.

'Why would you think that?' she demanded. 'What the hell makes you think I would lie about something as huge as this?'

'We're dealing with facts here, Amy. They don't lie either. David Gavin has been contacting Tucker Johnson. Special Agent Rivers found a letter in Johnson's house. It was written by your ex-boyfriend, and he seems to know all about what Johnson likes to do in his basement, including what he did to Danielle Colton. You were the only other person there.'

'I never told David anything.' Amy glared at Hickok. 'I never told him anything because I didn't remember anything. Hell, I wasn't even having the nightmares. He had no idea what had happened when he was with me and neither did I.'

'It's okay if you needed to keep it a secret,' Rebecca told her. 'You were fifteen years old, and it was a hell of a thing to deal with. You won't get into any trouble for not telling us. We just need to know the truth.'

'I'm telling you the damn truth.' Amy pushed back her chair, got to her feet and started to pace. The dog on the floor beside her whined, got up and slunk over to his bed.

'So, if you're telling us the truth, how does Gavin know?'

'I have no idea, Special Agent Hickok. If I did, I would tell you.'

Hickok glanced at Rebecca.

She shrugged in return, as truth was, she was un-sure. Hickok was right, the facts didn't lie, but this con-versation hadn't gone as she'd expected. Once confronted with the news about Gavin and Johnson, she had believed Amy would break down and confess to the lie. But she hadn't and Rebecca could tell from the pained look in Amy's eyes the accusation had stung.

Amy stopped pacing, pausing by the table and giving them both a fixed look.

'If I had remembered all along about Danielle and the basement, why would I have gone along with the charade of seeing Doctor Shinnick? And if I didn't want you to know, why am I not still keeping it a secret?'

She had a point. They were questions that couldn't be answered, and they left her apartment twenty minutes later no closer to the truth and having only succeeded in pissing Amy off. Rebecca had spoken with Jake shortly before arriving at Amy's apartment, learning of the twins' murder and that all clues pointed towards Gavin being responsible. They had purposely kept the news from Amy at this stage, knowing an official identification still had to be made.

Hickok's cell rang as they were getting into his car, and he stopped to take the call.

'Special Agent Hickok.' There was a brief silence as he listened to the caller. 'That was quick work.'

Rebecca watched his expression for clues, annoyed he gave nothing away. But that was Hickok all over, keeping his cards close to his chest.

Unlike Alan.

She remembered the hurt, bitter look on his face that morning. Despite catching her cheating he had begged to have her back. Mixed in with pity and regret at how things had ended, she was disappointed at his lack of self-respect.

Hickok killed the call, and she pushed Alan from her thoughts. 'Well?' she asked expectantly.

'That was Withers. He's already got us a match on the blood.'

'And?'

'And it definitely belongs to Troy Cunningham.'

Rebecca nodded, taking in the news and considering what it meant. 'You think he's another victim?'

'I don't know. We haven't found him, and I don't think we can say until we do.' Hickok was silent for a moment before starting the engine. He glanced at Rebecca, expression unreadable. 'What I do think, is that when we find Troy Cunningham the pieces of this puzzle are going to slot into place.'

* * *

Amy agreed to meet with Pastor Ralph shortly after Rebecca and Hickok had left.

Vic wasn't sure if she was doing it because she genuinely wanted to talk to someone after her gruelling from his colleagues or if it was just to shut him up. He had brought up the subject when he'd arrived that morning and gotten not much more than a non-committal grunt. Hickok's accusation had shaken her and, after mooching around her apartment for a while, she asked Vic if he could set up a meet.

Never one to look a gift horse in the mouth, he embraced the opportunity with both hands, eager to get Amy across to the church before she changed her mind, and he was straight on the phone to Pastor Ralph.

The pastor already knew he was playing bodyguard to a pretty lady and keeping her safe from a serial killer and Vic had told him that he thought it would help Amy to have someone to talk things over with. So when the pastor took the call he was already prepared and suggested Vic bring Amy to the church late afternoon.

Amy made them lunch, still a little sulky about Hickok and Rebecca's accusation, then went to get changed. Vic understood why she was pissed off. She didn't strike him as the type to tell lies and from spending time with her over the past week he knew she had been genuinely shaken up after learning the truth about her nightmare.

He had half-listened to the discussion, understanding Amy's ex-boyfriend and this Tucker Johnson guy were suspected of being behind the murders. He also understood why Rebecca and Hickok thought Amy had known, but they had to be wrong. There had to be another explanation.

He was waiting on the couch for her and groaned in dismay when she emerged from her bedroom and whistled for the dog.

'We're going to see the pastor. He doesn't need to come. I don't even think they let dogs in churches.'

Huckleberry was already on his feet and running to Amy who had hold of his leash.

'He hates being cooped up in the apartment by himself.' She smiled at Vic in an attempt to win him over. It looked a little forced and he could tell beneath it she was still peed off. 'I figured you could walk him while I speak with the pastor.'

'Can't we take him out later? My car is already covered in dog hairs.'

'He'll be fine. And he doesn't shed that much hair so your car will be fine too.' Amy clipped the leash on Huckleberry, headed over to the door. 'Come on. Don't want to keep your pastor friend waiting.'

Although he knew he was fighting a losing battle, Vic still grumbled all the way down to the car, and on the ride out to the church he kept one eye on the rearview mirror, making sure Huckleberry was behaving himself.

Pastor Ralph was waiting for them, and Vic made the introductions before leaving him and Amy alone. The pastor gave him a cookie from the tin Mrs Michaels had made fresh that morning and Vic nibbled on it as he made his way back to the car, while Huckleberry danced around him, whining for a piece.

'No way, buddy. These are too good to waste on an idiot dog.'

As Vic finished the cookie and wiped his fingers on his jeans, Huckleberry let out a frustrated sigh.

Damn dog was trying to put him on a guilt trip now.

Still irritated he'd been made to bring him along, Vic walked him up and down the parking lot a couple of times before deciding they would both wait in the car. He let Huckleberry in the back, climbed in the driver's seat and got himself comfortable, cranking the window open a couple of inches and retrieving his newspaper from the glovebox.

While he was pleased Amy had agreed to talk with Pastor Ralph and trusted the pastor was saying lots of good things about what a stand-up guy he was, he hoped they wouldn't be inside too long. Waiting around with just Huckleberry for company was dull. Even visiting Heidi Pearce had to rank higher than this for excitement.

He glanced around the parking lot, noted that aside from his car, there were two other vehicles. He recognised Pastor Ralph's Buick, the other vehicle was a dark van parked at the far end of the parking lot. Vic couldn't remember seeing it there when they had arrived, so guessed it had showed up while they'd both been talking to the pastor. It probably belonged to one of the two caretakers the church employed. Vic often saw them wandering around the grounds.

He opened up his paper and decided to open the door too. It was another warm day and the stillness in the air threatened a storm on the way. It was about time. Vic couldn't remember the last time they'd had this kind of heatwave.

He read the sports pages of the paper, ignoring Huckleberry's periodic whines, then tuned into the radio, found the country station he liked, rolled back his seat and closed his eyes. Comfortable and relaxed, with the sun burning through the glass and Tim Mc-Graw singing about the stars going blue, he started to drift.

He was jolted awake a minute later by the sound of Huckleberry's bark, which was followed by a low guttural growl.

'Damn, Huckleberry, what the...'

He stopped, catching sight of the figure approaching in the rear-view mirror. Although he couldn't make out the features, he knew it wasn't Amy or Pastor Ralph. The figure wore dark clothing and held something that glinted in the sunlight.

A knife.

As carefully as possible, Vic reached for his sidearm. He almost had it out of the holster, when he saw the shadow fall over him. Realising there wasn't time, he knocked his elbow back into the figure, using the element of surprise, heard the satisfying whoosh as bone connected with the soft flesh of belly and his assailant lost his breath, dropping to his knees.

Vic turned, took a look at the man who had tried to attack him, immediately recognising him.

'It's you.'

He seized the knife, reached for his cuffs, and climbed from the car, pushing his attacker's face down into the dirt. As he reached for his hands, the man rolled over, catching him by surprise – and Vic felt something: a sharp sting against his chest.

The fucker had a taser.

He wanted to yell out, but couldn't seem to find his voice as the shock pulsated through his body. The knife fell from his grip and he collapsed to the floor beside it. As he lay on the ground, he was aware of the knife being picked up again, was helpless to stop his attacker from plunging the blade hard into his belly. He felt sharp pain in his gut, the burn of the sun on his face and heard the sound of Huckleberry's growl over the Tim McGraw track still playing on the radio.

Then his eyes dropped shut and he felt and heard nothing.

40

Amy thanked the pastor and stepped out of the church, her head spinning and a mix of emotions creeping over her.

She appreciated Pastor Ralph taking time to speak with her, but the man was a stranger to her problems and had no idea what it was like to be in her shoes. Add to that the religious spiel he had thrown at her, about finding God and letting him guide her down the right path – well, she found it hard to swallow. She had given up believing in God the day her parents had died. Now she only believed in chance and hope and working hard to make things right; something that was presently out of her control.

Guilt, fear, anger, worry and frustration all

churned in her belly. Guilt for the victims who had been murdered because this sicko had a vendetta against her; fear of what might happen next; anger at Hickok and Angell's accusations; worry that Sullivan thought she had been lying too; and frustration because she didn't know what to do or how to act, given there was still one book left to go.

Glancing across the graveyard towards the parking lot, she noticed the dark van parked next to Boaz's car. Maybe a maintenance man or caretaker. Heading down the stone path, she breathed in the scent of the heavy air. The wind had died, and the sun was too hot. Dark clouds overhead suggested a storm was approaching.

As she neared the parking lot she could hear Huckleberry barking.

Damn it, Boaz, you were supposed to be giving him some exercise, not locking him in a hot car.

And then she saw Boaz, on the ground, between the car and the van, and her heart caught.

Had he collapsed?

Without thinking, she ran the remaining distance down the path and into the parking lot, over to where he lay. He was on the ground and curled in a foetal position.

'Jeez, Vic?'

Amy dropped to her knees; put her hand to his throat, feeling for a pulse.

He was cold, so cold.

Damn, Boaz. What happened?

She was about to call for the pastor, when she noticed blood pooling from underneath him.

Someone did this to him.

The thought caught in her throat, along with the scream. If someone did this, where were they now?

With shaky fingers, she reached carefully, quietly, into her purse for her cell phone.

As she did so, a shadow fell over her.

Amy froze, catching her breath, the phone clenched in her hand. It was a trap. As she understood, as her brain instructed her to scream, she felt an arm lock around her, a stinging pinprick against her throat, and her limbs immediately went numb. The arm tightened around her as she lost control, felt her body go limp, then only darkness.

* * *

The vibrations shook her awake.

Amy had no idea how long she had been out, but as she gradually came to, she became aware of two things. Firstly, she couldn't move. Her arms were mostly still numb, but a dull aching pain was slowly making its way down to her fingers. Her wrists were bound, her arms pulled uncomfortably tight behind her. Secondly, she was in a moving vehicle, lying down with her head against the floor, the vibrations rattling through her and causing her belly to roil. A wave of nausea hit as the fog started to lift and she retched forward, realising something was tied across her mouth.

Panic took over and she tried to scream, fought frantically to sit herself up and pull her wrists free. The binding was tight and with another jolt of the vehicle – some kind of van – she lost her balance, falling back down.

Stay calm. Don't let the fear take over.

She fought to gain her breath, to control her breathing.

Baby steps, Amy, baby steps.

She forced herself to still, getting her breathing under control, but couldn't stop her body from shaking. As she gradually became more lucid, understanding her predicament, the shaking increased. She remembered seeing Boaz lying on the ground, the blood, and the van she had assumed was the pastor's. She had been grabbed from behind, had blacked out.

Huckleberry; where was Huckleberry? He had

been in the car barking. What had happened to him and Vic? Were they okay?

Her throat was sore and dry and she became conscious it was difficult to swallow, probably due to the fear.

Deep breaths and stay in control. If you freak out, you have no chance of escape.

She closed her eyes, took in a couple of breaths. The shaking wouldn't stop, but her brain was working. She needed to use it, figure out how best to help herself.

Amy continued to draw deep breaths through her nose, focus her mind; she forced herself to roll over, to see exactly where she was. She saw dark walls, could smell the coppery scent of blood.

And then she saw the body on the floor next to her.

Oh my God, Boaz.

He was lying face down and there was no movement, other than the bumps and jolts from the van as it sped along.

Was he dead?

Amy noted he hadn't been tied up; his hands were loose. Whoever had put them in the van must have believed him to be dead.

She worked to get herself into a sitting position,

leant back against the wall of the van. A curtain separated the back from the front seats, so she couldn't see the driver. Whoever he was he wanted to keep his cargo hidden. Is this what he had done to Kasey and Ben, and to Shannon Castle and Leon? Had they all endured a ride in the back of this van, not knowing what was going to happen to them?

She heard him cough. It wasn't distinguishable enough to recognise him.

What was he planning to do to her?

She thought of her last book, tried to recall the murder scenes she had created, and told herself to stop. Scaring herself by thinking about what he had planned was not going to help her. She needed to focus on escaping.

Gingerly she reached her foot over and nudged Boaz. She needed him to be alive. Right now, he was her only hope.

There was no movement, no reaction at all.

Please, Vic. Please don't be dead.

She thought of Huckleberry. Was he still back in the car? She hoped her attacker hadn't hurt him. And then she thought about the heat. Even if he hadn't been hurt, he was trapped in the car in the blazing sunlight with no water.

What if no one finds him?

The pastor would, she told herself. Pastor Ralph would find Huckleberry and the pool of blood from Boaz, and her purse. She no longer had it with her, so she must have dropped it in the parking lot when she was reaching for her phone. Pastor Ralph would alert the police, and they would come and find them.

If it wasn't too late.

Shuddering, unable to stop thinking about what the man had planned, Amy tested the bond around her wrists. It was uncomfortably tight: rope, she thought, from the way it scratched into her skin, and her hands were growing numb. She wiggled her fingers, trying to get the feeling back in them, twisted her hands and wrists, trying to work the knots loose.

There were various tools in the back of the van: an axe and a couple of wrenches. Plus, she didn't know if Boaz still had his sidearm on him. If she could get her hands free, she could attack the driver.

She worked on the rope for a while, but there was no give and the knots were no looser than when she had started. Exhausted from struggling, she fell back against the wall of the van and sighed in frustration.

Think, Amy, think. You're a writer. What would you have your characters do?

She remembered reading a police safety thing

about tail-lights. You were supposed to kick them out, alert the car behind that you were trapped.

All very well, except she was in a van and the lights appeared to be hidden behind a panel she couldn't reach.

Unless she could get untied, she had no chance of escaping her situation.

She glanced again at the axe. It looked old and a little rusty. Would it cut through the rope? If she positioned herself, placed the axe between her wrists? A long shot, but anything was worth a go.

She scooted towards the axe, grabbed it with the toe of her boot and pulled it towards her.

The van took a sudden sharp turn, and she fell back, landing uncomfortably on her wrists; the axe sliding away from her.

Dammit!

She tried again, shimmying towards where it lay. Her foot had just made contact when the van slowed, turned another corner then pulled to a halt. The man killed the ignition and she heard the sound of his door opening.

Amy froze, her heart jumping into her mouth. The shaking started again.

She was too late.

Oh God, no.

She waited, listening, expecting the door to open. Instead, she heard the sound of another door, this one outside the van. It sounded like a garage door being shut. She held her breath, dreading what was to come, but the footsteps she heard subsided and she heard another door slam, then silence.

Where the hell were they? What was happening?

It sounded as if they were in a garage. Where had the man gone? What was he planning?

As the silence set in, her heartbeat settled and she tried to force the shaking to stop again.

She felt exhausted and just wanted to lie down, close her eyes, pretend none of this was happening.

You can't give up. If you give up, you're dead.

She thought of Huckleberry, of Boaz. She had to do this for them too.

Boaz isn't moving. He's dead.

She couldn't think that. She had to believe he was still alive, still with her. If he was dead, it meant she was in this all alone. She didn't want to be alone.

Using the toe of her boot again she brought the axe towards her. Now the van wasn't moving, it should be easier to position the blade. The shaking wouldn't stop and it made it difficult to hold the axe in place, but finally she managed to get herself on her knees and, securing the axe handle between her calf muscles, she started sawing at the rope.

It took forever, twisting her limbs at an awkward angle to reach the blade, and she could feel pain shooting down her neck and into her shoulders. The axe was blunter than she had expected and the interior of the van stifling and airless. Sweat rolled down her forehead and into her eyes and she longed to be able to spit the gag out of her mouth; would give anything for a drink of water.

She was tired and the rope didn't seem to be wearing. If the man came back, she would have no strength to fight. It was no good. She couldn't do this.

Emotion hit and she choked down a sob. Dropping the axe, she slipped to the floor and began to blub like a baby.

Pull yourself together.

Exhaustion rolled over her, the enormity of the situation taking hold.

You have to fight. You can't give up.

And she would. But first she needed to gather her strength. Closing her eyes, she let oblivion take over.

41

Ryan Caparelli was either dead or had staged it to look that way. Joel had left officers covering the ground near where Caparelli's cell phone had been found. Seeking any trace of him, they had initially searched the surrounding woodland, before turning their attention to the neighbouring farm. It was in the pigpen that Caparelli's fraternity ring had been found. At least they assumed it was his ring; it bore the initials RC inside. Tomorrow they would return with a team and try to find any other remains the pigs might have left.

If Caparelli had planted the ring, he had wanted them to believe he was dead, so what was he up to? If he had been murdered, his killer had been careful not to draw attention to the death. It was not showy like the killings from Amy's books, and this posed the question, were the incidents related?

The camera footage of Caparelli with Troy Cunningham at his gym on the morning he disappeared taken, together with the unfinished and unsent text suggesting Caparelli had seen David Gavin, made Joel certain they were. There were too many coincidences otherwise, and he didn't believe in coincidence.

* * *

It was getting late, and Jake was ready to head back to the motel after a long day spent with the medical examiner.

Rivers was still over at the Johnson place with Wagner, overseeing the recovery of remains from the well. Jake had spoken with him, learned they were close to calling it a day. Wagner would drop Rivers off at the motel on his ride home.

For now, it was just him and the two deputies, Wayne Rawlins and Emily Benson, in the sheriff's office. They were waiting for their shift cover, then both would head home for a few hours' rest. Rawlins looked dog-tired, but Benson was still perky and full of life. Jake had learned over the past day that she rarely shut up. It got a little distracting, but he couldn't knock her enthusiasm. She was a small-town girl, having grown up in Melford, and this was probably the most exciting case she would see in her career.

'Do you remember much about the Cunninghams?' he asked her, finishing the dregs of his coffee and switching off the computer he had been using.

'Sure. Everyone knows everyone around these parts. I was not long out of diapers when they moved to town. City folk. George never spoke much, but Mary was nice. I remember trick or treating when I was a kid. She would always give us candied apples she'd made. After Troy left town with Nadine, it was just the two of them. He didn't come back to visit much and they moved east a few years back.'

'What about Troy? Do you remember much about him? Did he have anything to do with the Rooney twins?'

Benson screwed up her nose. 'He pretty much kept himself to himself. They were all older than me. I remember thinking Leslie and Crystal Rooney were pretty cool when I was a kid. They dressed the same, had a lot of boyfriends and they were very popular. Troy didn't run in their circle.' Getting up, she gathered the coffee cups, took them to the sink. 'You want another cup before I empty the pot?'

'I'm good, thanks.'

'I don't remember Troy having many friends. It wasn't that he was unpopular. He didn't want to join in. Used to take himself off into the woods, fishing and hiking. There was one kid he was friendly with for a while. Rawlins, you remember that kid Troy Cunningham hung around with one summer?'

Rawlins glanced up from the drawer he was returning files to. 'Virginia's nephew you mean?'

'Yeah, he's the one.'

'I remember him. He was only here one summer. Creepy kid.' Rawlins nodded, thinking back. 'Into all his sports and used to insist everyone call him Cap or Captain.'

'So he was friendly with Troy?' Jake asked.

'Yeah, they were always off in the woods together. Troy was harmless enough, but that Cap kid was bad news.'

'Bad news how?'

'Like I say, he was only here one summer but we had more trouble in those six weeks than we usually do in six years. Caught him shooting a crossbow at Judy Kemp's dog. He said it was an accident, the little fella got in the way. Then there was the incident with the young Landry girl. What was her name, Emily?'

'Victoria Landry.'

'He kept following her around and she claimed he broke into her bedroom, stole a pair of her panties. Of course we could never prove it. We had a couple of fires too and reports of vandalism. You know, punctured tires, graffiti, that kind of thing. Pretty sure that was Cap. Might have been Troy too. As I say, Troy Cunningham was harmless enough when it was just him, but Cap was a bad influence. Damn glad when the boy left town.'

Jake nodded, taking the information in. Was there a connection?

'The summer Cap was here – was it the same summer Danielle went missing?'

'No, I was really young when Danielle disappeared,' Benson told him. 'Don't remember her much. I do remember Cap. Would have been four or five summers later.'

Jake got up, stretched. It had been a long day, and he didn't think he would have trouble sleeping tonight, if he could get his mind to switch off. There was still something missing. Something not adding up.

Benson walked out with him to the car.

'Is Marcie looking after you boys, okay?'

'She is.'

'Hope you've been staying for her breakfast. Her pancakes are legendary.'

'I'll be sure to give them a try.' Jake opened the car door, paused. 'You said Cap stayed with his aunt.'

'That's right. Virginia Martin.'

'Is she still in town?'

'No.' Benson shook her head. 'Virginia passed away a couple of years back. House still belongs to her family. I've heard they're rich folks from back east. They rented it out for a while, but it's been empty for the last six months or so.'

'Okay, thanks. You have the address?'

'Sure.' Benson seemed a little surprised Jake wanted it, but gave it willingly.

'You take care now and see you tomorrow,' she said as he got into the car, closing the door. 'And don't forget to try some of Marcie's pancakes.'

Jake assured her he would and gave her a wave as he pulled out of the parking lot.

Did Cap fit into this picture somehow or was he chasing a dead lead? It would be worth checking out the Martin woman's house, even if it was just to tick it off the list.

Right now, he needed food and sleep. He would check it out in the morning.

* * *

Joel and Angell were alerted to Amy Gallaty and Victor Boaz's disappearance early evening.

Pastor Ralph Michaels had found Boaz's Camaro when leaving the church, with an unconscious Huckleberry on the back seat, and a pool of blood and Amy's purse in the dirt next to the car.

The dog was rushed to a nearby vet and treated for dehydration, while Joel and Angell convened with Withers at the crime scene.

They interviewed the pastor, who confirmed he had spoken with Amy. After she had left, he had pottered about in his office, sorting out paperwork. It was a good couple of hours before he made the discovery.

The blood came from a stab wound, probably stomach Withers guessed, and they needed to establish whether it belonged to Amy or Boaz. One certain thing was, they were both missing.

The killer had already re-enacted all six books. What was he planning?

They were still working on the basis their unsub

was David Gavin. Had this been his plan of revenge: to kill from each of Amy's books, then come after her?

The twins had been found earlier that day. Plenty of time for him to dump the car with their bodies and head back to Juniper. The pastor told them it had been Amy's idea to meet, and while he wouldn't go into the specifics of their conversation, Joel understood it had probably been prompted by their meeting with her earlier that morning, when he had accused her of lying to them.

Gavin had to have been watching her place and followed them to the church. He had probably over-powered Boaz first, before taking Amy when she returned to the car.

'We need to tell Jake and Rivers.'

Angell was right. And they needed to establish where Amy and Boaz had been taken, and fast. Caparelli's place was a possible. It had been used for murder before. Troy Cunningham's beach house would need to be checked again also. They had been missing now over three hours and their killer had already proven he was a fast worker.

Hickok nodded grimly. 'I'll go make the call.'

* * *

Tucker Johnson hadn't been found and, while it was unlikely he would return to the house, they had to be prepared for such an eventuality, so Wagner maintained a police presence. Having a squad car outside also kept the kids at bay. Too many of them were ghoulish little snoops who would think it a good idea to check out the murder house.

The deputy covering the first part of the Monday night shift was Howie Cox, one of the newer recruits to the sheriff's department. It was his second time sitting guard outside the Johnson place and, though he would never admit it, the job scared the shit out of him.

Howie wasn't a little guy; give him a bar brawl or a traffic incident and he was your man. He wasn't afraid of confrontation and could hold his own in a fight, but stick him in the dark outside a creepy house where God knows how many people had died, he completely lost his bottle.

The first night he had made the mistake of bringing only a newspaper for company. The silence had been the worst thing. He couldn't keep the car stereo on for fear of running down his battery, and soon learned that every sound was magnified when you were in the middle of nowhere. By the time

Rawlins had arrived to relieve him, he was about ready to pee his pants.

This time he had brought a portable radio and a flask of coffee, as well as the newspaper. Dusk was only just starting to settle and it was going to be a long six hours.

He spent the first hour reading the sports pages, had a cup of coffee and texted his girlfriend, while listening to the local radio station and tapping his foot to the beat of Christina Aguilera and Eminem.

He made a point of having a pee before it got pitch black, locking the doors of the car when he got back inside. It was stupid, but he couldn't help it. Nothing was going to attack him in the woods. There were no dead spirits in the house and Tucker Johnson was probably long gone. He just had to keep his cool until the shift change and then he could head home.

Around nine-fifteen the sheriff radioed in, told him the author and her police guard had gone missing in Juniper. He asked Howie if he had seen anything untoward, telling him to keep his eyes peeled. It was likely they were still somewhere in Juniper, but they couldn't be certain. Howie assured Wagner there had been nothing out of the ordinary and went back to his crossword.

His phone pinged and he smiled as he read the

latest message from his girlfriend, Carlene, about keeping his spot warm in bed. He texted back a dirty response he knew would have her blushing and set the phone down.

It was then he saw the flashlight in the trees, heading towards the back of the house.

Oh shit.

Howie's mouth dried up. He glanced at the radio, wondering if he should call it in.

Don't be an idiot. It'll just be stupid kids.

He still had to check it out. Reluctantly he reached for his flashlight, exiting the car. The night was warm, the trees still. Overhead the sky let out a low deep growl. The storm was close.

Clicking on the flashlight and drawing his sidearm, Howie made his way around the side of the house, following the direction in which he had seen the beam. He shone the light around, saw no one. Maybe whoever it was had been passing by, or they had seen the police car and decided not to approach. It had to be stupid kids, and he was overreacting.

Still, he made himself do a walk around the perimeter of the house, relieved when he saw the safety of the car come back into view. He would lock himself back inside, finish his crossword, see if Carlene had responded to his text and maybe have another cup of coffee. Four and a half hours to go and then he could get out of this creepy place.

A rustle came from behind him. Before he could react, a hand clasped across his forehead, yanked his head back and he felt the slice of a blade against his throat.

For the briefest moment Howie struggled to catch his breath, tasted blood in his mouth, and then he was gone, slipping to the floor, his moment of passing marked by another ominous rumble in the sky.

* * *

Taking the deputy out had been easy. It was dragging him back to the car that proved hard work. He was a heavy son of a bitch and, while it was tempting to leave him where he'd fallen, it was safer to have him positioned back in the car, make him look as if he was still on duty. Although it was unlikely anyone would pass by, it was better to be prepared.

Finally getting him into place, leaving the window slightly ajar and radio quietly playing, he hoisted open the garage door before heading back to where he had left his car. Knowing the coast was now clear, he drove it straight up to the house, quickly parking it in the garage and killing the lights. He closed the door, clicked on his flashlight and opened the trunk, smiling at the man inside.

He had already transferred him between cars, knew his strength was ebbing and he wouldn't put up a fight. Acting quickly, he pulled him from the trunk, lifting him over his shoulder, pushed the lid shut and made his way through the side door into the main part of the house. Sitting the man down in the hallway, he took a moment to catch his breath before opening the door to the basement.

He hit the switch, saw the faint flickering beam from the room cast a creepy glow over the staircase and he smiled, before turning his attention back to the man.

'Come on. Let's get you into place.'

* * *

After learning Amy and Boaz had gone missing, Jake found it impossible to settle.

His initial reaction had been to drive back to Juniper.

'There's nothing you can do,' Hickok told him. 'I have everyone out looking and we will find them. Keep looking for clues in Melford. We need to connect the dots.'

Jake knew the Fed was right, that by the time he'd driven back to the city it would probably be too late. He had to put faith in Rebecca and Hickok; hope they would somehow find them. That still didn't mean he would be able to rest.

Unlike Rivers.

The federal agent had been shocked when they'd received the news, but had retired to his room shortly afterwards, telling Jake that as there was nothing they could do, they might as well get some rest.

Jake couldn't believe Rivers was going to be able to sleep, knowing what had happened, but then he guessed the man hadn't gotten himself personally involved with the girl who was now missing. So while Rivers slept, Jake paced the motel room, making call after call, needing to know everything possible was being done, as anxiety and frustration knotted in his gut. Amy had to be okay. They had to find her.

Eventually, no longer able to stand the confines of the four walls of the motel room, he snatched up the keys to the car. He couldn't do anything to help Amy or Boaz, but he could put himself to use in Melford, and he would start by checking out the address Emily Benson had given him for Virginia Martin's place.

* * *

Amy had somehow managed to drift off, her crying fit and the exhaustion of trying to free herself having proved too much.

The sound of the van door opening and then slamming shut brought her to, and quickly.

Raw panic clawed its way up her throat as she remembered where she was and what had happened.

He was back.

She rolled over, struggling against the rope, while trying to scoot back into the corner, expecting the door to open at any second. Instead, she heard the engine start, felt the van move again.

Where was he taking her now?

She glanced over at Boaz. There was still no sign of life, and she couldn't see him breathing.

God, I've got to get out of here.

The van turned a corner sharply, picking up speed, and Amy lost her balance, found herself rolling down the floor towards the doors. She managed to steady herself, started pummelling at the doors with her feet. It was stupid to think they would open, and they didn't, but she had to try.

She glanced around the floor as her eyes readjusted to the dark, frantically looking for something she could use. The axe hadn't worked and it had been her best shot.

Then she saw it. On the floor, partially hidden beneath Boaz's foot, the blade of a hacksaw. Using her foot to nudge his away she pulled the blade towards her. It was broken in half and, like the axe, didn't look sharp, but she might be able to get the teeth to cut into the rope.

With difficulty she managed to get back onto her knees, holding the blade between the heels of her boots and, pushing her hands down, began to saw at the rope. The van hit a bump in the road and the blade slipped, cutting flesh. Amy yelped, the noise muffled, and squeezed her eyes shut against the pain.

Keep going. Don't give up.

This time she was more cautious as she started to saw.

Keep it steady. Don't let the blade slip.

After a couple of minutes, she sat up straight, attempted to roll her shoulders and twisted her neck, needing a moment of relief. She tested the rope, her heart skipping a beat when she realised it had loosened. Not enough to free herself, but it was a start. She forced herself to try again, managed to cut through another strand of rope before the van braked sharply and she took another nick to her wrist, dropping the blade.

The driver killed the engine, and she heard the door open.

No, please, no. I need more time.

Frantically, Amy yanked at her wrists. There was more give in the rope, but she couldn't quite get her hands free.

She heard footsteps, heard the sound of the lock and squinted against bright light as the doors opened, and the beam of a flashlight was thrust in her face. As the man caught hold of her ankle, started to pull her out of the van, Amy used her free foot to kick out blindly. It connected with bone, and she heard a grunt, as the hand briefly released her. She scrambled back, her fear bubbling over as she fought desperately against the knots. They were getting looser, but not enough.

The man set the flashlight down. It was still bright, but not blinding her, and she blinked hard trying to pull him into focus. Then he had hold of her ankles again, this time both of them, and was dragging her from the van. Amy squealed and struggled, determined to keep fighting even when he pulled her to him, banded an arm around her chest to hold her in place.

'Shush,' he whispered, his breath hot against her ear and the gesture sickly intimate.

In response she stamped the heel of her boot hard on his foot. He grunted, loosening his grip, then shoved her hard, and she found herself face down in the dirt. She groaned as pain shot through her, then she drew in a breath, and gingerly rolled over to face her attacker.

Troy Cunningham smiled down at her. 'Hello, Amy. Ready to play?'

42

The Martin house appeared unoccupied. Weeds grew in the front yard and there was no car on the drive, no light coming from any of the windows. Benson said the place had been rented, but not in a while. If the owners wanted new tenants, they would need to clean it up a bit first.

Although it seemed a futile lead, Jake was here now, so might as well take a quick look around. He clicked on the flashlight he had brought, and followed the trail of the beam as he walked around the property. The house was at the end of the row and set apart from the nearest neighbour by tall conifers offering plenty of seclusion. If someone wanted to hide out, it was the perfect place.

Dust was on the windows; the blackness of the interior revealing nothing.

This was a wasted trip. No one was here and his time would be better served elsewhere. Deciding to head over to the sheriff's office, Jake made his way across the driveway, back to his car. The beam of the flashlight shone over the brickwork, picking up a dark patch.

He stopped, frowning. It looked like oil.

Dropping down he ran his finger over the patch. Definitely oil and it was fresh. Someone had been here, and recently. That thought on his mind, he headed over to the sheriff's office.

* * *

Wagner was still at his desk, burning the midnight oil.

'Any news?'

'Not from Juniper.' Jake dropped down into one of the two chairs facing Wagner's desk. 'They're still looking.'

'Guess you'd like to be back there helping with the search.'

It wasn't a question. Wagner understood.

Jake smiled tightly. 'I couldn't sleep so I took a drive out to Virginia Martin's place.'

Wagner nodded. 'You think there's a connection?'

'Troy Cunningham was friendly with her nephew, Cap?'

'That'd be right.'

'The place is supposed to be empty. Deputy Benson said there have been no tenants for at least six months.'

Wagner laced his fingers and looked Jake squarely in the eye. 'Where's this going, detective?'

'Someone has been there recently. There's oil on the drive.'

'Okay. There could be a simple explanation.'

'There could, but given everything that's happened and knowing who Virginia Martin's nephew is, don't you think it's worth checking out?'

Wagner was silent for a moment, considering the question. Before he had a chance to answer they were interrupted.

'Sheriff Wagner, Detective Sullivan.'

Deputy Benson stood in the doorway. She was out of uniform, her dark hair loose around her shoulders.

'What's up, Emily?' Wagner asked, for the moment ignoring Jake's question.

Benson dropped into the chair facing Jake, her eyes bright, her expression eager. She had found something.

'What is it?' he asked.

'It's Cap,' she said a little breathlessly. 'I figured it out.'

*   *   *

Declan finished dressing, slipped on his shoes.

Sullivan had been shocked he'd been prepared to get some sleep, given that Amy and Boaz were missing. Quite what the man expected them to do about it while stuck in a small pissant town like Melford, Declan didn't know; he had tried to point that out to Sullivan, but succeeded only in flaring his temper. So Sullivan had gone off to brood and Declan had retired to his room. He could hear Sullivan through the wall, making calls, heard him leave his room and disappear off in the car.

Where had he gone?

Feeling restless, Declan tore a sheet of paper out of his new notebook and scribbled a brief message.

Couldn't sleep. Gone for a walk. I'll head out into the woods in case there's any sign of Johnson or Gavin.

Before leaving the room, he slipped the notebook

into his suitcase, padlocked it and pocketed the key. He was still irritated he'd left his other notebooks in Juniper. The information he had documented in them was important and he only hoped he wouldn't need to refer to his case notes.

He locked the door behind him, folded the message he'd written for Sullivan and slipped it under his door before setting off down the road towards the woods.

* * *

Amy rolled onto her side as Troy reached for her, attempting to get away.

She knew he had been a suspect, but hadn't honestly believed it could be him, especially after Nadine had been murdered.

He force-fed his girlfriend acid. What is he going to do to you?

She squealed and wriggled as he caught hold of her shoulder, butting him in the belly with her head, and he momentarily let go, clutching at his stomach. He looked in pain. Did he have an injury she could attack?

Grimacing, he caught hold of her by the hair, yanking her to her feet and marched her towards the house. For the first time Amy took in her surroundings and realised where she was. The house in the woods, where Tucker Johnson lived, where Danielle had been murdered. She couldn't go inside. She could never go into that house again.

Terrified, she struggled to break free, only to feel his arm tighten around her. Up above, the sky flashed bright, lighting up the house with its dirty white walls and dark soulless windows. A threat of what was to come.

Troy leaned in close and ran his tongue down the side of her face, his touch warm, wet and repulsive against her skin.

'Ready to relive your nightmares, Amy?' he whispered, as a roll of thunder grumbled overhead.

No. How did he know?

The shaking began again as he dragged her inside the house, kicking the door shut behind them. Recognising the layout of the building, and with the familiar smell of dust and damp clogging her senses, she thought she might pass out.

Fight it, Amy.

She struggled in Troy's arms, fought frantically as he pulled her down the hallway and into the kitchen, towards the basement door.

No, I can't go down there.

She pulled at the rope. Each time it gave a little more, but never quite enough. And then she was heading down the stairs from her nightmare, half falling, half being dragged.

This wasn't happening. It couldn't be happening. Not again.

She pulled again at the wrists, her left hand jerking free. Using her elbow, she rammed it hard back into Troy's belly, aiming for the spot where she knew he was hurt. He screamed, let go of her and she turned, kneeing him in the balls before fleeing up the stairs. He gave an agonised growl and then she heard him right behind her.

It was a repeat of twenty years ago, into the kitchen, her foot catching the chair leg and bringing it down, into the hallway towards the safety of the front door.

It wouldn't open.

Panic poured through every vein. Amy turned, saw Troy heading towards her. Her only option was the stairs. She took them two at a time, aware he was only a heartbeat behind her, heading for the first room, getting inside and slamming the door shut.

He already had his hand on the doorknob, was trying to push it open.

Amy glanced down, saw the latch and locked it in place.

She saw she was in a bathroom. The room was sparse and dirty, with spiders in the bathtub.

Troy was throwing his weight against the door. It was holding, but wouldn't for much longer.

She glanced at the small window. Even if she smashed the pane there was no way she would fit through it. Taking a moment to pull the cloth from her mouth, she sucked in a deep shaky breath and considered her options. There were only a few toiletries in the bathroom, a shower curtain, a toilet brush and a couple of threadbare towels. Nothing she could use.

She needed a weapon. And fast.

Think, Amy, think.

She glanced at the toilet, recalled seeing a movie where the lid of the cistern had been used as a weapon.

Troy launched himself against the door again. It was starting to bow with his weight and would either splinter or the lock would give.

She grabbed hold of the lid. Floating in the cistern lay a rat and she stifled a scream.

Keep it together, Amy. You've more to worry about than a dead rodent.

The cistern lid was heavy, probably porcelain, and

she held it tight, standing to the side of the door, waiting for it to give.

Then thought, why not give Troy a helping hand?

She waited for the next thump against the door, quickly reaching across and unbolting the lock. When he launched himself again she was ready and waiting.

The door flew open, catching him off guard, and he stumbled into the bathroom and crashed against the basin.

Not allowing herself time to think, Amy slammed the cistern lid hard against the back of his head, watching as he dropped to the floor like a dead fly. Gingerly she stepped over his body, the cistern lid still in her hands in case he tried to get up again.

He didn't.

She made her way downstairs, remembering the front door was locked, and searched the rooms for another exit. There was a door towards the back of the house, but that too was locked. In the living room, she tried the window, relieved when it opened.

As she slid across the sill, she heard shuffling upstairs, realised Troy was gaining consciousness. She needed to get away from the house and fast. Following the walls of the house she found herself out front; spotting the police car, she ran across the front yard wondering when it had arrived and why the officer hadn't come to her aid. As she approached the car, she heard Mary J Blige playing on the radio, saw the officer sat in the driver's seat.

Why hadn't he helped her?

She understood why as she pulled open the door and a flash of lightning momentarily lit up his sightless eyes, the slash in his throat.

No.

Troy had done this. Troy had killed him. And he was going to kill her if he caught her.

Where were the keys? She could take the car.

She checked the ignition, felt in the officer's pockets, trying to ignore the fact rigor mortis had already set in and his body felt cold and stiff.

Where the hell are the keys?

Noise came from the house.

Troy.

Understanding she had to move quickly, she reached for the officer's holster and found it empty.

No keys. No gun.

She was on foot without a weapon, and needed to get away from here fast. As she had done twenty years ago, she headed for the woods. This time she had the advantage that her pursuer was further behind her.

Just get away from here, Amy. Find a car, find a house, and alert the authorities.

The sooner she found help, the sooner she could get help for Boaz, could check up on Huckleberry and see Sullivan.

She really needed to see Sullivan.

Another growl of thunder rumbled overhead as she ran into the safety of the trees, trying desperately to remember the route back to town.

Twigs snapped underfoot as she made her way blindly through the darkness, her breath ragged, but not daring to stop. Another flash of lightning showed she was still on the path, but she had no idea where it was headed.

Was Troy behind her? Was he close enough to catch her?

Up ahead in the distance she saw a faint beam.

Was it a flashlight? Was there a search party out looking for her and Boaz?

Knowing it couldn't be Troy she ran madly towards it.

* * *

Declan cut down the wooded path he had followed earlier, knowing it led to Tucker Johnson's house. He had spent much of the day there with Sheriff Wagner, watching as the remains of Johnson's victims had been pulled from the well.

The man had been killing for a long time, and it would take a while to make formal identifications. So far, they had recovered eight victims and both Declan and Wagner suspected that number would probably double.

The woods were dark and he was glad he'd had the foresight to bring his flashlight with him. As he made his way towards the house he thought about how surprised Sullivan would be when he found out Declan had turned out to help after all. He knew the detective didn't like him, thought he wasn't up to the job and wanted an easy ride. It would be good to see the look on Sullivan's face when Declan came through, was the one to solve the case and be painted as a hero.

Sullivan would hate that and so would Hickok. He would show them both.

Thunder growled overhead and he questioned the wisdom of not bringing a jacket. The night was warm, and he hadn't thought he would need one. It looked like he could be wrong.

Wagner had been stationing cruisers outside the house and he briefly wondered which of his deputies had pulled the first shift. It wouldn't be the irritating

Benson, as she'd been on shift and annoying him with calls throughout the day. As he pondered the question, he heard a rustling sound in the distance.

Was someone in the woods?

He shone the flashlight ahead of him, saw only trees and bushes. Then the crunch of feet against leaves; the sound of heavy breathing. Who the hell was out here in the middle of the night? He swung the beam around again, this time highlighting the figure heading madly towards him.

Amy Gallaty? What the hell was she doing out here in the woods?

He kept the beam trained on her as she ran towards him, almost collapsing in his arms.

'Jesus, Amy? What happened?'

She was struggling to get her breath, glancing behind her, terrified.

'It's Troy Cunningham. He's after me. You have to help me, please.'

Declan flashed the beam in the distance, saw she was alone. 'Hickok called, told us you were missing. Is Officer Boaz with you?'

'He's hurt. Troy hurt him. He might have killed him.'

She looked about ready to lose it and that wasn't

going to help either of them while they were out here, so Declan tentatively put his arm around her, the gesture making him feeling awkward. Offering comfort was something he wasn't good at.

He glanced around, knowing he had to get her out of the woods.

'Come on. There's a deputy at the Johnson house. We can get a ride back into town.'

'No!' Amy pulled away, flinching as if he had hit her. 'He's dead. Troy killed him too.'

'The deputy's dead?'

Shit.

'Yes, I found him. It was just me and Troy.'

'He took you to the house?'

'Yes, me and Officer Boaz, but he's hurt pretty bad. He might be dead. We have to go into town. We have to get help.'

'Is Officer Boaz at the Johnson house?'

'Yes. Come on.' She sounded impatient, irritation overtaking her fear. 'We need to go get help.'

Declan nodded, pulled out his gun and clicked off the safety. 'Okay, but first we have to go check on Officer Boaz. We can't leave him.'

'No, we have to get help.'

'Amy, I have a gun. I will keep you safe. Town is a

twenty-minute walk. The house is only two minutes away. If Troy is there, I'll take him down.'

'I'm not going back there.'

'We can't leave until I have assessed the situation.' When she shook her head, looked like she might lose it again, he forced himself to soften his tone. 'Look, I can't leave you out here, especially not if Troy is looking for you. I promise I will look after you.'

She looked doubtful, which had his temper rising. Why did no one think he was capable of doing his job?

The sky lit up with another flash of lightning and the first spits of rain started to fall. Wasting time fighting, he was going to get wet. Declan hated getting wet.

'Come on, Amy. Trust me. We need to go check on Officer Boaz and stop Troy.'

'Where's Sullivan? Is he with you?'

'He's back in town and worried sick about you. Once I've secured the scene I'll call him on the radio from the police cruiser; let him know you're okay.'

'I don't know if it's working. Don't you have a cell phone?'

'Not on me.' He was getting impatient with the questions now. They needed to find Troy before he left the house. 'Come on, Amy.'

He put his arm around her again, shining the beam of the flashlight down the forest path, and pushed her forward, guiding her back towards the house, gun drawn and ready should he need it. As they reached the clearing where the house stood, the rain fell heavier, the storm now directly overhead. Lightning crackled across the sky, as thunder roared above them.

'Where's Officer Boaz?' Declan demanded, pushing Amy towards the house as he used his gun hand to wipe rainwater from his eyes.

'He's in the van.' She pointed towards the dark vehicle parked in front of the yard, seeming unwilling to move any further forward.

'Come on.' Declan caught hold of her elbow, urged her forward, eager to get out of the rain. Damn woman was getting him soaked and he didn't have a change of clothes.

As they neared the van, a dark figured stepped out of the front door.

Troy?

Seeing him, Amy screamed, and Declan held her close. Another bolt of lightning lit up the sky, illuminating the man's features.

It was Troy.

He watched the man cross the front yard, heading towards them.

This was it. This was going to be his big moment.

'It's okay, I've got a weapon. I promise you, Amy, everything is going to be fine.'

As Troy neared, Declan raised his gun.

* * *

Rebecca arrived back at the precinct about ten minutes after Hickok, having spent much of the evening searching for Amy and Vic.

He glanced up, met her eyes as she entered the office and she knew straightaway he hadn't found anything either. Frustration was kicking in. Amy and Vic had been missing for several hours and with each one that passed the chances of finding them alive grew slimmer. They had always suspected Amy would be a target and should have known to step up her police protection as the killings progressed.

'So what's our next move?' she asked, dropping into her chair. Her eyes were sore, her brain tired and she rested her elbows on the desk, head in hands, and exhaled.

They were running out of places to look, but Rebecca knew they couldn't give up. Amy and Boaz were counting on them, and so was Jake. He was in Melford, unable to do anything, and she had promised him they would find Amy. She couldn't let her partner down.

'Go home and get some rest, Angell. We've got everyone out looking for them. You can't do any more tonight.'

'I'm not going home while they're still out there.'

'You're dead on your feet and you look like hell.' Hickok narrowed his eyes in warning when she scowled at him. 'You're no good here unless you get some rest.'

Rebecca knew he was right, but couldn't bring herself to leave. She would never sleep anyway, knowing the clock was ticking.

'What about you? Are you gonna go get some rest too?'

'No,' Hickok admitted.

'Well, if you're staying, I am too.'

'Damn stubborn woman.'

Rebecca sighed heavily, frustration kicking in. If they weren't against the clock, she'd be kicking back at Mahoney's, nursing a glass of bourbon and trying to figure the puzzle out. Unfortunately, time was not a luxury.

'We have to find them, Hickok. I can't let anything

happen to Amy, for Jake's sake as well as hers. And Boaz, I know he can be an idiot, but he used to be my partner.'

Hickok dropped down beside her, caught hold of her hands. 'Hey, it'll be okay. We'll figure it out.'

Rebecca looked at him, studied his expression. It was one of those rare moments where the cocky mask had dropped and revealed the man underneath. The one she wanted to know better.

'How are we gonna do that?'

'I'm working on it. You're right, you know.' When her eyes narrowed, he grinned. 'Boaz is an idiot, but we'll find him. We'll find Amy too.'

He squeezed her hands, got to his feet and the moment was gone. Muttering under his breath he went over to the desk Rivers had been using, tried the drawer.

'What are you doing?'

'I want to get at Boy Wonder's notebooks, those ones he keeps scribbling in. He must have written a book by now. Maybe we've missed something.'

'You're clutching at straws, Hickok.'

'You have a better idea?'

Rebecca didn't, so shut up.

Hickok swore, shaking his head. 'Can you believe the anal little prick has locked his drawer?'

It didn't surprise Rebecca. From what she'd learned about Rivers over the past couple of weeks, he bordered on obsessive compulsive disorder. He was a neat freak, a little paranoid and exactly the type of person to lock his desk drawer.

'Maybe he didn't want you snooping through his stuff,' she pointed out drily, rolling her eyes as Hickok reached in his pocket for a set of keys, finding the right one to work the lock. He opened the desk drawer, pulled out half a dozen notebooks; he opened the top one and started to read.

'Jeez, Angell, the kid even writes down what he had for breakfast. No wonder he's filled so many of these stupid books if he's documenting pointless crap.'

'Come on, put them back. You're not gonna find anything. This is a waste of time.'

Ignoring her, Hickok turned the page, chuckled.

'What's so funny?' Rebecca snapped.

'He's written about you.'

'What do you mean he's written about me?'

'Bossy and self-righteous, generous ass, but nice pert rack, she's an eight out of ten.'

What the hell?

'Let me see.'

Hickok held the book out of reach when Rebecca made a grab for it, grinning at her.

'Don't worry Angell; I'd give you at least an eight and a half.'

'That little shit.' How dare he write about her? When she saw him, Rebecca was gonna kick his ass. 'Give me the book.'

She made to grab it again, succeeded only in knocking it out of Hickok's hand. As it landed on the floor, a picture fell out.

Hickok plucked it up from the floor, stared at it.

'Jesus Christ.'

'What?' Rebecca demanded.

He handed her the photograph. There were two men in the picture, and they had been fishing, proudly holding up their catch for the camera.

'Declan Rivers and Troy Cunningham know each other,' she murmured, staring at their faces and immediately understanding.

'That's not all.' Hickok was still looking at the notebook. 'He's got a list here. Ben Hogan, Kasey Miller, Shannon Castle, Leon Pruitt, Nadine Williams, Wesley Peterson and Leslie and Crystal Rooney are all on it, their names crossed out.'

'Jeez. How the hell did we not see this?'

'Why would we?'

She guessed Hickok was right. Rivers had been an

outsider brought in, his sole purpose for being in Juniper to help catch a killer.

'There's one more name on the list. It hasn't been crossed out.' Hickok shook his head, closing the notebook and meeting her eyes. 'We need to find Amy before it's too late.'

* * *

As Troy approached, Amy tried to pull away, but Rivers tightened his grip.

'He's going to kill us. For God's sake, shoot him.'

'Hush, it's gonna be fine.'

There was no fear in his tone. Why was there no fear? This was wrong. Something was very wrong.

'What the fuck did you do, Troy?' he demanded. 'You let her get away.'

What?

'Shoot him, dammit. Please, shoot him.'

Instead, Rivers did the opposite, flipping the gun and handing it to Troy.

'She managed to get loose and caught me off guard.' Troy scowled at Amy. 'The bitch smashed me over the head with the toilet lid.'

'All these years without making a single mistake and now you do this?'

What was going on? Rivers was a Fed, he was working the case. How did he know Troy?

'Why are you talking to him?' she asked, panic burning her throat.

Rivers tightened his grip around her, but didn't answer, instead continuing to address Troy.

'You're a fucking stupid idiot. We've been so careful and now when it counts the most and all you had to do was get her here and down into the basement, you mess up. This is how people get caught, Troy, and we're better than that.'

'I have a goddamn stab wound and the pain is killing me. It's not my fault I had to step in when you got sent here. She got me off guard, caught me right where the knife went. I nearly fucking passed out. But we have her now.' Troy used the gun to trace the outline of Amy's jaw, before holstering the weapon. 'It won't happen again.'

'Damn right it won't. You're lucky I ran across her before she made it back to town, found her boyfriend.'

No.

This was wrong. It was a trap.

Instinct kicking in, Amy smacked Rivers in the shin with the heel of her boot and he yelped, loosening his grip. She tried to break free, but he pushed her forward and she slipped on the wet ground, Troy easily catching hold of her in a headlock, before she regained her balance and could run. He yanked her back against him as Rivers shone the flashlight in her face, leaned in close, his eyes wide.

'Surprise.'

'No.' Amy breathed hard as she pulled at Troy's arm locked firm around her neck. 'What the hell are you doing? Let me go.'

'Why would we want to do that? We want to have some fun with you.' Rivers nodded to Troy. 'Let's get her inside.'

'No, no, God, no.' Fear shot through her. 'Not inside, please, no.' Rivers and Troy; had they done all of this together?

She continued to struggle as the rain fell harder, fought against Troy as he tried to drag her back towards the house, kicking out hard at Rivers when he stepped forward to help. He managed to catch hold of her ankles, lifting her, and between them they carried her into the house, back through the hallway, into the kitchen and towards the basement door.

Amy screamed and thrashed, trying to break free, but it was hopeless against two of them.

'No, no, please don't make me go down there.'

Rivers grinned at her, pulling open the door and

leading the way down the stairs and into the basement room.

She recognised it from her nightmares, saw once again the tools hanging on the walls, the spot where Danielle had died and the bloodstains on the floor. Nausea took hold.

I'm gonna be sick.

Rivers dropped her ankles and, as Troy pulled her back in a tight embrace, she took in the rest of the room, saw the figure lying on the concrete floor. At first she thought it was Boaz, but then the man rolled over, groaning.

David.

'Oh my God, what have you done?'

Her ex-boyfriend lay bound on the floor, tape around his wrist and ankles, across his mouth. He looked ill, weak and barely conscious.

Troy hugged her close, as Rivers crossed the room, kicked David hard in the belly, making him grunt in pain, before grabbing hold of a handful of his hair and yanking him upright.

'Say hi,' he taunted, smiling at Amy, lips twisted and eyes mean. 'Remember him, your darling ex?'

'Why is he here? Why are you doing this?' Amy could hear the fear creeping into her tone, was aware she was shaking. She wanted to stop, to be brave, but right now she was so damn scared.

Troy ran his thumb across her lips, leaned in close and pressed his face against her hair. He gently kissed her cheek.

'David is here because he has an important role to play tonight. When we're done playing, he is going to kill you.'

43

Declan Rivers was born into a family of wealthy Maryland bankers with a silver spoon in his mouth.

Son of Charles Montgomery Rivers, Chuck to his pals, Declan grew up wanting for nothing, raised to believe what he wanted was his to take, regardless of who stood in the way.

His grandpa, Henry, was a ruthless business tycoon, the one who had built the family's riches from nothing. He was a shrewd businessman, lacking emotion when it came to the benefit of his company, earning many powerful allies along the way.

Chuck grew up in a privileged world; he was the playboy of the family, partying and enjoying life, who took his wealth for granted and treated it with a more carefree attitude than his harsh taskmaster of a father.

His cavalier attitude to money rubbed off on his son Declan, who was enrolled in the top schools and given anything he wanted that money could buy. The one thing he didn't have, and what he grew up without, was a mother figure. Irene Lowell had been a dancer, hoping to make it big in theatre. She was ambitious and pretty, and Chuck had taken interest in her long enough to get her pregnant. She hadn't wanted Declan, had fought with Chuck for an abortion, before eventually agreeing a settlement which would see her giving birth and relinquishing all rights to the baby.

Chuck wanted an heir to the family business, but had little idea how to raise a child, and Declan spent the early part of his childhood in the care of nannies who were instructed to give him what he wanted.

When Declan turned ten his father decided to marry Elizabeth, another wannabe in the world of show business. Chuck started to take more of an interest in family life, wanting to create a unit with his wife and son. He insisted on Declan referring to Elizabeth as 'Mom', something which galled Elizabeth, who didn't care about parenting. She wanted the family name to carve herself a career and she and Declan quickly developed a mutual dislike for one another.

The only joint passion Chuck and his son shared was their love of sport, and Declan craved for the weekends when they could get out of town, and it was just him and his father.

Chuck was a hunter. He enjoyed fishing, he liked to shoot, and he had a cabin in upstate New York where he would sometimes take his son. They both enjoyed the hunt, chasing down the prey and putting a bullet in its head. Declan learned early on that he also enjoyed using his knife. There was something intensely satisfying about toying with a life, choosing when and how to wipe it out and with each kill he made, he would fantasise about it being Elizabeth.

He also shared Chuck's passion for ball games, with basketball his forte, and he had the Rivers genes: tall and lanky in build, but deceptive in strength and fast around the court. He soon became captain of his team in high school and Chuck affectionately referred to his son as Cap, a nickname that stuck.

Declan was fifteen when his father decided to divorce Elizabeth. They had been fighting a lot in recent months and when things turned ugly the boy was sent to stay with his Aunt Virginia. The woman wasn't his real aunt; Declan's father was an only child. She was the niece of his grandfather and Chuck's cousin, a mousy spinster who lived alone in a small town called Melford out in Oregon.

Declan was furious. This was all Elizabeth's fault, and he hated her for seducing his father, for upsetting his life.

Women were all the same: vile creatures with hidden agendas. They pretended to be weak and helpless, luring men in with the promise of sex.

He hated them all.

He had written off that summer before it began, determined to sulk his way through it, causing trouble wherever he could. Then he met Troy Cunningham, a boy a couple of years older than him and someone he could identify with. He recognised the darkness within Troy, was drawn to it. And the two of them bonded, growing close.

Then came the day when Troy told him about the Johnson house and what had happened to Danielle Colton in the basement. Instead of feeling fear when he visited the house, Declan experienced excitement. He also felt disappointment, wished it had been he who had witnessed what happened, not Troy. Danielle had been the prey. How would it have felt to end her life? He wanted to know. He wanted desperately to know.

He returned to New York, took his first kill on his seventeenth birthday.

Chuck had bought him a Ferrari and as he took it for a drive, he saw her. She was a prostitute, reminded him of Elizabeth to look at, and his mind went into autopilot, picking her up and driving her to a desolate spot on the edge of the city where he strangled the life out of her. He wished he'd had a knife; regretted she was dead and he hadn't been able to cut her. Next time he would be prepared. Next time would be different.

Next time turned out to be with Troy.

They had run into each other in New York. Troy was attending Cornell, while Declan was hanging out at his dad's apartment. They reconnected instantly, the bond between them as strong as before. Again, Declan saw the darkness, and understood that Troy hadn't yet accepted it. He invited Troy to his father's cabin for a weekend of fishing and hunting, taking with him a gift in the form of Melanie, a girl he had picked up the night before.

At first Troy had been in denial, still conditioned to believe killing was wrong. Declan had to show him, had to force him to take the knife, but once he had gotten a taste, had understood the beauty of being in control, he had gone a little crazy with the blade, and then Melanie was dead and Troy was sobbing, trying to come to terms with who he was.

After Melanie they took trips to the cabin a couple of times a year, each time with a different girl. Declan taught Troy they had to pick girls who wouldn't be missed and girls who didn't live anywhere near the cabin. If a hooker went missing in New York City, no one would think to look for her upstate. They used acid to destroy the bodies, kept the teeth as souvenirs.

But then as always, Declan grew bored.

Killing was enjoyable, but it was all too easy. He wanted for people to notice, he wanted a challenge. He wanted to prove he could get away with the perfect murder. Around the same time, he started looking at a career in law enforcement. Chuck wanted him to go into the family business, but Declan's mind was set.

He found murder fascinating, loved studying cases, learning about serial killers, their drive and their methods, what their downfall had been. There was a perverse craving to be on the inside looking out, to track other murderers, understand what made them tick and use what he learned to harness his own skills. He applied to join the FBI, almost flunked out, and had to rely on his father's influence and his close friendships within the Bureau to get him through the door.

Not long after being accepted he decided to pay a surprise visit to Troy at his home in Juniper, Oregon.

The two of them had a rule never to socialise together, to lead their lives separately outside of the weekends away at the cabin. It was for safety, Declan had insisted. If people weren't aware they knew each other, they could never be connected and linked to any murder. Troy had his life in Oregon, Declan had his back east – and that was how it should stay.

But rules were made to be broken, so when he was in Oregon on business, he decided to look his old friend up at his beach house.

Troy hadn't been home and he soon learned his killing buddy had been holding out on him, as Nadine Williams had invited him in, told him to make himself at home until her boyfriend returned. He passed himself off as an old school friend, introduced himself as Cap, and she was quick to welcome him.

Declan was surprised at the woman his friend had chosen to spend his life with, knowing he had a type: liked the pretty but quiet girls with soft features, long hair and little make-up. Nadine was sharp and brash and there was nothing understated about her at all.

What had drawn Troy to her?

And then he learned, over coffee with her on the deck, that they had met in Melford, that she had been the cousin of Danielle Colton, and it all made sense. Nadine was Troy's connection to the past, to what he had witnessed in the basement. That was why he kept her close.

It was following her back into the beach house, as she took their cups through to the kitchen, that he noticed the books. There were six books and they were the only ones on the shelf. It was too much of a coincidence for it to be a different Amy Gallaty.

This was the girl from the basement, the one who had gotten away, and Troy knew who she was, knew she was an author. Rage simmered as Declan understood his friend had kept this from him.

'Have you ever read any of her books?' Nadine had asked, wandering back into the living room where he stood with one of them in his hand, glancing over the back cover.

'No, I've never heard of her,' he lied.

'She's brilliant. I love her stories. They're so suspenseful and keep you on the edge of your seat. I've met her a few times, you know.'

'Have you, now?'

Nadine took down a framed photograph in which she stood beaming next to a pretty woman who had wide almond shaped eyes, a warm smile and long tawny brown hair. She was exactly Troy's type.

'This is Amy Gallaty?'

'Sure is. Troy was the one who introduced me to her; he bought me a copy of her first novel one Christmas. I'm her biggest fan and he takes me to all of her signings. He took this picture.'

What perverse little game are you playing here, Troy?

He had the opportunity to find out when his friend returned twenty minutes later and was shocked and surprised to see him sitting on the couch. Troy had been quick to get Nadine out of the house under the pretext of a shopping errand.

'What the hell are you doing here?' he had hissed. 'I thought we had a rule?'

Declan picked up the framed picture of Nadine and Amy, raising his eyebrows.

'And I thought we had no secrets. You've got some explaining to do, Troy.'

And so, the truth came spilling out: about Nadine and how Troy had been drawn to her because of the connection to Danielle Colton; the truth about Amy and how he had been watching her, obsessing over her for years.

He had been living and working in Spokane when a business meeting had brought him back into Oregon, to the city of Juniper, and it had been by chance he'd happened across an article in a local paper about an aspiring novelist whose first book had just been released. Troy had recognised Amy immediately, had kept the cutting from the paper and tracked down her book, giving it to Nadine as a present. When he had learned Amy was going to be doing a book signing, he used a ruse of a surprise weekend to take Nadine to Juniper and they just happened to be in the area to drop in.

She was even prettier than he remembered, those amber eyes drawing him in and kicking him in the gut, and although he shouldn't have been surprised, he was disappointed when she didn't recognise him.

Their paths had only crossed briefly as kids, and even back then she had barely noticed him, but given the secrets he knew about her it still hurt there was no connection. Nadine had been beside herself, getting to meet the author of the book she had loved, oblivious of the connection tying her to Amy, and Troy played along, the supportive boyfriend trying to keep his girl-friend happy.

Back home he could think of little else. Amy plagued his thoughts and filled his dreams. He wanted her to notice him, wanted to have her for himself – to smell her hair and taste her skin, feel her against him. And then there was the small dark part of him wanting to control her and hurt her; make her understand who he was, and see that same fear in her eyes that he had witnessed all those years ago, as she understood he was going to end her life.

He wrote her a letter, anonymous of course, signing it from Mr X. She wouldn't know it was him, but she would understand he was out there watching and that gave him some comfort.

A few months passed and he started hunting for work back in Oregon. He was good at what he did, and it didn't take long to secure a job with a decent firm. Initially Nadine didn't want to go, but he sold it to her on the promise of a bigger wage and a beachfront house; three months later he was living in the same city as his favourite writer.

Initially Declan was furious with his friend for holding out on him. They had talked about Amy over the years, had even discussed how she would make a satisfying kill, given she had narrowly escaped death once before.

Had Troy been planning to go after her alone? Had he wanted her for himself? They were a team, they worked together.

Initially Declan considered killing Amy himself, getting Troy back for not telling him. He could take her somewhere remote, have his fun, then call his friend up and tell him what he had done. But despite Troy's secrecy, he still felt a sense of loyalty. He was also growing bored with the kills they were doing. It frustrated him that no one had any idea of what they had done or of the body count they had achieved. It wasn't that he wanted to be caught. He couldn't bear the thought of being locked up in a cell and scrutinised by doctors and behavioural therapists, but he still wanted people to look at what he had done, to go down in history like Jack the Ripper or the Zodiac Killer.

He returned home, his mind in overdrive as he began to hatch a plan. Juniper was already renowned for the Alphabet Murders. They could emulate Rodney Boone by creating their own trail of death, bringing the city to its knees once again. And they could do it by using Amy's books, re-enacting a murder scene from each novel.

When he suggested his idea to Troy, his friend was initially against it. Troy was happy to continue with their secret weekends at the cabin, but had no desire in bringing their kills to the attention of the public. It was the promise of the final kill that got him on board. The understanding that once the book series had been completed there would be a final death to conclude the murder spree. They would take Amy back to the house in the woods and relive the murder of Danielle Colton.

With Troy now a willing accomplice, Declan set about putting his plan in motion.

If they wanted to return to the basement, use it for their fun with Amy, they would have to take out Tucker Johnson. They did the deed one cold weekend not long after Christmas, driving out to Melford and attacking the man in his house, dragging him into the basement and using the knives he had tortured his victims with to butcher him to death. Once his body had been destroyed they returned to their lives, content in the knowledge Johnson was a loner and no one would come looking for him.

Declan had done his research on the Alphabet Murders, knew the federal agents who worked the case were Max Sutton and Joel Hickok. Max had just retired, and Hickok was in line for a new partner. What Declan wanted, Declan got, and a word with his father about how much he felt he could learn from this man, and the pulling of a few strings with Chuck's friends at the Bureau, saw Sutton's replacement being reassigned and Declan stepping into his shoes.

Anything was possible if you knew the right people.

It was too dangerous to leave the case open, so

they would need a fall guy to take responsibility for the murders. Troy was the one to suggest David Gavin. He had been watching Amy closely enough to know the volatile relationship she had endured with her ex, and although Gavin had relocated to Chicago, Troy was convinced his jealous streak, and the fact he was far from over Amy, would be enough to lure him back to Juniper.

They did so by playing on his suspicions that Amy had been cheating on him with her close friend, Ryan Caparelli. Gavin's paranoia about the two of them had brought about the end of the relationship. Troy attended the same gym as Caparelli, had already struck up a casual friendship with him, and learned all the details over time. They would lure Gavin back with an anonymous note supposedly from Caparelli's ex-girl-friend, suggesting he had been right about the two of them. Once he was in town they could begin the murder spree.

The plan worked and Gavin returned. It was almost too easy. But then he threw a curveball, going after Caparelli.

Of course, Caparelli had denied everything and punches were exchanged. It was after Gavin had left that Troy found Caparelli unconscious in his apartment with injuries requiring hospitalisation. If he took the man to hospital it would lead to questions, and the police would be on the hunt for Gavin before their killing spree had even begun.

That couldn't happen.

Troy had used a pillow to smother Caparelli and then, with no acid to hand and needing to act quickly, he bundled the man's body in the trunk of his car and under the cover of darkness took him out to a nearby farm and dropped his body in the pigpen. Caparelli was supposed to be heading out to Europe and, while he would be missed eventually, it would hopefully buy them the time they needed.

Gavin was proving dangerous and unpredictable and there was concern he would go after Amy next or confess to what he had done. Fortunately, he retired to the motel room he had rented and another anonymous note from the alleged ex-girlfriend, asking him to lie low and wait for her to get in touch, seemed to do the trick.

The first victim selected was Ben Hogan, a student at Juniper College and the nephew of Senator Blaine Hogan, a close personal friend of Chuck Rivers. That Hogan had a pretty girlfriend who happened to work in the place Amy sometimes bought coffee was a coincidence, albeit a rather fitting one.

Troy was responsible for kidnapping the two students and carrying out the first murders. It was the first time he had killed alone, aside from taking care of Caparelli, and Declan knew it would be a test. If he pulled it off, they were good to go. He did, and Declan once again used his influence with his father, persuading him to convince Blaine Hogan that Special Agent Joel Hickok was the best man to help catch his nephew's murderer, given he had already worked closely with the Juniper Police Department to apprehend the Alphabet Killer. It was an argument that made sense and Hickok was personally recommended, with Declan along for the ride.

From then on it had been plain sailing. Gavin had behaved himself enough to avoid detection and Declan was able to keep tabs on him, luring him to Troy's beach house and taking him out of the picture when the investigation began to centre on him.

Nadine had been the only other problem.

Oblivious to her boyfriend's extra-curricular activities, she lived in her own little bubble and was unfortunately a little too obsessed with Amy Gallaty. Amy's book series was complete, and she had moved on to new projects, something Nadine took badly, and she started to cause scenes that drew attention to her and Troy.

The final straw had been the night of Leon Pruitt's

murder. Declan and Troy had been careful to give each other alibis. For Ben and Kasey's murder, Declan had been back east and he only arrived in town the night Troy killed Shannon Castle. Leon's murder was supposed to give Troy an alibi and he had been out in town with Nadine, in sight of dozens of witnesses. Declan had used the ruse of the Trail Blazers game to pretend he was out of town, hiding out in Ryan Caparelli's apartment before going after the doorman and Nadine had nearly ruined the whole set-up, hell-bent on going after Amy at the Velvet Lounge and putting her boyfriend at the scene of the abduction.

It was after that night Declan knew she was a liability and had to go.

Troy protested, claimed he loved her, but when it came down to a choice between him having Nadine or having Amy, he chose Amy. For twenty years Troy had longed for Amy Gallaty and, as he watched her struggling in his friend's arms, saw the fear in her eyes and that terrified understanding, the knowing of what awaited her, Declan knew he had made the right choice.

44

'She says the cop, Boaz, is alive.'

Rivers was circling Amy, watching her closely, but his comment wasn't directed at her.

'He's not alive. I stabbed him. There was no pulse.'

'Well, you'd better check, Troy, make sure he's not, and then get rid of his body. Put it down the well. That's what David would do.' Rivers winked at Gavin, who was still only half-conscious on the floor. 'Isn't that right, David?'

There was something different about Rivers. He had always been rude and self-important, but the air of incompetence was gone and the man standing be-fore Amy seemed capable and domineering. Had it all been an act? The smile he gave was cruel and he showed no hesitation. She could see it in his eyes that he wanted to hurt her. And while her mind worked overtime, trying to figure a way out of the situation, she knew time was running out. She had seen Danielle, what Tucker Johnson had done to her, and knew what they were planning. She had to get away again.

How had she been so stupid as to trust him out in the woods? She hadn't questioned what he had been doing there or why he was so desperate to get back to the house. She'd just been relieved to see him, had honestly believed he was going to help her.

But no one could help her now.

Sullivan was in town, but oblivious to her predicament, and Boaz mostly likely dead. She could only help herself.

There was no reasoning with Rivers. He was enjoying this. Could she work on Troy? From the way he kept caressing her face and leaning in close to smell her hair, she suspected he wanted her on a more personal level than Rivers.

As Rivers wandered over to David, to check on his bonds, she rested her head back against Troy's shoulder. She heard him hitch his breath as he drew in the scent of her hair. Although it repulsed her to do so, she forced herself to quit struggling and relax into him. He stiffened, his arms still tight around her, and she felt him grow hard against the small of her back.

Stay calm. Even breaths, Amy.

Turning slightly, she rested her forehead against his cheek.

'Please help me, Troy,' she whispered, careful not to let Rivers hear. 'If you want me, I'll be yours.'

She swallowed hard as his arms tightened around her, crushing her against him. One of his hands slipped down to cup her breast.

Oh, God. Keep it steady, Amy.

She forced herself to look up at him.

Sorry, Sullivan.

She owed Sullivan nothing, had no reason to feel guilty, but still, she did.

This was self-preservation and she was fighting for her life. 'Please. You, but not him. Just you and me.'

'What the fuck?'

Rivers had hold of her hair, was yanking her head back. He slapped her hard across the face.

Amy squealed and winced.

'You think you can come between us you sly little bitch?'

Troy didn't react. His hard-on still poked into her back as he continued to hold her.

'We already have you,' Rivers continued. 'What makes you think you can bargain with us?'

He shook his head, turned to Troy, disgusted. 'Go upstairs and get rid of Boaz. I'm going to get our friend here ready for some fun.'

* * *

Jake got the call from Hickok as he was heading out with Wagner. He listened as the Fed told him about the picture and the list, before explaining Benson had already recognised Rivers and made the connection.

His weapon was drawn as he kicked open Rivers' motel room door. The room was empty, and he was unsurprised to see the bed hadn't been slept in.

Did he have Amy?

If he did and he hurt her, Jake was going to kill him.

Wagner stepped in behind him, nodded grimly. Benson and another of his deputies were close behind. 'I'll take Anderson. Head over to Virginia's. They could be there. Benson, you go with Detective Sullivan over to Leslie Rooney's place. I'm thinking if they're not at Virginia's they will have returned to Troy's old family home.' He looked at Jake. 'I'm guessing these boys are in it together?'

'It's looking that way.'

* * *

Benson drove, gunning the engine and taking corners at breakneck speed. Leslie Rooney's house was in darkness. There was no need for lights, as she wouldn't be coming home and if Troy and Rivers were inside with Amy, they would want to be discreet.

Benson tried the front door and, as expected, found it locked. Jake eased her out of the way, drew his gun, before kicking it hard. Wood splintered as the door flew open. They were met with dark silence.

'Take downstairs,' he instructed, before heading to the first floor.

The house was small and didn't take long to search. They were wasting their time. Amy wasn't here.

'I'll radio the sheriff,' Benson said as they headed out to the car. 'See if they've turned up anything at Virginia's.'

They hadn't and agreed to reconvene back at the sheriff's office. Jake was quiet on the ride back, frustration kicking in and his belly jumpy. The clock was ticking and they were running out of time. Amy had to be okay. As they headed through the woods, passed the junction that led down to Tucker Johnson's place, his mind worked overtime.

And then it hit him.

'Stop the car.'

Benson glanced over, eased her foot off the gas. 'Why? What's up?'

'The house in the woods: Johnson's place, that's where they would take her.'

She nodded, swung the car around sharply, headlights thrashing ahead, the car bouncing as road became dirt track.

There was a loud bang, the car skidded and Benson fought to keep control. Jake grabbed the wheel, turned it into the skid and they slid off the road, their path halted by a giant oak. Smoke fizzled from the hood.

'You okay?'

'Yeah, I think so.' Benson nodded. 'The tyre must've popped.'

Jake helped her from the car, stopped long enough to be sure she wasn't hurt.

'Radio Wagner, tell him to get backup and meet me at Tucker Johnson's place.'

'You should wait for them to get here.'

'No time. I need to get to Amy.'

Leaving Benson with the car, he took off at a sprint towards the house.

* * *

As Troy disappeared upstairs to find Boaz, Amy made a final attempt to break free, again using her feet to kick out at Rivers. He had already wised to her tactics and easily manoeuvred himself, so she missed. Managing to work her left arm behind her, she grabbed at his groin, squeezed hard.

He screamed and let go, and it was all the time she needed to grab the knife she'd seen sitting on the table and plunge it at his shoulder. She caught flesh, enough to have him howling again, but not inflict any real damage. As she pulled back for a second shot, his fist flew out, catching her in the face. Amy stumbled back, losing her balance and landing on the floor, the knife still in her hand.

She tasted blood, put her hand to her cheek and tried to get up, her head swimming. Rivers reached down, plucked the knife from her fingers and yanked her to her feet.

'You'll pay for that,' he snarled, dragging her across the room to the spot where Danielle had once stood.

No, God, no.

She screamed, still trying to struggle as he forced her arms above her head, and she felt hard, cold steel lock around her wrists. She yanked hard at the chains, knew it was too late. Rivers reached out with the knife she had attacked him with, ran the blunt edge of the blade down her cheek and smiled gloatingly, and Amy's heart jumped into her mouth.

Stay strong. Don't show fear.

She drew her head back, spat in his face. His expression turned dark, but he didn't react.

'He's in love with you,' he said conversationally.

Who was he talking about? David? Troy? She didn't ask; waited for him to elaborate.

'But then I guess you know that. It's why you tried to trick him and turn him against me.'

He was talking about Troy. 'It's not the kind of love you think it is. He doesn't want you in the way you think he does. He's infatuated with you and has been ever since he saw you and Danielle Colton down here.'

What?

Rivers caught the shocked look on her face, smiled.

'You didn't know, did you? That he had followed you into the woods; was in the basement when you found Danielle.'

Was he being serious? Had Troy seen? On one level it made sense. How would Rivers know if no one had been here? Amy thought back to that night, remembered being in the basement with Danielle, and Tucker Johnson coming in. It had just been the three of them, hadn't it?

She remembered the scent of damp, the taste of fear, the horrifying sight of Danielle. And then she saw eyes, watching, staring from the darkness.

Someone else had been there.

'He's obsessed with you, Amy, and yes, he wants to fuck you. I will let him, but you have to understand, for Troy, pain and pleasure go hand in hand. He wants to fuck you, but he also wants to hurt you, to kill you. And we will, but we'll take our time. He's waited a long while for this. By the time we're done you will be begging to die.'

Amy shuddered, tried to take a step back as Rivers raised the knife; pointed the tip into her chin. The chains stopped her.

'You're a sick fuck,' she whispered. 'You won't get away with this.'

'But we will. We've been killing for years and no one realises. David is going to take the blame for your murder. Everyone knows he has a jealous streak and has been bitter because you dumped him. He made it easy for us, following you around and taking your picture. The police will think David snapped. He remembered what you'd told him about the basement, about Danielle's murder—'

'I never told him about this place. I didn't even remember it had happened until a couple of weeks ago.'

'Really?' Rivers ran the blade down her throat. 'I don't believe that. I think you knew.'

'I didn't know. I swear.'

'Well, it's irrelevant anyhow, because everyone already believes you've been lying. They've found the letter I planted upstairs in Johnson's bedroom, the one they think David wrote to him trying to blackmail him over what he had done. David wanted Johnson to help him kill you, get you back for dumping him.'

'What?'

Amy knew Hickok and Angell thought she had lied about not remembering the basement. But did Sullivan believe that too?

'You see, David killed all those people to get back at you and when I call this in, your boyfriend and his pals are gonna think he killed you too. I will find the scene, take him down, and save Troy's life. He'll be badly injured, but alive. The police have already found blood in his house, know someone hurt him. He will tell them that

Gavin showed up a few nights after killing Nadine, stabbed him and brought him here. So your ex-boyfriend will go down in history as a serial killer, Troy will be his surviving victim and I will get a fucking gold medal.'

'You're sick.'

'Maybe I am.' Rivers nodded in agreement. 'I prefer creative, but we can go with sick. Rather sick than dead, Amy. Like you're going to be.'

He flicked the knife down, ripping open the neckline of her T-shirt to her bra, grinning when she sucked in a breath.

Don't react. He wants you to show fear.

'You won't get away with it. They'll figure it out.'

The sound of footsteps on the staircase had them both looking at the door.

Troy entered, sounding out of breath.

'He's gone.'

Amy's heartbeat quickened. Was he talking about Boaz? 'What the fuck do you mean, he's gone?' Rivers snapped, slamming the knife to the floor in a rage. 'I thought you said he was dead.'

'I thought he was. He wasn't breathing.'

'For fuck's sake, Troy.'

'He can't have gotten far. We'll find him.'

Shaking his head, Rivers followed Troy to the door.

Before he disappeared, he turned back to Amy, twisting his lips. 'Don't go anywhere.'

* * *

Hidden in the safety of the bushes, Vic had watched Troy go back into the house.

He had no idea where the hell he was, knew only he had woken in a van, pain shooting through his belly and his mouth drier than the Sahara.

He had groaned, tried to move his head, was hit by a bout of dizziness and had to wait a couple of minutes before trying again to sit up. There was blood all sticky over his shirt and then he had remembered – being in the parking lot at the church, Troy Cunningham attacking him with a knife.

And Amy. Where the fuck was Amy? She had been inside with Pastor Ralph. Was she still at the church or had she left and been attacked too? It made no sense for Troy to just attack Vic. Amy was the one he was protecting. She was the one most likely to be in danger.

Where was she?

He had felt for his sidearm, unsurprised to find his holster empty, and grimacing in pain, forced his hand down to his ankle, felt for the second smaller gun he kept as backup, relieved when his fingers touched metal. Fucker hadn't thought to check for a backup weapon.

Grumbling and swearing at the pain, angry at being caught out and taken for a fool and not wanting to admit he was a little bit scared right now, he had pushed himself out of the van, sucking in the scream as he hit against the ground. He wheezed out a breath, took a moment to overcome the wave of nausea and looked around before forcing himself to crawl for the safety of the bushes. From there he had watched Troy come out of the house and go to the van. Heard him curse when he found it empty. A couple of minutes passed before he headed back inside, and Vic let go of the breath he hadn't realised he'd been holding. He bit down on the pain as he forced himself to his feet.

It was time to find out where the hell Amy was.

* * *

Amy waited for several long, agonising minutes, her arms aching and her face pounding where Rivers had hit her. She was desperate to know if Boaz was okay, hoping against hope he was and had managed to get help. She knew it was a long shot. He had bled pretty bad and been unconscious for a long time.

The metal dug into her wrists and she knew there was no way to escape this time. Boaz was her only hope.

Eventually she heard the sound of footsteps, her heart sinking when Troy entered the room. He looked mad as hell, and she tried to shrink away as he approached.

He skimmed his fingers down her face, into her hair and Amy jerked back as he caught hold of a handful of her hair, forcing her forward and pressing his mouth hard against hers.

No.

In a gut reaction she brought up her knee, caught him sharp in the balls. He groaned, falling back, took a moment to recover, cursing and swearing at her. Managing to get himself upright, he pulled out a pocket knife, flicked open the blade, and took a step towards her.

* * *

Jake stepped into the basement room, saw Amy chained up and Troy heading towards her, the glint of a blade in his hand, and his heart almost stopped.

'Stop where you are. Put the knife down, Troy.'

The man froze, both he and Amy looking over to

where Jake stood; then it happened quick, Troy was behind her, using her as a shield, as he pressed the blade to her throat.

'Put the knife down, Troy. It's over.'

'Fuck you. Drop the gun or I'll slit her throat.'

Jake hesitated, memories of Denny flashing into his mind.

'Shoot him,' Amy urged. 'He'll kill me anyway.'

She was being brave, but he heard the edge of fear in her tone. Still, she wriggled against Troy, anger flashing into her eyes.

'Shut the fuck up.'

'It's true. And if I'm going to die, I want you to die too. You're not a man; you're a worthless, lowlife, pathetic excuse for a human being.'

'Shut up!' Troy repeated, pressing the knife tighter, drawing blood.

Jake sucked in a breath, squeezed the trigger.

He closed his eyes for a brief second, opened them to see Troy's grip slip on Amy as his eyes went wide, blood gushing from the bullet hole in his head as he fell to the floor.

Amy let out a breath.

She was okay. Thank God she was okay.

Relief lit up her face, then her eyes went wide. 'Oh my God.' She started screaming.

Jake felt the pain in his back, was aware of the blade twisting inside him. His gun dropped to the floor and, as the room started to swim, he dropped to his knees. Blackness took hold and then he felt nothing.

* * *

Amy continued to scream as Rivers walked slowly towards her, the bloody knife he had used to stab Sullivan, dripping in his hand.

No, he can't be dead, he can't be dead. Please no.

Rivers' focus was on Troy, his face contorted with pain and anger. 'No!'

As he howled in anguish, sobbing over the body of his dead friend, Amy cried for Jake, wanting to go to him, needing to know if he was still alive.

When Rivers finally calmed, stepping in front of her with red-rimmed eyes, he had regained his composure, his expression cold and calm, his eyes dead.

'It's your fault.'

'Go to hell.'

Amy glanced past him at Sullivan's body, inwardly cursed herself, as another tear rolled down her cheek. The tears weren't for Rivers. He could do what he wanted; she no longer cared.

'I'm gonna cut you up into little pieces.'

'Do what the hell you want.' She spat the words in his face. 'I don't care.'

He pressed the knife into her cheek, nicked it, drawing blood, and she flinched. 'I'm going to make you care.'

A shot rang out, making her jump.

Rivers looked at her, the impassive look on his face changing to one of surprise. Blood ran between his lips and he blinked heavily, taking an unsteady step back before dropping forward. As he crashed to the floor, Amy saw blood seeping from his back, and then she saw Boaz, on his knees, one hand clutched at his belly and his gun still aimed.

'Vic. You're okay?'

He grinned at her, more strained than usual, but still that dopey Vic Boaz grin she had gotten used to over the past couple of weeks.

'That showed the little shit.'

Amy wanted to weep, relief and grief washing over her.

'I'm so glad you're okay.'

'Me too.'

And then he gave her that dopey grin again, his eyes dropping shut, and he hit the floor.

EPILOGUE

Victor Boaz became something of an overnight celebrity, having been directly involved in both of Juniper's serial killer cases.

The first time hadn't been so great. He had played a part in the Alphabet Murder investigations, but it was his partner who had been applauded for catching the killer, while he learned he shared genes with the sick son of a bitch.

This time round he had saved a victim and brought down the Storybook Killers, as the press had dubbed Declan Rivers and Troy Cunningham. And this was after being injured in the line of duty. He had spent five days in intensive care before being given a private room, his own TV, which meant he could catch up on the soaps, and he had the nurses fawning over him. They told him reporters had been calling, all wanting the scoop, and a couple of the younger nurses had slipped him their numbers, saying when he had recovered, they would love to have a drink with him, hear all about how he took down the rogue FBI agent and saved Amy Gallaty's life.

He had seen Amy once since that night. She had visited him in hospital the day after he was admitted, thanking him and saying she would never forget what he had done for her. He had heard Sullivan had also been admitted to hospital, had spent time in intensive care after being stabbed by Rivers.

Vic understood at that moment her feelings for him, knew where her heart lay, but it no longer mattered. He was already over Amy, aware his new hero status promised plenty of new opportunities with his female fans.

After what they had gone through together she would always be a friend, but nothing more, and Sullivan could have her.

Vic didn't need a girlfriend cramping his new lifestyle.

* * *

Three anxious days Amy waited to find out if Sullivan was going to be okay. She had been certain he was dead, but the paramedics said the knife had missed his heart by a couple of inches. It would be touch and go, but he would hopefully pull through.

There had been questions and more questions.

Troy Cunningham and Declan Rivers were both dead and the clues they had given that they had killed before were of great interest to the police, who were scouring missing persons reports and investigating the lives of both men in great depth, much to the irritation of Chuck Rivers, who claimed the whole matter to be a big misunderstanding and had already involved lawyers to try and clear his son's name.

David had been admitted to the same hospital as Sullivan and Boaz, suffering from dehydration. Despite his request to see her, Amy declined.

Hickok and Angell told her he would face questioning and possible charges once he had recovered, and she took the news impassively. That chapter of her life was over, and she didn't wish to open it again.

Although his body hadn't been found, the police were also certain Ryan was dead; an unwitting victim of Troy and Rivers' gruesome legacy. Amy had taken the news numbly, crying tears for her friend when she was alone with Huckleberry. He, thank God, was okay, back from the vets and bursting with energy, and she took comfort in having him home again. He was a pain, but he was hers now, and she would honour Ryan and look after his dog as best she could.

Her friends were her rock: Heidi, Fran and Gage were there for her while she waited for news about Sullivan and Boaz, taking turns to stay with her. It was going to be okay, things would get better, and Amy knew that for sure the morning Sullivan regained consciousness, asking to see her. She had been at home when she got the call and when she arrived at the hospital Angell and Hickok were in the hallway outside his room, having already seen him. There was another lady with them. Older, pretty, with dark hair.

'This is Jake's mom,' Angell told her, making the introductions. 'She just flew in.'

Amy shook her hand, a little apprehensive, but the woman had kind eyes and a warm smile.

'He's been asking for you. Why don't you go see him,' she suggested gently.

Sullivan was pale, his jaw stubbled, and he looked drawn, but the spark was back in his eyes, and he didn't attempt to stop Amy as she went to him, holding on tight and not prepared to let him walk away from her again. She breathed him in, needing to know he was really with her.

'You scared me,' he admitted.

'You scared me too.' She traced a finger over his jawline, across his lips. 'I just met your mother.'

'I figured.'

'She seems nice.'

'She is.'

Amy was silent for a moment, the question she didn't want to ask, but knew she had to, playing on her lips. She had to know.

'So, tell me, Sullivan—'

'Jake.'

'Okay, tell me, Jake. Are you going to push me away again? Tell me this is wrong?'

He was silent for a moment, dark eyes studying her face. 'It was never wrong,' he said eventually, reaching out and brushing her hair away from her face. 'It was just wrong timing.'

'What about now?'

His lips curved and he cupped her head, pulled her to him, kissing her softly.

Resting his forehead against her, his lips curved against her mouth.

'Now? Now I guess we will find out.'

* * *

Hickok stopped by Rebecca's townhouse on his way to the airport.

She hadn't been expecting him, wasn't sure how things were going to end between them this time. In his typical Hickok way, he had breezed into town, destroyed her relationship, and had her questioning her feelings for him all over again.

Okay, so that wasn't necessarily fair. Perhaps she and Alan had been wrong from the offset, but still, it shouldn't have ended the way it did.

She'd told Hickok when the case was done, they needed to talk, but things had been crazy busy, and the opportunity hadn't arisen. Now they had run out of time.

There would be no vacation. Rebecca understood that. Rivers' involvement had rattled the FBI and Hickok was needed back at Quantico to help them understand how a serial killer had slipped through their net.

'So, I guessed I'd drop by and say hey before I left.'

'Okay then. Hey,' Rebecca repeated, her tone dry.

No word of whether he planned on coming back to relieve the unresolved tension between them.

It galled Rebecca to admit it, but she was incredibly frustrated they'd never gotten to finish what they started the night they'd been interrupted. The case had distracted her, but now it was over she could think of little else.

Joel Hickok might be an irritating asshole, but there was no denying he was great in the sack.

He studied her for a moment, that cocky expression making her want to slap him and kiss him at the same time.

'So say hi to Sullivan for me. And tell Boaz he did okay. Tell him he's still an idiot, but yeah, he did okay.'

'Anything else?'

He looked her up and down. 'Nope.'

'Okay, then I guess it's goodbye.'

'Okay, bye.'

'Damn it, Hickok. We said we were going to talk.'

He looked at her then, really looked at her. 'We will.' He loitered for a moment, hesitated. 'I'll come back and we'll talk. When things are clear, I'll come back. I promise.'

'What about now? You're just gonna go?'

He arched a brow and she could see from the smug look on his face he had clocked exactly where her frustrations lay.

'I've got a flight to catch, Angell.'

Rebecca shook her head, turned and walked back into the house, heading straight for the living room.

She waited a beat, heard the door close. Then the sound of his footsteps.

He caught her from behind and her breath hitched. 'The couch?' he asked, lips brushing her neck.

Rebecca smiled. 'Yeah, the couch, for old times' sake.'

* * *

MORE FROM KERI BEEVIS

Another book from Keri Beevis, is available to order now here:

https://mybook.to/KerisnewBackAd

ACKNOWLEDGEMENTS

First and foremost, my thanks go to my brilliant editor, Caroline Ridding, and the rest of the fantastic team at Boldwood Books.

It would have been difficult to complete *The Story-book Killer* without the help of certain individuals and, while I am grateful for everyone's support, there are a couple of people I would like to acknowledge personally.

Thank you to Jonathan Curtis Dip Hyp, Clinical Hypnotherapist, for guiding me through Amy's hypnotherapy scenes. I appreciate you taking the time to meet with me and talk me through the process, and for then patiently answering all of my follow-up questions as I was writing the book.

It is handy to be related to a police officer and my thanks also go to my sister, Detective Sergeant Holly Beevis, for doing her best to ensure I did not trip up on the technical details.

To Jonathan and Holly, if there are any mistakes in *The Storybook Killer*, they are my errors, not yours.

Finally, I would like to acknowledge Paul Shinnick, winner of my competition to have a character in the book named after him. Thank you for entering and I hope you enjoy reading about your namesake. Thanks also to fan Faith Gallaty, for letting me 'steal' her surname after I took a liking to it, and to all of the readers who have supported me over the past year. I couldn't have done it without you.

ABOUT THE AUTHOR

Keri Beevis is the internationally bestselling author of several psychological thrillers and romantic suspense mysteries, including the very successful *Dying to Tell*. She sets many of her books in the county of Norfolk, where she was born and still lives and which provides much of her inspiration.

Download your exclusive bonus content from Keri Beevis here:

Visit Keri's website: www.keribeevis.com

Follow Keri on social media here:

- facebook.com/allaboutbeev
- x.com/keribeevis
- instagram.com/keri.beevis
- bookbub.com/profile/keri-beevis
- tiktok.com/@keribeevis

ALSO BY KERI BEEVIS

The Sleepover

The Summer House

The House in the Woods

Trust No One

Every Little Breath

Nowhere to Hide

The Cottage by the Sea

The House Sitter

Dead of Winter

Dying to Tell

Deep Dark Secrets

The Detective Rebecca Angell Series

The Alphabet Killer

The Storybook Killer

THE *Murder* LIST

THE MURDER LIST IS A NEWSLETTER DEDICATED TO SPINE-CHILLING FICTION AND GRIPPING PAGE-TURNERS!

SIGN UP TO MAKE SURE YOU'RE ON OUR HIT LIST FOR EXCLUSIVE DEALS, AUTHOR CONTENT, AND COMPETITIONS.

SIGN UP TO OUR NEWSLETTER

BIT.LY/THEMURDERLISTNEWS

Boldwood

Boldwood Books is an award-winning fiction publishing company seeking out the best stories from around the world.

Find out more at www.boldwoodbooks.com

Join our reader community for brilliant books, competitions and offers!

Follow us
@BoldwoodBooks
@TheBoldBookClub

Sign up to our weekly
deals newsletter

https://bit.ly/BoldwoodBNewsletter